Praise for
The Iron Druid Chronicles
by Kevin Hearne

"Kevin Hearne's Iron Druid Chronicles has grown from strength to strength since its publication in 2011. Kevin's writing style along with his characterization has made him the darling of urban fantasy readers all over the world."

—Fantasy Book Critic

"They are clever, fast paced and a good escape."
—JASON WEISBERGER, Boing Boing

"It may be possible that Hearne and Atticus could be the logical heir to Butcher and Dresden."
—SFFWorld

"Celtic mythology and an ancient Druid with modern attitude mix it up in the Arizona desert in this witty new fantasy series."
—KELLY MEDING, author of *Three Days to Dead*

"Kevin Hearne breathes new life into old myths, creating a world both eerily familiar and startlingly original."
—NICOLE PEELER, author of *T...*

Hounded

"This is the best urban/paranormal fantasy I have read in years. Fast paced, funny, clever, and suitably mythic, this is urban fantasy for those worn-out of werewolves and vampires. Fans of Jim Butcher, Harry Connolly, Greg van Eekhout, Ben Aaronovitch, or Neil Gaiman's American Gods will take great pleasure in Kevin Hearne's *Hounded*. Highly recommended."
—JOHN OTTINGER III, editor of Grasping for the Wind

"Filled with snarky descriptions . . . comradely characters, thumping action and a plot as stylized as a Renaissance Faire, this tale is outrageously fun."
—*The Plain Dealer*

"A superb urban fantasy debut . . . with plenty of quips and zap-pow-bang fighting."
—*Publishers Weekly* (starred review)

"Fans of fantasy and urban fantasy will eat this one up. . . . *Hounded* is a series debut that is absolutely not to be missed!"
—My Bookish Ways

"For both the urban fantasy and non–urban fantasy geekoids, *Hounded* is a tremendous read. Fun, well-written, and entertaining."
—Blood of the Muse

"A page-turning and often laugh-out-loud-funny caper through a mix of the modern and the mythic."
—ARI MARMELL, author of *The Warlord's Legacy*

Hexed

"Kevin Hearne . . . cranks out action and quips at a frenzied pace . . . in this fun and highly irreverent read."
—*Publishers Weekly*

"Hearne's writing is fast paced and spot on . . . *Hexed* is steeped in magic and wrapped in awesome. It really doesn't get much better than this!"
—My Bookish Ways

"The humor in *Hexed* is non-stop. . . . Hard to read without a smile plastered across your face."
—Blood of the Muse

Hammered

"In this adrenaline-spiked third Iron Druid adventure . . . Hearne provides lots of zippy plotting and rocking action scenes. . . . Fans will be thrilled."
—*Publishers Weekly*

"I love, love, love this series, and *Hammered* is the best so far. . . . You'll be turning pages in warp speed until the final battle, then you won't be able to turn them fast enough."
—My Bookish Ways

Tricked

"Kevin Hearne's *Tricked* manages to combine the fun aspects of the previous books and give the saga a darker turn to make this book more akin to a thriller."
—Fantasy Book Critic

"*Tricked* is packed with thoroughly engrossing characters, fascinating mythology, creatures that will make your head spin, lots of action, and a ton of heart."
—My Bookish Ways

"Hearne understands the two main necessities of good fantasy stories: for all the wisecracks and action, he never loses sight of delivering a sense of wonder to his readers, and he understands that magic use always comes with a price. Highly recommended."
—CHARLES DE LINT,
The Magazine of Fantasy & Science Fiction

Trapped

"*Trapped* is another amazing book for the series. Kevin Hearne is on a roll and I can hardly wait to see what trouble Atticus, Oberon, and Granuaile get into next!"
—Blogcritics

HUNTED

Don't miss the first five and a half books
of The Iron Druid Chronicles
by Kevin Hearne

Hounded
Hexed
Hammered
Tricked
Trapped

Two Ravens and One Crow:
An Iron Druid Chronicles Novella

Books published by The Random House Publishing Group are
available at quantity discounts on bulk purchases for premium,
educational, fund-raising, and special sales use. For details,
please call 1-800-733-3000.

HUNTED

THE IRON DRUID CHRONICLES

KEVIN HEARNE

DEL REY

BALLANTINE BOOKS • NEW YORK

Hunted is a work of fiction. Names, places, and incidents either are products of the author's imagination or are used fictitiously.

A Del Rey Mass Market Original

Copyright © 2013 by Kevin Hearne
Two Ravens and One Crow by Kevin Hearne copyright © 2012 by Kevin Hearne

Published in the United States by Del Rey, an imprint of The Random House Publishing Group, a division of Random House, Inc., New York.

DEL REY is a registered trademark and the Del Rey colophon is a trademark of Random House, Inc.

Two Ravens and One Crow was originally published seperately as an eBook by Del Rey, an imprint of The Random House Publishing Group, a division of Random House, Inc., in 2012

ISBN 978-0-345-53363-0
eBook ISBN 978-0-345-53877-2

Printed in the United States of America

www.delreybooks.com

9 8 7 6 5 4 3 2

Del Rey mass market edition: July 2013

For the Confederacy of Nerds:
AK, Barushka, Alan, Tooth,
and Pilot John

Pronunciation Guide

As always, please remember that while I provide these for reference, I'm completely okay with you pronouncing these names however you wish, because the entire point of reading is to enjoy yourself and not stress out about unusual names from mythology. If, however, you enjoy knowing how to pronounce them, here you go:

Irish

Aillil = ALL-yill (In *The Wooing of Étaín,* this name is held by both Étaín's father and the brother of Eochaid Airem. It's used here to refer to the brother.)

Amergin = AV er ghin (legendary Irish bard whose name is spelled and pronounced many different ways. The modern Irish spelling is *Amhairghin* and pronounced something like OUR yin, but the Morrigan would use the Old Irish spelling and pronunciation.)

Brí Léith = Bree LAY (the *síd* or home of Midhir)

Eochaid Airem = OH het EH rem (High King of Ireland once upon a time)

Étaín = eh TEEN (so epically hot they wrote an epic about her)

Fódhla = FOH-la (one of the poetic names of Ireland
  and the name of the Irish elemental)
Fúamnach = FOO am nah (Midhir's wife)
Midhir = ME er (member of the Tuatha Dé Danann; half
  brother to Aenghus Óg and Brighid)
Orlaith = OR la (Yep, that –ith on the end is just to
  make it look pretty)

Polish

Dukla = DOOK la
Gościniec pod Furą = gohsht NEE etz pohd FOO roh
  (basically long o wherever you see oh)
Jasło = YAHS woh
Katowice = Kat oh VEET suh (city in southern Poland)
Pustków Wilczkowski = POOST kov wiltch KOV ski
Sokołowska = SO ko WOV ska
Wojownika = Vai yov NEE ka
Wrocław = Vroht SWOF
Żubrówka = Zhu BRUF ka (bison grass vodka, popular
  in Poland and available here, quite tasty mixed with
  apple juice or cider)

Translation Note

There is a passage in the novel where Atticus recites some verses from Dante's *Purgatorio* in the original Italian, but he neglects to share an English translation. I have duplicated the verses here and followed each with a translation by Henry Wadsworth Longfellow.

From Canto V:

> *Là 've 'l vocabol suo diventa vano,*
> *arriva' io forato ne la gola,*
> *fuggendo a piede e sanguinando il piano.*

There where the name thereof becometh void
Did I arrive, pierced through and through the
    throat,
Fleeing on foot, and bloodying the plain.

> *Quivi perdei la vista e la parola;*
> *nel nome di Maria fini', e quivi*
> *caddi, e rimase la mia carne sola.*

There my sight lost I, and my utterance
Ceased in the name of Mary, and thereat
I fell, and tenantless my flesh remained.

HUNTED

Chapter 1

It's odd how when you feel safe you can't think of that thing it was you kept meaning to do, but when you're running for your life you suddenly remember the entire list of things you never got around to doing.

I always wanted to get blindly drunk with a mustachioed man, take him back to his place, do a few extra shots just this side of severe liver damage, and then shave off half his mustache when he passed out. I would then install surveillance equipment before I left so that I could properly appreciate his reaction (and his hangover) when he woke up. And of course I would surveil him from a black windowless van parked somewhere along his street. There would be a wisecracking computer science graduate from MIT in the van with me who almost but not quite went all the way once with a mousy physics major who dumped him because he didn't accelerate her particles.

I can't remember when I thought that one up and added it to my list. It was probably after I saw *True Lies*. It was never particularly high up on my list, for obvious reasons, but the memory came back to me, fully fantasized in Technicolor, once I was running for my life in Romania. Our minds are mysteries.

Somewhere behind me, the Morrigan was fighting off two goddesses of the hunt. Artemis and Diana had decided that I needed killing, and the Morrigan had pledged to protect me from such violent death. Oberon ran on my left and Granuaile on my right; all around me, the forest quaked silently with the pandemonium of Faunus, disrupting Druidic tethers to Tír na nÓg. I could not shift away to safety. All I could do was run and curse the ancient Greco–Romans.

Unlike the Irish and the Norse—and many other cultures—the Greco–Romans did not imagine their gods as eternally youthful but vulnerable to violent death. Oh, they had nectar and ambrosia to keep their skin wrinkle-free and their bodies in prime shape, changing their blood to ichor, and that was similar to the magical food and drink available to other pantheons, but that wasn't the end of it. They could regenerate completely, which essentially gifted them with true immortality, so that even if you shredded them like machaca and ate them with guacamole and warm tortillas, they'd just re-spawn in a brand-new body on Olympus and keep coming after you—hence the reason why Prometheus never died, in spite of having his liver eaten every day by a vulture who oddly never sought variety in his diet.

That didn't mean a fella couldn't beat them. Aside from the fact that they can be slain by other immortals, the Olympians have to exist in time like everyone else. I'd tossed Bacchus onto an island of slow time in Tír na nÓg, and the Olympians took it personally—so personally that they'd rather kill me than get Bacchus back.

I didn't think for a moment I could do the same to the huntresses. They were far more adept in combat, for one thing, and they'd be watching each other's back while doing their best to shoot me in mine.

"Where are we going?" Granuaile asked.

"Roughly north for now. Situation's fluid."

<I may have left some fluid back there when I saw

those arrows coming,> Oberon said. The Morrigan had taken both arrows in her shield and told us to run.

"I almost did too, Oberon," Granuaile said. She could hear his voice now that she was a full Druid. "I should have been ducking or tackling Atticus or almost anything else, but instead I was just trying my damnedest not to pee."

"We'll have to take a potty break later," I said. "Distance is key right now."

"And I'm guessing stealth isn't? This is going to be an easy trail to follow the way we're moving through the forest."

"We'll get crafty when we have the space to do so."

The Morrigan's raspy voice entered my head. It wasn't my favorite habit of hers, but it was convenient at the moment. Her tone was exultant.

Here is a battle worthy of remembrance! How I wish there were witnesses and a bard like Amergin to put it down in song!

Morrigan—

Listen, Siodhachan. I can keep them from pursuing you for some while. But they will hunt again soon enough.

They will? What about you?

I am better than they. But not immortal. My end is near; I have seen it. But what an end it will be!

I slowed down and looked back. Granuaile and Oberon paused too. *You're going to die?*

Don't stop running, you fool! Run and listen and do not sleep. You know how to stave off the need to sleep, don't you?

Yes. Prevent the buildup of adenosine in the brain and—

Enough with the modern words. You know. Now you must either find one of the Old Ways to Tír na nÓg— one that isn't guarded—or make your way to the forest of Herne the Hunter.

The forest of Herne? You mean Windsor Forest? That's a hell of a run across Europe.

You can always die instead, the Morrigan pointed out.

No thanks. But Windsor is not much of a wilderness anymore. It's more like a groomed park. People drink tea there. They might even play croquet. That's not a forest.

It will suffice. Herne is there. He will defend it. And he will bring friends. And, Siodhachan, remember that Gaia loves us more than she loves the Olympians. They have given her nothing in all their long lives. Even now they traumatize her with pandemonium. I am unbinding their chariots; they will be afoot for some while until their smith gods can make them anew. Take advantage and give yourself as much of a lead as possible.

Something didn't compute. *Morrigan, if you saw this coming, why didn't you warn me?*

You were with your woman.

My woman? If I tried to call Granuaile that, I would promptly lose some teeth. She's not mine. You can't possess anyone.

I have learned that lesson very well.

Fine, then what does that have to do with this ridiculous fight with the Olympians? We could have avoided it all.

No. It was always going to come. Delaying would do no good.

Are you kidding? That's what living is. Delaying death. Let's get you some Prozac.

Hush. I have for you what modern people call a lovely parting gift.

I shuddered to think what the Morrigan considered lovely, so I simply said, *A parting gift?*

In Tír na nÓg there is a Time Island with the following address. A vision appeared in my head of a short stone obelisk etched with Ogham script. *Do you see it?*

Yes, but—

Record it well in your memory. Circle the island. On the side facing upstream, look closely at the tree line and

*you will see someone there you might wish to retrieve. If
you do, ask Goibhniu for help.*

Morrigan. Why?

*Because I am trapped and this is the only way out.
And because you have chosen, and you have chosen
well. I cannot fault her.*

I lost a step or two as the import of her words sank in.
Granuaile shot a worried glance at me and I shook my
head once, reassuring her that nothing was wrong.
But . . . Morrigan, you never said anything.

Would it have mattered? Would you have ever chosen me?

I don't know. But I didn't get a chance.

*Every day was a chance, Siodhachan. Two thousand
years of days. If you were interested, you had ample opportunity to express it. I understand. I frighten you. I
frighten everyone, and that is a fact I cannot escape,
however I may wish otherwise.*

Well . . . yeah. You're fighting off two Olympians right
now and having this conversation. That's frightening.

*They came prepared. Their fabrics are synthetic. I
cannot bind them. And they are very skilled, trying to
wound my right side and affect my magic.*

Morrigan, just get out of there. You saved me and we
have a lead now.

*No. This is the choice I have made. It is only recently
I have tried to change in earnest—I mean since you slew
Aenghus Óg—and discovered that somehow change has
become impossible for me. I cannot make friends. I cannot be gentle except under the most extraordinary circumstances. My nature will not allow it. All I can do is
terrify, seduce, and choose the slain. Is that not strange?
Long ago I was merely a Druid like you and could do
whatever I wished. But once I became a goddess, certain
expectations came with the power. Call them chains,
rather. I didn't notice them until I tried to break free. My*

*nature now is no longer my own to do with as I please.
I can be only what my people want me to be.*

I'm sorry. I didn't know.

*I tell you so that you may grow wiser. It is a hidden
law of godhood, and woe unto she who finds it. I have
been trying to deny its reality, but it has asserted itself
too often to be anything but the truth. Yet I have some
comfort now.*

You do?

*Here is my victory, Siodhachan: I am permitted to do
battle, and I do not need a reason. Still, I usually have
one, and that reason can be whatever I wish. So today I
do not fight for glory or honor or bloodlust or vengeance. I fight for . . . something else.*

I understand. But say it anyway. For the win.

Love.

Morrigan, I—

I felt as if something popped softly in my head, like
the release of tension when a taut cord is cut. Or a binding. There was a sudden emptiness, and an overwhelming sense of vertigo caused me to stumble over a root
and execute a graceless face-plant.

Morrigan? The silence in my head pointed to only one
conclusion. Our mental bond had been like the soft elec-
tric hum of kitchen appliances or computers that you
never notice until they stop. During a rather painful ritual that had regenerated an ear I'd lost to a demon,
she'd slipped in the binding that allowed her to speak to
me telepathically. It was gone now.

"Atticus, what happened?" Granuaile helped me to
my feet and gasped when she saw my face. "Are you
hurt? Why are you crying?"

She let go of my arm and then had to grab it again
when I swayed on my feet, still a bit dizzy. "The Morrigan is dead," I said.

Chapter 2

"Think you can carry your staff in your mouth as a horse?" I asked, to forestall any questions about what happened. I rubbed away my tears with the heel of my palm. Granuaile understood and didn't press the issue, though her voice sounded hollowed out by shock.

"I suppose I could."

"Good. Leave your clothes here." I began to strip and tried to clear my head of its dizziness by taking several deep breaths. "We really need to make time. We'll hoof it and recharge from the earth as we go."

Granuaile peeled off her shirt. "The Morrigan said the Old Ways would be collapsed or guarded," she said, recalling what the goddess had said to us before we took off running. "Are we going to fight our way through and use one of those?"

"I think we'll be running all the way to England. Or to France, anyway, then we'll swim the channel."

"We're seriously running there from *Romania*?"

"That's right."

"We can't take a train or boost a car or something?"

"No. You heard what the Morrigan said. The only way she saw us survive is running the whole way."

"That doesn't make sense."

"When it comes to our survival, I don't want to bet

against the Morrigan's visions. She tends—I mean, tended to be accurate on matters of life and death."

"I'm not trying to argue the truth of what she said. I just want to understand why it's true."

I shrugged. "I don't know the answer yet. We'll find out as we go. My guess is that we'll have to figure out everything on the run."

Once divested of our clothing, with our weapons lying on the ground in front of us, we shifted to our hooved forms—a stag and a chestnut mare—and picked up our weapons in our mouths.

<Heh! You guys better hope we don't run into a thick patch where the trees grow really close together,> Oberon said.

I didn't have a reply for that, but Granuaile must have, because Oberon followed that up with an outraged <What? Seriously? Do I have to?> She obviously said he did, for he continued, <We need to get you some saddle-bags or something.> He picked up one of Granuaile's thigh holsters, where she kept three leaf-bladed throwing knives. <You know how ridiculous we look, right? I know a horse whisperer, and I'm totally going to give him a call about you.>

The one-sided banter continued as we began to run, and I was grateful for it. Someone I had thought of as eternal had abruptly ended, and it rocked me. I couldn't have summoned a single playful riposte to Oberon's comments. There was simply too much else for me to deal with, not least of which was figuring out how we would continue to survive.

Once out of the foothills of the Apuseni Mountains, we were able to pour on the speed, skirting along the edge of a small plateau and then, descending out of the wilderness, running across flat cultivated lands. We bore northwest to avoid crossing more hills and slowing down. We kept to the vineyards and alfalfa and cereal crops and avoided the villages. We swam across two rivers and crossed into Hungary by running south of Oradea as the sun set. Through Oberon, I relayed to Granuaile what the Morrigan had said—the bits about getting to Herne's forest, anyway.

Her question to me: <What route shall we take to get there?>

Our best chance was in simple speed, unless we could somehow find an Old Way to Tír na nÓg that wasn't monitored. I had no doubt that those would all be watched. The people behind planning this wanted to make sure they got us, and they wouldn't be able to if we could get to Tír na nÓg and then shift to another plane entirely. The Romans had done the same thing to the ancient Druids when they tried to wipe us out with the help of vampires and the Roman goddess Minerva. Step one had been to burn all the sacred groves on the continent, which were the only tethers to Tír na nÓg at the time; step two was to guard all the Old Ways; and step three was to use Minerva's aid to see through our camouflage. I'd managed to escape them by running north beyond the boundaries of the Roman Empire. I would not be surprised to learn that Minerva had advised Pan, Faunus, and the huntresses how to hunt us now.

But I had never tried to run across Europe before. I'd hiked it once and stayed in youth hostels and put little patches on my backpack because I thought it was a funny disguise, but I took my time doing that, and climbing up mountains was an experience to be savored. I rather thought dealing with mountains now would do nothing but slow us down, and, besides, I didn't want to telegraph our intended destination. To get to the Strait of Dover directly, we could simply run north of west and hit it. But that route would present us not only with several mountain ranges but plenty of well-paved cities like Budapest and Vienna. We needed misdirection and the ability to keep in touch with the earth at all times. That's why I took a sharp turn north at the Hungarian border: Once we crossed the Carpathians, we could stick to flattish land or, at the worst, low rolling hills all the way to France. While we moved northwest through Poland and Germany, we'd keep them thinking we were headed for Sweden via Denmark. To get the best possible route, however, avoiding the majority of villages while also minimizing our exposure to survivalists in the woods awaiting the apocalypse, I would need to consult elementals along the way. Using my Latin headspace, I reached out to the Carpathian elemental, who was dominant across several human political borders that were meaningless to Gaia.

//Druids run / Need guidance / Avoid people and cities if possible//

After some back-and-forth with Carpathia, we settled on a route that would take us north through rural areas of Hungary and Slovakia until we reached the proper Carpathian Mountains.

With a plan in place and an hour of trail behind us, I had time to feel, and much of that feeling leaked out of my eyes as I ran. I had spent nearly my entire life worshipping the Morrigan, and, in recent years, more than that. She was the darkness for me, an unexpectedly beautiful harbinger of doom and pain who forced me to struggle, who pushed me to improve myself. She was a necessary balance to Brighid, not something merely to be feared but to be treasured. As Brighid brought light and craft and poetry to our lives, the Morrigan brought an edge, a tangible sharpness to my existence by sharing hers with me.

With the clarity of hindsight, I saw the signs that the Morrigan had favored me far more than she had the average mortal. Six years ago, especially, when she took me away from Granuaile to repair the tattoos on the back of my hand, she'd been uncharacteristically candid with me, but I had dismissed it because we were in a room enchanted with bindings that encouraged harmony. Now I saw that our interlude there had been haunting her ever since. As soon as she left that room, she reverted to her cruel self, when she had not necessarily wished to do so. And that was what made her snap—not her love for some dude but her lack of freedom to love or not as she desired.

I'd tried to be her friend, which probably made it all worse. We'd gone to a few baseball games together simply to hang out, and she couldn't keep herself from remarking on the fear of failure the players felt, or their guilt or despair at poor performance, and only noticed their triumphs when I observed them aloud. Each time I did, she cringed, taking it as a rebuke. She seemed to think she should have seen it first, or at least at the same time, but she had a filter blocking all such things from her sight. Each time we'd gone out to the ballpark, she began the night flushed with optimism, convinced that this time she would be able to enjoy the competition and my company on a purely superficial level and ignore all the feelings she was attuned to feel as a goddess associated with death and war and lust. Usually that optimism had fled by the third inning and she sat in silence, distrusting herself to say anything lest it be perceived as accentuating the negative. My attempts to cheer her up with happy observations only emphasized that she lacked the social facility to engage on that level.

We caught a game in St. Louis once, and after a quick visit to the team shop I was struck by how different she looked in a Cardinals jersey and cap. She looked damn cute—not hot or sultry or sexy but the sort of innocent, wholesome beauty that lifts your spirit and makes you grateful to be alive to see it. But when I told the Morrigan she looked cute, she didn't understand the nuance, nor did she appreciate it when I tried to explain it to her. She thought I was asking for sex, discovered that I wasn't, and then we both felt frustrated and embarrassed. Despite these failures, I thought that we were making progress, becoming friends after two millennia of being uneasy allies against Aenghus Óg. I suppose the Morrigan didn't feel the progress was sufficient or of the right kind.

Perhaps just as frustrating for her was the inability to enlist the aid of an iron elemental in binding a cold iron amulet to her aura. No matter how she tried, she could not free herself from the conditions of her godhood and project friendliness.

I supposed she was free now—most importantly, free of those constraints and, to a lesser extent, of an idiot Druid who never recognized her true feelings. If I had looked at her in the magical spectrum, I might have seen those emotional bonds, much as Granuaile had seen them between us soon after she'd gained her magical sight. But I never dared to look at the Morrigan that way. She would know and consider it an invasion of privacy, and she dealt with such invasions harshly.

I supposed I was free now, too, but, unlike the Morrigan, I didn't want to be. Ridiculous as it seemed, I wanted to see her eyes flash red at me again and tell me I was doomed. I wanted to see another baseball game with her and train her in the hallowed yet disgusting art of chewing sunflower seeds.

And, admittedly, I wanted to feel protected again. She'd been the only one looking out for me. Without the Morrigan's aegis, I was once again vulnerable to violent death. That had been the case for the vast majority of my long life, of course, but I knew I would miss the last twelve years of relative security. The frequency of attempts on my life had increased dramatically since I'd

decided to stop running from Aenghus Óg, and having a
goddess in my corner had been a comfort. Her aid had
been sporadic and never free of pain, but without it I
would certainly already be dead. With her gone now
and two immortals on my trail, perhaps the sand in my
hourglass was finally running out.

We quickly discovered that all three of us running in
concealment was impractical. We lost one another and
spread out unintentionally or even bumped into each
other. I remained visible, since a stag running through
fields was not all that remarkable and decidedly no
cause for alarm. Someone might try to round up Granuaile as a horse, however, and Oberon might be reported
as a stray. It was easiest for Granuaile to remain completely invisible and Oberon camouflaged, and in such a
fashion they followed my lead.

Unaided, we were pretty fast critters; each of us could
reach thirty miles an hour and maintain that for perhaps
a mile or three before we had to rest. But with Gaia's
help, we could push that to forty to forty-five miles an
hour and keep it up indefinitely, replenishing spent muscles and preventing oxygen debt.

The eastern half of Slovakia is largely rural and we
had an easy time of it, especially after everyone had
gone home for the evening. We slowed down to cross
the occasional road or vault a low fence but otherwise
stayed in a zone and ran without speaking, hopefully
developing a gap that the huntresses would never be
able to close. Our first trouble waited for us to the north
of a lake called Veľká Domaša.

Domaša was oriented north to south, formed by a
dam on the Ondava River. It was about eight miles long,
and its surface, silvered with reflected moonlight, had
slid by on our left as we ran through the forested hills on
its eastern side. It was one of those mature forests that
give humans a sense of security, because the under-

growth had been either choked out or taught to mind its manners and couldn't hide large, man-eating predators. People hiked through it and preyed on wild mushrooms instead.

We slipped down from the hills after we'd cleared a wee town on its northeastern shore, a village of maybe five hundred people that I later learned was called Turany nad Ondavou. At that point, Oberon's nose picked up something and so did mine.

\<Hey, Atticus. Either something's dead or there's a vampire around here somewhere.\>

\<I smell it too,\> I replied.

\<Clever Girl says she smells it.\>

\<Okay, let's just chill here a second, and tell her not to shift. If she switches to human, the vampire will sense her.\>

\<Doesn't he sense us now?\>

\<We're harmless animals now, and he's probably looking for humans.\>

There was a road ahead of us that led to a border crossing—and thus a pass through the Carpathians. The plan was to follow roughly along its eastern side. I saw nothing on the road heading north, but, scanning to the south, back toward the town, I saw four figures—two on either side of the road. They were all looking south and clearly waiting for something. They wore jeans and hoodies with the hoods pulled up, hands jammed into their pockets.

Triggering magical sight, I saw that one had the telltale gray aura of a vampire. The other three were far more dangerous, in my view. \<Dark elves,\> I said.

\<Granuaile says she wants to set them on fire.\>

I gave a sort of mental snort. The dark elves wouldn't remain solid long enough to burn. \<I should probably quip here that revenge is a dish best served cold.\>

\<You need to explain that saying sometime. You say it

like it's a bad thing, but to me it suggests ice cream, because that's also best served cold. I think more people would seek revenge if it were served with ice cream. Or maybe gelato or frozen yogurt, but not the kind with fruit mixed in—>

<Oberon.>

<Yeah?>

<Ask Granuaile seriously if she wants to take them out or keep running.>

There was a pause before the answer came. <She says yes. She doesn't want them joining up with the goddesses and ganging up on us. But we need to do it quick if we're going to do it.>

She was right about that. The huntresses would be coming along and we couldn't delay. It occurred to me that perhaps the elves' sole function was to delay us.

The last time we'd encountered dark elves was in Thessalonika, and we barely escaped. There were fewer of them here, however, and Granuaile was now a full Druid with powers they probably did not expect.

Did the vampire know what we could do to him? He might be a young one and somewhat out of the loop regarding Druids. But I saw his utility to the group: He was a sensor array. We would not be able to sneak up on them unawares. He'd smell us or hear us far in advance.

<I'll unbind the vampire first and charge from here in plain view. Granuaile should stay invisible and flank the dark elves. If she uses magical sight, she should be able to keep track of them in the dark when they turn to smoke.>

Granuaile shifted but remained invisible and evidently had a complaint when she asked Oberon for her throwing knives, for I heard my hound say, <Slobber is just one of the many fine services I provide for free.>

<Oberon, please stay here. There's nothing you can bite down there.>

<Okay, that's fine with me. I've been meaning to do some serious maintenance of the undercarriage, if you know what I mean, and you guys always freak out when I go downtown.>

<Tell Granuaile she can go. I'm going to unbind the vampire now.>

I shifted to human and focused on the vampire, speaking the words that would separate him into nothing more than carbon, water, and trace elements. With him gone, the dark elves would have to rely on their more limited senses. I heard Granuaile's footsteps fade as she ran down the slope toward the road. She would flank them to the north while I would be charging in from the northeast.

Alerted by something he either smelled or heard, the vampire turned and pointed in my direction, but he crumpled inside his clothing once I energized the binding, and his jeans dropped to the ground with a sort of red sludge spilling out the legs. I dropped my camouflage, drew Fragarach, and charged, naked and howling, just like we Celts used to do in the good old days.

For their part, the dark elves dropped all pretense of being human. Upon the vampire's demise, they pulled out page one of their playbook from *Sigr af Reykr,* the martial art that means Victory from Smoke, and turned incorporeal to avoid getting stabbed or shot or otherwise ambushed. It would have been a fabulous tactic against someone who couldn't view them in the magical spectrum; they would have melted into the night and been untraceable. But I could see them plainly as clouds of white energy, and, furthermore, I knew they could maintain their smoke forms for only five seconds. They could spend as little as one second in corporeal form before turning to smoke again, but for that one second they would be vulnerable, and if I was right, once they were wounded, they couldn't go smoky again until they healed.

Each would have a black knife bonded to him that could dissolve and re-form like his body, but as such it was magical and couldn't penetrate my aura. Granuaile and Oberon could be hurt by those knives, however, so I wanted the dark elves to try to stab me all they wanted while Granuaile bushwhacked them.

As I pelted down the hill and crossed the field to their position by the road, I noticed that they weren't heading for trees on the far side of the road or forming up to face me. They were remaining in their positions, solidifying briefly and then going smoky again but waiting for me to close the gap.

That was odd. Alarm bells went off in my head and I stopped yelling as I tried to figure out what was up. There were no telltales of a magical booby trap, but perhaps they decided to go with something more mundane. They could have planted mines around their position and I would blow myself up.

Oberon, tell Granuaile to approach on the road. There might be mines.

I contacted Carpathia. //Query: Shallow buried metal ahead of my current path?//

//Yes//

I stopped running. //Show me//

The images filtered into my head. A semicircle of M16A2 bounding anti-personnel mines surrounded the dark elves on either side of the road but easily two hundred feet from their position. It was an American design; they were scattered throughout the Middle East and Asia. Step on one, remove your foot, and the mine would pop out of the ground about three feet into the air before detonating and spraying shrapnel for a hundred feet in every direction. To avoid detection, they would have been wiser to plant the modern blast mines that used a minimum of metal, but they probably were counting on me being stupid. I was still a safe distance away and could detonate them remotely. I'm not brilliant at shifting earth, but I can move a bit of topsoil when I need to.

Oberon, tell Granuaile to stop and hit the deck for a few seconds.

Targeting a circle of sod near me, I bound it to the top of the first mine. The turf flew through the air and triggered the bounder when it landed and rolled off. The explosion boomed in the night, and shredded bits of iron sprayed out and fell harmlessly between us. I repeated the exercise until all the mines had been detonated.

Silly dark elves. Earth is for Druids.

Still they refused to move. When they solidified, they were looking in my direction, but they kept their positions by the road. That meant they had some other kind of protection and wanted me to charge in. I wouldn't do that, because doing what the enemy wants is tantamount to taking a bath with a kitchen appliance. They might have another ring of those plastic mines after all. Carpathia would have a tough time sensing them, except perhaps as displaced soil.

Warn Granuaile to look for more booby traps. They're too comfortable there. Take them out from the maximum distance possible.

<Okay,> Oberon said.

I beckoned the elves to come forward, but once they saw this—which proved they had excellent night vision—they remained solid and copied the motion, white smiles splitting their faces. I smiled back and watched one on the far side of the road take a throwing knife in the side of his neck. So nice of him to remain still and present a target like that for Granuaile. His partner immediately went smoky, but the remaining dark elf on my side didn't see it happen, because he was facing me. I kept smiling at him and gesturing, and in another couple of seconds he went down too. The last dark elf had to turn solid after his five seconds were up, but he tried to be clever about it and solidified in a crouch, presenting a smaller target. Granuaile anticipated it and nailed him anyway. It wasn't a fatal shot, catching him in the shoulder, but my theory proved true: They couldn't dissolve their substance once their skin was broken. He clutched the knife and cursed in Old Norse, remaining crouched on the ground.

Tell Granuaile to head back to you and leave the knives. We'll get her some more. He's neutralized now, and I don't want to risk walking into a trap we can't see.

After a pause, Oberon replied, <She says last one to the hound is a really old guy.>

I grinned and sprinted back up the hill, leaving the lone dark elf behind to watch the bodies of his comrades melt to black tar. A regular infusion of Immortali-Tea might be keeping my body from aging, but Granuaile made me feel young again.

Chapter 3

The only way dark elves and a vampire could have been waiting at that particular spot long enough to plant land mines was if somebody had known we'd be running through there. That suggested a couple of things: Either the Olympians tipped them off—which I thought unlikely because they wouldn't achieve their measure of glory if they let someone else kill me—or someone was following the Morrigan's movements and made an educated guess about our route. That someone was most likely Fae. Few others would have a chance to move around the Irish planes without being seen.

Guessing our route wouldn't have been that difficult if one assumed we were headed north; there were few passes through the Carpathians, and following a river was one of the easiest ways to shake a tail—you cross it, you cross it again, you pretend to cross but really you just run in the shallow water until you reemerge a bit upstream on the same side. Sitting on a river that led more or less straight to the pass was a fair gamble.

I said to Granuaile, "We may have a faery tail."

<Yeah! This is the kind of faery tale with children who wander off and get in trouble in the forest. Usually they die because they don't have a wolfhound along—or parents. You ever notice the rampant child neglect going on in faery tales?>

"No, Oberon, I said we might have a faery tail, as in a faery who is tailing us."

My hound whined. <English is stupid sometimes.>

"Look up once in a while. It's clearly not only the goddesses hunting us. We still have vampires and dark elves to worry about, and I think they're getting help from someone in Tír na nÓg."

"Does *anyone* like us?" Granuaile asked, an edge of bitterness to her voice. "Because I'm thinking maybe we should go hang out with them if we survive this."

"Yeah. We should probably get out of Europe for a while if we can."

Grauaile exhaled quickly, banishing wishful thinking and returning to practical matters. "But first things first, right? We have to get out of this fix. Would it be ridiculous to booby-trap our trail?"

"No, I don't think so. In fact, I think it's strategically necessary."

"Agreed. Even a failed trap will cause them to slow down and be wary for more. We should make a pit trap with spikes in the bottom. You make the pit and I'll make the spikes."

I grinned at her. "A cold suggestion of mayhem? That's hot."

Granuaile dropped her staff, stepped forward, and placed her hands flat against my chest. Her face darted toward mine for a quick kiss but then pulled back at the last instant, leaving me with the heat of her breath and the scent of strawberry lip gloss. I don't think she was wearing any—beauty products tend not to survive the rigors of shape-shifting—but I always smelled it now, regardless; the memory of it was indelibly linked with the sight of her lips. She pushed me away, hard, and shape-shifted to a horse. She picked up her staff in her mouth and galloped north at full speed, leaving me bewildered and more than a little wistful. Oberon's mental groan came a few seconds later.

<She says if you want any, you have to beat her to the other side of the Carpathians.>

I broke into a wide smile before dropping Fragarach's scabbard on the ground and shape-shifting to a stag. <Giddyup!> I said to him, picking the sword up in my mouth.

<Have I ever shared with you my opinion of human mating habits?>

The race, I eventually discerned, was in earnest. I spent half of it like a cockfident waffle dolphin, thinking she would slow down and let me win. But then I tried to close the gap and found that she hadn't been going full speed after all; she had a sixth and seventh gear.

<Clarify some slang for me, Atticus?> Oberon asked.

<Sure.>

<Is this what humans call a "quickie"?>

The horse in front of me whinnied in amusement— Granuaile could of course hear Oberon too—but I wasn't gaining on her, so I didn't think it was funny. We were running either in or near the trees on the east side of Highway E371 to keep from drawing the attention of drivers crossing the border between Slovakia and Poland. This was Dukla Pass, site of one of the bloodiest battles of the eastern front during World War II. Farmhouses and memorials for the dead sat like squat chess pieces on squares of pasture framed by stands of timber.

Once past the border and safely on the other side of the pass, Granuaile paused to gloat at the edge of an alfalfa field. "Guess you'll have to rechannel all your sexual energy into making a death trap for immortals," she said.

<Eh, you guys have fun constructing impossibilities in the dark. I'm taking a nap.>

A nap sounded like a great idea to me, but we couldn't

afford the time. If we slept now we might never wake up, so we concentrated on our task.

Normally a pit trap would take many hours and a handy tool like a shovel or a backhoe—or at least a spade—with which to move the earth. But it doesn't take that long and requires no tools at all when the earth is willing to do all the work for you. The trick is to be smart about it when you have two expert huntresses on your tail.

"We can't have you cutting down branches here and sharpening stakes," I said. "If they have night vision or they come through here after dawn, there's too much chance that they'll see it and be wary. Let's cross the pasture on the hoof and leave a clear trail. Once we get to the other side, we pull a wascally wabbit and tunnel back, you see?"

"I surely do." She shifted to a horse, took up her staff, and galloped across.

<Oh. I guess this means I don't get that nap.>

"Not here, anyway. Across the field of joy. Here. Take Fragarach with you too. Tell Granuaile to get started and I'll be there soon. I need to snag some flashlights from the border station." Oberon opened his mouth extra wide to carry both my scabbard and Granuaile's knives.

<This is getting ridiculous. I want a deluxe package at a doggie day spa to alleviate my trauma,> he said.

"Enough complaining."

<I'm not complaining. I'm lobbying. It's this whole other word.>

I doubled back in camouflage, not caring if the huntresses saw the footprints. Let them follow me to the guard station at the border and wonder what I did there.

What I did was throw a couple of rocks at the guardhouse windows. Two guards obligingly came out with flashlights shining into the night, resting their hands on the butts of their guns and calling out warnings to the dark. I snatched their flashlights away, turned them off, and then cast camouflage on them. From the guards' point of view, the flashlights had leapt out of their hands and disappeared. They drew their guns but they couldn't find a target in the dark. I was already running back to the alfalfa field, chased by Polish curses that seemed to Doppler-shift bizarrely into "Never Gonna Give You Up," and after I thought of it I couldn't believe I'd just rickrolled myself.

Once I reached the field, I kept trucking across it with my human feet. There was no need to switch up my form for consistency; all the goddesses needed to do was follow me across. Underneath the opposite cover of trees, we made contact with Carpathia. Granuaile wanted a bit of help and some permission to harvest some living tree branches, while I explained the tunnel we needed and then the pit in the middle of the pasture that needed to be hollowed out while leaving the surface undisturbed. Artemis and Diana needed to see that swath of trampled alfalfa and follow directly in our paths.

Despite Carpathia's aid, building the trap took an hour. Moving the earth and hidden rocks in the ground wasn't that much trouble for the elemental—only the work of a few minutes or so—but it took us multiple trips through the tunnel to populate the pit with sharpened stakes. We could carry only so much, because we had to carry the flashlights too. Our night vision was sufficient for the work outside, but that wouldn't cut it in the total darkness of underground. Planting the stakes in the bottom of the pit so that they'd remain steady took the majority of the time.

The pit itself was rather deep at twenty feet, and Oberon was impressed. To him it was an epic feat of engineering.

<How deep is this compared to that one in Sparta where the Persian diplomats got kicked?>

"Not nearly so deep," I replied.

<What if you were like an evil cyborg longing for redemption and you wanted to throw the emperor with lightning fingers down here? Would he go *fwoosh* when he hit the bottom?>

"He'd go something, but probably not *fwoosh*." I was worried that the goddesses would avoid the stakes somehow. Their teams would fall in first, after all, and they might land on their teams and thereby avoid injury. I wanted it to be difficult to hop out if they somehow managed to avoid the stakes, and even I don't have a twenty-foot vertical leap. But what if they had some sort of levitation enchantment on their chariots? In the brief glimpse of the chariots that I'd had before the goddesses fired at us, I thought the chariots were floating slightly off the ground. I couldn't recall if their teams had been floating too. If so, then we'd probably wasted an hour. But if not, then the stags would fall in and drag the chariots down by their harness. Maybe. I hoped that, one way or another, falling into the pit would cause the goddesses at least an hour's inconvenience, if not more, in addition to slowing down their subsequent rate of pursuit. The Morrigan had bought us a few hours of time when she had unbound their chariots, since they had to wait awhile to get new ones from Hephaestus and Vulcan. We were eating into that time now. With luck, the pit trap would gain us half a day's lead on them.

The roof of the pit was nothing but a finely woven carpet of alfalfa roots strengthened with a binding in the middle to prevent sagging. Carpathia closed up the tunnel behind us as we left.

We hoofed it out of there to the northwest, loping downhill now, planning to skirt the Polish city of Jasło to the southwest. By following that general course—

keeping to rural areas as best we could but darting into villages here and there to get what we needed—we would avoid all the mountainous terrain of Poland and Germany. Once into the Netherlands, we could swing south and west through Belgium until we hit Calais, France.

Journeys sound so easy when you string together destinations in a sentence. But one does not simply run into Britain.

Chapter 4

I don't think people today fully understand the genius of *The X-Files,* a sci-fi show that dominated much of the nineties. It had a way of getting into your head. At least, it got into mine in ways that I didn't realize until later. Smoking men in suits now fill me with existential dread, for example. Whatever I'm doing when I see one calmly sucking hundreds of toxins into his lungs, I feel somehow that the smoking man manipulated me into doing it. I then have to flee and do something random in order to feel that I am not a pawn in his master plan. And let's just not talk about bees, okay?

Mostly the series taught me to fear silhouettes in open spaces backlit by strange lights. That's why a thrill of fear shot down my spine when I saw thirteen figures waiting in an onion field to the west of Jasło. Maybe they had Mulder's sister. Maybe we wouldn't be able to kill them unless we stabbed a shiv into the base of their skulls. Maybe they were dark elves.

The light providing the silhouettes wasn't coming from behind them, I saw as I drew closer, but rather surrounded them in various shades of purple. They seemed like silhouettes because they wore black, but the lights swirling around them were familiar and lit up some faces I knew. They were wards I recognized; these were the Sisters of the Three Auroras, the Polish coven led by

Malina Sokolowski, with whom I had signed a nonaggression treaty years ago.

Malina was in front, her wards the most colorful and undoubtedly the strongest, and her long blond hair was still breathtakingly beautiful. She hadn't aged a day in twelve years, and neither had I. But circumstances had certainly changed. The other members of her coven that I recognized—Roksana, Klaudia, Kazimiera, and Berta—were grouped close to Malina.

She had eight new members of the coven who had never signed the treaty, and I had Granuaile, who hadn't signed it either. If Malina wanted to get nasty, she technically could, via her proxies. Granuaile wasn't protected from spells, as I was, but she could get nasty too.

Through Oberon I communicated to Granuaile that we should shift back to human and slow down. She shifted simultaneously with me and we approached at a slow jog, weapons in hand. "They fight with silver knives," I muttered to her before we came into hailing distance. "Faster than human."

"Got it."

"And don't stare at their parts. They use alluring charms to control people."

"How lovely."

<Sounds complicated. They could control me by using kielbasa.>

Malina sounded surprised when she addressed me, though it might have been an affectation. "Mr. O'Sullivan? What are you doing here?" She did not add, "naked, in an onion field," but it was in her expression.

"Miss Sokolowski. I could ask you the same."

"It's Sokołowska in Poland. There are genitive endings on names here that I didn't bother with in America."

"Ah. Thank you. I really do need to learn Polish. It

seems congratulations are in order. Your coven is strong again."

"Yes, we are. And it appears there is another Druid in the world."

"Indeed. Malina, this is Granuaile."

The two of them exchanged pleasantries, and then Malina, as was her habit, got straight to business, ignoring our nudity.

"We divined some great cataclysm to come. Might you know anything about that?"

"Well, yeah. It's Ragnarok."

She thought I was being flippant. "I'm serious, Mr. O'Sullivan."

"So am I. The last time we met, at Four Peaks Brewery in Tempe, I was about to screw everything up for everybody. I'm fairly certain I succeeded. Now I'm trying to do what I can to delay its coming or soften the blow if I can't stop it. I think we have a year left before it all goes pear-shaped."

"Why a year?"

"Well, Loki is free from his long imprisonment, and Hel has a massive army to deploy against the nine realms. They could have started it already, you see, but they haven't because we've distracted them and wounded their confidence. And I'm counting on a prophecy, which pointed to next year."

Malina scoffed. "Whose prophecy?"

"The sirens who tempted Odysseus."

Malina exchanged a look with Klaudia, the waifish witch who always looked like she'd just completed erotic exercises. She managed to wear her clothes in such a way that you were certain she hadn't been wearing them a minute ago. "The sirens told Odysseus that Ragnarok would begin next year?"

I shrugged. "Not in so many words, but the evidence does point that way. They said the world would burn.

Loki is quite the pyromaniac, and I have no doubt that, once Surtr leaves Muspellheim, there will be much aflame. But, honestly, I don't know what the prophecy truly means. Maybe they're talking about lots of forest fires during an especially hot summer."

"I doubt that. The sirens did not speak idly to heroes of insignificant events."

"Ah, so you've heard about their accuracy?"

"Indeed. Is there something we can do? Because our divination suggested some sort of fire would be started here."

"It did?"

"Yes. You know I do not joke about such things."

"Well, yeah, but I don't know why a fire would start—what?" Granuaile had tapped me on the shoulder to get my attention. Once she had it, she pointed up. "Oh," I said. "Now it makes sense. Incoming!"

A large ball of fire was headed straight for us, arcing out of the western sky. We gave ground, and a palpable shock wave buffeted us when the fireball hit the earth. A twelve-foot-tall madman cackled in the midst of it while clasping his hands together in glee.

"There!" Loki said, his face intensely pleased. "Fff-fff-fffound you!"

Chapter 5

I drew Fragarach and charged him; there was no time to talk. He could set everyone on fire with a wave of his hand, so I preferred that he focus on me rather than watch him cook Granuaile and Oberon to ashes.

I was a little fire-shy after getting cooked myself by some dark elves, but Loki's fire was the magical sort and I knew my cold iron aura would protect me from it. He giggled as his right hand disappeared and the stump of his wrist became a flamethrower. Heat rained down on me as I leapt at him and slashed down with my sword. He was quick and stepped back, but I opened up a long wound down his right thigh.

Loki roared and turned off the flames. His eyes boggled at me as his head twitched. I should have been barbecued but clearly wasn't. "You can't burn us, Loki Firestarter," I said. "We're all protected."

You're not protected, I told Oberon with a quick thought. *Get Granuaile out of range.*

<Right.>

Loki waggled a finger at me and squinted. "You are nuh-no construh-uh-ukt," he stammered. "Dwarf-ff-fffs sssay they don't nuh-know you. Lllliar!"

"Who cares what the dwarfs know or don't know?" I smiled in a fashion that I hoped was unsettling. He was already mentally unstable and might therefore be more susceptible to intimidation. "All you need to know is this: I'm the guy who's going to kill you."

Loki's eyes widened and he took a couple of steps back as I advanced. But then his right arm disappeared behind him, he arched his back a bit, and the arm reappeared holding a very long sword that ignited from guard to tip as I watched.

I frowned. "Now, where, exactly, did you pull that from?" His daughter, Hel, had done something similar; she kept her knife, Famine, lodged between her lower ribs on her left side. She must have learned the trick of using the body as a scabbard from dear old dad. As shape-shifters, they would have the knack.

<Kind of recasts the meaning of the word *badass*, doesn't it?>

Oberon, tell Granuaile to talk to the witches. They need to charm Loki if they can.

<Okay. But it makes you wonder what he'd look like on one of those airport body scans.>

Loki's eyes went dark and he raised his sword. *Hurry, Oberon!* The flaming blade fell, but I wasn't there. I leapt directly at him again, because the best thing you can do when facing someone with enormous reach is to get inside it. I didn't hack or stab at him but delivered a straight kick between his hips, right in his center of gravity. He doubled over, let go of the sword as he staggered, and then fell heavily. I heard Polish behind me but kept my eyes on Loki. He shrank and morphed and sprang to his feet—this time as a Vedic demon with blue skin, four arms, and a blade that he pulled directly out of his body in each hand. He smiled with especially sharp teeth and twirled the swords at me, and I didn't have time to wonder until much later how he'd ever come across that particular form.

I had to fight my feet not to give ground. It had been quite some time since I'd practiced against more than two blades. When I was younger and everyone had a sword, you were more likely to run into that sort of thing. Nowadays you were more likely to run into multiple guns than multiple swords.

Loki's newly black eyes shifted from my face to a point over my right shoulder. He blinked hard, blinked harder, shook his head, and his swords stopped moving. He tried to refocus on me but his eyes drew away once more, and this time he flinched backward and dropped a couple of his weapons. The hands slapped at his eye sockets, and then he pressed his palms into them.

"Nuh! No! Ssstop!"

Worried about me, he lowered his hands and peeked over his fingers to make sure I wasn't about to run him through. That's when Malina stepped in front of me and tossed her hair at him. That did it. His hands dropped, his jaw dropped, and the other two hands still holding swords dropped as well.

"He's charmed now," Malina said over her shoulder, her gaze locked on Loki. "You can kill him and get this over with."

"No, we don't want to kill him," I said.

"Why not?"

"Because if we do, Hel will know it and launch her army out of spite. Ragnarok will begin. Hel would much rather start the show with Loki than without him, see. She has daddy issues and doesn't want to win without his approval and participation, so if you keep him busy we'll be in good shape."

"How do you know this?"

"Loki's been looking for me for about four months now. Well, he's been sleeping for most of it, but still. Hel didn't make a move in all that time except to protect him."

Roksana, the witch with a mass of curly hair tightly bound behind her in a ponytail, spoke up in her proper diction: "You want us to keep him charmed for an extended period?"

"Yep." I grinned at her.

Malina snorted. "This man is extremely unstable, and it will take a lot of work to keep him calm. You saw that it took several of us to subdue him just now. What do we get out of this, Mr. O'Sullivan?"

"Well, you get a world without Ragnarok, for starters. And I can buy you all some of those shiny black boots you tend to like."

"That is unacceptable. I might as well let him go right now."

"You'd help bring about the end of the world?"

"He seems to want to end you first, Mr. O'Sullivan. So tell me why shouldn't we let him go."

"I can score you some Girl Scout Cookies. You can't get Thin Mints in Poland, can you?"

"Be serious."

"Samoas, then?"

Malina simply glared at me.

"All right," I said, "what do you want?"

"You have given me the impression that we'd be not only saving your life but saving the world. We need more than cookies for that."

<I knew it. If you give a witch a cookie, she's going to ask you for a glass of milk.>

"Understood, Malina. But what? I don't know what you think I can give you."

"I want Poland to be free of vampires."

A silence grew in the field and Granuaile eventually broke it by saying, "Is she trying to be funny?"

"When and for how long?" I asked.

"After Ragnarok comes and goes or in a year: If we are here, and you are here, and vampires are here, you keep Poland vampire-free by whatever means necessary."

"All big ifs. But, all right, it's a deal: One month of keeping Loki captive equals one year of vampire-free Poland."

"That is acceptable." We shook hands on it.

"By the way," I said. "Hel has this hound called Garm, who can track anything, even across planes. She will send him to find Loki. When he does, Hel will bring an army of the damned to protect her father. Good luck with that. Oh, and Artemis and Diana are on my tail, so they'll be coming through here soon looking for someone to shoot. Bye. Gotta run." I gave her a short wave and took off running west. Granuaile and Oberon followed.

"What?" Malina's outrage was plain. "Mr. O'Sullivan! Come back!"

I grinned and kept running. It wasn't every day I got the best of Malina. I was sure to pay for it in the future, but in the meantime you have to surf the waves that come your way, and this one was super shaka nar nar.

Chapter 6

I cannot share the euphoria I feel, because Atticus would take me to task. His eyebrows would draw together and he would attempt to convey through his expression how very, very old he was, and as a comparative youngster—even a whippersnapper—I could not possibly know how inappropriate it would be to feel euphoric. But I cannot help but feel that way, even though we are running for our lives. Because we are running fast through satin darkness with strength coursing through our bodies, a percussive corps of hooves and paws tapping out a rhythm of flight, clods of earth kissing us farewell and swishes of grass caressing our ankles, like the soft fingertips of mothers who don't want to let their children leave home but know that they must; they let go but keep contact as long as they can, extending hands and arms until their children finally pass beyond their reach, and then they feel sad yet proud and live on a kernel of hope that someday their children will come back to them and say, Mother, I am home. That is the source of my euphoria: I feel a mother's love with every step I take on the earth. Wherever I go now, I am welcomed home, embraced and adored and supported. I am a Druid of Gaia, beloved of the earth, and the wonder of it is still fresh in my heart.

When I was a child unbound—in my old life—my mother and stepfather used to take me to places with mountains and trees for family vacations, since we lived in the flattest part of the country and saw little of nature but the sky and amber tops of wheat fields. Walking through the forest and touching the white trunks of aspens, I suspected that the trees kept secrets, but they would tease me, using the wind in their leaves to whisper of mystery and then rustle and fade, dry chuckles of merriment at my expense, the ginger girl from the plains. I thought the aspen groves must know something important, something cool, because when they loomed over my head and whispered amongst themselves, they shook slightly in their excitement. But now the world is undressed for me, naked and gorgeous and waiting for me to explore it, and all its secrets would be vouchsafed to my ears if I simply took the time to ask.

I know we're in terrible danger. It's the kind that Atticus kept warning me about—he tried to scare me into quitting my apprenticeship so many times. And it's true we have been in a whole lot of danger ever since he began the binding process. Still, though we are running for our lives, it's all I can do to keep from busting out a barbaric yawp like Walt Whitman.

Now, there was a man who knew how to celebrate life and tell us about it. Atticus prefers the British poets and has memorized all of Shakespeare, but, while sublime, the Bard dwells too much on the dark side of human nature to capture my unswerving devotion. During my training, I had to memorize a large body of work as a first step to learning how to operate in different headspaces, so I chose Walt Whitman's. Whitman saw the world for the endless wonder it was. He called grass *the handkerchief of the Lord*.

I wish I could go back in time and tell him how deliciously close to the truth he'd been. It's Gaia's handkerchief, Mr. Whitman, but you got the rest right. *The smallest sprout shows there is really no death, / And if ever there was it led forward life . . . / All goes onward and outward, nothing collapses, / And to die is different from what any one supposed, and luckier.*

Not that I look forward to dying anytime soon. Or that the Morrigan's death was lucky. But I think she must be well on one of the Irish planes now, at peace in the green somewhere. I will ask Atticus later, when the shock of her end is not so fresh. It is an object lesson that even gods are not eternal.

I do look forward to a long life, if I can secure it. For one thing, I still want to memorize the works of T. S. Eliot in addition to those of Whitman—I need to keep adding new headspaces. And there are more languages to learn. Plenty of love to be made. And Gaia to protect with all of my skill.

Considering Atticus, though, I can see that eventually my giddiness will fade. I'm not sure that, having lived so long and seen so much, he has the ability to feel wonder anymore—well, except where I'm concerned. For some reason he thinks a freckly girl from Kansas is something new, and I confess that my vanity is content to let him think so without protest. He is a man unlike any other, and I love him. And I know without doubt that he loves me back. We are bound, he and I; I have seen it.

Yet he is still a mystery to me. If he feels the love from Gaia that I feel, as I know he must, then how can he maintain his laissez-faire attitude toward pollution and extinction? He only bestirs himself to outrage if a magical threat to the earth presents itself, but I think most of the mundane threats are every bit as horrific. If we can somehow outmaneuver the Olympians and our other enemies, I will defend the earth from those who defile it. Fiercely. Starting with my stepfather's oil company.

Atticus thinks I overreact to such things. Perhaps I am an extremist. Or perhaps he's fallen prey to apathy like so many others, worn down and weary and too worried about who's chasing him to muster any outrage at desecrations petty or grand.

He has a point. There is plenty to worry about now. But there is so much to cherish, too, like the smell of turf and the wind in my mane—I have a mane!—and the effortless way I can leap over fences. This run has been a salve for what Bacchus and Hel left raw; Atticus and I enjoyed a nice interlude in Mexico, but that was more about us than about my bond with Gaia. Now, touching a new patch of earth with every step and feeling the energy waiting there, I am beginning to understand the scope of my gift and the size of my new responsibility.

The number of obstacles and changes of direction required to stay hidden in Poland far exceeds anything we saw in Hungary or Slovakia. Granted, our route is taking us roughly parallel with E40, a major thoroughfare in the southern end of the country. It is no wonder that we find it more densely populated. But it has slowed us down a bit, and I'm sure our average speed has dropped as a result. We do not know how fast the huntresses are moving or even if they are still behind us. I keep thinking they will drop down from the sky and put an arrow through our chests and all our running will come to naught. But in the absence of information we must act on the vague instructions of the Morrigan.

We snuck into Katowice about an hour before sunrise, a bona fide metropolis of millions. Atticus worried about our disconnect with the earth the entire time, and I empathized completely but pretended it wasn't that big a deal. Inside, I was all *ew*. I didn't like the dead feeling of asphalt. Honestly, I didn't know how he managed to

wear sandals on a regular basis when he didn't strictly
have to. I'd go barefoot all the time if I could.

But the sneaking was necessary. I needed some more
throwing knives, since they had proven their efficacy so
well; we had no other ranged weapons, short-range as
the knives were. We found a sporting goods retailer by
snatching the smartphone of a despondent clubber and
conducting a search. Said clubber wore a gray suit and a
forlorn expression. I think it was near dawn, like five-
thirty, the hour when early risers are brewing coffee and
making bacon, though the sun had yet to hint that it
would be arriving soon. The clubber had yet to find a
bed where he could get started gestating a legendary
hangover. He was weaving uncertainly on the sidewalk
and softly slurring his way through a song of self-pity.
He must have struck out on his quest to score, because
he was staggering through the streets alone with a half-
empty bottle of Żubrówka—a favored drink in Poland
that Atticus claims is a rather tasty vodka.

And thus I added the Polish drink of choice to my
bucket list and learned that other people's electronic de-
vices can be a fugitive's friend. Traffic was still light to
nonexistent, consisting almost entirely of early-morning
delivery vehicles. While the street was clear, Atticus put
the phone back in the man's pocket as I dispelled my
invisibility for a few seconds in his full view, a finger
resting provocatively on my lower lip, giving him a
come-hither look under a streetlight. His jaw and the
bottle of Żubrówka dropped at the same time. It shattered, drawing his eyes to the sidewalk, and I took the
opportunity afforded by his distraction to disappear
again.

<That was mean,> Oberon said, watching the man
look wildly around for me and pawing at his eyes as if
to clear them.

Why? I asked. *I've done him no harm.*

<Yes, you have. You will haunt him for the rest of his life. I know from experience.>

You're haunted by someone flashing you on a street corner?

<No. It was a dog park. Atticus and I were just arriving and she was leaving.>

Oh, here we go.

<She was so fit and her coat was tightly curled and she had a perfect pouf on the end of her tail like a tennis ball. I saw her for maybe five seconds, until she hopped into a Honda and her human drove her away. And now I can't see a Honda without seeing her.>

But that's a good thing, isn't it? Kind of romantic? A vision of perfection you can treasure forever, unspoiled by reality.

<Well, I don't know. In reality I'd like to try spoiling her, if she was in the mood.>

Look, Oberon, that man is lonely. He's too skinny and sweaty, and I'm willing to bet you five cows that he's socially awkward or he wouldn't be staggering drunk at this hour. But now, for the rest of his life, he will remember the naked woman on the street who looked at him with desire. When people treat him like something untouchable, he will have that memory to comfort him.

<Or obsess over. What if he starts wandering the streets every night looking for you?>

Then he's misunderstood the nature of beauty. It doesn't stay, except in our minds.

<Oh! I think I see. That's true, Clever Girl! Sausage never stays, because I eat it, but it's always beautiful in my mind.>

We left the man and hurried to the sporting goods store, a place called Wojownika, which turned out to be only a few blocks away. I toyed with the idea of snagging some other weapons, but they were impractical in this situation. We had no way to carry them, and cinching me up with saddlebags would be a terrible idea once I shape-shifted to anything else. Our best bet was to stay fast and unencumbered.

I didn't like stealing, but I didn't see an alternative. No one offers traveler's checks for Druids on the run. I would prevail upon Atticus to send the targeted store an anonymous windfall later, if there was a later.

Oberon bellyached a bit about carrying knives in his mouth again—a pointless complaint since Gaia's strength ensures our jaws never cramp or ache—but he has been uniformly delightful otherwise. I think his ability to live in the present keeps Atticus from panicking.

<I've never run this far before,> he said at one point. <Or this fast for so long. It's better than sticking your head out a car window, that's for sure.>

My theory is that Oberon might be a master of Tao. He always sees what we filter out. The wind and the grass and something in the sky, sun or moon, shining on our backs as we run: They are gifts that humans toss away like socks on Christmas morning, because we see them every day and don't think of them as gifts anymore. But new socks are always better than old socks. And the wind and grass and sky, I think, are better seen with new eyes than jaded ones. I hope my eyes will never grow old.

Chapter 7

I really wish castles had never become passé. I didn't shed a tear at the passing of the feudal system or the chamber pot, but I've always loved the castles themselves. They're so much fun to invade and take down from within, and they often have secret passages and catacombs and a tower, ivory or not, in which Someone Important usually lives and rarely comes down. Sometimes they have libraries with old tomes written in a crabbed Latin script full of alchemical recipes or musings on the mysteries of magical arts, complete with idiosyncratic spellings. I get nostalgic for the old days whenever I see European architecture that evokes the age of castles, and Poland is liberally peppered with those sorts of buildings. Perhaps it was nostalgia, along with a gnawing rumble of hunger, that encouraged me to stray from the fields and enter a small town in search of food. Well, that and the insistence of my hound. Aside from a side trip into Katowice to snag some knives for Granuaile, we had run all through the night, and Malina's coven—presumably with Loki—was more than two hundred miles behind us. Around midmorning, my hound snapped us out of the running zone we were in.

<I am going to eat these knives if you don't feed me soon,> Oberon said.

I immediately felt guilty. With Gaia replenishing our

strength and with so much else on my mind, I hadn't thought much of food. Our ability to snag three squares a day had been destroyed. We had become opportunists, snatching melons or whatever we could along the way, and once we scarfed it down, even though it was never enough, we kept thinking we'd run across something else soon. Too often we didn't.

<Okay. You've certainly been patient. How does prime rib sound?>

<Ack! Um, sorry, Clever Girl, I just drooled all over your knives. Blame it on Atticus. He said, "prime rib." For breakfast. I'm all for that, as long as there isn't any horseradish on it.> After a moment he added, obviously speaking to Granuaile, <You *like* horseradish? Well, I guess you have a good excuse, being a horse, but that doesn't explain why anybody else likes it.>

<I'm not guaranteeing prime rib, mind you. I just wanted to know how it sounded.>

<What? You mean you were messing with me?>

<Well, not exactly. We'll look for it, but I'm not sure we'll find a place that serves it. I'm just saying you may have to settle for something else.>

<I hope not, but I'm hungry enough to settle.>

We were about fifteen miles southwest of Wrocław, crossing more farmland, when we came across a road marked E67. Looking south along the road, we saw some buildings; it was one of the many wee villages scattered throughout the country.

<Let's see if they have a place to eat in that town,> I said. A couple of minutes brought us into a hamlet called Pustków Wilczkowski, and there we found an interesting rural hotel with a restaurant attached called Gościniec pod Furą. It was a white building with black boards accenting it in diagonal slashes, Tudor style, which was a surprise in itself. Wagon wheels braced the sign, so I guessed the name of the place had something

to do with wagons. Red and pink flowers in hanging pots dangled from the eaves, and the property thrived with burgeoning hedgerows and cultured gardens. We went around to the back, where the garbage and the woodshed were, and spied the kitchen door. It was open to let out some of the heat from the grill fire, only a screen door present to keep out insects, and through it we could hear sizzling and the clack of a pair of tongs by a chef waiting to flip a breakfast steak. The breakfast grill looked shoehorned into the layout of the kitchen, a clear afterthought and a recent addition. Since it was the only restaurant in town, demand for breakfast must have eventually convinced the owners to supply it.

A waiter called out an order, but it was lost on me: I still needed to learn Polish. Granuaile and I shifted to human and leaned our weapons against the back wall, leaving Oberon to guard them. We camouflaged ourselves, and Granuaile drew on my bear charm to keep her spell powered, since she didn't have her own charm yet.

Interesting fact: It is really fun to sneak into a restaurant kitchen stark naked. I nearly collided with a stern-looking waitress, who would have no doubt kicked me in the package if she saw me. She had a severe beauty that was probably softened by a smile in the dining area or when surrounded with good company, but out of sight of the customers—customers who may decide not to tip well—her face was taut and unforgiving. There was one other waiter, a younger man who clearly feared the waitress and made way for her, and a chubby, jolly cook in an apron and sweatband working two grills: one was a wood fire for steaks and pork chops, and the other was the flat metal kind for scrambling some eggs and frying bacon. I liked him instantly because of the faint smile on his face as he worked. Maybe he was just thinking about a funny joke or the smile on his lover's

face, but my intuition was that he was a soul at peace
with the artistry of his job.

A few minutes' observation revealed that he never
turned around to face the server area unless he had a
plate to deliver or a ticket to look at. He kept his attention on the grills otherwise. The two servers spent more
time out in the dining area than they did in the kitchen.

The cook eventually put up four plates, two with pork
chops and eggs and two with pancakes and bacon.
Oberon would be grateful for any of that. But a place
like this might serve prime rib sandwiches for lunch. If
so, they had to put the slow-cooking prime rib in the
oven in the morning. That meant it was available for
breakfast if you liked it ultra-rare, which Oberon did.

The oven was behind the serving area but also behind
the wood-fire grill's stone walls, which allowed me to
tiptoe back there and open the oven without being seen.
The large hunk of meat that greeted me elicited a smile,
because I knew how happy Oberon would be. I removed
it and rested the prime rib on a prep area next to the
oven. I found a couple of carving knives and a plate and
sliced off a generous hunk of bloody beef for my friend.
Granuaile snagged the pork chop plates and stole the
bacon sides from the pancakes while the waiters were
out of the kitchen, and the cook never noticed. The pancakes she left behind utterly failed to raise the alarm.

I felt sorry about the inevitable argument that would
erupt when our theft was discovered—especially sorry
to give the waitress an excuse to yell at the cook—but
we were hungry and in a hurry and nobody's lives were
at stake but ours.

Try to chew it slowly and enjoy it, I said, putting the
plate down for Oberon.

<Oh, great big bears, Atticus!> he said as he laid into
it. <This is the best prime rib ever!> He gave a soft whine
of appreciation. <Stolen and succulent, like forbidden

fruit when I'm already starving. This shall be known as the Great Meat Heist of Poland That One Time. All future meals will be measured against this one. It's even better than the Big Juicy Barbecue of Atlanta That Other Time, remember that? Or the Beloved Boar Sausage of Scotland We Had Once. And do you remember the Heinous Worldwide Bacon Shortage of 2013? This totally makes up for it.>

Glad you like it, buddy. There's no shortage of bacon here. In fact, you can have mine.

<You're giving me prime rib *with a side of bacon*? I love you, Atticus. If I ever have puppies, I'm going to tell them stories about this food. It's legendary.>

A heated exchange of Polish boiled through the screen door, and my pork chops tasted of guilt sauce. We had to chow down anyway. Any meal at this point could be our last. The waitress and the cook eventually broke it off and she exited the kitchen, no doubt to inform her customers that their breakfasts would take a bit longer.

We were just about finished when two large ravens descended with thunderous backwings that sounded like chopper blades. Each of them had a familiar white gleam in one eye. They landed on the woodpile and squawked at me.

"Hugin and Munin," I said. "To what do I owe the pleasure?" One raven—I couldn't tell them apart—squawked and shoved his beak in my direction, then squawked again while pointing with his beak to the other raven.

"You want me to talk to that one? Hi there. Oh! I see." It wanted me to mentally bond with the other raven. Activating my charm for magical sight, I had to blink a little bit at the intensity of white magic emanating from the two birds. But once I could focus, I found the consciousness of the indicated raven and reached out to it. Images slammed into my head, aerial views of Artemis and Diana racing across the Polish border near

Dukla, each of them in a fancy new chariot pulled by four golden-horned stags. They were running side by side, following our trail across a familiar alfalfa field, when the earth gave out from under them and they fell into our pit trap. They tried to leap out of the chariots and make it back to solid ground but weren't in time; they'd been moving quickly, and the stags pulled those floating chariots down. A grind house of gore and screaming ensued. Though I felt sorry for the stags, I didn't feel the least bit distressed at seeing the goddesses impaled on the wooden pikes we'd left at the bottom. They'd have to heal up from that, somehow get out of the pit, and get yet another brace of chariots and new teams to pull them. They'd be going a bit slower, but they would never give up now that I had personally wounded them. I needed a long-term solution more than ever, and I didn't have one.

The scene shifted; Artemis and Diana in the gray sky of an early dawn—it must have been the same one we experienced a few hours ago—looking none the worse for suffering what would be mortal wounds to anyone else and gathering themselves to begin again outside the pit. They had new chariots, new stags, and now a pack of seven hounds each. I remembered the hounds from mythology; they had been gifts from Pan and Faunus. Each goddess blew into a horn, and the hounds leapt ahead on our trail. They waited for a few seconds and then followed behind in their chariots. If we tried another pit trap, the hounds would fall in first and the huntresses would be able to see that in time to avoid it.

But it had worked. It had taken us about eight hours to get from the pit trap to here, and it was about three hours after dawn now, so if the huntresses began at dawn, that meant they were about five or maybe six hours behind us now.

The link broke and the raven I'd bonded with—clearly Munin, since I'd seen a memory—pointed at the other one, Hugin. Hugin's aura was a bit more intense—the current thoughts of Odin would of course be more active than his memories. I didn't think Hugin represented the totality of Odin's thoughts, but it had to be a relatively huge chunk of his consciousness, or else it wouldn't have put Odin in a coma for years when I'd speared the first Hugin back in Asgard. I had no idea how Odin thought of him, but from a Druidic perspective, Hugin was a headspace in Odin's mind—with wings. And in a similar sense Munin was a headspace as well. Both ravens had to report back to Odin periodically to recharge and reunite all the fragments of his consciousness, but it wasn't as if he sat with all the life of a mannequin while they were gone. Though they did embody the mind of Odin, they weren't the full sum of it.

I connected with the bird's bright threads of consciousness, and the aged whiskey voice of the Gray Wanderer filled my head with Old Norse.

<Keep running. You cannot ever stop for long. We are doing what we can to prevent the Svartálfar from interfering further.>

That's very kind. But how did you hear I was in trouble?

<The Morrigan told me.>

The Morrigan is dead.

<Precisely. Nine months after we met in Oslo, she returned and gave me a ruby that was bound to her. It glowed with power. "Someday," she told me, "this ruby will cease to glow and you will know that I am dead. And when that happens, you must protect the Druids from the dark elves if you wish them to fight with you in Ragnarok." It did not make sense at the time—she said "Druids," but there was only you. And I did not understand why the Svartálfar would be so important. But now it makes sense. You have enough problems without the Svartálfar on top of them.>

She foresaw this five or six years ago?

<She was a deeper one than any of us suspected.>

I let that eulogy pass unremarked. *Odin, how did you find me? I'm shielded from divination.*

<Your woman isn't.>

She's not mine. She belongs to herself.

<I care not. Run now. I want you to fight in Ragnarok. Or I want to watch the huntresses flay you alive. I find myself deliciously ambivalent.>

You've been watching?

<Of course. The view is quite lovely from Hlidskjálf,> he said, referring to the silver throne from which he could observe events in most of the nine realms. <I am not the only one with an interest here. And you should probably be informed: The Olympians have claimed the right to take your life. But there are gods of other pantheons who wish to keep you alive for other purposes—myself among them.>

What other gods?

Odin continued as if I hadn't spoken. <After the Morrigan fell, these other gods informed Olympus that if you are to die, it must be accomplished through skill and not overwhelming force. They are permitted to hunt you, in other words, and if they are successful, so be it, but the Olympians may not fly here en masse to confront you.>

Who can dictate this to the Olympians?

<Humanity has created more powerful gods. The Olympians would not wish to cross them, nor would I. Zeus and Jupiter saw you building that pit trap, you know. And we saw them see it. They were going to warn the huntresses and spoil the surprise. But we stopped them. That wouldn't have been fair. Or half so amusing.>

Thinking back to a particularly vivid dream I had twelve years ago in Flagstaff, I asked, *Might one of those gods be Ganesha?*

Odin ignored me again. <It works the other way too,

so I caution you against using modern transport. The Olympians insisted you must escape under your own power. Should you board an aircraft or a vehicle, the Olympians will be allowed to stop you.>

So we are entertainment for the gods? We run for your sport?

<You must understand how rare this is. Your actions cannot be divined or reliably predicted. The outcome cannot be known, and thus it is exciting. And there are others interested in your demise apart from the Olympians, which makes this more interesting.>

What others?

<You have already seen them. Vampires. Dark elves. As to the latter, the Ljósálfar are coming to Midgard to keep the Svartálfar out of your way. They are anxious to fight their dark brethren on neutral ground, and, for once, they know roughly where to find them—wherever you're headed.>

So we're not only entertainment, we're a method by which someone gets to pursue a personal grudge?

<It is a role you've played before. The Æsir were on the receiving end, if you recall. A small matter involving Thor.>

I recalled. It was not my finest hour.

I suppose you won't be helping us, then.

<On the contrary. As I said, we will do our best to take care of the dark elves. And I also told you to run, which was outstanding advice.>

The link broke and the ravens' wings blatted into the morning sky like fat motorcycle engines.

The Morrigan's assertion that we had to run the whole way made a bit more sense now. The gods had decided Europe was their Colosseum and we were the gladiators.

"No rest for the Druids," I said. "Come on, let's go."

Chapter 8

So much for my theory about faery tails. We were being watched constantly through divination, and Granuaile was the antenna. What Odin could do, others could do just as well, so Odin's point that there were other interested parties was well taken. The reason we had a vampire and dark elves waiting for us near the Slovakian border was because someone in Tír na nÓg was coolly divining Granuaile's location, quite correctly assuming I'd be nearby, and then dispatching assorted evil minions to slay us. They'd done this repeatedly in Greece while we were trying to get Granuaile bound to the earth; we'd shaken them for a while in the French Pyrenees, perhaps because we were spending nights inside a mountain and the scryer could not figure out where we were, but eventually they must have zeroed in on us. We'd left just ahead of an oncoming horde of vampires, if Oberon's nose could be trusted, and it usually could.

After we raided Hel and killed Fenris, Granuaile and I had been left alone in Mexico for a couple of blissful weeks—why was that? I'm sure her presence there would have been as easy to divine as anywhere else, and I was most certainly very close to her during that time. It must have been because the puppet master, whoever it was, couldn't get minions out to us in Mexico. If that was correct, then that told me quite a bit.

I had bound Mexico to Tír na nÓg long ago, back when the Maya were still running around and building future tourist sites. The Fae could have shifted and found us in short order if they wished. And Mexico certainly had its share of vampires; if they had wanted to find us, there would be no reason for it to take two days to locate us, much less two weeks. So this mysterious person was not using local vampires and wasn't shifting minions around using tethered trees. Instead, he or she was using a specific set of vampires—perhaps a specific set of Fae and dark elves too—and shifting them around using the Old Ways in Europe. That meant Mexico was safe territory. The whole New World was safe territory. And now that I knew that, Faunus had made sure that safe territory was unreachable.

It also meant that there was something important about the Old Ways that I was missing.

<Hey, Oberon.>

<Hey, Atticus.>

<Ask Granuaile if she's willing to investigate one of the Old Ways in Germany and see if we can escape through one.>

<Escaping would be good.> A few moments passed and then Oberon said, <Clever Girl reminds you the Morrigan said they were all collapsed or guarded.>

<Most likely that's true. I'm actually more interested in finding out who's guarding them. This is recon more than a genuine attempt to escape.>

<I've been meaning to tell you that when I chew on things it's recon more than a genuine attempt to destroy your stuff.>

<Just tell her, please?>

<Okay, she says let's do it.>

<Follow me.>

Eastern Germany had an Old Way to Tír na nÓg—several, in fact, hidden among the river valleys of the Ore Mountains, which divided Saxony from Bohemia. But the nearest was a wee bit southwest of the city of Hoyerswerda in Dubringer Moor, a wetland populated around the edges with birch, pine, and alder, spreading their roots in its marshy soil. Unlike the vast majority of the Old Ways, it wasn't in a cave. A few, like this one, were open-air mazes without walls. Walk through the birches in a certain pattern, end at a particular alder tree and circle it thrice, and you'd be in Tír na nÓg. It wasn't the sort of Old Way that you could collapse with an earthquake. You could clear-cut the trees or set fire to the landscape, and perhaps we would find something like that had happened, but it was more likely to be guarded.

Or not. How do you guard a place that's open to the air—and open to the public—without generating some attention? With caves you can hide the guardians inside.

We had to turn due south to get to Dubringer Moor, skirting a huge lignite strip mine at Kausche but otherwise enjoying the mixed evergreen and deciduous forests that surrounded wee hamlets until we arrived at the moor. Trees grew out of some juicy ground around the edges of it, but near the center it was a swampy marshland. I stopped at a birch tree that had three knots reminiscent of a triskele on one side. After looking around to make sure we were unobserved, I shifted to human and drew Fragarach from its scabbard.

"Ready?" I asked.

Granuaile shape-shifted and held Scáthmhaide at the ready. "Yep. Go."

In the magical spectrum the Old Way was plain to see, but Oberon couldn't see it at all and I didn't want him to step off. "We'll go slow. Look and listen for guardians. Don't forget the treetops. And, Oberon, if you smell anything weird, let us know."

<Okay.>

"And stay close to us. Single file. No chasing squirrels or anything else."

<Aww!>

We advanced ten paces to another birch, directly south of the first one. "Walk around this counterclockwise," I said, demonstrating, "and then we go west." They followed me to the tree next door and then we turned south.

Oberon asked, <Can I go smell that bush over there?>

"No, you can't, buddy, I'm sorry. The path itself is the tether to Tír na nÓg. It can be walked both ways. If a tree dies, then the path gets adjusted a tiny bit, but it essentially remains the same. The alder tree at the end of this must be the twentieth different tree anchoring this Old Way since I learned about it. And the same goes for the birch where we began. But if you step off the path, you have to start over."

We crept through the birches, following a sinuous trail and stopping periodically to listen and watch for trouble. Nothing alarmed us, aside from the paranoia that every step brought. We kept expecting faeries or some sort of monster from Greco–Roman myth to jump on us, but we had this portion of the moor to ourselves. When we reached the alder tree, I grew super-cautious, peering up into the canopy.

"There has to be something here," I said. "It can't be that easy."

"What's easy?"

"This is it right here. We walk around that tree three times and we're in Tír na nÓg. Boom. Escaped. We shift to the New World and send all these ass bananas a postcard that says, suck it, you'll never trap us again. But it doesn't make sense."

"Maybe they forgot about this one?" Granuaile ventured.

"Maybe. Maybe they're just being clever with their ambushes. Maybe someone's invisible?"

"Let's check the magical spectrum."

"Already there, but go ahead, you might see something I didn't."

Granuaile scanned the tree and noted it had a whisper of color about it as a tether, but there wasn't anything else to be seen. Nothing glowing in the canopy. Nothing glowing on the ground.

"Oberon, what do you smell?" Granuaile asked.

His nose twitched for a few moments before he gave a mental shrug. <You guys. Swampy birchy grassy stuff. Nothing to eat.>

"All right, we'll just take it slow." I crept forward and led them toward the alder tree. We had to go clockwise around this one. I peered up into the branches but spied no threats. The first orbit around the tree was uneventful, and I began to hope. But the second trip around put us halfway between the planes, and we saw what was waiting for us if we kept going: A semitransparent second world overlaid the one we were walking. And waiting there, in Tír na nÓg, one more circle around the tree, was the guardian we'd been expecting all along.

I should say, rather, that we expected *a* guardian—but not this particular guardian.

"Eep!" Granuaile squeaked, startled. Oberon barked at it. I raised Fragarach and watched it carefully. It smiled at us with three rows of jagged teeth but did not move, except to raise its tail. The end of it was blackened and bristling with what looked like very large cactus thorns. Except for the tail and the human face with an abnormally toothy grin, it had the body of a red lion. The face was framed all around by a magnificent mane, with the lush hair growing out from the neck reminding me of nineteenth-century American Romantic poets.

"If that's what I think it is, then it's not Greco–Roman," Granuaile said, "and it's not Fae either."

"No, this guy would be Persian," I said. "But I have no idea why he's involved in this."

<What is it, Atticus? I don't like all those teeth.>

"It's a manticore," I said. "And it shouldn't be in Tír na nÓg."

Oberon growled low in his throat, a steady rumble of warning. <I don't think it should be anywhere. That thing looks wrong. And hungry.>

"Can it attack us?" Granuaile asked.

I lowered my sword. "Not from where it currently is."

"It's right in front of us."

"No, it's in Tír na nÓg and we're not quite there yet. We'd have to go around the tree once more, and then he could attack us."

"Or he could go around the tree the other way."

"No, that wouldn't get him here. He can't get out of Tír na nÓg without walking the proper path—it's just as complicated from that side as it is from here. We had to take many steps to get this far, and he would have to take as many to get to us. And I bet you he doesn't know the way. He can't see the path in the magical spectrum like we can. He was placed there by somebody else, and he has to wait for us to come to him."

"But he's in Tír na nÓg, right? So if we get past him we're golden, correct?"

"Well, yes. But getting past a manticore is next to impossible. Their venom is supposed to be a death sentence. Doesn't matter if it comes out of the tail or from his bite. Even the claws are deadly, if reports are accurate."

"Reports or myths?"

"Myths, you're right; I'm sorry. There are no reports

of people surviving manticore attacks, because they would have to survive to report it."

"Couldn't we break down the venom ourselves by unbinding it? I mean, we're sort of immune to poison, aren't we?"

"I suppose we are in some sense. But that takes concentration, and while you're working on not dying from poison, he'll spill your guts on the grass or bite your head off. And the third member of our party is not immune."

Oberon stopped the barrel roll of his growling. <Wait. If this is a party, where's the snack tray?>

The manticore's face, a malevolent visage promising painful death, abruptly turned to one of earnest appeal. He raised a paw to beckon to us, indicating that we should come through.

"Okay, that's really creepy," Granuaile said.

"Yeah. It's kind of a 'step into my parlor' kind of thing, isn't it? Well, we're not going to play his little manticore games. We have our answer now. The Morrigan was right—everything's being watched. But it's a bit staggering."

"You mean, all this effort to kill us?"

"Yeah. It could be done in a simpler fashion, but whoever's behind this wants to make sure no blame accrues to them."

<I wonder what happens when this guy goes to the dentist.>

"Huh. Atticus, could every Old Way in Tír na nÓg be guarded without Brighid's knowledge?"

I considered. "Probably not for an extended period of time, but for a short while I don't see why not."

"Well, I don't see why. How can she be unaware?"

"She has to be informed, just like a president or a prime minister does. She won't know there's a problem until somebody tells her."

"Okay, so that means she could conceivably be the one behind this, or she's aware of it and complicit, or she's flat-out clueless."

"Don't forget aware and incompetent. Conceivable, but doubtful."

"All right. I want to talk about it some more, but let's step away from those teeth first."

<You know, he can't floss without thumbs. Think of the halitosis.>

"Yep, good call. We need to move on." We'd doubtless ceded some ground to Artemis and Diana during this little side trip, and we could ill afford to give them any more.

The manticore's face melted into desperation once we began to backpedal, and then he gave up all pretense of pacifism and sprang at us, mouth agape and claws extended. It was entirely silent and phantasmal: He passed right through me, not being quite on the same plane as I was.

<Ha! No Druid for you!> Oberon taunted him.

The manticore faded entirely from view once we stepped off the path. We agreed to resume our run and continue northwest through Germany until we safely cleared the Harz Mountains, and then we'd head straight west for the Netherlands according to the path laid out for us by the elemental Saxony. It was already somewhere around midday, and we wouldn't get out of Germany before night fell.

"Can we run as humans for a while to save Oberon the effort of relaying our conversation?" Granuaile said.

I shrugged. It would be slower going, but we had a bit of a lead and we needed to talk. "Sure." We adopted a ground-eating pace and trusted Saxony to guide us around developed areas as much as possible. With any luck, our streaking would go unnoticed. Or, if someone did see us, they might reasonably conclude we were running away from the very large dog behind us.

"So who's in charge of the Old Ways on the Tír na nÓg side?" Granuaile asked. "Who would inform Brighid if there was a problem?"

"Ah! The rangers. I see where you're going with this now. If Brighid isn't responsible and no one's told her what's going on, then someone has suborned the rangers."

"Exactly. And remember when we first went to Tír na nÓg together, and there was that one Fae lord who told us the rangers had reported all the tree tethers were malfunctioning throughout Europe?"

"Yes! Snooty, foppish type. I called him Lord Grundlebeard."

"Right, and so he's not a good buddy of yours. And he's in charge of the rangers, or he wouldn't have been reporting that at the Fae Court."

"Gods below," I breathed, realizing she was right.

"Yeah. Would Lord Grundlebeard have the power to do all this?"

I thought aloud for her benefit. "Use the rangers to organize some sort of obstruction at every Old Way throughout Europe? Yes. He could do that. But reliably divine your location the way that the Tuatha Dé Danann or other gods can do? That's doubtful. And consider what we've had thrown at us in the past few months: dark elves, Fae assassins, vampires, and now the Olympians. You'd have to have vast resources and serious power to push all those buttons and still keep yourself hidden. Grundlebeard can't have that kind of juice on tap."

"Wait. You think this person is working with the Olympians?"

"Now that we're talking through it, I think they have to be. Just remember how this all went down. I was giving you a tour of the Old Ways. We got to a specific spot in Romania and the trap was sprung. The Olympians were already there waiting for us—and so was the Morrigan. Now, the Olympians have their own methods of divination and they could have figured out where to find you in advance, and of course it's Pan and Faunus who are spreading pandemonium and preventing us from shifting through tethered trees, but there's no way they could have set a manticore to guarding one of the Old Ways in Germany from the Tír na nÓg side. They have to be colluding with someone on the Fae Court, but I don't think it's Lord Grundlebeard. I think he's involved, don't get me wrong, but it's more likely that he's getting his orders from someone higher up."

"Okay, I won't argue with that. But the manticore tells us something else."

"What?"

"Whoever's after us, they're spread really thin. You don't use manticores as mercenaries unless you're desperate, am I right?"

"That's a good point," I said. "I think we should address that and other points with Lord Grundlebeard at our earliest opportunity. Find out who's giving him orders."

"Agreed. Who knows what revelations would follow?"

<Hey, Atticus? Clever Girl? I've just had a revelation.>

"What is it?" I asked him.

<I know why humans wear clothes! It's because you look ridiculous when you run naked. You both have all these floppy jiggly bits and—>

"Okay, that will do."

<Victory is mine! Hound 1, Druids 0.>

"Oberon, we can't play that now."

<Well, what else are we going to do? I like a good run as much as the next hound, but we have been running for a really long time. I don't get to stop and smell any-

thing or chase pine martens or talk about my favorite movies, because you guys are wound up tighter than a Yorkie's back door. Can't we lighten up a bit while we run?>

"What do you want? A story?"

<Sure! A good Irish story.>

"All right. There's one that may be relevant to our current situation. I just thought of someone amongst the Tuatha Dé Danann who might have the means, motive, and opportunity to arrange all this."

<Well, that doesn't sound like a story to me. It sounds like you want to obsess some more about who's after you.>

"Obsess? I'd call it dutiful attention to self-preservation. Come on, Oberon. It has birds behaving badly, love rectangles, and even a cameo appearance by the late, not-so-great Aenghus Óg."

<That god you killed a few months ago?>

"That was twelve years ago, Oberon, but, yes, that god."

<Months, years, whatever. He was in a love rectangle?>

"No, Aenghus wasn't, but his half brother, Midhir, was. They were both sons of the Dagda. And it's Midhir who might be behind all this."

"I haven't met him, have I?" Granuaile asked.

"No, he was at the Fae Court the day you were introduced, but he did not introduce himself. I remember seeing him seated with the Tuatha Dé Danann on the right side of Brighid, but he didn't come up to say hi with the rest of them."

<Maybe he's a little bit sore about you sending Aenghus to hell.>

"That's my theory."

<Okay, lay it on me.>

"All right. I don't think I should tell you the whole

thing—it would take too long. It's practically an epic, called *Tochmarc Étaíne*, or *The Wooing of Étaín*. These events took place before I reached my first century of life. I had already discovered the secret to Immortali-Tea, thanks to Airmid, daughter of Dian Cecht, but I had yet to acquire Fragarach. Ready for the short version—the version I heard from people living at the time, not the one written down by Christian monks centuries later?"

<Yeah! Go!>

"Okay. Midhir desired a woman who was not his wife—a beautiful woman named Étaín. With Aenghus Óg's help, he got her, and he lived with her for a year and a day—which effectively divorced him from his first wife, Fúamnach, according to the laws of the time. Fúamnach disapproved of the match, as you might expect, and being no slouch at magic herself, she turned Étaín into a large purple butterfly that was blown about on the wind for seven years, until the poor lass landed on the shoulder of Aenghus Óg.

"Realizing it was Étaín and that Midhir was especially talented in shape-shifting others besides himself, Aenghus warded Étaín with wild magic and tried to return her to Midhir, in hopes of saving her. But Fúamnach again summoned winds and blew Étaín away. This time the butterfly fell into a flagon and was consumed by the wife of a warrior who'd been trying to start a family. Aenghus Óg's wards preserved Étaín's life in singular fashion: She made the leap from digestive system to womb, shifted from butterfly to egg, and was eventually reborn to this woman, still beautiful but remembering nothing of her former existence."

<Whoa, Atticus, hold on. Étaín was a large butterfly and this woman didn't notice that floating in her drink? The wings and the little insect legs didn't tickle her throat on the way down?>

"Well, it was a big-ass wooden flagon, Oberon, not a glass brandy snifter. You don't take dainty sips out of a flagon. You gulp giant draughts at a time and let rivulets of mead flow out the sides of your mouth. If she felt anything at all, she'd probably chalk it up to something going down the wrong tube."

<All right, but come on. How do you jump from stomach to womb? And shift from an insect to a fertilized human egg?>

"That was Aenghus Óg's wild magic ward at work. It's supposed to protect you, but its effects are unpredictable since it improvises its responses to danger. Most of the wards I craft are simply wards of repulsion, to prevent certain kinds of beings from passing—like a ring of salt can prevent the passage of spirits but not much else. Wild magic is capable of doing most anything."

<And this all really happened?>

"As far as I know it's true. The details were given to me by the Morrigan and Airmid after the fact. The Morrigan heard part of it from Aenghus Óg, and Airmid heard part of it from her father, Dian Cecht, whose role in this I'm kind of skipping for brevity."

<Okay, what happened after she was reborn?>

"Years later, the High King of Ireland, Eochaid Airem, had his pick of the most beautiful women in Ireland for his bride and naturally chose to wed Étaín. The Tuatha Dé Danann always took note when the High King took a wife, and that is how Midhir learned that his old love was walking the world again. Midhir still loved her, but she, of course, didn't remember him at all. So he set about wooing her in epic fashion.

"The story here goes on for quite some time about the love rectangle between Étaín and three men: Midhir, King Eochaid, and Eochaid's brother, Aillil. Aillil was basically a puppet in all of this, his behavior controlled by Midhir and Aenghus Óg, but he at least escaped from the whole mess with only a few months' suffering. Not so the High King.

"Midhir performed four magical tasks for the High King on behalf of Ireland and also gave away vast sums of wealth, all with the goal of winning Étaín. Once he figured that she rightfully belonged to him, he showed up at court in Tara, turned both himself and Étaín into swans, and flew away in full view of the monarch.

"King Eochaid searched for her for many years, tearing up the faery mounds of the Tuatha Dé Danann until finally he hit upon the correct one: Midhir's *síd,* called Brí Léith. He demanded the return of Étaín, and Midhir eventually agreed, saying he'd bring her to Tara forthwith.

"He was as good as his word—he brought Étaín to Tara. But he also brought forty-nine other women whom he had enchanted to look just like Étaín. He presented the fifty women to King Eochaid and said, Go ahead, dude, choose your wife.

"The High King chose one and they had a kid together, and for a minute you think, aww, how nice, a royal successor and a happily-ever-after! But Midhir returned after a year and a day and said, 'So, King Eochaid, how do you like your wife?' And Eochaid replied that he was vastly pleased. That's when Midhir crushed him forever. He said, 'Did you know that Étaín was pregnant when we took wing together all those years ago? She gave birth to a daughter—your daughter, though the child was never told this. And it was she whom you chose, in the likeness of her mother, to be your queen. You are now married to your own daughter and have lain with her and brought forth issue with her. And you have given me Étaín once again. So you are paid for trifling with the Tuatha Dé Danann.'"

<Auggh! You didn't say it was going to be gross!> Oberon said.

"Yeah, Atticus, I'm with the hound on this one," Granuaile said. "Turbo ew, okay?"

"Why are you blaming me?" I said. "I didn't make it up. That is what Midhir did to the High King of Ireland."

"Well, if that's how it happened, I don't like how Étaín was never given a choice. Both Midhir and Eochaid should have been kicked in the marble bag for behaving like her hoo-ha was something they could buy and sell."

"Should you ever meet Midhir, I urge you to deliver that kick to the marble bag and tell him why," I said, "but, again, it's not my story. It's an illustration of Midhir's character and abilities. What did you learn?"

<He's so powerful that he can turn you into a newt!>

"Well, not us—that would be a direct spell, and your cold iron talisman would protect you from that. It's not preventing people from divining your location, but it does protect against targeted magical attacks. What I hoped you'd learn is something about how Midhir operates."

"He's shady," Granuaile said. "And patient. Once he knows what he wants, he's willing to wait to get it and will set up everything so that his victory will be assured. Not afraid to do his own dirty work either—though he hasn't shown himself to us yet, if he's the one behind this."

"It's a different situation," I said. "He can't afford to be directly involved. Remember that, until recent events, the Morrigan was very much in my corner. He had to tiptoe very carefully to make sure she wouldn't discover his involvement. And there are others among the Tuatha Dé Danann who are favorably disposed toward us. Goibhniu, for one, and Manannan Mac Lir, who are powerful and influential in their own right."

"But wait a second," Granuaile said. "If he's doing all this to avenge his brother's death at your hands, shouldn't

he have been destroyed years ago when Brighid and the
Morrigan did their purge? They went around putting
people down after Aenghus Óg tried to take over, didn't
they?"

"Excellent point. He must have concealed his alle-
giance very well."

"Unless he was never allied with Aenghus at all. If he's
Aenghus's half brother, then he's Brighid's too, isn't he?"

"Yes."

"So he might have been in Brighid's camp all along."

"True. But if that's the case, that would still make him
antagonistic to us now, since we are not Brighid's favorite Druids."

"Speak for yourself," Granuaile said. "She likes me
just fine."

I grinned, acknowledging that she had a point there.
"Either way, he's still around and could have both the
means and motive to wish us harm. We need to investi-
gate when we get the chance."

<You know what I think? I think Brighid's only jeal-
ous of Atticus because I'm so much smarter than her
wolfhounds. And I'm more handsome by an exponen-
tial factor of shepherd's pie.>

"What? Oberon, that doesn't make any sense."

<It makes perfect sense to me.>

"Do you perhaps mean pi, the mathematical sym-
bol?"

<No, Atticus, I mean shepherd's pie. I'm not going to
confuse that with math. Shepherd's pie is delicious and
desirable, and math is not.>

My efforts over the years to instruct Oberon in basic
timekeeping and other mathematical concepts had failed
utterly—except in the realm of vocabulary, I suppose.
He soaked that all up and spouted it out later in unpredictable combinations. He had tried, for example, to
rate dry dog food on "the quotient of the beef correla-

tion coefficient" and sausage on a "pork echelon matrix." But he still got confused if you asked him to count beyond twenty.

"Oh, I think I see now," I said. "You are using shepherd's pie as a unit of measurement."

<That's right. It measures how awesome something is.>

"But that's math."

<No, it's food. It makes perfect sense to dogs, Atticus. You're human, so you wouldn't understand.>

"Didn't you use gravy in this manner before?"

<Shepherd's pie *contains* a rich beef gravy. So pie is on another level than gravy, see?>

"I think so. This means that cold chicken, for example, would be a kind of gravy, while a slow-roasted tri-tip would be . . . ?"

<A big slice of pie. Or, looked at another way, greyhounds are gravy. Poodles are pie.>

"Got it. I think you're right, buddy," I said. "Brighid is totally jealous."

Granuaile and I shifted to our hooved forms and we picked up our pace again.

Chapter 9

It was unfortunate that we had no time to savor our surroundings on such a beautiful day. The mixed woods of Germany were the sort that deserved a good savoring—no, a *savouring*, with a British *u* in there for the sake of decadence, as *colours* are somehow more vibrant to me than mere colors. It was in the woods of Germany that big bad wolves ate grandmothers and girls who dressed in red. It was Germany that hid the gingerbread house of a witch who hungered for children to roast in her oven. And somewhere in the mountains that we were doing our best to avoid, Rübezahl still wandered with his storm harp, shaking the earth or fogging the skies as the notion took him.

We had successfully navigated northwest through farmlands and river crossings and had recently threaded the space between Bergen on the north and Celle on the south. As we headed into a lovely wooded stretch that gave way to dank moors here and there, the sun sank before us and filtered through the needled branches of evergreens.

Usually there are only two kinds of script one sees in forests: signs that warn off trespassers and hunters, and carved hearts in the trunks of trees with the initials of a couple who felt there was no more romantic thing they could do to celebrate their love than scar the local plant life. So when I saw a neat white envelope pinned to a tree, addressed to *The Shakespearean Scholar* in a neat calligraphic hand, I stopped to check it out and shifted to human.

"Hold up," I called to Granuaile and Oberon. "I need to take a look at this. Stay alert."

Granuaile shifted to human also. "What is it?" she whispered.

"A note."

The envelope was sealed with red wax and the Old Norse word *hefnd*. Vengeance. The paper inside was a fine linen. There was no date or salutation or signature, just two lines from *The Merchant of Venice,* written with ink and quite possibly an old-fashioned quill. I read it aloud: *"Thou call'dst me dog before thou hadst a cause; But, since I am a dog, beware my fangs."*

<Fangs? They're called *canines*. Duh!>

"It's Shakespeare, Oberon."

<Oh, so that makes it okay? Of course it does. He could call a wolfhound a kitten and you'd make excuses for him.>

There was no postscript. Nothing written on the back. Nothing else in the envelope.

"He expresses himself with economy."

"What?"

"Never mind. Thinking aloud. Unwisely." The clue was in the quote: Vampires ahead. The last time I saw him, back in Thessalonika, Leif Helgarson had told me that he would try to warn me with Shakespeare when Theophilus was getting close. Theophilus was the old vampire who'd set the Romans after the ancient Druids and had, until recently, thought we were all dead. Now that he knew we were alive he wanted to finish the job. But it wasn't quite dark yet on our second day of running: That meant if Leif had left this note for me, he had to have left it before dawn, while we were still chugging

through Poland. That spoke of an uncomfortable prescience regarding the route I was taking, even if someone in Tír na nÓg was doing the divining. The wind was
behind us and I was sure he wouldn't be able to tell, but
I asked my hound anyway:

Oberon, do you smell the dead? Vampires?

My hound paused to sniff the air. <Nope. You smell
kind of rank, but not dead.>

Smell this envelope. Any trace of the dead on it?

<Huh. Maybe a little. Smells more like a regular dude.
But, wait—let me see the note. Yes. The paper smells
like a dead guy.>

So Leif had written the note, but someone human had
left it here, most likely at his instruction. Oberon confirmed this after snuffling around a bit at the base of the
tree.

<There was a guy here who smelled like cabbage and
milk. He came from that direction,> he said, pointing a
paw south, <and left the same way.>

"Well, there are some kind of bad guys ahead," I told
Granuaile, "if this note is to be believed. It suggests
vampires, but they still have a while to sleep."

"Let's go around."

"Around where? We don't know how far away they
are or anything else. This note may be intended to make
us change our course. If we go south, in the direction of
the mysterious note delivery man, we'll be in the Harz
Mountains, and that won't be fun. If we go north we
risk getting pushed into the sea before we're ready. What
we do know are two things: There are two huntresses on
our tail, who are gaining ground while we talk, and
heading due west is the fastest route through this piece
of country since it presents the fewest obstacles."

"I'm sure the vampires know that too," she said. "We
should go around."

"It's just now dusk," I pointed out. "They can't all be up and waiting for us yet."

"It's not worth the risk," she responded. "Let's swing a single mile to the north and then turn west again. We'll avoid whatever's waiting ahead and lose no more than a few minutes."

"All right. But let's go as humans so our weapons will be ready. Oberon and I in camouflage, you in full invisibility. Oberon, if you smell anybody but us, you let us know."

Granuaile disappeared from my sight and her disembodied voice said, "After you."

I cast camouflage on my hound, and he shook as if he'd just gotten out of the bath. <That spell always tickles.>

Are you going to giggle? We can market an invisible plush doll of you and call it the Tickle Me Oberon.

<Who wants an invisible plush doll? You always want to be able to see what you're cuddling. Besides, giggling isn't my thing. Now, if you came out with a Feed Me Oberon or a Hump Me Oberon, that would sell like nothing else. Especially to people with poodles. Poodles would demand a Hump Me Oberon.>

I laughed and cast camouflage on myself. "Let's go," I said aloud, so that Granuaile would hear as well. I headed north and continued the silly discussion in hopes that it would help me relax.

How would poodles even know about it? They haven't learned language like you have.

<Love is the universal language, Atticus. Put the Hump Me Oberon in those pet stores where they let dogs inside and they'll figure it out.>

You mean put your toy in the aisle with all the other plushies?

<Exactly. Except the Hump Me Oberon isn't a toy. Oh, no, it's not for puppies! It's for grown-up poodles, know what I'm sayin'?>

Ha! Oh, my gods, Oberon, the imagery . . .

We had gone about three hundred yards when we found ourselves at a wooded lakeshore. The water looked inhospitable; we would fight both submerged plants and scum on the surface should we attempt to swim it. If we wanted to continue north, we'd have to go around. If we circled east we'd be heading back toward the huntresses; if we went west it would be toward whatever nameless threat waited for us.

"Bugger. Boxed in and we didn't even know it," I said. "You okay with turning west, Granuaile?"

Her voice answered from my right. "We don't have too far to go. It doesn't look like a long lake. We can swing back north on the other side of it. If vampires are waiting for us, I'd rather get past them if we can before they rise."

"Good call."

After clearing the lakeshore and turning north, we broke into an odd-shaped field that might have been natural at one time but had clearly been cultivated in the past. Now it lay fallow, with random weeds and grasses sprouting out of it. It was the sort of place one expected to find deer and the like, but no whitetails bounded away from us. No birds chirped either. Despite being in camouflage, I felt exposed. When moving quickly like this, I wasn't exactly invisible; the camouflage couldn't keep up with the constantly shifting background and I could be seen as a distinct blur, especially since there was still a bit of sunlight left.

Oberon, do you smell anything?

<No, but the wind behind us isn't helping. All I can smell is stuff we've already passed.>

I don't like this meadow. There's something out—

Chapter 10

When the blurred shape of Atticus fell in front of me, at first I thought he'd simply tripped and I almost laughed, because pratfalls have been amusing since the Stone Age. Then I heard the belated crack of a rifle to the south and Oberon's startled cry: <Atticus!>

Stay with him, I said, as the training kicked in and I turned toward the direction of the shot. *I'm on the threat.* There was nothing I could do for Atticus that he couldn't do for himself, except address the sniper. And by *address* I meant destroy him, no shriving time allowed. My scruples regarding the taking of life evaporate when people try to kill us.

<Atticus? Atticus! Clever Girl, he's not answering me!> Oberon said. He sounded truly panicked and it began to worry me. But I had to worry about the sniper first. Especially after I felt a bullet whip by my ear and then heard the report right afterward.

I was still invisible, but that was way too close for a random shot—especially since he'd obviously hit Atticus while he was in camouflage. Logic dictated that the sniper must be able to see us—probably using an infrared scope. Our spells did wonders in the visible spectrum but did nothing to mask our heat signatures.

Though I was reluctant to do it, I dropped my staff and said goodbye to my invisibility. Atticus had taught me that superior fighters sometimes lose because of a failure to adapt to a shift in the enemy's tactics. The enemy had clearly come prepared to fight against camouflage and invisibility, so it was time to mix it up. Sniper rifles are usually mounted on stands or pods and are ill suited to taking out fast-moving aerial targets. So I shifted to a peregrine falcon and flew as fast as I could. I still wasn't terribly good at flying, but I figured it would get me above the canopy in one piece. Once I was above the trees, he'd have more trouble finding me than I would have finding him.

<There's all this blood on the ground! Can you help him, Granuaile? Please?>

Stay and guard him, Oberon. Trying to make sure we don't get shot at anymore. I'll be there as soon as I can.

I hoped it wasn't serious. Blood on the ground sounded serious, but I couldn't begin to think about what that might mean yet. If I allowed myself to get distracted, I wouldn't survive. Fight now, feel later.

Another shot boomed through the early evening, but it wasn't close enough for me to sense its passing. I saw the muzzle flash and banked around in that direction.

My eyesight as a falcon made me feel half blind as a human by comparison; I could see three times the detail with my black eyes that I could with my green eyes. I could clearly track the sniper abandoning his stand and rifle and running through the forest from two hundred yards away. From that distance, he was one hell of a sniper to hit Atticus on the run.

He pulled a sidearm from his vest—one of the bullet-proof type, not a waistcoat—and loaded a round into the chamber. All black gear, no natural materials for me to bind, and if I'd been trying to follow him with human eyes, even with night vision, he'd be tough to spot. But I was looking at him through a raptor's eyes: His silhouette stood out against the forest floor like ink on bristol board.

The sidearm would be a problem if he got a chance to use it. He hadn't exhibited any supernatural powers yet—nothing vampiric, anyway—but he clearly had some paramilitary training at the very least, if not the real thing. I couldn't take him out as a falcon, so I considered my alternatives as I closed the distance between us. If I swooped down on him and changed to human, he might be able to get a lucky shot into me despite my training. I needed a quick kill. Dropping onto him as a sea lion was obviously a nonstarter, and horses are not generally known for their mad assassination skills. I did have a jaguar form, but it was problematic for me. It came with an extraordinary sense of smell that triggered uncontrollable sneezing fits—at least, it had the first time I tried it. I hadn't taken the form since shortly after my tattoos were complete. I'd been too afraid to smell all those horrible things again. What if I turned into a jaguar, all snarly and toothy, and just sneezed on the guy instead of slaying him? He'd shoot me for sure, and that would be such a stupid way to die.

But I had done some reading on how jaguars hunt. They had a surefire kill move, and I was fairly certain I could pull it off if I didn't think about it too much.

The guy looked up over his shoulder and I saw the infrared goggles. I dove in response, assuming he'd take a wild shot. He didn't; I'm not sure he spotted me. I threaded my way through the canopy and then leveled out underneath it, gaining on him fast and still maintaining some altitude above him. He was changing directions, little jukes here and there to try to fake me out. That wasn't going to happen. He might be a trained soldier, but there was no way he could hope to be faster than me as a falcon—or as a jaguar, for that matter, or even in my normal form juiced up on the earth's magic.

I pointed myself to a spot ahead of him and folded my wings in tight against my body, gaining speed as I dove and keeping silent. I quietly opened my beak to its full extent as I approached the top of his head and shifted to a jaguar an instant before landing heavily on top of him. I rode him down to the ground, my jaws clamped around his skull, and bit down as hard as I could. He screamed and shot the gun once, a spasm of his finger more than anything else, and died with his blood filling my mouth. He twitched a few times, and that, coupled with his blood and brains on my tongue, freaked me out. I shifted to human and couldn't control my revulsion: I spat a couple of times, felt the chunks of brain pass my lips, and then vomited right on top of his body. It was so much worse than sneezing. I crawled away as soon as my stomach gave me half a chance.

Threat neutralized, I told Oberon.

<Good, now come back and help Atticus! I don't know what to do.>

He still hasn't moved or said anything to you?

<No. I don't see how he can. He's been shot in the head.>

Something lurched in my stomach again, and I suddenly felt cold. I heard a tiny voice wail, *no no no,* but there was no one else around to make those sounds but me.

You didn't say that before! I scrambled to my feet and pelted back toward the meadow, leaving the sniper's body to rot.

<I'm sorry! I can't think straight! You can heal him, right? He's not really dead?>

Wait. What does he smell like?

Oberon held his head low, his ears and tail drooping

as he paced worriedly around a still form. The wailing voice that said *no no no* got louder.

<He smells dead, but my nose has been wrong before. I think. I hope.>

Oh, gods, I hope you're wrong too.

The enormity of what had happened began to catch up with me. Leif's warning of an ambush had been legit—it just hadn't manifested itself as vampires, the way Atticus had thought. I reached Oberon in the next few seconds and my throat tightened at what I saw. Atticus was sprawled on his right side, blood pooled underneath his head. His eyes were open and unblinking. The entry wound near his left temple was a small black hole, not red or a bruised purple. A small black hole.

I knelt next to him and put a finger underneath his nose to see if he was breathing. He didn't appear to be, and I felt no puff of air on my finger. I searched for a pulse on his neck but found nothing. I tried his wrist. I put my ear down to his chest and hoped I could hear something over the voice saying *no no no*. All was still. And though these indications were all of a kind and pointed to a terrible conclusion, the worst for me was that Oberon was plainly visible, and so was Atticus. They had both been running in camouflage and Atticus had been the one to cast it.

<Is he dead?> Oberon asked.

A small black hole. No vital signs. That should have done it, but it was having to answer Oberon, saying it aloud, that broke me.

"Yes," I cried, my voice quavering. "He's gone. I can't do anything." And then we both howled. We howled the way people do when they don't care about speaking anymore because the words don't exist that can properly convey their emotions. Only ragged, broken, discordant noises could come close. And there are always tears and snot and gasping too, gasping because there isn't enough wind to cry all that they feel in a single breath.

For what else was there to do? CPR wouldn't help with a head wound. I couldn't make his heart beat if his brain wasn't *fucking there*. Druidry only gave me the power to heal, not resurrect.

He'd died before he finished falling. The little black hole in the side of his head swelled until it filled my vision—a distortion brought on by my tears. Knowing I'd already avenged him gave me no satisfaction.

I had him for only a few weeks. I'd thought we would be happy together forever. And I think I might have said that out loud, to his body, in a sort of high-pitched, incoherent keening that approximated speech but wasn't intelligible. Twelve years of longing and being with him every day—closer to thirteen if you counted the year of flirting at Rúla Búla before I began my training—thirteen years of repression and stupid surrogate boyfriends so that I would be a stronger Druid, but only a few weeks of openly loving each other, ended by a small black hole in the side of his head. No chance to tell him goodbye or let him know one more time how grateful I was to be bound to the earth. No chance to let him tease me and then tease him back harder. No chance to cuss at him in Old Irish because he said it made him feel young again, or put on strawberry lip gloss and watch him go dizzy. He'd always had a thing about that for some reason.

I don't precisely know how long we cried over Atticus, but the moon was high in the sky, probably close to midnight, and my throat was raw before I remembered that Artemis and Diana were still after us. We'd probably cried away much of our lead.

Oberon, I said, *we have to go.*

<No. I'm not leaving him.>

We have to. The huntresses are coming.

<I don't care.>

Atticus would care. You know that. He would want us to run and thwart them. We will bury him and say our farewells, and then we will honor him by sticking it to the Olympians.

<How are we going to do that?>

By making it to England. Surviving will piss them off and make Atticus proud.

<But I don't want to go to England. They're not Irish. And he's my friend.>

I know, Oberon, but staying here and letting the Olympians kill us won't make him happy. Us either, for that matter.

Oberon ignored my wisdom and asked, <Where is he now? In Tír na nÓg? Mag Mell? Can we go see him there?>

I didn't know where he was. Normally the Morrigan would escort spirits to their final resting place, but she was dead now. Perhaps Manannan Mac Lir would know. Maybe Atticus and the Morrigan were together somewhere.

I'm not sure where he is, Oberon, but I'm sure we can't see him. The dead and the living can inhabit the same planes in the Summer Lands, but they do not mix.

<Wherever he is, I want to go there too.>

No, Oberon. I need you to stay with me. Please? Let's send him off properly.

<But we don't have any whiskey. We can't have a wake without whiskey.>

We will have whiskey as soon as we find a liquor store.

Fragarach was lying a short distance away, so I retrieved it and placed it on the ground in front of him. I didn't roll him over or anything like that. I couldn't bear to see the other side of his head. The small black hole would haunt me forever as it was; I didn't want to see anything worse.

I closed my eyes, pressing tears down my cheeks, and used my Latin headspace to contact the local elemental, Saxony.

//Druid needs aid / Bury body and sword here / Keep surface undisturbed//

//Harmony// came the reply. Atticus and Fragarach sank into the earth, and the turf nearby sort of stretched and closed over him, adjusting itself to make it appear as if nothing had ever happened there. No blood. No marker to indicate that the finest Druid to ever walk the earth ended his walk in this nameless field.

My voice wasn't up to speaking aloud, so I spoke mentally to Oberon. *Here lies Siodhachan Ó Suileabháin,* I said, *known as Atticus to us. He changed my life forever—for the better—and I can never repay the debt I owe him. All I can do is honor his memory by protecting the earth.* I paused, confronted by the impossibility of doing justice to my memories of him, so I simply ended with, *I loved him and will think of him every day, no matter how long I live.*

I sobbed once and then did my best to weep silently so that Oberon would know it was his turn. He whined, indecisive, before he gave form to his thoughts.

<Atticus was the best human being ever,> Oberon said. <And I'm not just saying that because he gave me sausages. He taught me language, for one thing, so I could enjoy movies while he was at work. He told me stories in the bath and took me hunting and for jogs around the neighborhood. And once in a while, if I kept bothering him about it, he would give me some time with a really hot poodle bitch. And you know what else? He gave the best belly rubs, because he knew what it was like. He was a hound too. The best part about hanging out with Atticus was when we went running together as hounds. We felt the wind on our noses and ran until we found a field of clover, and then we'd flop on our

backs and wriggle around in it and take a nap in the sun. He knew how to be a hound's best friend. I loved him. I don't think I'll ever wag my tail again. That's all.>

I petted Oberon and stood shakily. I sniffled and looked up at the moon. Its cold light gave me no comfort. It only reminded me of Artemis and Diana. I cast my eyes back down to the ground and shook my head. There had been no vampires waiting for us. Only a sniper, probably in their employ, determined to wipe out the last of the Druids. And even the vampires were being directed by some shadowy figure in Tír na nÓg.

I really need to run now. I need to get out of here.
<I'm with you.>

I shifted to a horse and found Scáthmhaide where I'd dropped it. Then I lit out for the Netherlands with Oberon as if we could somehow catch up with what we'd lost, as if the desolation we felt could be left behind and wouldn't grow inside us with every mile.

Chapter 11

A pair of horns blast behind me, I am chilled with a premonition of my own death, and I wish for the thousandth time that Atticus were here. Did he find horns to be harbingers of death and sorrow? I cannot ever ask him now.

Instead of "When the Saints Go Marching In," I always hear "Taps" at funerals, and somehow the collective sorrow of so many final farewells builds in my mind, a great Jungian unconscious flood of tears and roses thrown on caskets and folded flags given to widows by a pair of crisp white gloves. That horn that plays in the John Williams score after Luke Skywalker finds the smoking ruins of his aunt and uncle—such a mournful sound, full and hollow at the same time, a surfeit of emptiness. And the call to charge never rouses me but rather signals that someone is going to die a violent death soon—or, if it starts a race or contest, it means there can be only one victor.

The horns that blasted behind me were dim, nasal, and stuffy sounds that nevertheless meant the goddesses were gaining on us, and they weighted down my legs, which were already straining, not from fatigue but from dolor. These were the sounds of horns and hunting that, according to myth, brought Actaeon to Diana as she was bathing. He'd been lost in the woods and thought that by following the sounds of horns he'd be saved. But Diana had turned him into a stag and set her hounds on him instead. Those horns had called him to his death.

Is she still sounding the same horn all these centuries later?

And is there anything more horrifying to the hunted than the sound of horns? Even the baying of the hounds is not so terrible; they are animals and following their instinct and training. But the murderous intellect behind the horn, the creature coldly orchestrating my doom—that's what makes me feel like prey and sets icy wings of fear fluttering inside my throat.

I probably would have given up already if it weren't for Oberon. And he is probably thinking the same thing regarding me. In truth, we are running only because Atticus would have wanted us to. I think we are only marginally more scared than we are depressed, and we aren't running as fast as we had been before. The urgency is gone. I don't see how I can survive this if Atticus and the Morrigan couldn't. The powers of a Druid are awesome, but the powers arrayed against me are too numerous and in a different league. I'm not going to quit, but I feel like I'm on a soccer team losing 3–0 with ten minutes left on the clock. While winning in that scenario is still theoretically possible, I don't see a way to make it happen all by myself and I half-wish that the end would hurry up and get here, banishing the dread of its approach.

We crossed the border into the Netherlands, and the elemental directed me to turn sharply to the southwest to avoid the bulk of cities by the sea. We'd have had to turn south at some point anyway to reach the French coast.

It's odd, sometimes, how a border can seemingly change the character of the land. The German landscape had been sharp, clean, and precise, whereas the Dutch, even at night, had a bit of a gauzy filter over it, as if the ghost of Rembrandt had pulled his brush across it to soften the edges just a little bit. The colors I saw in my night vision, too, appeared subtly textured and mixed by the master, not so stark as they had been in Germany. Or perhaps it was no different at all, and only my melancholia made it so.

Noting the change of direction, Oberon said in a subdued tone, <Hey, Clever Girl?>

<Yes?>

He let some time pass, and all we heard was the pounding of my hooves and the pads of his paws on the earth. They beat out a rhythm of cycling thought, the percussive notes repeating *Atticus* over and over if you were inclined to hear it that way, and we were. Then he said, <Do you know how far we still have to go?>

<Not precisely. Why?>

<Do you think we'll make it there before the huntresses catch up to us?>

The horns sounded again. Perhaps my imagination magnified the sound a bit.

<I'm not sure, Oberon. I hope we do.>

<I hope so too. But I'm wondering how realistic it is. I've been thinking that if I have to go out, I'd like to go out fighting instead of running. I want to face the Predator. I don't want to "get to the choppah!" with Arnold. You remember those guys? Well, they weren't real guys. What I mean is, did you ever see that movie?>

<You mean *Predator*? Yeah, I've seen it.>

<Really? It's no wonder Atticus thought you were perfect.>

<He thought . . . ?> I felt as if my eyes should be flooding with tears, but horses don't cry the same way humans do. Oberon continued, not waiting for me to finish.

<There was that one character who decided to take

off his guns and meet the Predator with just a knife. I forget what his name was, but I'll never forget what he did. Everybody was crapping their pants and scrambling for the choppah, but he was like, hell with that, homies, I'm not running from my problems. I'm going to face them, even if they kill me, but first I'm going to slowly cut open my own chest and make some crazy eyes. And then the Predator did kill him—and pretty fast too—but I always respected his decision to take that stand. He was like, fuck the choppah, Arnold! Oh. Will you excuse my language?>

<You're excused.>

<Thank you. So that was his attitude, except he never said a word. You just knew what he was thinking. And now I'm kind of thinking the same thing. When the goddesses first appeared and shot those arrows at us, I was so startled that I peed, and I feel ashamed of that now.>

<You don't have to be, Oberon.>

<I think I do. I think I have had a longer and better life than any hound has ever had, and I shouldn't fear death. Am I right, Granuaile? I'm not very good at time, but I'm pretty old for a wolfhound, aren't I?>

<The oldest ever,> I told him. <You're legendary.>

<Well, I don't feel legendary. But I do feel old. So old that I probably shouldn't be here. I have had more than my fair share of sausage and bacon and steak. And I don't feel like running anymore. I feel like stopping here and putting up the fight that Atticus never got a chance to put up himself.>

Oberon abruptly quit running, and I had to stop too. We were in the middle of a large barley field.

<You go on, Clever Girl. Get to the choppah.> He turned to face the northeast and growled. <We'll see who pees first this time.>

My instinct for self-preservation spoke up. It told me I could survive this. I could drop Scáthmhaide, abandon

Oberon, and turn into a peregrine falcon. I could fly straight across the channel to England, find a tethered tree, and shift away to safety. They couldn't have pandemonium going on over there too, I thought. Somewhere in the New World, maybe even back in Arizona, I'd bind my amulet to my aura the way Atticus did, and then the playing field would be a bit more even.

Except I'd never be able to live with the guilt. And I'd never have the stomach to fight again if I didn't fight now.

<Oberon, this isn't the place to take a stand.>

<You can't talk me out of this. I'm doing it.>

<I'm not trying to talk you out of it. I'm with you one hundred percent. Fuck the choppah, okay?>

<Well, okay then. What's the problem?>

<This isn't the right place to do it. You have to choose your battleground more wisely. The huntresses have hounds now, remember?>

<So?>

<So you're standing in open ground, where they can surround you.>

<Oh.>

<We need to get to a place where we can put our backs to a wall and not get flanked. Make them face you. Remember how the guy in the movie chose his spot carefully?>

<Yeah! It was this river valley or something with a log across it. He stopped there.>

<Exactly. And do you see why he did it?>

<The Predator had to come straight at him. Couldn't get across without going through him first.>

<That's right. And that's what we need to do. We need to find a spot like that where we can do the most damage possible.>

<Whoa, horsie. We?>

<Silly dog. Didn't you hear me? I'm not going any-where without you.>

<Awesome!> I had thought Oberon's tail might wag at that, but it didn't. He simply pricked up his ears. <Do you know a good place around here?>

<No, but I'm sure the elemental does. Let's keep going while I figure it out.>

The ears drooped. <Hey, wait a minute, Clever Girl. You're not trying to trick me into running away, are you?>

I raised my right front hoof. <Pretend I'm raising my right hand. I swear by all that's holy—>

<You mean sausage and bitches?>

<I swear by sausage and bitches that I am not trying to trick you. We will find a good place to fight and then that's what we'll do.>

<Okay! Let's do this!>

We ran, and I consulted the elemental about a suitable place to defend ourselves. Images of the path ahead flashed through my mind until I saw a likely spot.

//There / That place / Query: Where is that?// It was a small precipice—only fifteen or so feet high—but if we could get our backs to it, we would have a relatively unobscured line of sight and no one would be able to sneak up on us. There were trees on top of it, but at the base a small clear space before the trees broke up the view—and the approach was on a gentle slope as well, so we'd have the high ground.

//Remain on current path// the elemental said. //Will guide//

//Query: Distance to destination?//

Elementals are not excellent at using human units of measurement, but I figured it was about eighty miles to the southwest, skirting cities and keeping to rural areas as much as possible. If we sped up, we could make it in a couple of hours.

<Two hours' run,> I told Oberon. <That's not bad. We can stay ahead for a couple of hours.>

<Sure, no problem! Atticus drilled me on this. An hour is the one with sixty seconds in it, right?>

<Never mind. Just keep up with me and we can do this.>

Chapter 12

Our minds are all that defend us from the horror of the void. The majority of the time we simply think about something—anything—else, and that itself is an act of defiance against the vast nothing of the universe. But minds break down and stop thinking sometimes. They feel instead: A looping, gnawing monster eats away confidence and goals and even a sense of duty until we are in a dry bleak place of ennui, unable to focus on the minutiae that used to keep us moving. Tongues taste chalk and ashes, and eyes see only gray washes occasionally penetrated by bright stabs of panic.

Depression is a prison to which you have the key except you never think to look for it.

I do not know how long I stayed in the gray, afraid of the nothing and cycling through the long list of my trespasses. I cannot conceive of a judge who could grant me forgiveness. There are some shames I can never outlive. What good would it do to continue? Had I not brought enough ruin to the world—especially in the recent past? But it was the panic that saved me. Panic that Granuaile and Oberon would die. I could not bear to have their deaths added to the vast number that already weighed down the scale of my spirit.

My eyes opened onto darkness, which was not precisely heartening but an improvement over the gray.

Adrenaline coursed through me as I attempted to get my bearings. Cold earth shifted under my right side, and I winced at the pain this small movement caused in my head. Stretching out with my left arm and feeling the boundaries of the space with my fingers, I quickly discovered that I was in a small chamber underground, obviously with some rudimentary air circulation. Fragarach rested in front of my face in its scabbard. Beyond that I had no idea where I was, except that Granuaile and Oberon weren't with me. We had been running for our lives. Why was I not running? Why had I been reviewing my life with such self-loathing?

//Query: Carpathia?//

//No. Saxony//

Saxony was a German elemental. Why was I in Germany? We'd been in Poland, and Hugin and Munin had visited us. Then we'd run, and . . . yes, we had crossed into Germany. There had been that attempt to find an Old Way to Tír na nÓg, and then we found that envelope on the tree—Oh.

//Query: How did I get here?//

//Fierce Druid placed you here / Thought you deceased//

I blinked as I processed the fact that elementals had decided to refer to Granuaile as Fierce Druid. //Query: Then why do I have space and air to breathe?//

//I provided / Druid had not moved on//

No, I hadn't. And apparently I didn't rate an adjective in front of my title. I was just plain old Druid.

//Query: What happened to me?//

//Projectile impact to head//

Someone had shot me? So *that's* why my head ached. My fingers trailed up to my head and gently traced their way around it. There was a dimple near my left temple that hadn't been there before, and it was tender. I was sure the exit wound on the other side had been heinous, but I didn't want to lift my head and probe it. I was still healing.

I let my hand drop down to my necklace, where I groped for the last charm on the left side of my necklace, the one I'd never used before.

"Guess you worked after all," I said.

Granuaile had asked me what it was for once. I told her it was my version of a soulcatcher. I'd made it in response to Napoleon's invasion of Russia. I was a medic for the Russians during that time and saw what musket fire could do, what it meant for an old Druid who had protections against magic but not against high-velocity hunks of lead. I'd seen guns before that, of course, but had avoided them as best as I could. Joining the Russians had been a sort of fact-finding tour, with the sterling bonus that I got to wear those fun furry hats.

I decided I'd be able to survive most any hit to the body, given time to heal, except for a direct hit to the heart. I could armor myself against that. Shots to the head, however, presented a rather monumental problem. Brain death didn't allow one time to heal, and the brain was the warehouse for the spirit. Punch a hole in that and you'd shuffle off your mortal coil right away.

Keeping your coil unshuffled was the problem. Healing of the gross physical body could happen on autopilot as long as my tattoos had contact with the earth; I didn't need to consciously direct that, and it technically didn't require a beating heart. But keeping my spirit anchored to my body with a hole in my head—well, that was tougher and, as it happens, entirely necessary to keep the healing happening.

It was sometime during the process of binding my cold iron amulet to my aura that I realized I was really altering the nature of my spirit, and if I could do that to my spirit, I might be able to do other things as well. I spent years perfecting my other charms, until I decided

in the nineteenth century to attempt the soulcatcher.
(Despite the recent name I'd given to the charm, I am
reluctant to use the word *soul*—it has some pretty awful
baggage with it, the kind that's been roughed up quite a
bit and thrown around without any regard for what
might be inside.) As I told Granuaile once, I had no idea
whether it would work or not; to test it, I'd have to die.

And I guess I had died. With rare exceptions, people
who get shot in the head do that. Granuaile wouldn't
have buried me if my heart had been beating. So the
charm had worked precisely as I had intended.

All of my charms are triggered by mental commands;
without them, I'd have to speak the words aloud every
time for every binding, as Granuaile does. But you can't
very well trigger a mental command when your brain
has been blown out. So I had triggered it back in the
nineteenth century and hoped I'd never have occasion to
discover whether it worked or not.

The charm executed a series of bindings, three of
which were conditional: The first one bound my spirit
to my corporeal form even if my heart stopped beating,
a sort of soul cage using the framework I'd already es-
tablished by binding my amulet to my aura; the second
took a snapshot of my physical brain every five minutes,
accounting for every synapse and neuron, and that had
been ongoing since I triggered it in 1812; the third was
a healing command, automatically drawing upon the
earth (so long as my spirit remained) to heal my head in
accordance with the last stored image of my brain, down
to the last cell; and once those had been accomplished,
the fourth slammed my spirit back into its mortal coil—
my brain—and got everything working again. The theory was that my heart would start pumping, the lungs
would start breathing, and I'd hopefully rise from the
dead without fangs or a shambling gait and with my
personality and memories intact.

So much could have gone wrong. Getting decapitated, vaporized in a giant orange ball of flame, or losing so much blood that I couldn't ever get the heart pumping again. Getting shot on the roof of a building with no hope of contacting the earth. Heck, falling in the field in such a way that none of my tattoos touched the ground would have been disastrous all by itself. The charm was by no means fail-safe insurance against death. But the effort I'd spent on it had clearly paid off.

The gray wash abruptly returned to my vision, the black pitch of the earth fading. What would I do with a new lease on life? Find new and gruesome ways to doom everyone alive? Speak without thinking, make Faustian bargains with witches and frost giants? Save Granuaile and Oberon now, only to see them die at the hands of Loki later? That would be unkind. It would be more merciful to leave them to Artemis and Diana, who favored the quick kill.

I would never have allowed myself to think that way in the company of others. But one is never so alone as in the grave. I could feel all this and no one would overhear or suspect. For all that we may sometimes despise our fellows and be driven to rages and petty revenges, I think we are even darker creatures when we are alone. We can learn to fear our own thoughts more than the lash of the whip or the slap in the face.

At least that is how I imagine it is for people cursed with self-awareness.

Two regrets pulled me out of the gray. If I did nothing, I would never see Granuaile's freckles again. Or those green eyes. Or smell her strawberry lip gloss . . . Well, okay, it was more than two regrets. Three. Three regrets. And damn if Oberon didn't deserve a poodle or some kind of companion besides me. All right, four regrets. Probably more, the longer I thought about it.

A fair measure of pride had something to do with me

clawing my way to the surface as well. I couldn't stand the thought of Theophilus smiling a smug smile and drinking a goblet full of blood, toasting the final demise of Druids on the earth. He had a metric fuckton of bad karma due him, and I hoped I'd be the one to back up the truck and dump it on his undead ass.

And, gods below, didn't the Morrigan deserve a shred of effort on my part after what she'd done for me?

I clutched Fragarach tightly as Saxony helped me rise to the surface. //Query: Where is Fierce Druid and Druidfriend?//

//No longer in my realm//

They must have already left Germany. If Granuaile had decided to follow the plan, they could be in the Netherlands or even Belgium by now.

//Query: Plot straight line to them for me?/ Speak with neighboring elementals?//

//Pleasure / Harmony//

//Harmony / Tell Fierce Druid nothing// I didn't want Granuaile and Oberon to slow down or decide to wait for me when the huntresses would be close behind. And since they were still probably being watched, I didn't want to tip anyone off that I was walking the earth again.

//Harmony// Saxony said once more.

When I emerged into the air, it was deep night. If Saxony could trace Granuaile through a neighboring elemental, then it was probably the same night that I had been shot. It was entirely possible. Brain tissue is not so heavy or dense as muscle tissue, and I hadn't needed to replace all of it—just the few ounces of a bullet's path. Tracks led to the northwest—dogs and deer. The huntresses had been through here already, and their hounds were sniffing out Granuaile and Oberon.

Saxony pointed me just south of west. I shifted to a stag, picked up Fragarach between my lips, and ran, more worried than I'd ever been. Once, when I'd taken a knife in a kidney and another between the shoulders from the Hammers of God, no less a deity than Jesus had told me the pain I'd felt then was a fraction of what I'd feel if I followed through with my chosen course of action, and while I've never worshipped him, I do know he's not the sort of god who lies to people. At the time, I couldn't imagine anything worse than my current pain, because I was out of magic then and damaged kidneys fucking hurt. But now I thought I knew what Jesus meant. Free of the gray wash of depression and thinking straight, losing Granuaile and Oberon would be . . . well, I didn't have words for that kind of agony. Maybe I had my own dump truck of bad karma waiting for me somewhere ahead. I had certainly earned it, but I raced to avoid it if I could; there was no way I wanted to feel that.

Chapter 13

Oberon and I run much faster now that we have a destination and a purpose, even though the Netherlands has proven to be something of an obstacle course. We have had many more roads to cross, and skirting the population is a challenge, but it's aided by the night; millions of Dutch folk slumber in peace—spooning, perhaps, with someone they love, snoring the snores of the unhunted—and remain blissfully unaware that magic is real and a very old branch of it is doomed to perish in their borders.

As the sky broadcasts a pale gray warning of an incipient sunrise, I spy a sign welcoming me to Veluwezoom National Park, except that the Dutch spell it *Nationaal*—which I kind of like. The bonus vowel suggests abundance, as if their country is stuffed with a surpassing bounty of natural gifts. It is a not unreasonable conclusion. Veluwezoom is a serene stretch of heath and assorted trees, the latter huddled together around the perimeter of the park and giving shelter to innumerable critters that Oberon, were he not so forlorn, would have loved to harass. The leaves on the trees fly flags of red and orange and yellow, heralding with the brightest pageantry the decline of their vigor. Seeing that, Atticus would be smiling and starting to talk about celebrating Samhain soon. If he were here.

Missing people in our lives are like wounds we reopen with thoughts.

Our destination lay at the far end of a field of grass and heather that sloped ever so gently up to it. Once there, at the base of the small tree-topped cliffside the elemental had shown me, I shifted to human and turned to survey our trail. I beheld a vista of fading green and pale lavender, contoured slopes of plants crouching patiently in the predawn gray, waiting for the first blazon of the sun to light their edges with fire and joy. Oberon turned with me, nose in the air, sampling its scent, and ears twitching at the sound of birds waking up for the morning's natter. They were located in small handfuls of trees on either side of the cliff that constricted our view of the periphery. Perhaps they found the prospect of the heath as stunning as we did; it was a shy, muted beauty ready to be seen and applauded.

<Is this the place, Granuaile?>

"This is the place. Backs to the wall like I promised."

<And no choppah.>

"That's right, no choppah."

The great hound gave a sigh and stretched himself out on the grass, paws in front, sphinxlike, and kept his eyes scanning the horizon. <There are worse places where one could make an end.>

Much worse, I agreed, though this time I spoke mind-to-mind. If this was to be my final sunrise, I wanted to appreciate the soundtrack without my voice stomping on it.

I petted Oberon and he let me do it, but I noted that he didn't wag his tail even a little bit.

<You know what would be totally pie to have along right now, since we can't have Atticus?> Oberon said as we waited.

What would be pie?

<Some hogs-o-war. Mounted with special-ops spider monkeys. Nobody would expect that. Or the Spanish Inquisition.>

What are you talking about?

<You know what I mean! It's from that play by Shakespeare, and I figured Atticus would have appreciated that.>

Shakespeare had a hog-mounted monkey cavalry? In which play?

<I don't remember the whole thing, because it was very long, but Atticus recited it for me once, and there was a line that went like this: "Cry ham hock and let slip the hogs of war!" I know you might not agree, but for me that was the best thing Shakespeare ever wrote.>

You mean, "Cry havoc and let slip the dogs of war" from Julius Caesar?

<No, I don't think that's it. There was ham in there; I'm sure he was talking about ham. They were going to battle hunger.>

I think you might have been hungry when you heard it, Oberon.

A clipped puff of wind was echoed by another, and in another few seconds these could be recognized as the distant barking of hounds. A horn, much clearer than before, rode the air behind it. The huntresses were approaching the bounds of the park, with their pack leading the way. I wasn't looking forward to meeting the pack, but it was necessary if we wanted to have a shot at Artemis and Diana. And these weren't going to be cute little snuggly-wuggly puppies. They'd be trained killers. If I didn't treat them as such, I'd be dinner.

If I had my druthers, I wouldn't have minded some help either—some more modern, realistic help than what Oberon wanted. U.S. Marines, for example. I'd say, "Sorry, fellas, but these enemy combatants, Artemis and Diana, happen to be immortal. They can't be killed." The Marines would exchange glances, and then their platoon leader—who would be a nice young gentleman from the South, totally polite and unable to drink legally—would say, "Well, miss, we respectfully doubt their immortality, because they have yet to meet the applied force we can bring to bear. Semper Fi."

I sighed and banished the nice deadly Marines from my head. Atticus told me once that people never survive battle because they wish it. They survive because of their actions, the actions of their allies, or the inaction of their enemies. That is all.

I cast camouflage on Oberon and invisibility on myself. I gave us both the same speed and strength bindings. Oberon took point and I set myself up behind him, back against the tiny cliff. He'd break the charge, and if any of them got past and tried to turn and snap at him from behind, I'd be there to brain them with my staff. I had a throwing knife ready, though, and two more resting in the holster I'd strapped to my thigh. That would do for some of them.

I'm not very knowledgeable when it comes to dog breeds. The hounds given to Artemis and Diana in ancient days would probably not conform to any modern breed anyway. I wondered if these were the original hounds, kept eternally youthful like Oberon, or if they were descendants of the originals. When they appeared, I saw that they weren't bloodhounds with big floppy ears. They were more like big spaniels or retrievers and of varying coat colors. They were all smaller than Oberon, anyway, but there were fourteen of them and two of us.

Their inability to see us gave us a significant advantage, I must admit. All they could do was smell us. The first one ran into Oberon, and it went about as well for him as charging into a brick wall. All forward momentum ceased abruptly as Oberon batted him down with a paw and then followed up with his jaws. I threw two knives and they found their marks, then the pack flowed around us and it was all teeth and a whirling staff until they were still and we remained.

You okay, Oberon? I asked.

<Some scratches but nothing serious. You?>

The same. We need to move to one side now, away from the bodies, and keep low until it's time to pounce. They're going to be mad and pour some arrows in here, I bet.

<Are we going to try to take them one at a time?>

I guess so. Pick one and jump on her back. I'll try to make sure she stays down, as much as any of the Olympians can stay down. You have to watch out. They'll have knives and they're going to be super-fast.

<I don't care about facing the knives. That's kind of the point, heh-heh.>

Gods, Oberon. This time, when the tears came, I had proper eyes to let them loose, and I wiped them furiously from my cheeks. *You need to think strategically instead of suicidally. If Atticus were here, he'd kill me for even allowing you to risk yourself this much.*

Oberon gave a soft whine. <If he were here, I wouldn't be suggesting it.>

I reached for something positive to say but couldn't lay hold of a single word. I knew exactly what he meant. For all its manifold beauties, the world is never so fine once someone you love leaves it; instead, there is only the bleak prospect of loneliness and might-have-beens.

Look, the killer virgins are going to live through this and we won't, I said, *but I want them to feel ambushed. When it's over, I want them to shudder and realize that we would have owned them if they were mortal.*

<Okay, Clever Girl. That sounds good. I'll order a slice of that.>

We didn't have long to wait. Two golden chariots pulled by teams of stags glided over the heather as the sun crested the horizon in the east. Once they saw the bodies of their hounds, the goddesses reined the stags in and leapt out, each with a bow in hand and an arrow nocked and ready to go.

It was my first real good look at them. They'd been quite a distance away back in Romania, and the Morrigan had blocked my view before I had time to study them.

Based on my experience with Hermes and Mercury, I was pretty sure that Artemis was the paler of the two. Neither was dressed in bedsheets or the flowing skimpy dresses one sees so often in fantasy art—and they weren't rocking the hooded-elf look either. Lean and wiry, dark hair queued and gathered in golden circlets, Artemis wore a sleeveless, pale green tunic gathered at the waist with a broad belt. She had black pants tucked into some of those calf-high boots that looked like moccasins—but none of it was leather. All polyester and other synthetic materials. And the circlets in her hair weren't gold— they were plastic. I knew because I tried to create a binding between them and the earth, which would effectively pull her to the ground by her hair, but it didn't work. Same thing with her belt buckle, and her bow and arrows were man-made composites too. I had no doubt that the knife strapped to her thigh was a composite as well.

Artemis was a sharp and stringy sort, jaw like a hatchet blade and muscles in her forearms rippling like piano wires. She didn't head straight for the pile of hound corpses but circled to her right, where Oberon and I were hiding. She approached in a crouching step, eyes flicking around for signs of us. Diana circled the other way in a similar gait.

The Roman goddess was a bit softer around the edges

than her Greek counterpart, and she had made a bit more effort to find clothing that echoed her ancient origins. She was wearing one of those armor skirts centurions used to wear, except hers was made of black pleather or some other unholy creation of fabric science. She had some black greaves on over her sandals too. Like Mercury, her skin was bronzed and seemed to glow as if she'd been waxed and polished in a detail shop. She was hot, to a degree that was rather unfair.

They took very different approaches to their famous virginity: Artemis's complete lack of attention to her personal appearance meant she couldn't care less what men thought of her, while Diana appreciated the tease of looking desirable yet untouchable. I used to admire them both when they were simply myths, for they represented two of the world's earliest memos to men that women could get along quite well without them and enjoy a full measure of happiness besides, thank you very much. It was more difficult to admire them now that they were hunting me, however.

Artemis looked as if she might wind up stepping on us at one point, and that would have been dangerous when she had a bow ready to fire, but she changed her path to draw nearer to the hounds. I saw that in a few moments she'd be presenting her back to us.

Get to your feet silently once she passes us and jump on her back, I said to Oberon.

<Got it. This will be easy.>

I should have stopped him right there because he jinxed it. But he rose to his feet silently, as did I, gathered himself, and sprang at her back when she was no more than two yards away. And though I had granted Oberon extraordinary speed, Artemis was still faster. Sensing the attack somehow, she dropped her bow and arrow, raised her left arm, leaned to her right, and caught Oberon in a choke hold.

<Auggh! She got me!>

He tried to wrestle loose, but Artemis held fast and drew her knife. She held it up to his neck and said in English, "Be still. I can't see you properly, so be sure you don't cut your own throat." That prevented me from sweeping her legs, as I'd planned. The situation had changed. I began to sidestep to the left, still behind her but away from her knife hand. If she wanted to take it away from his throat and throw it in my direction, she'd have to do it across her body. But she was counting on her partner to keep me at bay, and I was all too aware that Diana was the more dangerous in this scenario. She still had a bow and could skewer me quickly if she sussed out my position.

Do it, Oberon. Don't struggle.

<How did she know where we were?>

I don't know, I said, and wished that I did. I wasn't as good at strategy and tactics as Atticus was. This entire scheme had been ill advised from the start, and I'd been stupid to think I could outwit two immortal huntresses.

Thirty yards away, Diana's eyes searched for me. They didn't fall precisely on my position, but they were close. I tried to move as quietly as I could but felt I had to keep moving. If she got a fix on my position, there would be no time to dodge.

"Your master is dead, young Druid, but you need not follow him," Diana called. It occurred to me to wonder how precisely they knew Atticus was dead. Did they find where I'd buried him and dig him up? Had someone told them? Or were they able to communicate with their hounds, like Druids could, and learned from them that they'd lost one of their prey? I answered my own question with my next thought: If it hadn't been one of the Olympians, then dryads had probably told them, or some other spirits of nature. We'd no doubt passed our share during our run. "Release Bacchus and we will spare you."

"And the hound?" I said, moving as I did so.

"Since you have killed all of mine, I think your hound should die too," Artemis answered, "but I will be generous if you bargain in good faith now. This is not simply a hound to you, is it? This is a friend."

"Yes, he is. If you kill him—or harm him in any way—you'll get nothing from me. Bacchus will be lost forever." Diana was doing her best to zero in on my voice, her head slightly cocked but her eyes tracking me accurately now.

"I understand," she said. "Bacchus is a friend of ours. Release our friend and we will release yours. Everyone lives. Everyone goes home unbruised. Our quarrel was never with you."

<I call bullshit!>

"And yet you've hunted me for many miles," I said.

"Only to recover Bacchus," Diana replied. She was inching closer, bow at the ready. "We never sought your death."

"If you wish to talk, then talk," I said. "Stop moving and drop your bow, Diana, or I might begin to suspect you do seek my death after all."

Diana gave a tiny smile and stopped advancing but didn't drop her bow. "Very well, mortal. If you're willing to be reasonable, we can talk."

"Diana, wait," Artemis said. "I don't think we're alone—"

Chapter 14

Artemis heard me coming, but it wasn't in time. Distracted sufficiently by the negotiation with Diana and Granuaile, she realized too late that there was, indeed, someone else out there.

It was me, the dead guy, with Fragarach in my left hand and approaching behind her right shoulder, swinging with all I had at the base of her neck. Slice through the spinal cord fast enough and the brain can't tell the right hand to slit the throat of a hostage, I don't care how godlike you are. I sent her head sailing toward the pile of corpses, and her body slumped to the ground. Oberon was free and confused.

<Hey! What? I smell Atticus! Atticus, is that you?>

I didn't answer him. There was still another huntress to dispatch. Not caring about the noise I made, I chased after Artemis's head, snatched it up by the hair, and then chucked it directly at Diana. Her bow was fully raised and drawn now and swerving to shoot. She had to duck Artemis's head, but she straightened right back up to fire, correctly assuming that I was charging her. She was about to release and I was about to drop and roll when something whacked her hard in the back of the knees, and her shot went high and wide. It was Granuaile, of course, and she'd done me proud, taking advantage of the distraction I'd provided.

All kinds of things can happen in a battle to make you freak out, I'd told her once. Freaking out over friends getting slagged, for example, is perfectly normal. Going Hulk because somebody ruined a picture or souvenir of your significant other, that's to be expected. And if someone returns from the dead to fight again, nobody will look down on you for losing a tolerable amount of your shit. But you always, always have to deal with the threat first and save the freaking out for later, preferably when some decent alcohol is at hand to numb your noggin.

Diana immediately rolled away when she hit the ground, and thus Granuaile's follow-up struck the earth with a dull thud. I wouldn't be able to get to the huntress before she regained her feet; she'd rolled with her bow and would be able to nock and fire another arrow at stupid speed if she made it. A blur in my vision announced that Oberon wanted her to stay down as much as I did; Granuaile must have refocused his attention. The huntress did manage to spring to her feet, only to be yanked back down as she reached for an arrow.

I heard Oberon say, <Got her left arm, you get the right!>

Diana's attempt to free herself by clocking Oberon upside the head met severe resistance from Scáthmhaide; Granuaile didn't miss this time, and her blow audibly snapped both bones in the goddess's forearm. The arm pressed into the turf, where Granuaile stomped on it. Diana shrieked and struggled to free herself, but I imagined that Granuaile and Oberon were both juiced on the earth's energy for extra strength and she had no leverage.

Before Diana could think of using her legs and possibly kicking Granuaile off her arm, I decided to redirect her attention. I dropped my camouflage and said, "Well, hello there, Diana," as I strode into her view. Her eyes rounded, and her mouth stopped making noise and just hung open.

<It's Atticus! I knew it!>

Stay on her, buddy. Don't let go, okay?

<I won't! She won't move!>

Thanks. We'll talk in a minute.

I smiled at the shocked expression on Diana's face. Normally I wouldn't behave this way, but something about the Romans brought it out in me. It probably had something to do with how they had helped to wipe out the Druids. "You gave us quite the chase," I said. I twirled Fragarach once in my hand and halted it abruptly, feigning surprise at an unexpected thought. "Oh! Hold on. Did you think you were hunting *us*?"

Her eyes narrowed and she took breath to speak, but she never got to say a word. I hacked off her head with one stroke and kicked it away from the body so she couldn't heal it back up.

"Whooo!" I shouted, allowing myself a fist pump. "That one's going on my highlight reel."

Granuaile dispelled her invisibility and Oberon's camouflage. Her knuckles were painfully white against the wood of Scáthmhaide, and I couldn't tell by her face if she wanted to kiss me or kill me.

"Right," I said. "You probably have questions."

Chapter 15

"Who are you, and why do you have Fragarach?" Granuaile said through clenched teeth.

That wasn't the question I'd been expecting. "I'm Atticus, and the sword is mine."

<He's Atticus!> Oberon's tail was wagging and he clearly wanted to jump on me, but he held back, seeing the tension in Granuaile.

Heck yes. Snack for you!

"Atticus is dead."

"I was only dead for a little while."

<He just helped us kill the unkillable ladies. He's on our side.>

Ignoring Oberon's comment, Granuaile drew a knife from her thigh holster—her last one—and raised it over her shoulder, ready to throw. "Tell me who you really are. Are you Loki? Coyote?" I was beginning to understand why the elementals called her Fierce Druid.

"It's easy to tell, Granuaile. Look in the magical spectrum. Loki's a mess of anger and white light. Coyote is a mix of all colors. And all you'll see from me right now is the iron in my aura because I'm not drawing on the earth at all."

<Or you could just smell him. That's Atticus. I can hear him in my head, and he promised me sausage.>

I said a snack.

<I will snack on sausage, thank you very much.>

Oberon's test was insufficient, and Granuaile knew it. Coyote was capable of talking mentally to Oberon—or at least hearing him, as far as we knew—and he could also copy my form all the way down to my scent. The latter ability was how we'd fooled Garm and Hel into thinking I was dead back in Arizona.

Granuaile exhaled sharply and then spoke the words for magical sight. I waited patiently while she checked me out.

"What's your real name?" she asked, still testing me, and now that I'd recovered from my surprise, I approved of her caution.

"Siodhachan Ó Suileabháin."

"I was once a vessel for another person. Name the person."

"Laksha Kulasekaran."

"And what was that one thing we did together that one time?"

"We don't discuss that in front of the hound."

<Hey!>

Granuaile dropped the knife. "It really is you."

I tapped the soulcatcher charm on my neck. "Remember this? It actually worked."

She dropped Scáthmhaide too and tackled me to the ground. Oberon took it as an invitation to dog pile and landed heavily on the both of us.

<This is so awesome! I'm so happy right now! Atticus is back!>

Granuaile kissed me, and I got to enjoy it for maybe two seconds before Oberon decided to drool on our faces.

"Ew! Oberon!" Granuaile said, as we both wiped away the slime from our cheeks.

<Side effects from doggie joy may include face lube and leg-humping.>

"Don't you *dare* hump my leg!" Granuaile warned. "And please give us some time to ourselves."

<Aww.> Oberon's tail was still waving madly back and forth, but he graciously removed his weight from us.

"Granuaile, it's okay, we need to go anyway."

"We do?"

"Oh, yes. This isn't over. They're not dead any more than I am. We have to keep running. We should be able to make it to France at least."

Granuaile rolled off me and stood, then offered her hand to help me up. "How are they going to heal up a decapitation?"

"They'll get help from the other Olympians. I bet Hermes and Mercury will put them back together again."

"Why not simply start over with another body?"

"Because their current bodies are in great condition. They're just missing heads. While I was running to catch up, I was thinking about their rules for regeneration—it can't be arbitrary. They can't simply wish themselves a new body. They have to suffer a certain amount of catastrophic damage."

"Decapitation isn't catastrophic?"

"Not for them. Remember the tale of Orpheus, whose head was washed out to sea and floated around until he was plucked out by women doing their washing at the shore? Their ability to remain functional is mojo on a scale we can only dream of. Probably has a lot to do with having ichor instead of blood. I bet you they're still conscious and can hear us right now."

"That is *so* disturbing."

"I have a plan," I said, picking up Fragarach. Granuaile retrieved her throwing knife and Scáthmhaide.

"Of course you do."

<Hey Atticus, do me a quick favor before we go? It's easy.>

"Sure. What is it?"

\<Hold Granuaile's staff for just a minute. You know, rest it on the ground so that it's like a walking stick or something and the top of it is near your right cheek.\>

Granuaile and I traded weapons to humor him and I stood as he instructed.

\<That's perfect! Now say this like Sir Ian McKellen: "I am Atticus the White, and I come back to you now at the turn of the tide."\>

It was too silly and I couldn't do it, though I tried. I didn't have the gravitas; I dissolved into laughter before I could finish.

"I'm sorry, Oberon. We really need to move."

\<That's okay, I enjoyed the attempt.\>

"So what's the plan?" Granuaile asked.

"Same as the last one, except now we run with heads tucked under our arms like footballs."

"We run naked in plain sight with severed heads? A murder streak?"

"Heh! No, we'll go camouflaged if we have to escape, but I'd rather keep in plain sight for now. It's part of the plan. And so is speaking in Old Irish from now on, to keep the goddesses from listening in. Either that or communicating mentally through Oberon."

"All right. Give me a sec."

She jogged over to the sad collection of hounds, presumably in search of her other two throwing knives. I found a way to keep myself occupied while she was busy doing that. The chariots of the huntresses, along with their teams, still waited a couple hundred yards away. Grinning to myself, I unbound the chariots to hunks of metal and set the stags free by unbinding their harnesses and giving them quick mental shoves: *You're free. Run.* They took off, and I wondered how willing Hephaestus and Vulcan would be to forge the huntresses yet another chariot.

Granuaile returned and declared herself ready.

"Okay, which one do you want?" I asked.

"I'll take Artemis."

"Watch out for the mouths. I'm sure they'll bite if you give them the chance. Old Irish from now on."

She looked doubtful. "Are you sure it's safe? What if they know it?"

"Old Irish never spread beyond Ireland, unless you want to count Scots Gaelic. The Olympians would have had no reason to learn it, especially since the Tuatha Dé Danann took pains to learn Greek and English. And by the time the Greeks and Irish intermingled in any great numbers, the language was transitioning to Middle Irish anyway."

"What about the Romans?"

"They never conquered Ireland. They called it Hibernia and left it alone for the most part."

"Got it."

We found the heads with little trouble and confirmed that the immortals were still very much alive. They didn't have breath to speak, lacking any physical connection with their lungs, so they did their best to glare meaningfully at us. We each tucked our grisly goddess head into the crook of a left arm and resumed running south. Soon we would swerve west again to head for Calais. The elemental promised to keep us on a rural route as much as possible to avoid being seen.

I apologized first to Oberon for excluding him from the forthcoming conversation, explaining that it was intended to taunt the goddesses and not to cut him out.

<That's fine, Atticus. I'm just happy you're back.>

Me too, buddy.

Switching to Old Irish, I said to Granuaile, "The main reason I know this isn't the end of things is because the Morrigan said we wouldn't be safe until we reach Windsor Forest. That's still a good run ahead of us."

"Why do you think the rest of the Olympians haven't gotten involved?"

"I'm sure it has something to do with pride. The huntresses want to claim our kills as their own, though they'd never be able to touch us if we were able to shift planes. And when it comes to the rest of the Olympians, Odin said they're under orders to keep out of it from other deities—though I don't know which ones. So I'm certain the Olympians are watching the hunt, but they're also acutely aware that others are watching it too. Odin isn't the only one keeping track, you can be sure."

"Oh. They're tracking *me,* you mean."

"Yes. You are not so anonymous as you once were. But my point was that this is now an inter-pantheon power play. We removed Bacchus from the board, so now they've killed the Morrigan and penciled in a hash mark under the column that says *badass*. If they can't finish us off, though, with everyone watching, then that makes the Morrigan's death a fluke—or what it truly was, which was suicide."

"Suicide?"

"Yes. The Chooser of the Slain chose herself."

"But why?"

I wasn't ready to discuss that with her yet. Primarily, of course, the Morrigan had felt all the weight of an eternal prison sentence; she could never change who she was, because of the constraints of belief. But the question of why she wanted to change would lead to a discussion of our strange relationship. The revelation that the Morrigan had loved me dumped a load of guilt ferrets on the back of my neck, and I hadn't managed to shake them free. I doubted it would be a comfortable topic of conversation. We'd have to talk of it soon, but now wasn't the best time.

"Let's talk about her later, if you don't mind," I said.

"Okay, as long as we don't forget."

"I won't."

"You were saying about the Olympians?"

"They're going to be anxious to keep this confined to the huntresses as much as possible. The more effort they have to expend in taking us out, the smaller their victory over the Morrigan and the more ridiculous they appear. I mean, entirely apart from the fact that they were forbidden to interfere, they would diminish themselves in the eyes of every other pantheon if they have to exert their full might to be rid of us. That's probably why they can't see past our camouflage; this time, Minerva is staying out of it."

"But they've already involved quite a few of them. Neptune started that earthquake back in Romania, and then you have Pan and Faunus spreading pandemonium to keep us from shifting. And the forge gods made them new chariots, right?"

"Exactly. It's bad enough as it is. But if snuffing us was all that mattered to them, consequences be damned, they could have done it by now. Say that Ares, Mars, Athena, and Minerva dropped down here right now in front of us, and both of the Apollos. Would we stand a realistic chance of taking them out if they were fully prepared?"

"Eek! No. I guess not."

"You guess right. They're all weakened compared to their glory days, but they are still powerful beings and more than a match for us if we can't surprise them. That means our deaths aren't paramount yet; *how* we die is still more important, so there's definitely politics at work here."

We spent some time after that catching up on what had happened between me getting shot and arriving in time to dispatch Artemis. I think Granuaile edited out some of what she felt and thought while she believed me dead, but that was okay. I didn't tell her everything I thought and felt when I was in the gray wash of depression either.

Our run southwest passed quite pleasantly until Hermes and Mercury paid us a visit. They accosted us before we could cross the border into Belgium. They dropped down from the sky on their wee ankle wings and hovered, keeping pace until we stopped. Mercury did all the talking, as usual, while Hermes stared on silently.

"Release the goddesses," Mercury demanded in English without preamble.

"Oh. Hi, guys!" I waved at them with Fragarach and smiled. "Are you speaking for yourselves or delivering a message?"

"These are the words of Jupiter and Zeus."

"Nice, very nice. Well, you might have noticed that I don't respond well to commands. Are you willing to talk a little bit this time, or are you here to deliver another ultimatum and then unleash some more Olympians on me when I refuse?"

Mercury seethed but confined himself to saying, "You wish to speak, mortal? Then speak."

"Thanks! Last time you didn't seem very anxious to listen. Kind of makes me wonder how much you care about Bacchus, actually, since if you kill us you'll never get him back. Did I make that plain earlier? No one knows where he is but us. You can't ask the Tuatha Dé Danann. They have no clue."

"So he is a hostage."

"No, he's not a hostage. I don't want any ransom in a bag of unmarked bills. I'm perfectly fine with leaving him where he is. And if you are fine with it too, which it seems you are since you've been busy trying to kill us, then we're actually on the same team here and I'm not sure why you're so hostile. Could you clarify that for us? Do you want Bacchus back or are you willing to write him off?"

The messenger gods exchanged glances and then Mercury sighed. "We want him back."

"Awesome. Thank you for admitting it. I will freely admit to you that I would like to be left alone. In fact, the entire reason we're here is because you won't leave me alone. I didn't pick this fight, okay? Bacchus and Faunus did. So the solution here is very simple, and I would appreciate it if you would relay my proposal to Jupiter and Zeus."

Mercury nodded and Hermes blinked to indicate that they were listening.

"There's only one rule: Don't fuck with the Druids. The best part about that rule is that it requires no effort to follow. Easiest rule in the world. You can have the huntresses' heads back when you agree you won't allow them to hunt us or pursue any kind of vengeance on us through surrogates or associates of any kind. And the same goes for Bacchus. I'll happily give him back to you once I'm assured he won't be allowed to pursue his inclination to destroy us. And just to be safe, that goes for all the Olympians. If Jupiter and Zeus give me their word that members of their pantheon won't keep attacking us, then we won't have to keep defending ourselves and humiliating your dumb asses." I thrust Diana's head out to him by way of punctuation. "Message ends."

Mercury sneered at first but then grew uncertain when he took a closer look at Diana. "We will deliver you even so." He and Hermes launched themselves into the sky and disappeared into the sun.

"That was less than diplomatic," Granuaile commented, using Old Irish.

I responded in kind. "I know, but there's nothing to be gained here with a soft shoe. The sky gods aren't being serious yet. They're sending minions to make demands of us. We're going to have to up the stakes to make them pay attention."

"How do we up the stakes?"

"We'll figure it out in England. The Morrigan saw a way out for us there, but damn if I know what it is. Until we're there, all we can do is buy time, and I just bought us a bit more. Let's keep running."

"Yes, let's." Granuaile's eyes dropped down from my face and landed on Diana's head, whereupon she gasped. "Atticus, wait. Is Diana, you know, still with us?"

"What?" I peered at Diana and saw that she was slack-jawed. She'd never struck me as the mouth-breathing type, and even if she was, there was no way she could breathe at the moment. Turning my body so that my back was to Granuaile—and therefore to Artemis—I untucked the head from my arm and held it in both hands.

Diana's eyes were closed and her mouth hung open. I lightly slapped one cheek to see if I got a reaction, even reflexive. Nothing. I shut her jaw and it fell back open.

Being careful to continue speaking Old Irish, I asked over my shoulder, "How is your goddess doing?"

"She's fine. I mean, she looks more than a little angry, but she's alive. Yours?"

"Well, we may have a problem." I cast magical sight and saw that the white glow of Diana's power was gone. So was her entire aura. She appeared to be truly dead. "Hold up your head for me?" I asked. I craned my neck around and saw that Artemis still shone with energy. "Okay, thanks."

Diana had none of that anymore, and it dawned on me that my cold iron aura must have slowly snuffed out the magic that was keeping her alive. It hadn't been quick, like the nearly instant disintegration of faeries when they touched me, but a gradual process that required prolonged contact. The question that worried me was whether she was forever done or if she would be able to begin anew at Olympus, an idea of virtue and ambrosia made flesh. Had I unwittingly turned her mortal, in other words, or was she only *mostly* dead?

The longer I lingered there the greater chance that a divine observer would figure out what happened—if they didn't know already. Thinking back to his reaction before he flew away, Mercury might have figured it out. I hoped not. It would be best if the Olympians didn't know I could do this.

Tucking her head back under my arm as if nothing had changed, I said, "Let's go, but you run a bit ahead. I don't want Artemis to see what happened."

Granuaile resumed running but called over her shoulder, "Is she toast?"

"Tough to say. I think we'll get some kind of reaction from Olympus soon. If they come for Artemis, bust her head before you let them have it."

"Ugh. Seems wrong somehow."

"You mean now that she's helpless? It's not murder if you can't kill her. It's more like redistributing her consciousness. Only other gods can kill them."

"Unless you just did it."

"Right. Aside from cutting off her head, though, I didn't really mean to kill her."

Granuaile laughed. "You know I'm on your side, but to an objective listener, that sounds like a less than convincing argument."

"I know. We'll have to wait and see."

As we crossed into Belgium and wove a sinuous path through farms and villages and around cities, occasionally earning a honk from a driver who spotted us along a rural road, storm clouds gathered overhead, darkening the Belgian morning commute.

"Hmm. I think Zeus and Jupiter have received our message. We can expect their reply shortly."

"What do you think they'll say?"

"I don't think they'll say anything."

"Then how is it a reply?"

Two thunderbolts lanced down from the clouds above and struck us. Our fulgurite talismans provided protection, but the sentiment was unmistakable.

"That's their reply," I said, and it was nothing more than I expected. But what followed was completely unexpected.

<Hey! Watch out!> Oberon said, running behind us, but it wasn't in time to prevent Hermes and Mercury from swooping in behind us and batting the heads out of our arms with their caduceus . . . es? Caducei? Who has ever had to deal with more than one caduceus before?

Neither head popped up helpfully and allowed the messenger gods to scoop them up on the fly. They dropped at our feet, merely dislodged, and tumbled along as we slowed to pick them back up. We couldn't let Hermes and Mercury escape with the heads intact; for one thing, they'd find out for sure what had happened to Diana. For another, they'd be able to put Artemis back together fairly quickly and then she'd be only an hour or so behind us. I was already carrying Fragarach in my right hand, so it was a simple matter to shuck it out of its scabbard and halve Diana's head before Mercury could circle around to pick it up. It was not so simple for Granuaile, however, to take care of Artemis. Hermes was a bit quicker on his second pass—or else the head had rolled a bit farther from her feet—and it was all Granuaile could do to fight him off with her staff and prevent him from picking it up. She was probably thirty yards ahead, and if I went to help we'd have Mercury trying to get involved too. I had to keep my eyes on him or else he would doubtless take advantage when my back was turned. His cursing in Latin certainly indicated he'd like nothing more.

Oberon, wanna play fetch?

<On it,> he said, understanding precisely what I meant. While Granuaile and I kept the flyboys at bay, he scampered over and scooped up Artemis in his jaws, grasping her ponytail like a tug toy and letting her head dangle off to the left side of his snout. Hermes shouted when he saw that and I stole a quick glance to see what had happened.

Good, I said, returning my eyes to Mercury, *now bring her over here and drop her at my feet.*

Both Hermes and Mercury tried to intercept Oberon by flying over us, but we backpedaled and Oberon dodged the one pass they had at him. He dropped Artemis at my feet, and I ended it with a wet chunky sound. The Olympians roared in outrage.

"Oh, stop," I said. "They'll be fine again before the day is through and you know it. If Zeus and Jupiter would come talk to me we wouldn't have to go through this."

They didn't answer and neither did they attack. Coming after the heads in an attempt to restore the huntresses was one thing, but striking at us and involving themselves in the hunt would violate the terms Odin had outlined earlier. They floated above us, quaking with the desire to show us what an airstrike truly meant, but we simply set ourselves and waited, saying nothing as the storm clouds boiled overhead. Eventually they flew back south toward Olympus and our tense muscles could relax.

<They're not very nice to animals,> Oberon observed. <How did they ever become the visual symbol of flower delivery?>

Chapter 16

There was no rest for us in Belgium. We stopped only once, and it wasn't for food, which prevented me from investigating a modern mystery: What do people in Belgium call Belgian waffles? Our Waffles, perhaps, or maybe National Breakfast Pastries? It remains for me an inscrutable conundrum. And so it goes for Belgian chocolate and Belgian witbier. I had spent very little time in Belgium since its rise to international fame for delicious foodstuffs. I supposed I would have to use the modern fallback position and Google it.

The reason for our pause was Hugin and Munin, who flew in to give us an update from the all-Odin all-the-time news channel.

Munin pointed at Hugin, indicating the raven with which I was to bond. Odin's speech filled my head like Oberon's did, though it was still a bit odd staring at a raven instead of his one-eyed visage.

<The Álfar have successfully destroyed thirty Svart-álfar who were lying in wait along your path. They have asked me to relay their gratitude for the opportunity.>

The Álfar took out thirty dark elves? *Oh. Well, they're very welcome. I'll send them some fine Irish whiskey as soon as possible, if you'll be so kind as to deliver it to them.* Because if someone saves you from a potentially life-threatening fight, you owe them booze. It's a rule that transcends time and cultures.

<Of course. Of more importance is the fact that the Olympians have ascertained you're heading for the English Channel. Neptune and Poseidon are stirring up the ocean there. I have heard this from my own god of the sea, Ægir. You should prepare for some sort of trickery—what's the Irish word I'm looking for?>

"Shenanigans."

"Yes, that's it," Odin said. "Shenanigans."

My aquatic form was a sea otter, and Granuaile could shape-shift into a sea lion. While we could swim the channel like that and Oberon could dog paddle, we weren't going to kick a lot of ass if the Olympian sea gods got involved. And I could see already how they would rationalize what they were doing; if we were eaten by sharks, well, that happened all the time. It wasn't direct interference in the hunt.

Though I'd already determined it would be unwise, I asked anyway to see what Odin would say: *Can't we just take the Eurostar train underneath the channel and avoid all that?*

<You can try. If you think you can sneak past the sentries they have at the station and wish to trap yourself in a metal container with plenty of innocent people, and if you wish to break the rules of engagement that prevent them from flying down in front of your current location, by all means, go right ahead.>

He knew very well I wouldn't do that. *What about Artemis and Diana? Any word on them?*

<They are back in Olympus, breaking in their new bodies, awaiting yet another set of chariots to be made. They will not be on the trail again for some time.>

I breathed a private sigh of relief—and not just for the extra time. I was glad Diana hadn't died a true death, for if she had, there would have been no possibility of a negotiated peace between us.

Odin added, < I found your treatment of their heads to be amusing.>

Yes, well, I'm sure they found it less so. Listen, Odin, I need a favor if you can manage it. Get word to Manannan Mac Lir of the Tuatha Dé Danann what's been happening—and Flidais too, I guess. We need some Irish help to get across the channel, because we don't have anything that can skate us past Poseidon and Neptune, and we'll probably need Flidais to help us in the UK after that.

The raven squawked at me, and Odin's voice said, <I am not your errand boy.>

I know, and I said it's a favor. I sensed that Odin wasn't opposed to helping me, but I'd failed to throw a sufficient sop to his ego first. Thanks to a meal I once shared with Odin and Frigg, I remembered that the Norse diet in Valhalla was quite restricted and unvarying, and Odin might be tempted with gustatory delights. *In thanks for which, I'll send you some Irish whiskey too, plus some Girl Scout Cookies.* He could no doubt secure such items on his own if he truly wanted them, but things always taste better when they have the added flavor of contraband.

<Oh, well, if we are exchanging services, that's entirely different. I want a gross of those Samoas I overheard you mentioning to the witches in Poland and a case of Redbreast. And I mean the fifteen-year-old stuff. Not negotiable.>

Done. As long as Manannan shows up and we survive.

<I will do my utmost to ensure he appears. A question before I go: Do you know anything about the vampire situation?>

What vampire situation?

<Rome is in an uproar. Or, rather, I should say the

rest of the world is—Rome itself is now silent. Twenty-
seven vampires, all of them quite old and part of the
vampires' power structure, were slain yesterday during
daylight, their heads missing.>

I frowned. *Only vampires? Didn't they have human
bodyguards?*

<Thralls, yes. Also dead. Their deaths are not causing
the uproar.>

"Interesting."

<You know nothing about it?>

I knew all about it. I'd asked Goibhniu to arrange the
whole enterprise the last time we were in Tír na nÓg.
The idea was to put a bounty on vampire heads, starting
with the heart of their power in Rome, and let all the
pods of mercenary yewmen know. I couldn't have
known it would work so well or that they'd coordinate
and take out every vampire in the city, but I'd hoped for
a significant disruption to the vampire chain of command. This sounded like a complete decapitation of
their leaders—literally—and it might explain why we
hadn't seen any more vampires since the Polish border,
as well as why Leif might be too busy to deliver his own
messages. Odin didn't need to know that, however.
There was no telling who else he was talking to, and I
didn't need to have the mysterious puppet master in Tír
na nÓg hearing about it and letting the vampires know
that I was paying for their heads.

Nope, I said, *not a thing beyond what you've told me.
It certainly brings me joy to hear it, though.*

<They were looking for you, weren't they? This should
ensure that they remain preoccupied with their internal
affairs for the near future, which coincidentally benefits
you, doesn't it?>

It's a happy coincidence, I agreed. Theophilus struck
me as the sort who preferred to rule from the shadows
and not get directly involved, but I bet he would either

be required to rule himself now or expend all his efforts in putting some puppets in charge. One of those might be Leif. And I'm sure Leif would be figuring out how to turn the situation to his advantage, as would every other vampire.

<Yesss,> Odin said, Hugin's head cocking to the side and managing to convey that Odin didn't think it was a coincidence at all. <Well. I'm off to find your sea god. You can leave the cookies and whiskey at the drop point in Colorado.>

Many thanks, Odin.

<I am grateful to you for the entertainment. The Einherjar are betting heavily on the outcome, and your return from the dead caused settled bets to become unsettled. The fights that have broken out have been inspired. How did you manage to come back from a bullet to the head, by the way?>

I shrugged as if it were nothing. He didn't need to know that. *How are the odds?*

<In your favor now,> Odin replied. <But they're betting the woman and the dog don't make it. Three to one against.>

I broke the connection before I said something unforgivably rude.

Chapter 17

We arrived in Calais, France, around one in the afternoon. Timing and mental exhaustion required an interlude. We needed to give Odin time to find Manannan Mac Lir, and we had a comfortable lead on the huntresses, so we could afford to relax—or at least, not run—and have a decent meal before crossing the channel at night. We snuck into a clothier to grab some duds and walked out looking at least civilized if not fashionable. We also lifted six leather belts for later use. I took note of the name to make sure the establishment got paid later for what we took. Not trusting ourselves to nap briefly, we chose to remain awake and explore the city for a few hours. I kept my eyes peeled for possible enemies but tried to conceal my paranoia. We all studiously avoided talking of the immediate past or the future; we were both desperate, I think, for a thin slice of normalcy. I taught Granuaile a few French words here and there and taught Oberon that the food he wanted was called *saucisse*. We pulled off another meat heist in a café, but the food was rather pedestrian in Oberon's view compared to what he'd had in Poland. It took the edge off our hunger until we could enjoy something later, however.

After sundown we walked to a spot near the channel and found a likely looking place to have dinner, called

Le Grand Bleu. Before walking in, I asked Granuaile
and Oberon to wait while I made arrangements. Casting
camouflage on myself, I borrowed a cell phone from the
purse of an unsuspecting teenager to call my attorney,
Hal Hauk, back in Arizona. I walked a short distance
behind her as I called; she missed the phone a bit quicker
than I had hoped, due to an addictive need to check for
texts or something every few minutes. Her cursing in
French was entertaining, but I couldn't appreciate its flu-
ency once Hal answered his cell phone.

"Whoever you are, it's four in the morning here," he
said without preamble. "This had better be good."

"Hi, Hal!" I said, sounding as cheerful as possible.
"It's me, Atticus. On the run in France without ID or
money. Need the money right away. Know anybody in
Calais?"

Hal groaned. "You're going to give me a headache,
aren't you?" his gruff voice rumbled.

"Your kind don't get headaches," I reminded him. We
stuck to vague words because it wouldn't be wise to
have terms like *pack* and *werewolves* bouncing around
communications satellites.

"That doesn't mean you aren't one," he said. "To answer your question, I believe there is someone nearby,
yes."

"Can someone meet us at a restaurant called Le Grand
Bleu and drop a wad of euros in my hand and you wire
them some reimbursement from one of my accounts?"

"Of course I can. But what sort of trouble are you in
now?"

"Everyone's trying to kill me. So far they've only managed to do it once."

"What?"

"The good news is that Granuaile is now a full Druid."

"That's great, but who's after you?"

I couldn't very well tell him plainly without making

eavesdroppers raise a red flag, so I improvised a toupee for the bald truth. "Well, I'm running from several different LARPing troupes."

Hal caught on and said, "Of course. Which ones?"

"The Fae, the Svartálfar, all the vampires, and the Olympians. Plus Hel and Loki."

Hal ignored everything except the last. "Loki! Loki is free in the world? LARPing, I mean?"

"Well, to some extent, yeah. The backstory for his role is that he busted out of his binding a few months ago, but he's been napping for much of that time, trying to heal up a bit after centuries of scarring and sleep deprivation. I've been able to distract him from the business of Ragnarok with one shenanigan or another, and right now he's under the control of Malina's coven in Poland. Oh, and before I forget, do you remember that cabin in Colorado I had you buy for me?"

"Yes."

"Good. I need you to buy a case of fifteen-year-old Redbreast whiskey and somehow get your hands on a gross of Samoas and put them in the cabin right away. Send Greta to do it or something."

Silence greeted this for several seconds, and I began to fear I'd lost the connection. Just as I was about to check, Hal said, "Pardon me, is this some kind of social experiment? You want me to get a hundred and forty-four Samoans and cram them into your cabin with a case of whiskey?"

"No, I said Samoas. The Girl Scout Cookies with chocolate and coconut. Luxury item outside of the States, you know. I've seen them go for fifty bucks on the Malaysian black market, but they're only four dollars a box for us. The problem is they're out of season right now, so it's going to be tough."

"Out of season?"

"Yeah, they don't sell them year-round, Hal. It's usu-

ally January through April and here we are in October.
I'm sure you can find them somewhere, but it's going to
be tough. This is a major quest I'm giving you here."

"I'm too old to be chasing after Girl Scout Cookies."

"Well, I'm older, and I'm paying you to be my lil'
cookie monster."

"This is not why I have a law degree."

"No, but the law degree is why you get to charge me
that hourly rate."

Hal sighed audibly through the phone. His frustration
carried across the Atlantic very well. "How did our conversation get to this place? I mean, didn't we start with
everyone trying to kill you? Let's go back to the part
where you said they already killed you once."

"Hal, I don't have time to explain. I borrowed this
phone and need to give it back. Just have an associate of
yours show up at Le Grand Bleu with a fat stack of bills
and get that contraband to the cabin. Pretty please."

"Fine, but I'm going to bill you for my therapy ses-
sion."

"You do that. Oh, and we have a few local vendors
who would probably appreciate some reimbursement
for my activities today. Have your dude also drop off a
few hundred euros at this store." I gave him the address
of the clothier as well as the café from which we'd snaf-
fled lunch, and he quickly rang off before I could think
of anything else for him to do.

I slipped the phone back into the teen's purse and then
dissolved my camouflage. Granuaile was about a half
block away with Oberon sitting by her side, and he was
getting plenty of attention.

<Ah, the French are so lovely,> he commented as a
pair of women paused to smile at him and scratch him
behind the ears. <Great food, amusing little bulldogs,
and super-hot poodles. They have made their mark on
the world, have they not? But yet they also appreciate

the greatness of the Irish—me—and that is why their hands are so soft. They honor me with their soft hands.>

Oberon, you're doing that thing again where your ego replaces your reason.

<Sorry? I didn't get that; I'm too busy being adored. What's that they're saying right now? They're telling me I'm a good boy in French, aren't they? They sound so sweet. It's like they're feeding my ears with sugar while massaging them with those wonderful fingers at the same time—>

Don't get carried away, now.

<I can't help it. They moisturize. Haven't you ever heard of lotion, Atticus?>

I ignored his gibe and said, *We're going to be heading indoors to eat. Ready to squeeze underneath a table?*

<Not really. Can I take a nap while you go do your knife-and-fork thing and then you can bring me something in a doggie bag?>

Okay. Where do you want to plonk down?

Oberon wandered around to the rear of the restaurant and stretched out against the wall. <Unconsciousness in T-minus five minutes! Five! Four!>

You mean seconds?

<Whatever.>

I cast camouflage on him to prevent someone from calling in a stray and then took Granuaile's hand and squeezed it gently. For another hour, perhaps two, we would have some time to enjoy our lives instead of running for them. She smiled at me and leaned in for a quick kiss. We decided, however, to give it an extended run.

<Oh, barf! Human mating habits. If this was a movie, I would skip to the next scene.>

You're supposed to be asleep.

<Well, I would be, except that there are these people mashing their faces together in front of me.>

We granted him mercy and circled the building to get

a table in the restaurant, camouflaging our weapons and taking them inside. Tables of a light wood awaited us, along with rattan-style chairs in a cold gray. We eschewed alcohol—we'd be swimming soon—but ordered some challenging items for our digestive systems.

I opted for something that translated literally to *monkfish in an algae shirt,* but monkfish are famously unconcerned with wearing clothing. It really meant that the monkfish was wrapped in seaweed, but privately I thought the Algae Shirts would be a great band name. Incredible merchandising potential.

Granuaile wanted fish too but wasn't feeling up to the monkfish, so after asking me for a wee bit of coaching on pronunciation, she ordered *"turbot Hollandaise au citron vert, écrasée de pommes de terre, crème de ciboulette."*

The waiter, a tall gentleman with heavy eyelids, bobbed his chin and said, *"Oui, mademoiselle."*

She grinned with victory as he departed. "That was fun to say. I've enjoyed all these little phrases I've picked up today. I think I should learn French next."

"I agree. Let us begin. Repeat after me: *J'ai l'air ridicule quand je ne sais pas ce que je dis.*"

"Wait. I heard a cognate in there. Something about ridiculous. You're setting me up to say something stupid, aren't you?"

"Auggh! You caught me."

She smiled briefly before her expression turned serious. "How long do you think it will take us to cross the channel?"

"It's a twenty-one-mile swim, so however long it takes Oberon to dog paddle the whole way. It might be a very long time, unless you think you'd be strong enough to kind of tow him along and speed up the process?"

She pursed her lips in uncertainty. "I haven't even tried to swim yet. I have no experience with that form;

we haven't been by the sea in the past few weeks since I've been bound. But towing a hundred fifty pounds of wet dog doesn't sound easy."

"Well, it won't be deadweight. He's going to be helping. Hopefully we'll have time to experiment. We'll use the belts to jury-rig a harness for the weapons first, and then if we can figure out something for Oberon too, great. But if not, we'll basically swim circles around Oberon to make sure nothing's coming at us."

That earned me a Billy Idol lip curl. "Something's going to come at us, isn't it?"

I nodded. "Odin revealed that it's Poseidon and Neptune's job to make sure we never make it to England. I don't think they'll content themselves with waves."

"So what do we do?"

"The same thing that Poseidon and Neptune will do. If they can influence the animals of the sea, so can we. You look at them in the magical spectrum and attempt to communicate with them, the same way you made the initial connection with Oberon. Try to convince them that we taste like ass or there's something shiny waiting for them in the Black Sea or whatever, just don't eat us."

"We're not going to have access to magic while we swim."

"Nope. Whatever I can store in my bear charm will have to last us the entire way across. We should cast magical sight while we're still in the shallows and keep it on all the way."

"We need to make like ten more of those bear charms."

"Yeah, it's tough to argue that. But it might be more important to bind your amulet to your aura first. Everyone who wants to find me can do it now by finding you. The only reason we're staying mildly ahead of them is because we keep moving. But that's not sustainable."

"Tell me about it."

"Well," a cultured voice said, "I found you the old-fashioned way. A wiretap."

Our heads swiveled in alarm as our hands reached for weapons. Leif Helgarson, living embodiment of a frenemy, stood stiffly with his hands clasped together in front of him. He was out of reach beyond the neighboring table, but he could get into reach quickly if he wished.

"Though I admit, I was informed ahead of time which city you would be in. Hal is not so security-conscious as Gunnar was, have you noticed? He should be using a scrambler."

What I noticed was that Leif had ceased trying to blend in—not that he had ever been especially good at it. He was wearing a black paisley waistcoat over a white shirt and a candy-apple-red cravat pinned with a pearl. Black skinny pants and shiny, pointy black shoes completed his look, which suggested to me mild mental illness.

"Since when did you start monitoring calls?"

"Working with Theophilus has given me access to technologies and methods I would not have used earlier. I have been monitoring all calls running through the cell towers near Hal's residence and place of business, so thank you for reaching out to him."

"It's not a wiretap if you're not actually tapping a wire," I said, in a peevish attempt to reassert control. A small part of me was relieved that Leif wasn't able to track me through all the blood we had shared—he used to drink mine in lieu of payment for his services and I think I probably ingested some of his once back in Flagstaff, so that had been a legitimate fear of mine after he'd surprised us that time in Thessalonika. Tracking Granuaile through divination and monitoring calls was annoying, but at least we could work on countermeasures against that; I couldn't take back the blood. "Now get out. We were trying to have a romantic interlude, and your cravat is ruining everything."

"Your conversation sounded rather prosaic and based on survival rather than procreation to me."

"Who said anything about procreation? The point, which you apparently missed, is that you're not welcome."

"Where are the dark elves this time?" Granuaile asked, looking over his shoulder. "Are they in the kitchen?"

"No dark elves at all," Leif replied, "though some other vampires may arrive shortly."

"Please wake Oberon and get him in here," I said to Granuaile, never taking my eyes off Leif. "Look out for threats while we talk." Leif wouldn't leave before he'd spoken his piece, so I ground out, "Say what you came to say."

<All right, coming,> I heard Oberon grouse in response to Granuaile's mental call.

Leif gestured to the empty chair next to me. "May I join you?"

"No. Over there." I flicked my eyes at the unoccupied table across from us.

"Very well." No sooner had he seated himself than our waiter swooped in to inquire about getting him a drink. Leif caught his eye, charming him, and said, "You will forget I am here. Ignore me." The waiter turned and shook his head once, wondering what he'd been doing, before retreating to the kitchen to see if the answer waited for him there.

Oberon, invisible to most everyone, joined us and squeezed in behind Granuaile's chair.

<Whoa, that's Leif,> he said. <We don't like this guy, right? Do I need to open a can of wolfhound?>

I decided to let Granuaile answer him and prompted my erstwhile attorney, "Why are you here?"

"I have been given a task to perform, which I have no intention of performing. It runs counter to my own interests, despite the attempts of Theophilus to ensure that I have a personal stake in its completion."

"And that task is what, exactly? Kill us?"

"Near enough," Leif admitted. "I am to prevent you from swimming the channel, or, at minimum, delay your crossing. I therefore urge you to depart sooner rather than later."

"Fine by me," I said, making as if to rise. Leif held up a pale, placating hand.

"Nonsense. Enjoy your meals first. The urgency is not so great as that, and we have other things to discuss."

"Such as the note you left for me in Germany?"

"I am glad you received it. I have heard that you killed one of the snipers."

"There was more than one?"

"There were five. The one you killed was at the edge of the net, so to speak. Had you continued straight ahead from the place where you found the note, you would have been caught in a crossfire."

I didn't bother correcting him on who had killed the sniper. "Whose idea was that, and how did they know to set up there?"

"As to the latter, you probably know better than I. It is someone in Tír na nÓg who is divining the future of your protégée." He waved a finger at Granuaile.

"Do you know who it is?"

"No. Theophilus is quite closemouthed about it. All I know is that he gets regular updates from his source on your future or current position. As soon as the sun set, we heard you would be in Calais this evening, and I was sent immediately to cut you off. I am supposed to coordinate with the local vampires and one other to prevent your escape. Naturally, you are the wild card in all of this. Your amulet prevents them from predicting your actions and thus they never know whether they will be successful."

The waiter arrived with our orders and placed the artfully arranged plates in front of us. We thanked him and he left without looking at Leif.

"Where is Theophilus now?"

A tiny shrug. "He is constantly on the move now, as am I, but I believe he is somewhere in Italy at the moment."

"Good."

Leif quirked an eyebrow. "Is it?"

"Yes," I said. Perhaps the yewmen would find him and deliver the vengeance of Druids. I wondered if Leif had heard about what had happened in Rome, but I didn't want to bring it up. "Was it his idea to send the snipers?"

"No, but he approved it. The idea came from one of his allies who rather concerns me—an Austrian fellow named Werner Drasche. You may have the misfortune to meet him shortly. He bankrolled the mercenaries and has the wherewithal to continue such activity. It is his opinion that modern military force would be most effective in bringing you down."

He was right about that. I noted that Granuaile fumed silently at this news, and I felt a bit sorry for Herr Drasche. He was now irrevocably on her shit list. "Interesting," I said. "Why would I meet him shortly?"

"Theophilus has sent him here with the same basic information I was given—namely, that you would be in Calais tonight. He is probably searching for you even now, as I would be had I not heard from a hireling about your call to Hal."

"A hireling?" Granuaile said. "Who talks like that?"

"A contracted employee," Leif amended, which was not much better.

"Why should I be worried about this guy? Is he a vampire?"

Leif shook his head once, curtly. "No. He is human,

or at least he once was. You cannot simply unbind him. Think of him as a vampire without the common disadvantages. He is not dead; he can walk in the daylight; wood is no more dangerous to him than any other substance. And yet he enjoys many of our advantages—superior strength, long life, extraordinary recuperative powers, and an ability to hide his feeding so that no one notices."

"What is he, then?"

"I cannot say with certainty. A horror born of madness, perhaps. I have only recently met him, and my investigations have yet to bear fruit. But if you ask him, he will say that he is an arcane lifeleech."

"An arcane lifeleech?"

Leif winced. "He does have a penchant for melodrama. And cravats."

"Oh." I dipped my chin at his throat. "So that thing on your neck wasn't your idea?"

"It was my idea to flatter him into thinking he influences my personal tastes. But it is not my idea that cravats are attractive."

"I'm relieved. So what does Herr Drasche do, latch on to his victims and drain their life?"

"He does nothing physically. He can do it from a distance. Hence his use of the word *arcane*."

I frowned. "How great a distance?"

"I cannot provide an accurate measurement, but within his sight, certainly. He cannot hide in Sri Lanka and drain a victim in the Seychelles. But he could stand at the door to this establishment, for example, and leech the very life from your cells. A little from you, a little from Granuaile, and a little from everyone else." He swept his hand around to include the entire restaurant. "You may not feel anything at all, except perhaps a mild fatigue. He is the perfect parasite. He thrives entirely on the energy of others now and has no need to ingest food—only water."

"So he can just drain a little at a time?"

"Oh, no, he can drain people completely. He refrains, however, because it is unnecessary. Imagine, Atticus: He can walk abroad in daylight and sample from everyone in public. He is sustained and kept youthful wherever he goes."

"This only works on people?"

"No. Plants and animals too. He can live until the end of days if he so chooses and have minimal impact on his surroundings. Yet if he needs unnatural strength, it is at his fingertips. He can grow stronger by draining the life of everything around him."

"Gods below, what a monster." Given enough time, he could snuff an elemental.

"Indeed. But apart from some odd cosmetic decisions, he does not look the part of a monster. Instead, he cultivates the aspect of a dandy."

I snorted. "Nobody calls people dandies anymore, Leif. We call them douche bags now."

"In sooth?"

"Verily. And in case you were wondering, you're dressed like a dandy."

"Alas! It is the least of my faults, I imagine."

Truer words were never spoken. I could never forgive his betrayal, but somehow I had slipped into bantering with him like old times. I looked down at my plate and realized I had yet to touch my food. Granuaile hadn't sampled hers either and became aware of this at the same time I did.

Leif noticed our gazes and said, "Please, eat."

The monkfish in algae shirts looked tasty, but I was no longer hungry. "I've kind of lost my appetite."

"Me too," Granuaile said.

Oberon spoke up. <What a shame! Happily, I've

found mine.> Granuaile picked up a fork, scooped a bite of turbot, and held it out to her right, over seemingly empty space. A couple of licking noises later, the turbot had disappeared from the fork.

"How can such a creature as a lifeleech exist?" Granuaile asked.

Leif grimaced. "I am uncertain. My only information derives directly from him and may be suspect. But to hear him tell it, he was an accident of alchemy—a by-product of a sixteenth-century search for the philosopher's stone. He represented a form of success, of course, but he drained to death the alchemist who created him, in the first few minutes of his newfound power. He is unique, which I suppose is a minor blessing, as there will be no others. Of more concern to us is that he is entirely in the confidence of Theophilus."

I noticed that Leif had subtly cast this as an "us vs. them" scenario, when in fact he was with them. Or, if that was not entirely accurate, he was certainly not with us.

"Huh. How'd that happen?"

"I do not know. I am not in confidence with either of them. I am also unsure of Herr Drasche's motivation regarding your pursuit and murder. He could not harbor an old antipathy for Druids, since he was born long after all Druids had disappeared from the earth save you—and he only heard of your existence recently. But it may simply be an issue of loyalty for him. His relationship with Theophilus has depths I cannot fathom."

"Well, how about the obvious?" Granuaile asked. "Are they lovers?"

Leif blinked. "Oh. Well. I hadn't considered that. Perhaps."

"Aha!" Granuaile said, pointing at him, her face lit with victory. "So that means vampires *do* have balls! Ever since the last time we saw you in Thessalonika, I've been wondering about that!"

Leif flinched as if Granuaile had slapped him. "You have?"

I grinned, because I knew what she was up to. Leif had a peculiar squeamishness about vampire biology and refused to discuss it. If she could cause enough discomfort, he might decide to leave.

"Well, yeah," she said, pressing the attack, "I mean, you're basically animated dead tissue, right, so why would any system from your human life still work if it's superfluous to the act of predation and converting blood to energy? I mean, I'm sure you'd have a vestigial sack dangling there, but there's no reason to suppose your nuts would still be churning out babymakers and testosterone like a regular dude's if that's not going to get you a night's supply of blood. But if Theophilus is sharing his sweet cadaver love with Werner, then I guess I was *dead* wrong about that, eh? Did you see what I did there? Hey! Where are you going?"

"Excuse me," Leif called over his shoulder, suddenly in a hurry to exit the restaurant. He was already halfway to the door.

I laughed. "I told him to get out and he ignored me, but bring up his pop rocks and he can't wait to leave. Good call." I gave her a fist bump.

"Thanks. I hope I didn't pounce too early."

"Oh. We never got an answer, did we?" I doubted I'd ever learn the truth about vampires.

"No, but we got an incentive to get out of here. I don't want to walk into an ambush outside, and I'm not anxious to confront something called an arcane lifeleech."

"Neither am I, but we can't go yet. We don't have any money to pay for this fabulous food we're not eating."

<I would eat it if you'd let me lick it off your plate.>

Granuaile said, "We'll feed you, Oberon, but in depressingly human-sized bites."

The waiter stopped by to make sure everything was

satisfactory, seeing that my monkfish remained undis-turbed.

"*Très délicieux,*" I told him. He removed himself from our sight, only to be replaced by a large man in a black beret with hyper-aggressive muttonchops. They were imperial expansionist chops, threatening to leap from his face onto mine and colonize it for the glory of a fill-in-the-blank god and monarch.

"Monsieur O'Sullivan?" he growled.

"*Oui.*"

He reached into his pocket and withdrew a large roll of euros. He dropped it onto the table and hauled his muttonchops away before they could execute an airdrop and establish a beachhead on my jaw. Apparently that was all the welcome I would receive from the local pack.

"Hmm," I said. "Taciturn."

"Aloof," Granuaile said.

<Or starving.>

"He was also in a hurry to leave, and that was a hint in itself. Let's go."

"Yes, let's."

<But . . . the food!>

Granuaile abandoned her earlier promise to feed him tiny bites and put her plate on the chair next to her for Oberon's easy access. I peeled off some bills and left them on the table as Oberon hoovered up the turbot.

We picked up our camouflaged weapons and the belts and exited, Oberon lamenting the waste of my monk-fish. <There are starving puppies in Iowa who'd be grateful for that food,> he said, <but I could be grateful on their behalf.> Privately, I mourned with him; dinner had not gone as I'd planned. I'd rather hoped to do my best to be a communicative male and verbalize a feeling or three to Granuaile, demonstrating that I, at least, had evolved beyond grunting, but circumstances had stolen my opportunity. I hoped I would have another soon.

The Strait of Dover—or, from the French perspective, the Pas-de-Calais—beckoned to us in the dark. The Morrigan had promised us a way out if we could make it to Herne's forest on the other side. Crossing the strait would leave us at our most vulnerable, and I seriously doubted Oberon's ability to swim twenty-one miles unaided.

We waded out a short distance into the cold surf, where Granuaile gave me Scáthmhaide, stripped, and donated her clothing to the tide. After a quick kiss—truly quick this time—she shifted to a sea lion.

I cast night vision. "All right, let's see what we can cook up. No matter what we do, we're going to increase your drag. But if we try to hook up something lengthwise, that's going to mess up your swimming motion. I think we're best off hooking you up bandolier style."

I asked Oberon to hold on to our weapons for us on the beach while I got Granuaile rigged. It would not do to lose them in the surf.

Using two of the belts, I slung them diagonally so that they passed over a flipper on one side and under it on the other, forming an X. I buckled them on her back and asked her to roll over. She did, presenting her belly. I fetched Scáthmhaide from Oberon first and laid it crossways near the top of the X, just above her flippers—the theory being that she would not need to twist and flex right there as much as she would on her neck or her tail. At the two contact points with the belts, I bound the wood to the leather so that there was no possibility of detaching. I admired again the craftsmanship of Creidhne and the cleverness of Flidais: The bindings on Scáthmhaide were carved in and "solid-state," immune to my cold iron aura. I didn't know if Fragarach was like that or not, but I had always avoided touching the blade for fear of ruining the enchantments that made it so powerful. "Give that a try," I said. "Can you swim okay like that?"

She heaved her bulk forward a bit awkwardly with the staff riding high on her chest and then dove into the waves. She disappeared for a full minute but then exploded out of the surf in front of me and soaked me in salt water.

"Very funny," I said. Granuaile laughed, but as a sea lion it sounded like braying, and that made me laugh too and eased a bit of the tension I felt.

"All right. Let's add on Fragarach and see what happens." I hadn't truly prepared it for a sea journey, but if we ever got to dry land again, I would pay plenty of attention to the blade and have Goibhniu give it some love. If nothing else, a gentle request to Ferris, the iron elemental, would allow me to pinpoint any problem areas and prevent developing rust.

I was just taking Fragarach from Oberon when his ears pricked up and he looked to the south. <Somebody's coming, Atticus. You might want to hold on to it.>

I followed his gaze and saw a slim silhouette approaching. I triggered my magical sight and saw that the figure had an odd, churning aura in green and orange. He had magical power of some kind, but there wasn't enough white in it to mark him as a god.

"Stay here," I said. "Be ready to go."

<Granuaile says we should bail and see if he can swim, whoever it is.>

Examining his clothing, I saw that it was composed of natural materials—cotton and silk, mostly. "Nah, I got this," I said.

As I padded across the beach, I crafted a binding between the back of his suit jacket and the sand but didn't energize it. I let it hang there, waiting for completion.

I dispelled magical sight to get a clear look at him. The moon conspired with the ambient light of Calais to provide some decent illumination, and night vision did the rest. He had on some of those slick ankle boots like Leif had been wearing, the kind with extra-long pointy toes. Not exactly beachwear. His suit was gray with a gray paisley waistcoat, and a silk cravat in an alarming soda-pop orange writhed around his neck, seemingly aware of its own hideousness.

It could be no other than Werner Drasche. I had to admit that Leif was right—he dressed like a dandy. But I think perhaps the idea behind the cravat was to distract from his face. His cheeks were entirely tattooed with alchemical symbols, the sort of squiggly signs that are reminiscent of astrology but based in elemental magic. They didn't cross his nose or mouth, but they continued above his brow and onto his shaven scalp. I didn't have time to examine them closely, but I'm sure they weren't a random configuration; they were equations. Formulae. And they represented a binding to the elements of life, the way my tattoos were a binding to the earth. Leif had called them "odd cosmetic decisions," but that was either an understatement or a failure to understand what they represented. Probably the latter: A vampire would have no need to understand alchemy.

I did not bother introducing myself. He knew who I was already. "Why are you looking for me?" I called while he was still twenty yards away.

He answered me in German. *"Manche Leute muss man einfach umbringen,"* he said, and then reached into his suit and pulled a Glock 20 from a shoulder holster. I energized the binding I'd made and watched him spread out his arms in a futile attempt to regain balance as he was yanked backward onto the beach and held there by his suit jacket. He held on to the gun, but he was spread-eagled now and unable to point it at me.

I was a little bit stunned at his stone-cold attitude; he'd simply announced his intention to kill me and pulled a gun.

If Leif had been telling the truth, this was the lad

who'd arranged to have me shot. Whether or not it was true, he'd just tried to kill me himself. And he was trying again, albeit in a different way. Raising his bald head from the sand and baring his teeth, he tried to drain me. I felt the hit on my cold iron amulet; it pulled away from my chest as if someone were tugging on it.

My patience bid farewell. Though I would have much rather spoken with Herr Drasche in an attempt to learn more about Theophilus, he had now put us on a kill-or-be-killed footing three different times. Removing Fragarach from its scabbard, I charged with the intention of decapitating him, but then a sudden thought caused me to change my mind. Instead, I brought the blade down hard on his right arm between the wrist and elbow, severing it and spraying blood on the sand.

"Manchen Leuten muss man einfach ihre Hände abhacken," I told him. He bellowed incoherently as I sheathed Fragarach and picked up his amputated hand. Making sure he could see me, I removed the Glock 20 from its grip and tossed it into the ocean. Admiring the simplicity of it, I shrugged and followed up by tossing his hand into the ocean too.

When Werner saw that, his roar went subhuman, and I felt through my tattoos that he was drawing energy from the earth—but not in the same way that I did. All the little microorganisms in the sand, any insects or small vertebrates nearby—he was draining them all since he couldn't drain me. I pointed Fragarach at him and said, "Stop that, or you lose the other hand." He stopped, taking loud gasps of breath between clenched teeth, but I noticed that his arm ceased squirting blood and a flicker of orange lit his eyes.

"Now that you're disarmed," I said in German, "I'm curious. You wish to kill me but appear to know very little about what I can do. It leads me to speculate on your source of information. Since your source obviously left out some critical details regarding my abilities, perhaps he or she was less than honest regarding other things as well. Now, I will freely tell you that I was informed of your existence less than thirty minutes ago. This intelligence came from a vampire named Leif Helgarson."

Werner Drasche cursed creatively and I smiled.

"Ah, yes. We have both been played, you and I. Leif expected me to kill you before I could learn of his role in sending you after me. Am I correct in thinking your removal would allow him to get closer to Theophilus?"

The lifeleech considered, then nodded.

"And he warned me of your coming in order to gain a measure of my trust. But I have had occasion to learn that Mr. Helgarson does nothing that does not serve his own self-interest. Any information he provides that appears to help you actually helps him. And the same goes for his services. Now that you have had occasion to learn the same lesson in a very painful way," I said, flicking a finger at his stump, "perhaps you and I can part without loss of life or further injury. Perhaps we can even find your hand. If I retrieve it, can you reattach it and heal?"

Drasche nodded. "I have done it before."

"Then, seeing as we are both victims of another's machinations, I propose a gentleman's agreement. First, we shall forgive each other our trespasses. Second, I will provide your severed limb so that you can be whole again. And third, henceforth we shall not trouble each other or conspire to do so with others. Live and let live in peace. Agreed?"

Werner Drasche needed little time to weigh the advantages of this.

"Agreed," he said. "Though I can speak only for myself and not for Theophilus."

"Understood," I said. "Your loyalty to him is admirable, though I would point out that right now Leif Hel-garson is a far greater threat to Theophilus than I am. And a far greater threat to you, I might add. But act or not on this information as you will. It is not my business. Our business together is easily concluded, and I am happy that we could find some ground on which to agree."

<Atticus, is everything okay?>

Yeah. A misunderstanding. Going to see if I can give this guy a hand.

Binding like to like—skin to skin—I created a bond between Drasche's left hand and his right, which floated somewhere in the nearby tide. The binding found a tar-get in the waves, and the right hand flew out of the water with a crab already attached to the trailing muscle tissue. Once Drasche was giving himself a low five, I dis-solved the binding and shooed the crab away.

"There you go, sir," I said. "I am a man of my word. Give me a moment to grant us both some space, and I will release you from the sand. I hope that if we ever meet again, we can do so amicably and partake of some-thing potable. May harmony find you."

Werner Drasche said nothing as I took my leave; he just fixed me with a glare of stone and watched me go. Once I reached the spot where Oberon waited, I dis-solved the binding on Werner's suit jacket. He sat up and cradled his stump, holding his hand next to it. I switched to the magical spectrum and saw the lifeleech swell with stolen energy, his arm suffused with the white light of magic. It took him less than a minute to com-plete the operation. I saw him hold up the hand and flex the fingers as if it hadn't been dinner for a crab in the recent past.

That was more than a little scary. He healed far faster than I did—faster than vampires and werewolves too. And it was entirely at the expense of other living creatures nearby. By all rights, I should have killed him for the abomination he was. But that was a moral path through deep woods that kept spiraling in on itself until there were no more abominations to kill but myself. Maybe Werner Drasche would give me another reason to kill him in the future—a reason that hadn't been conveniently provided by Leif Helgarson. I could not expect a second confrontation with him to be so easily won as the first. But let that song be sung when it would: For now, refusing to be a pawn in Leif's power games would suffice to keep me happy.

The arcane lifeleech stood, brushed himself off, and nodded once at me before turning toward the lights of Calais. I expected he would give Leif a little bit of trouble or, at minimum, speak some poison into the ear of Theophilus, and that would be satisfying as well.

Silhouettes rushed out of the city to meet Herr Drasche, and I saw by their gray auras and the red lights in their heads and chests that they were vampires. Werner Drasche was definitely not a neutral figure; he was an enemy to whom I'd shown mercy. Three of them remained with Drasche, but two passed him and ran in my direction—further evidence that his circle of acquaintances knew very little about me.

I unbound both vampires before they could get close. They melted messily into the sand. I was not neutral either.

<Can we go now? Because I'm really anxious to start asking you, "Are we there yet?">

Yeah, buddy. I waded out to Granuaile and bound Fragarach on top of Scáthmhaide, then tied the holster of throwing knives on top of that. *If we're going to drown our sorrows in the literal sense, let's get it over with.*

Chapter 18

The first hundred yards or so was largely an effort on Oberon's part to properly express how cold the water was.

<My nether regions have emigrated to my core and might never return. Maybe they'll send me a postcard.>

He was pretty slow in the water and I wasn't much faster; sea otters typically chase down sea urchins, which tend to have the top speed of a snail, so speed wasn't at a premium. But Granuaile's staff, sticking out horizontally from where we'd bound it, performed a valuable service: Oberon was able to drape his forelegs over it and keep his head above water and kick with his back legs. I did the same on the other side, and together we were able to make about ten miles per hour. Two hours wouldn't be so bad, I figured, if no one messed with us, but that was far too much to hope for.

Avoiding the shipping was a challenge in itself; the Strait of Dover was one of the busiest waterways in the world, and we had to add on a bit of distance by swimming outside those lanes.

We saw nothing for the first few miles except the next choppy wave that wanted to slap us in the whiskers. The white cliffs of Dover eventually appeared in our night vision; they had some white magic about them in the magical spectrum. Someone had cast wards over them, though I could not tell what kind at that distance. When we swam past the halfway point without incident, I allowed myself to feel the faint stirrings of hope. And, directly afterward, I felt faint stirrings in the sea.

Something was moving beneath us. The strait was twenty to thirty fathoms deep, and something down there was displacing a substantial amount of water. Something of leviathan proportions. Rising.

My imagination filled with a tentacled horror reaching up from the dark to pull us down for dinner. Krakens, to me, are so much more terrifying than sharks, though I do not know why it should be so. More people are bitten by sharks than eaten by krakens every year, but seeing a shark would have been reassuring right then. A shark, somehow, was merely a predator doing its predator thing, where a kraken was an unholy monster that sent sailors (and Druids) shrieking from their bunks.

I'm aware that my fear and loathing of krakens is unjustified—after all, they bear me no more ill will than I bear to lunch meat. But fear and rationality are hardly good drinking buddies—I'm fairly certain one of them doesn't even drink. When I'm on dry land, I can set aside my dread and even feel sorry for krakens because nobody loves them. It is a desolate feeling to crawl about the crust of the world unloved, and though most of us have never spent a single moment bereft of love, we can sense the emptiness of it and fear it, can sympathize with J. Alfred Prufrock and all such people unmoored from the shores of humanity. But my empathy for krakens dissolves in the water when we may be swimming in the same body of it.

Night vision, I discovered, does little good in the water past a couple dozen feet. If something decided to swim up from beneath us very fast, I would have almost no time to swim out of the way, assuming I could. And Oberon was about as agile in the water as a lily pad.

Magic sight was slightly better—the auras of living things have their own light and don't give a damn how far away they are from the sun or moon. But the sea is full of living things, and as I peered into the deep I had quite a bit of filtering to do before I could see anything more than visual noise and get a sense of distance. If I was having trouble, I imagined Granuaile was bewildered. She could interpret what she saw very well but still had difficulty penetrating the nonessential bindings.

When I finally identified the threat, it was so close that I nearly shat kine. It wasn't a kraken at all; it was a chorus of seven great serpents, spawn of Jörmungandr, swollen to monstrous size and rising below us to the left. Väinämöinen had told me of his encounter with one of them long ago; otherwise, I would not have recognized them. Sentient but shy creatures that preferred to dine on blue whales, they never would have pursued us without goading. They preferred the deep ocean and rose to the surface only in their youth to satisfy their curiosity. Poseidon and Neptune were whipping them doubly against their natures—to eat food they'd never seek out on their own, and in a portion of the sea they habitually avoided.

Frantically seizing on the threads of their consciousness one by one, I shouted the concept of *Poison!* to them as best as I could. One turned away. Then another. One that I hadn't shouted at turned away, so Granuaile must have been doing something similar. Four were still rising fast and opening jaws that would gulp us down like goldfish. I got one more, and two others peeled off to erupt from the surface nearby. But for the final one— a gigantic yawning darkness rimmed in teeth—there was simply no time. I had a Hamlet moment as death approached: The famous Dane had marveled in the graveyard at how *Imperious Caesar, dead and turned to clay, might stop a hole to keep the wind away,* and I wondered at how I could live so long and survive so many wars to wind up as snake shit.

Something massive rammed into the serpent's neck right below the head—it came in from the north and I never saw it coming, because I had been looking down. The collision caused the serpent to change course just enough to miss our tails. It still exploded through the surface along with the six other serpents, and the resulting turbulence tumbled us ass over teakettle deeper into the water. This wasn't a problem for Granuaile or me, but it was a significant issue for Oberon, who'd had no warning at all of the attack.

<Atticus! Help! The sky is gone! What's happening?>

I couldn't answer him specifically, because I honestly didn't know. The churning of the sea continued to pull me in directions I didn't want to go, and I was helpless to fight against it. I couldn't even see him. I caught a flash of Granuaile's sleek shape twisting away from me—either above or below, I couldn't tell which—and saw the shining trunks of serpents surrounding me like scaly towers. Everything else was dark and I couldn't tell which way was up. The huge creature that had butted into the last serpent flickered in my vision—a shark, perhaps, but strangely limned in white magic. And then the serpents crashed back into the sea again and made it all worse. That told me where the surface was, at least.

<Can't breathe! Atticus! Water!> Oberon's clear panic was infectious, and I struggled to right myself. I didn't know where he was and couldn't think of how to help him even if I did.

<Find Granuaile if you can,> I told him. It was his best hope, slim as it was. The serpents would be coming around for another pass; Poseidon and Neptune wouldn't let them give up.

<Oh! Wait—>

I didn't know what I was supposed to wait for. I began

to shout "Flee!" at the serpents, to try to clear them out, but all that accomplished was another short-term reprieve from becoming an hors d'oeuvre. The Olympians were urging the serpents to eat us as quickly as I could urge them to forget about it, and so for every time I convinced one to swim in a different direction, it would swing back around a few moments later as I switched my attention to another set of jaws. It wasn't sustainable; my magic was draining rapidly out of my bear charm. Soon I would have no way to communicate to the creatures, and that would be the end.

I missed one diving from above, but Granuaile must have spotted it, for a serpent plunged right past me, its scales scraping my fur and its tidal gravity pulling me deeper with it, tumbling me in swirls of current and confusing my sense of direction once more. My lungs burned, reminding me that breathing air was not optional, but the surface was a mystery to me now.

<Atticus, where are you?> Oberon's plaintive tone was heartbreaking.

<I don't know, buddy. I'm sorry.> I managed to fight free of the serpent's wake and searched for anything in the darkness that would tell me which way was up.

Two glowing white figures drew my attention—the lambent glow of godhood. Poseidon and Neptune, calmly floating in their element and directing the chaos. Their heads told me which way was up, and I began to swim desperately for the surface.

I didn't know anything was closing on me from behind until it plowed into my rear. It splayed my legs wide across its smooth bulk as it rose rapidly toward the surface. Energy abruptly flooded my tissues and I finally understood. It was Manannan Mac Lir in his aquatic form as a killer whale—a killer whale capable of magnifying his natural strength and speed and drawing Gaia's strength directly from the water. And as I had done many times in the past with Granuaile and Oberon, he was now sharing some of that strength with me through skin-to-skin contact that slipped past my aura, while giving me an express ride to the surface.

It was he who had delivered a head butt to the seventh serpent and perhaps had helped distract the others. Odin had totally earned his Samoas and whiskey.

The stars never shone so bright as when we splashed through the surface and the blackness sheeted away from my eyes. I gasped a lungful of sweet, salty air and then had to hold it in as Manannan dove again—so quickly that I slipped off his back as he darted away.

<He found you!> Oberon said, and the victory in his tone reassured me.

<Yes, but I think he's left me behind now.>

<He's coming back to fetch me, and Granuaile is here too. Follow north and he will wait for you to catch up. He says to climb up on his back with me and not to worry. He and Clever Girl are keeping the snakes busy.>

Indeed they were. A quick survey of my surroundings revealed that the spawn of Jörmungandr were thrashing about in the sea, tossing the waves as if apoplexed. The Olympians urged them to violence while we Druids urged them to peace, and it was in their nature to side with us. The Morrigan's words came back to me: *Gaia loves us more than she loves the Olympians.* They might have the power to coerce her creatures and usurp her magic to some extent, but in the end they were bound to their worshippers whereas we were bound to the earth itself.

Now that I was finally able to see them clearly, the children of Jörmungandr proved to be as beautiful as they were terrifying. Blue-green scales, just as Väinämöinen described, shedding sheets of water and glinting in the moonlight, covering everything except for membranous tissue stretched between five bony ridges that fanned out from the top of the head. I didn't see gigantic fangs;

I thought all the teeth were pretty large, and perhaps the ones on the edges were a bit plus-sized. And it hadn't been my imagination in the sea that their mouths were giant black holes—they really were. Inside, the cheeks and tongue were not pink or red but a scaly asphalt, as though something else flowed through their veins besides blood. Overlarge eyes like oil puddles helped them see in the gloom of the deep, and their gills flared beneath their jaws, horizontal shadows slashing across the scales.

Manannan's back and dorsal fin floated on top of the waves about a minute's fast swim from where he lost me. A sodden wolfhound huddled around the front edge of the fin, his paws hugging either side of it and his head resting against its left side, facing the tail. I scrambled up the side and bounded toward him until I could leap on his back and hold on with my otter paws.

<Okay, let's go!> I said. <If Granuaile is ready, that is.>

Oberon's mental voice spoke in an abominable caricature of pirate speech. <Arrr, that she is, matey! Swimmin' a fathom deep to starboard! Or port! Whatever direction that is! It matters not, because I'm a salty dog! Arrr!>

I didn't reply for fear I would encourage him.

Manannan pulled away from the boiling cauldron o' serpents, which were thrashing impotently under the conflicting commands of Olympians and Druids. For about fifteen seconds I harbored hope of a clean escape. And then two arrows fell out of the sky and sank into Manannan's back, right behind the dorsal fin. He shuddered and almost dove by instinct before he remembered he had to keep Oberon topside.

I squinted through the night and, past the writhing trunks of serpents, saw two white-veiled forms skipping across the waves on giant clamshells pulled by dolphins. Those were the chariots of Poseidon and Neptune, but they now carried Artemis and Diana, who had obviously regenerated and caught up to us. But they were out of their element now. It was an awfully choppy ride through the sea-serpent mosh pit and they couldn't be as accurate with their arrows as they wished, but they were still bloody dangerous, and I didn't want to give them any more free shots. Luckily, in their haste to catch up to us in the strait, they had forgotten to take proper precautions with their mode of transport.

Clamshells are all natural. If I could have grinned widely as an otter, I would have. Using energy provided by Manannan Mac Lir, I bound the shells to the bottom of the channel. That dumped the huntresses into the strait and prevented them from firing on us. I released the binding almost immediately, because I didn't want to hurt the dolphins towing them. But those poor sea serpents were probably working up an appetite with all that thrashing around. I shot an idea to Granuaile and Manannan via Oberon: *Monsters tend to like virgins in the old stories.*

Two things happened at the same time: Poseidon and Neptune realized that their goddesses were in trouble and stopped pushing the serpents to eat us, and we encouraged the serpents to eat the goddesses.

Oh, it was a thing of beauty. All seven of them whipped around and dove after the huntresses in a swirling eddy of scales and flesh and then disappeared beneath the waves. Mm-mmm! Goddess Tartar! Double down!

We had no idea if one snake had eaten both or if they'd gone into different digestive systems. It didn't really matter. We told all the serpents to flee, and that's what they did, streaking for the open Atlantic and deeper water. Poseidon and Neptune would rescue Artemis and Diana, of course, and the goddesses would eventually resume their hunt, but there was no way they'd keep us from reaching England now. I stupidly thought we had won.

Chapter 19

Manannan required a bit of triage once we reached the narrow strip of beach between the white cliffs and the western docks of the port. The arrows sticking out of his back weren't made of natural materials, and there was nothing we could do but tear them out. He would heal fine, but I suspected he would have precious little patience for the Olympians from now on. Through Oberon, he communicated that he would leave us there and remain in the strait to monitor developments. Though I wanted to ask him about the Morrigan—did he bear her to Tír na nÓg, was she at peace now, and so much more—it was neither practical nor appropriate to speak of such things through my hound, so we thanked him and bade him farewell. He swam off, the holes in his back already closed up. I shifted to human first and unbuckled the belts on Granuaile's back after unbinding our weapons. Granuaile shifted to human and waded out of the surf with Oberon, who shook himself and sprayed us with hound-scented salt water.

"All right, let's get the hell off this plane and thumb our noses at the Olympians," I said. "There should be a small coppice of trees tethered to Tír na nÓg nearby."

Skirting the city in camouflage, we crossed Military Road and then Folkestone Road, which led us to Elms Wood, a sliver of untouched forest that had served as a border between farms for centuries. We placed our hands (and paws) against the trunk of an elm and searched for the connection to the Fae plane. It wasn't there.

"No, not here too!" Granuaile said, slapping the tree trunk in frustration. "How'd they get here ahead of us?"

"They've known where we were headed for a while now," I said, then added, "Damn it."

"So they've managed to corrupt the forests here too?"

"Yes."

<What are we going to do? Go get some bangers and mash?>

"We'll go to Kent. There's an Old Way there that might not be guarded. And if it is, we'll go just a bit beyond and get what sleep we can during the day before pressing on to Windsor. There's not enough time to make it there before dawn, and I think we should hit it during the night if we can."

Following the procedures we used in our run across Europe, I shifted to a stag and remained visible while Granuaile and Oberon followed in concealment. Running through England was a bit nostalgic for me, having spent quite a bit of time there at various points of my life, but the countryside was far more developed. There used to be more Old Ways, but many had been destroyed in the name of progress, eaten up by the modern world, and there was no real incentive to make any more in protected areas when the system of using trees to shift had been so dependable until recently.

Still, even at night, we ran through some stretches of English countryside that were utterly sublime. Oberon spotted a herd of sheep sleeping in a pasture and begged me to let him go mess with them.

<Come on, Atticus. If we scare enough wool off them, you can make me a sweater with a huge O on the back. I'll wear it to the dog park and everything.>

<We don't want to wake anyone up, Oberon, including the sheep. And you don't really want to be a rascally sheep-biter. You would come by some notable shame.>

<But they're so fluffy!> When I didn't respond, he appealed to Granuaile. <Clever Girl, intercede on my behalf! We'll go over there and bark a bit and they'll all wake up and bleat in a charming British accent and then we'll move on. It won't take two years!> After a brief pause I heard him say, <Minutes, years, you know what I mean!>

<Oberon, I'm sorry we've had days and days with no fun at all, but I promise we will make this up to you with something really good.> Sensing weakness, my hound immediately switched into negotiation mode.

<I want a crazy cinnamon-coated poodle named Nutmeg! And I mean crazy. The kind that barks at fire hydrants and pees on mailmen.>

<I'm not sure we can guarantee something that specific, but it will definitely make up for all this.>

Kent had more preserved woodland than some other bits of England, with small named stands of timber breaking up the farmland and sheep pastures. A stretch of trees west of Sevenoaks called Mill Bank Wood was home to the only Old Way that lay across our path to Windsor. A boulder hidden under moldering leaves concealed a chute that led to a memorial for Lugh Lhámh-fhada in Tír na nÓg. We approached it cautiously, expecting it to be guarded by Fae or monsters or human mercs. None of that turned out to be true; instead, when we arrived, we discovered the boulder had been reduced to rubble and the earth churned around the place, effectively destroying the passage to Tír na nÓg. I couldn't muster the outrage to curse our luck; it wasn't luck, anyway, but further evidence of a carefully coordinated campaign against us.

We moved on, but I didn't tell Granuaile or Oberon

where we were going or why, in hopes of foiling attempts to divine our destination from here. Directly west, perhaps two or three miles, behind the French Street Burial Ground, the Long Wood offered concealment and a place to sleep, and it said something about my exhaustion that I was too tired to make an adolescent joke about its name. It was damp and smelled a bit of rot after a recent rain, but it was safe for the moment.

I shifted to human and said, "Let's sack out here for the day," since it was only an hour before dawn.

Granuaile shifted and said, "Can we afford the time?"

I shrugged. "I figure we have a little bit, yeah. The huntresses probably need brand-new bodies and chariots, and they have to pick up our trail somewhere on the Dover coast. We're coming to the end, though, and we can't let them be all refreshed when we're not. You and Oberon sleep. I'll watch for a while and then wake you up to take a turn."

Granuaile drew close to me and planted a soft kiss on my lips. "No arguments here. I'm exhausted." Granuaile curled up on the ground and Oberon sprawled next to her. Both of them drifted off in a couple of minutes, and I was left to think about how we would survive going forward.

If, somehow, we could defuse tensions with the Olympians, our priority had to be the mystery in Tír na nÓg. Whoever was divining Granuaile's location was also responsible for sending the dark elves and vampires after us.

Strangely, the safest place for us would be Tír na nÓg. Neither vampires nor dark elves would be tolerated there. Shuttling them through using the Old Ways was one thing and easily hidden—especially for someone like Lord Grundlebeard, who controlled the rangers— but keeping them in Tír na nÓg for an extended period as they came after me would raise all sort of alarms and

questions that this shady adversary would wish to avoid.
And as for the remaining threat—the Fae—I had a distinct advantage where they were concerned.

If I could find a safe place to leave Granuaile and
Oberon, I could go solo and perhaps surprise Midhir or
Lord Grundlebeard. If they were behind this, they'd expect me to stay next to Granuaile and wouldn't be able
to use divination to see me coming.

I let Granuaile sleep until midmorning before waking
her up to take a watch.

"I needed that," she said, stretching languorously and
perhaps a bit teasingly. "Thanks."

She levered herself up, but Oberon barely stirred. Poor
hound.

"You're welcome. Wake me up midafternoon. We'll
go get some clothes." I stretched out next to Oberon
and stopped fighting my fatigue.

Chapter 20

An odd shudder traveled up my right leg and rattled my ribs, shaking me all along the length of my tattoos. It woke me with a start and made Granuaile jump.

"Gah! What the hell was that?" she asked, staring at the tattoos on her arm as if they would provide an answer. Frowning, she turned to me and saw I was awake. "Did you feel that?"

Oberon roused and yawned. <Feel what?>

"Yeah, I felt it."

<What's happening? Are we about to be trampled by a herd of English football fans?>

"So what was it?" Granuaile said.

"The last time I felt this was when Perun's plane died."

"Oh, no."

"Yeah. Some plane connected to earth has been destroyed."

"Does that mean Loki is free?"

"Probably. Unless someone else is destroying planes."

The shuddering continued, and I extended my thoughts to the English elemental, Albion.

//Disturbance detected / Query: Source?//

The reply confirmed my fears. //Old plane of the Finns / Burning//

"Albion says it's a plane of the Finns."

"How many do they have? Not as many as the Irish, I hope?"

"No, I can't think of many. Unless it's Tuonela, their land of the dead."

"Why would Loki even care about that?"

"No idea. But if he's free again, what happened to Malina? Did she let him go, or is she a crispy critter now? Or maybe Hel found them and threatened her, or paid her off, or killed her—who knows." Annoyed by the lack of answers, I looked up at the sky, assuming that Odin was looking in on us from Hlidskjálf. "And, hey, Odin! Are you listening? I thought you were supposed to be keeping an eye on Loki, since he's such a potential problem."

Granuaile considered. "The Finns had a thunder god, didn't they, sort of like Perun?"

"Yeah. I saw him once. His name is Ukko, which basically translates to *old man*. God of the sky and thunder. He was part of the crew that came to kill me in Arizona and instead hacked up Coyote into tiny pieces. He seemed a bit more laid back than the other thunder gods, though. Probably because the Finns are just cool like that. Want to guess where they say thunderstorms came from?"

"Oh, ew. I'm not sure, judging by the grin on your face."

"All that noise and precipitation gets made when Ukko and his wife, Akka, have thunderous sex. Isn't that awesome?"

Granuaile shook her head. "No, it's gross. You are such a guy sometimes."

<Isn't he a guy all the time?>

She's not saying I'm occasionally female. She's implying that I'm shallow.

<Oh, I know. So why did she say only sometimes?>

Hey!

Granuaile couldn't have heard what I said, but Oberon's comment, plus the outrage that must have shown on my face, caused her to laugh.

<Burrrrn!>

"Good dog," she said, petting him.

"Well, I hope Ukko's all right," I said, steering the conversation back to safer territory, "if indeed he was the target and if this was Loki's doing."

"Ukko wanted you dead and you're worried about his welfare?"

"Well, yeah, I guess. He also cheered when the Morrigan cut Vidar in half. I think he was more bored than truly angry with me. He tagged along for the entertainment value."

"If he calls ganging up on people and watching them die entertainment, I'm not predisposed to like him."

"Few of the old gods are truly friendly. Goibhniu is a notable exception."

<Don't forget Fand! She gave us both bacon and sausage.>

Granuaile brightened, agreeing with my hound. "Yeah, I like Fand, and Manannan Mac Lir. They tend to save our asses, so what's not to like?"

"Count them amongst the few, then," I said, and squinted west toward the sun, now low on the horizon. "You let me sleep a bit long, didn't you?"

"You needed it. I was just about to wake you."

Two large ravens swooped down from the sky and landed on the branch of an ash tree. "Ah, Odin was watching us after all," I said, pointing at Hugin and Munin. "Perhaps we can get some answers."

In the mundane spectrum I still couldn't tell them apart, but in the magical spectrum they were easily distinguished now, since Hugin glowed with more magic as the mind of Odin. Hugin jerked his beak at Munin, indicating that I should bind my consciousness with his.

Once I did so, Odin's memories caught me up with recent events. I saw Loki still dazed by the charms of the Sisters of the Three Auroras, specifically by Klaudia's lips, to which I myself had succumbed once upon a time. They were decadent. Sultry. So very, very kissable. And, damn, they almost snared me through the replay. The witches and the god of mischief were still in the same field where we had left them, which surprised me to some extent. I had expected Malina to move the operation elsewhere, but perhaps she had decided that moving was more trouble than it was worth, and it's not as if onion fields are subject to constant scrutiny. The view expanded to show me Garm, Hel's gigantic hound, similarly entranced by a couple of other witches. I smiled appreciatively. With Garm occupied, Hel wouldn't know where to send her *draugar*. Malina had done well.

Garm's gaze was fixed on a stick held in front of his eyes by one of Malina's younger coven members. Clearly it had been enchanted with the same beguiling charm they had used on their body parts to ensnare humans. With both Loki and Garm preoccupied—Garm being Hel's eyes and ears on earth, much like Hugin and Munin often served as Odin's—Malina could conceivably stave off Ragnarok indefinitely, keeping Hel uncertain of victory.

Provided, of course, she wasn't interrupted.

Ukko provided the interruption. Somehow, he'd discovered that Loki was unbound from his long imprisonment and located him—a mystery that begged to be solved, since no one else had beaten him to it. Why was Ukko the first to discover this? He flew down from the sky, landed a short distance away, and, without so much as a howdy-do, threw lightning at Loki.

His motivation wasn't a mystery at all. Like Perun, who held an equivalent position amongst the old Rús tribes, the Finn would have very little love for the Norse pantheon, being a sort of direct competitor for the hearts and minds of people in that region of the world.

Loki flew bodily through the air, his torso folded and his long flailing limbs reminding me of a squid. He landed fifty yards away, far outside the range of Klaudia's lips or Malina's hair or any other charm capable of calming him. His body bloomed in flames and the madness returned.

"Hah? Who?" he cried, then saw Ukko advancing. "Thhhhunder god! G-g-guh, good!"

Malina shouted something in Polish, but Loki and Ukko ignored it, focused as they were on each other. Loki took a deep breath in the way a trained opera singer would, chest rising faintly but lungs filling like a bellows. He threw back his head and roared as his hands flew up and an inferno exploded from him, a burnin' ring o' fire that lifted Ukko off his feet and set the field alight. Here, then, was the great conflagration that Malina's coven had foreseen.

"S-s-set your world on f-f-fire!" Loki spat before launching himself into the air and streaking north, presumably toward Finland. Ukko, having no choice and forced to play defense, followed him without ever acknowledging—or perhaps even realizing—that he had flipped Loki's switch from "Neutralized" to "Unchained Sociopath."

Odin's vision didn't chase after them but rather panned back to the witches. They had their purple wards up, protected from the flames but clearly feeling the heat. Garm, however, had no such protection. His fur was aflame and he sprinted, howling, for the river that bordered Jasło's western edge, some two hundred yards away. The witches ran after him, cursing in Polish and sounding far more angry than scared.

Munin broke off the images and squawked at me. I disconnected with him and then switched to Hugin to speak with Odin.

All right, why was Ukko there? I said.

The Gray Wanderer's voice lacked the casual tone he'd employed when Loki was safely occupied. Even the raven looked a bit more concerned. <I was hoping you could tell me.>

Are you suggesting I had something to do with it? Not only would that be against my own interest, but I've been a little busy lately.

<Someone had to stir him to action. Ukko is not what one would call vigilant.>

Well, what about Hel?

<She didn't know where he was. Her hound was ensnared by those witches. Besides, she wouldn't need to send anyone if she wished to free her father. She would have come herself and brought *draugar* along, as she did when Loki invaded Nidavellir.>

Maybe she just told Ukko that Loki was free and Ukko used his own methods.

<Possible, perhaps,> Odin granted, <but not really her style. This seems more like the sort of string-pulling favored by the Tuatha Dé Danann, if you don't mind me saying.>

Oh. Right. Midhir, I said.

<Who?>

I shared my suspicions about Midhir's motivation to want me dead and his relative ability to do it.

<Interesting. This will set off a whole new round of betting in Valhalla.>

This time I didn't curb my tongue. *The Einherjar can go toast their foreskins.*

Odin laughed at me. <I'll be sure to tell them.>

Do. What happened to the witches and Garm?

<The witches reached the river safely. Garm shifted to Hel before he got there, so I assume he is recuperating now.>

Great. One more thing to worry about.

<Garm is of no concern at present, and neither is Hel. Loki is. He's burned out the Finns and presumably he's now free to look for you. He'll scour the continent for you because of what you did to Fenris.>

That reminds me. How is Freyja doing? The Norse goddess of beauty and war had been severely injured in our raid on Hel.

<Recuperating. Frigg is looking after her.>

Does she even know we were successful?

<I do not believe she has regained consciousness yet.>

I frowned. *Is she in a coma or something?* I knew that she had lost a lot of blood and had some shattered bones when we evacuated her, but perhaps she'd suffered more head trauma than was immediately evident.

Odin huffed impatiently. <I don't know. I haven't checked today. What you need to worry about is Loki's next target—and that's you. He'll want you dead before he starts Ragnarok. I think he sees you as a bigger threat than me right now. The best thing you can do, therefore, to delay the onset of the world's end is to make yourself scarce. Get off this plane.>

Thanks, I said dryly. *We've been working on that. Gotta go.*

<No, stay there.>

Why?

<There are dark elves on the way. You've remained in one place long enough for them to pinpoint your location.>

Like I said, gotta go.

<The Ljósálfar are coming too. And one other.>

Who?

<You've met.> The rainbow bridge from Asgard shimmered into existence on the pasture next to the Long Wood, and we saw distant forms in the sky growing larger. I broke my link with Hugin and turned to Granuaile.

"On your guard. Dark elves coming," I said. "And apparently some standard elves and a bonus dude to help us somehow."

Oberon perked up. <Awesome! I've never seen a base-model elf before! But they come with bonus dudes?>

In this case they do.

Granuaile hefted Scáthmhaide. "Going invisible," she said, before speaking the binding and winking out. I cast camouflage on Oberon but left myself visible.

The Ljósálfar, when they stepped off Bifrost onto Midgard, both disappointed and delighted me. They weren't wearing leaf-shaped green and gold armor with curlicues or long robes with overlarge embroidered sleeves. They didn't glow with backlighting or come with their own soundtrack by Enya. Their hair wasn't long, straight, and silky, and their eyes weren't limpid pools of oh-my-god straight out of manga. But they were tall and slender and very shiny, and they sounded like wind chimes when they moved.

The sound came from their light-blue enamel armor—that is, glass fused to a metal base. It draped their forms in layered scales so that they reminded me of pangolins, if pangolins could blind you like metal mud flaps on a semitruck. In the center of each enamel scale, a single rune had been etched with acid, and so far as I could tell, it was always the same rune. On a practical level, I couldn't imagine the benefit to enamel; basic blunt force would shatter it, and the metal backing each scale looked to be either aluminum or a thin wafer of steel. But the runes must offer some protection. Their helmets had no metal backing: Each was a solid piece of shaped glass in light blue, etched with the same rune over and over, lending the impression that someone had found some defective fishbowls at an outlet store and shipped them to Álfheim. A grid of thin holes had been drilled through the glass around the nose, mouth, and ears, which had the effect of blurring out those features, but otherwise I could see that their heads were closely cropped and the tops of their ears did have the famous pointy cartilage. They had swords swinging on their left hips, but I wondered if they weren't ceremonial. Their primary weapons rested in holsters strapped to their thighs—large flechette pistols.

Two dozen such elves were led by a thick, diminutive fellow in heavy steel plate. His armor was also etched with runes, but these were many and varied and flickered with their own light. Four small axes were strapped to his back, handles peeking over his shoulder. His voice was muffled somewhat by his helmet, but I still recognized the diction.

"I greet you, Druid, Wolf Slayer, Freyr's Bane, Loki Shepherd. May you walk from battle unbruised and exult in the death songs of the slain."

There was only one person I knew who would assign me such epithets and string them together. "Fjalar? Is that you? Runeskald of Nidavellir?"

<The dwarf who made us nom-noms?> Oberon said.

"Yes. I have come with the Glass Knights, the Ljósálfar elite, rune-warded and ready for battle, to meet the Svartálfar who pursue you. Axes have I brought, newly forged and blazoned, to cut the smoky black and tear flesh out of vapor."

"What? I beg your pardon, but you lost me there."

Fjalar drew one of the axes fixed to his back. It had a barb on the handle that triggered a release on the holder as he pulled it up so that the blade wouldn't get caught. Clever design. He pointed at the runes seared into the blade of the axe and said, "These are experiments in craft and war, an attempt to cleave through magic mist and wound the flesh, to sunder smoke yet slice through bone and sinew."

"You're saying if you hack a dark elf in his smoke

form with that, he'll show the wound when he turns solid?"

"I will not know until I attempt it, but it is my hope. The runes are supposed to end their vaporous state and then the blade cuts them, which binds them to their solid form. Should any of the axes prove successful, more will I make and teach the craft and song to other Runeskalds."

"That sounds fabulous," I said, "but what if none of the axes perform the way you hope they do?"

The dwarf's armor twitched, signaling a shrug underneath all the steel. "I will return to my forge and try anew."

"No, I mean, the dark elves are not going to allow you to experiment on them."

"They will have no choice in the matter."

"I mean they're going to fight back."

"And the lamb will cry before it's slaughtered. There is no difference." Fjalar's helmet twitched, indicating his eyes had been drawn elsewhere. "Ah. See where they come. Remain here and do nothing until you are ordered to drop to the ground."

"I beg your pardon?"

"You need do nothing but attract them. Let us take care of this."

I cast my eyes across the pasture separating the Long Wood from the copse to the east and spied a sizable group of dark elves approaching—equal to the number of elves on our side. Dressed in what appeared to be shimmering white warm-up outfits that basketball teams favor—except with tunics instead of jerseys—they ran in an undisciplined mob until they saw Fjalar step forward, brandishing an axe. Responding to some unseen cue, they formed into a wedge and sped up, moving at double time.

Behind me, the Glass Knights spread themselves into

six half squads of four elves each and drew their flechette pistols, one in each hand. Fjalar strode forward a
few more paces, until he was perhaps twenty yards in
front of us. If anyone had been dressed in modern combat gear, I would have felt a bit silly standing there naked
amongst all that armor, but aside from the flechette pistols we were all rocking it old school, and I felt like a
proper Celt.

"You seriously don't want me to do anything?" I
called.

"You will ruin our tactics if you do," the Runeskald
replied over his shoulder. On the one hand I felt a tad
hurt that they didn't want my help, but on the other I
was happy to let them assume all the risk if they wanted
it. I was also curious about how this would unfold. This
was the most disciplined bunch of dark elves I had seen
to this point, and if I was not mistaken, they were carrying standard steel weapons because they had learned
they couldn't pierce my aura with their magical knives.

*Oberon, I'd like you and Granuaile to hang back be-
hind the elves if you're not already doing so.*

<We are, but I'll tell Clever Girl.>

With thirty yards to go until they reached Fjalar, the
dark elves stopped and drew steel scimitars, holding
them above their heads. They paused for a few beats
and then charged on a silent signal. Fjalar rushed to
meet them, one dwarf against twenty-five dark elves,
and he wasn't silent. He sang something fierce, and a
yellow energy began to coalesce around his armor. When
he met the point of the phalanx, his axe whiffed through
the clothes and smoke of the point man, as the rest of
the wedge flowed to either side and flanked him, their
swords arcing down onto his armor. Their blades rebounded away from his helmet and pauldrons as if they
were rubber and made clunking noises instead of an expected clang; yellow light exploded at each contact. Fja-

lar swung again with his axe, slicing ineffectually through smoke. I suppose he'd managed to make a few of them drop their standard weapons, and his armor had clearly been enchanted to withstand their blows, but neither side was doing any damage.

Undaunted, Fjalar dropped his first axe and drew another one. While he reached back, the point man solidified, nude, and stabbed at him with the black knife that all Svartálfar carried. This weapon rebounded as well. And when Fjalar hacked at him with his new axe, the villain evaded it again by turning incorporeal.

Some of the dark elves moved beyond Fjalar, reformed a smaller wedge, and charged up the slope at me, their true target. They all still had gleaming steel in their hands. Seeing this, one of the Ljósálfar barked a command in Old Norse and the elves raised their weapons, but no one ordered me to get down. I readied Fragarach and cast a final worried glance at Fjalar. He was drawing his third axe, bellowing his skald and snarling at his opponents, who continued to rain down blows as useless as his own—until he swung at them with the third axe.

As before, the dark elves dissolved to coal-black smoke in advance of his blow, but this time, when the axe passed through, it seemed to pull and rip them into solid form as it moved through the air, the way a zipper will part and reveal something hidden in its journey downward. And the dark elves who had been so torn back into the world were split by the axe, and inky innards slithered out of their torsos onto the earth.

"Victory!" Fjalar shouted, and the Ljósálfar leader behind me commanded that I get down. The dark elves in front of me were awfully close, but I dropped to the earth in curiosity—and so did Fjalar.

The elves began to shoot their flechettes in a prescribed pattern at the dark elves, in set intervals—once every half second, though it took me a couple of seconds to realize it and understand the strategy. The first volley caught some of the dark elves unawares, but most saw it coming and dissolved, dropping their steel in the process. The subsequent shots passed above my head and through them without harm—but that wouldn't continue. The dark elves could maintain their incorporeal forms for only five seconds, so the Ljósálfar just needed to spray the field with flechettes for six, and they would catch all of them solid at some point.

Four seconds in, one of the Svartálfar materialized at my side with his black knife held high. He was blown away before he could bring it down. Others saw that the Ljósálfar were a threat and took shape behind them, but when the dark elves lunged in for the kill, the runes on the glass armor activated and repulsed them with a blue shock wave that sent them staggering backward. And then, in the fifth second, the ones below in the field all had to beef up, and they were hit by a double volley of flechettes: The first rocked them and anchored them to flesh, and the second mowed them down.

The stragglers behind the line of Glass Knights—only three—melted away and fled.

<I want to see that again in slow motion!>

Fjalar and I rose from the ground and stepped away from the mess of dark-elf corpses, before their inherent instability caused them to melt and turn to an oily goo.

"Did you see that, Druid?" the Runeskald crowed. "The order of runes triumphs over evil!"

"Well, yeah, I guess. What happened there?"

"The third axe worked! Now that I know the proper runes and skald to use, I can create more such weapons and arm the Glass Knights for their mission, honor-bathed and glory-steeped."

"I'm sorry? What mission?"

"Our kings, Aurvang and Gedelglinn, have decreed it

should be so. Deep into Svartálfheim the Glass Knights shall delve, wreaking ruin and smiting those who would oppose us during Ragnarok."

Something didn't compute. "Hold on. How do you know who will oppose you during Ragnarok? Have the Svartálfar said they would fight with Hel?"

"Is this not proof enough, Druid?" Fjalar said, gesturing at the field where the dark elves were dissolving into tar.

"No, it's not. These are clearly assassins or mercenaries in someone's employ, but they do not represent the hearts of all the Svartálfar. There may be some who would oppose Hel, and, if so, they would be valuable allies."

Fjalar growled and yanked off his helmet with his left hand. His chin was still bald and his hair in braids, in accordance with his culture's mourning practices. He stepped up to me. "Are you such a good judge of character now? You who sent Loki Fire Hands to Nidavellir to kill thousands of my Shield Brothers?"

"I didn't send him there to kill anyone. He did that without my urging and you know it. But what does Odin say about this plan to invade Svartálfheim?"

"Did he not tell you to wait for our arrival? Did he not send us here on the Bifrost Bridge? Is that not Bifrost, even now, waiting to take us back to Asgard?" he said, pointing behind me. The rainbow bridge shimmered in the late-afternoon sun. "What am I doing, arguing with a nude man?" he groused, stalking past me and attempting to stalk on the rainbow too, except that it wasn't the sort of surface that allowed stalking. The Glass Knights turned and followed, denying me any more time to discuss the matter. I frowned after them, because it was a disturbing development. I wasn't a particular fan of dark elves, but that was only because I hadn't met any nice ones yet. From what Manannan

Mac Lir had told me, some of the Svartálfar had nobility
in their nature. They tended to be the ones who didn't
take mercenary contracts.

"Odin, are you on board with this?" I shouted. The
bridge retracted without an answer, though I hardly expected one.

<Atticus, those last three dark elves didn't really go
away for good.>

Interesting. Where are they?

<Behind you, picking up steel swords from the
ground.>

Thanks. Tell Granuaile she can fire at will.

I turned around and raised Fragarach in time to see
three dark elves with scimitars loping my way, wearing
grim expressions and nothing else. I winced when one of
Granuaile's knives sank into the groin of the leader and
he went down screaming and clutching the ruins of his
junk.

I'm going to have nightmares.

<Word.>

The remaining two Svartálfar whiffed into the air, an-
ticipating more knives from an invisible assailant, but
Granuaile stayed her hand. Their steel dropped to the
ground and I pursued one of the clouds, swishing Fragarach through it, thinking I would catch him as he turned
solid. I missed high. Sensing what I was up to, his substance dropped to the ground and he solidified, where
he promptly swept my legs and blocked the wild swing I
made, with his forearm staying my wrist. His right hand
poked me in quick sequence along pressure points across
my chest and froze up my muscles—where the hell had
he learned that? But then it was easy for him to pin my
sword arm and wrap his other hand around my throat.
His buddy came back, retrieved a scimitar, and took two
steps with a mind to finish me, before a throwing knife
abruptly sprouted from his chest. It didn't kill him, but

its appearance caused him to focus on prolonging his own life rather than ending mine. Oberon jumped on him and ended it—at least, that's what I think happened, judging by the growl and the takedown. Granuaile wouldn't have growled; she would have clocked him upside the head with her staff, which is what she did to the fellow choking me. She put a whole lot of energy behind that swing, because his head exploded like a melon and he slumped on me, leaking black blood.

"Thanks," I gasped. "I was just about to take care of him, but, yeah, you know. That was good."

Granuaile dispelled her invisibility and kicked the dark elf off me before kneeling at my side. "Did he paralyze you or something?"

"Partially. I'm working on it." The muscles were locked up and I had to patiently relax them, one fiber at a time.

"That's Far Eastern supa-sekrit martial arts, isn't it? Where did a dark elf learn that?"

"In the Far East, I expect, just like I learned a few things there. We don't know how long these guys live or what access they have to instruction, but it shouldn't be a shock to discover that they're well trained. We've managed to surprise them a few times and I think these Glass Knights are something new to them as well, but they're equally capable of surprising us." I'd seen plenty of the dark elves get taken out in ambushes so far, but I reflected that I hadn't done too well against them in head-to-head combat. They were extraordinarily fast and strong, and if I hadn't had Granuaile's help a couple of different times they would have snuffed me. It would be better to avoid future conflict—or even have them fight on our side. "I'd rather get to whoever's sending them after my ass than meet any more of them."

"I hear that. But let me speak a word into your ear: clothes."

"Yeah. We should get some. No one takes you seriously when you're naked."

"That's wisdom right there. Hold on, I'm going to get my knives." The first Svartálf she'd hit had bled to death, and his hands were still cupped around his groin. I turned my head away so I didn't have to watch her yank out the knife, but the sound it made caused me to cross my legs. His body turned to a sticky puddle as Granuaile stepped away and wiped her blade clean on the grass.

I was capable of free movement after another few minutes, and we jogged through the Long Wood toward a road called Hosey Hill. I took note of the birds in the wood and paused to watch them.

"What's up?" Granuaile asked, seeing my gaze directed at the treetops.

"Augury, if we're lucky. We're due for some luck, don't you think? I'm not a proponent of augury as a rule, but since I have no other methods of divination available to me, I'll take what I can get."

Granuaile flicked her eyes upward, tracking the finches flitting around in the branches. "What are you aiming to get out of all that noise?"

I sat on a thin carpet of leaves and kept my eyes on the birds. "A guess about our pursuit. How long before the huntresses catch up."

She sat next to me and rested her staff across her lap. "You never taught me how to do that."

"I rarely use it. I prefer casting wands, because it's quicker and you can ask multiple questions. With augury you have to wait and observe for about fifteen minutes per question and hope you didn't miss something."

<Can I sniff these trees while you're doing whatever you're doing?> Oberon asked.

"Sure, buddy, just don't bark at anything."

Oberon trotted off, and I spent the next fifteen minutes trying to guess the future according to the behavior of the ten or so birds I could see frolicking above us. The theory behind augury was akin to chaos theory in that actions in one place can have profound effects elsewhere, and birds were acutely sensitive to changes in their environment—they could anticipate storms and dry spells and figure when it was best to migrate. Thus, if one was properly schooled in how to interpret their behavior, one might be able to tap into their sense of the future. These birds would see not only me pass underneath them but the huntresses as well. The question was when?

I wasn't sure I caught everything that their fluttering and pecking order had to tell me, but my best guess was that, once we made it to Windsor Forest, we'd have a few hours to kill before dawn, and the huntresses would get there shortly after sunrise.

In camouflage, we resumed our run, following Hosey Hill north to Westerham. I washed off the remains of the dark elf in a public fountain and then we entered an Orvis store—a kind of outdoorsy UK chain—just before close of business. I found a black Havana shirt and jeans and declared myself satisfied; there was no use finding any shoes. It was the next best thing to camouflage when running at night. Vowing to pay them back when we could, we exited, dropped our bindings, and allowed ourselves to be seen.

Granuaile had found an all-black training outfit, a form-hugging kit that would let her move silently without restriction, as long as she didn't wear the noisy Windbreaker that came with it. She stuck to the running tank, proudly displaying the full tattoos on her right arm.

Granuaile's eyes roved up and down. "Mmm. Druid is the new black," she said.

"Did you just make a yummy sound?"

<Yes, and I would like to point out that she didn't do that when you were nude.>

Chapter 21

We floated onto the grounds of Windsor Park like shades, unnoticed in the dark of night. On Snow Hill, two miles to the south of the castle, we paused by the statue of George III, which gave us a view of the Long Walk to the castle, tree-lined and coiffed according to royal wishes.

"See this guy?" I said, my hand slapping against the stone of the pedestal. "Not only did he lose the American colonies and usher in the twilight of the British Empire, but he pulled down Herne's oak back in the eighteenth century. It was already dead, so I guess that was some excuse, but I can't help thinking it was kind of a dick move. But there are still oaks there to this day, replanted by this monarch or that. We should be able to go there and call him."

<Atticus, these oaks you speak of, are they . . . uh, you know—off limits?>

"Well, it might be wise to refrain from marking them. Herne had a whole pack of hounds. They might take issue with you claiming their trees as your own."

<But they're dead, right? So what's the big deal?>

"Not sure, but it's best to be polite."

"How do we call Herne, exactly?" Granuaile asked.

"We'll ask Albion to help us out."

I did my best to sound confident. In truth, I didn't

know how we were supposed to call him or how he could possibly help us against two immortals. The Morrigan's assurance that Herne could help us somehow seemed hollow now that she was dead and we'd been unable to do anything to the Olympians except inconvenience them. But I knew he was for real. Just before the whole business with Aenghus Óg exploded, Flidais had come to visit me with a warning, and she casually mentioned that she'd been guesting in Herne's forest. She wouldn't have called it that if Herne weren't a force to be reckoned with. She would have called it a forest in Albion, or perhaps simply Windsor Forest.

Like most of the world, Windsor Great Park used to be wild, but its size had dwindled over the centuries to the present 4,800 protected acres. North of Frogmore House—which was itself a bit south of the castle—lay the historical location of Herne's death. The oak that had been pulled down on the orders of King George III had been replanted by King Edward VII. It was there I would attempt to call him.

I didn't know much about Herne, having never met him; I'd heard the same legends as everyone else. The attempts to explain his existence were many and varied. In the view of some, he was a corrupted form of the horned god Cernunnos, or perhaps a twist on Odin, who also led a form of the Wild Hunt and had experience hanging from trees. Many of these theories had something to do with Herne's penchant for wearing antlers and connecting dots between the name *Herne* and old words for *horn*. To others, he was an historical figure, a ranger or gamekeeper for one of the old kings, led by disgrace of some kind to hang himself and haunt the woods ever after. Shakespeare gave him a shout-out in *The Merry Wives of Windsor,* but he didn't lay down the definitive legend so much as give Herne a different kind of immortality.

We padded down the grass from Snow Hill into the row of trees lining the eastern side of the Long Walk, where puffy strands of mist clung to the trunks like torn cotton balls. Some insects buzzed and an owl hooted, but otherwise the only sound was our soft footfalls on the turf.

We veered to the northeast, across trimmed expanses of grass to the slightly more verdant grounds of Frogmore House, a sometime residence for members of the royal family. A serpentine pond wound behind it, with plenty of willows weeping on the banks and hedges growing to please the gardener who loved them.

We must have tripped a passive security alarm on our way across, because a couple of guards with flashlights and guns came looking for us. The flashlights told us right where the guards were, and Granuaile and I decided to mess with them a bit. Approaching in camouflage, we snatched their guns and chucked them into the pond.

"Bloody hell!" one shouted. A trip, a takedown, and a Druid Doomhold later, and they were both sleeping peacefully on the exquisite back lawn.

"They had guns," Granuaile remarked. That was somewhat unusual for security in the UK. "But I guess they weren't MI6."

"No, they were pretty low-rent. Means the royals aren't here. That's good."

The few oaks north of Frogmore were truly magnificent, even if they looked a bit lonely in the too-tidy landscape of Home Park. We were in a restricted area now but had already subdued the closest security. Thick trunks and wide, strong branches formed impressive canopies, and in the mist they managed to take on a slight character of menace. Despite this, they were as susceptible to the ravages of pandemonium as the rest of the world's trees. I hoped the efforts of the Olympians wouldn't prevent Herne from appearing now. His specific tree—or rather the big tree that was supposedly planted in the precise spot of the original—was circled by an iron fence that bore a plaque linking it to supernatural history.

//Druid requires aid// I sent to Albion. //Request: Contact Herne / Old steward of this place / Express our wish to meet//

//Done// Albion replied. //Soon he will come//

"Oh," I said aloud. "That was fast."

"What?" Granuaile asked.

"Apparently Albion has a direct line to Herne." That intrigued me. I was curious to know if Albion granted Herne any of his magic, or if Herne was living like the gods, suckling at the magical teat of belief. If it was the latter, then it was a highly localized belief. "He should be coming soon, but I don't know from where."

I doubted he would ride in from the north, where there was a golf course now. We scanned the landscape around us until Granuaile spotted something moving to the south, and she chucked my right shoulder to point behind me. "Over there, I think." Even with night vision, it was difficult to see. She was pointing at something that had detached itself from the shadow of a veteran oak tree even more ancient than the one marked as Herne's. Behind it, several other somethings moved. The figures brightened as they got closer—that is to say, they took on a minimal albedo, reflecting moonlight and providing faint outlines. There were three men on horses and hounds walking alongside. The figure in the center had a large rack of antlers floating over his head, but his features were largely occluded by a hooded cloak. Part of me wondered how he'd managed to pull a hood over those antlers and added that there was no good reason for a ghost to wear a cloak or anything at all, but another part reasoned that one of the few perks to being an unhoused spirit must be the ability to wear impractical clothing for effect.

The riders became clearer as they approached, but it wasn't merely a function of shrinking distance; they were becoming brighter, flaring into luminosity as the spirits manifested fully. The horses and hounds were supposed to be black, according to legend, but in the light of the moon and their own ghostly glow—perhaps aided by a certain transparency—they took on more of a midnight-blue color.

Herne rode in leathers of the hunt. His eyes, visible under his hood once he drew near, lacked pupils; they were holes made of lambent cobalt.

The bottom half of his face billowed with a dark thicket of a beard. Trimming it would require pruning shears.

The antlers were quite imposing up close, and taken together with his face and disturbing eyes, they suggested what Bambi's dad would look like if he ever decided to kick the ass of anyone who dared to be stupid in his forest.

His companions lacked headgear, but their eyes and beards were of a kind with Herne's. Evidently, men's grooming products had yet to penetrate the spectral market.

Herne looked first at me, then at Granuaile. "Wich is the Druyd?"

I blinked and was slow to reply. I'd been kind of expecting to hear something raspy and whispery out of his throat, or something choked with phlegm, the way ghosts always seem to sound when they vocalize in popular entertainment, but Herne spoke in a perfectly clear baritone—in Middle English. If he used short, simple sentences, he could probably make himself understood to a speaker of Modern English, but longer sentences would be difficult for contemporary speakers to decode, since half the vowels would be pronounced differently. Amongst the tales of him that purported to be historical, this fact suggested that he was much more likely to have been a subject of Richard II than of Henry VIII.

"Did he ask which was the Druid? We're both Druids," Granuaile said.

Herne's brow furrowed at first, perhaps trying to process Granuaile's modern pronunciation, but then it smoothed out and his mouth quirked up on the left side.

"Bothe of yow?"

"Is he okay?" Granuaile asked.

"Yes. It's Middle English," I said.

<Did Middle English hounds bark with an extra syllable on the end? Like "woofe"?>

I ignored Oberon's question and addressed Herne. "Aye, bothe."

"An Druides be, thanne answere me: Whos love in Eire is moste fyn and fre?"

"Did he just rhyme on purpose?" Granuaile whispered.

I replied in kind, though Herne could easily hear us. "Yes. It's a riddle in verse. If I can't answer in the same fashion, then I'm not the old Druid I claim to be and I'm trespassing here. Even though Albion's obviously told him I'm a Druid, it's a sort of challenge."

"Do you know the answer?"

<Of course he does. It's bacon. Bacon is the answer to everything.>

Oberon had a point (Why are we here? Bacon), but that wasn't the kind of answer Herne needed. He wanted to hear the name of an old hunting partner with a legendary libido, so I said, "Whether in bedde or in feeld do ye meet, Flidais awaiteth your limbes to greet."

At this, laughter erupted from the ghosts to the point where one of the hunters started coughing uncontrollably, which I thought completely bizarre since he no longer had a pulmonary system.

"Wait," Granuaile said. "Flidais isn't funny. I missed the joke. Why was that funny?" The easy grins of the hunters faded, replaced with a look of discomfort.

"If I explain it to you, then it won't be."

Granuaile noticed that the hunters now looked a bit embarrassed. "Do it anyway."

"In Middle English, when referring to a man, a limb was a euphemism for a penis, and the verb *gretan* didn't simply mean *hello*—it had a rather strong connotation of a sexual embrace. So I'm sorry to say I was being a bit crude."

"Ooooohhh."

"Perhaps more than a bit."

Granuaile's mouth tightened in prim disapproval, and she turned narrowed eyes on the hunters. One began to inspect his boots, and the other found something fascinating up in the sky. Herne abruptly decided that now would be a good time to pet his horse. They might speak Middle English, but it appeared they could follow Modern well enough, and Granuaile's body language needed no translation. "I know all you boys are old school," she said, waving her finger around to include me while looking at the hunters, "but let's try to remember what century this is, shall we? Any ass you can kick, I can kick better, and so can Flidais."

"Aye!" Herne barked, and glared at his men as if they had been the only ones laughing. Then he turned to us, smiled, and said, "Honored Druids, you are welcome to my forest." His old diction sloughed away. "I have learned to speak Modern English over the years, so be at ease. You are my guests. Hunt or rest as it pleases you."

Once he called us his guests, I finally understood what the Morrigan intended. Herne would take little to no convincing to join our side. His honor—his *raison d'être*—demanded that he protect both his forest and his guests.

"Is my hound a guest as well? He likes to hunt with us."

"Aye, he is."

I thanked him and said, "It is more likely that we will be hunted than have time to hunt anything else."

Herne's friendly smile disappeared. "Hunted? By whom?"

"Olympians. At least one is plaguing Albion even now—either Pan or Faunus."

"The goat-footed god? He has passed through here recently."

"And because of that we cannot shift to Tír na nÓg. He spreads pandemonium and upsets the order of Gaia, distresses the forest. He keeps us here so that Artemis and Diana can slay us."

Herne scowled, and the cobalt eyes flared brighter for a moment. He dismounted and squatted, pressing the fingers of one hand into the earth. I noted that this process made no noise whatsoever—no creak of leather, no thump of foot on the forest floor. He and his companions made noise only when they wished to. After a few seconds of contemplation, Herne said, "It's true. It's not visible, but it can be felt. The goat disturbs my forest." He looked up at me. "And they come to hunt my guests?"

"Aye. And it is not only your forest they disturb but all forests in Albion."

"It shall not stand," Herne vowed, rising. "My guests are few, and none have dared trespass on my goodwill for some time. No one attempts to hunt my forest anymore."

That was more likely due to protections laid down by the Crown Estate than anything else, but if Herne wished to believe it was due to his badassery, I wouldn't disabuse him of the notion.

"If any attempt it now, they shall feel my wrath. Rest now and recover your strength. Should Olympians appear to despoil my forest, day or night, we will ride."

"My thanks. Um . . . forgive my ignorance, but do you have power to wound the corporeal?"

Herne stared at me in silence for a time, unable to believe I'd asked him, but then withdrew a knife from a sheath at his belt. It was barely visible, and its outlines were suggested only by reflected light. Stepping forward slowly, he raised it casually and pressed the point into my chest just enough to draw blood.

"Do you feel its bite?" he growled.

"Yes. Fair enough. I am answered."

He nodded—a rather dangerous gesture when one is sporting antlers—and returned the knife to its sheath. I triggered my healing charm to close up the small wound.

One of Herne's hunters spoke up suddenly, his voice surprisingly high and nasal and amused. "Ha! What means your hound to sniff thus?" he said. Herne and I turned our heads to discover Oberon with his nose snuffling at the rear end of a bewildered ghost hound.

I sighed. "Oberon, you're embarrassing me."

<Huh,> Oberon grunted. He raised his snout and swung his head around to look at me. <Can you believe this, Atticus? Scentless asses. What will they think of next?>

Chapter 22

Together we left the Home Park and ran southwest to the proper Windsor Forest, which was only a mile or two long these days. On the northeastern side of it there was an amusement park, which struck me as an odd juxtaposition. To a Druid, the forest was the amusement park.

Herne left us near the edge of a field in the middle of it, far from prying eyes, and told us he and his hunters would leave us for now.

"Again, you are welcome. Call my name if you need me," he said. "Otherwise, rest or prepare yourselves as you will."

We thanked him, and he faded out of sight as slowly as he had originally appeared. As soon as they were gone, Oberon flopped onto his back and said, <The royal hound's belly demands rubbing. Step lively, humans, neglect me not.>

Granuaile laughed and knelt next to him to oblige. I smiled and took a look around. This wood was a comfortable place. Not sensual comfort of any kind—merely a quiet spot where we could repair and nurture those parts within us that had been damaged or neglected during the run. I approached an old beech tree twined with ivy, plucked a couple of strands, and plonked myself down on the ground next to Granuaile and Oberon. My hound twisted his head to see what I had in my hands.

<What are you going to do with that?>

"Arts and crafts," I replied.

<So you'll be at it for a while?>

"I guess so."

<Good. Thanks, Granuaile, the belly is sated.> He rolled over and pulled himself closer to me without getting up. Using my lap as a pillow for his giant head, he stretched himself out on his side and sighed in contentment. <Ahhh. Nap time.>

Granuaile shook her head. "You slept all day."

<Not all of it. We woke before sundown. And now it's, uh, after sundown. So there.>

She smiled, got to her feet, and then addressed me. "What are we going to do now?"

"Relax while we can. There are a few hours before dawn."

"Shouldn't we be preparing to meet two very pissed-off huntresses? Building booby traps or something like that?"

"Probably. But there is some time to be creative—or at least some time that I can steal—and so I'm going to take it. Ever notice how you never have time to do something until you decide that you do?" Granuaile peered at the twisted strands of ivy in my hands and looked doubtful that they could serve as anything beyond compost. "Come on. Sit back down for a sec." I patted the ground next to me, on the side where Oberon wasn't stretched out. She sighed and sat in the indicated spot, resting her staff on the ground. I smiled at her. "There. Isn't this nice?"

She looked at the canopy above, with the moon peeking through the leaves, and listened to the soft whisper of the night from grasses in the nearby field. "I can't argue the point. It's lovely."

"Gaia has left us wonder wherever we go, if we only open our eyes to it."

"Oh, I agree."

"Now, I know I am not much of a craftsman," I said, busily knotting the vines into a circle, "but greatness is in the act of creation and not necessarily in the finished product. Creating is the yin to the yang of our consumption and the doorway to beauty that we all want to walk through. Creating is how I tell the world I love it." I handed the completed wreath to Granuaile, and she smiled as she took it.

"You're very sneaky, you know."

"Am I?"

She placed the ivy wreath on her head. "I thought you were being philosophical, and then you pivoted to mushy."

"I have +20 verbal dexterity."

Granuaile leaned in for a kiss, but Oberon interrupted. <Stop now or I will yak on your lap.>

We were saved from both yak and further mush by the arrival of Flidais, who called to us from the small field and revealed herself when our eyes followed her voice.

"Well met, Druids." Her tone mocked us gently. "Is it safe to approach?" She stood in her chariot, nearly identical to that of the Olympians in that it was pulled by stags. It wasn't a flashy design, more utilitarian than anything else. I'm not sure how she had muffled the noise of her movement; we should have heard her coming. Or perhaps I'd been simply too absorbed in Granuaile.

I beckoned her over and we all rose from the ground to meet her, Oberon grumbling about naps he'd never get back. I cautioned him to keep his thoughts to himself, since Flidais could hear him if she wished. She was dressed for battle—that is, she had her standard hunting leathers and bow and quiver, but she also wore two long daggers for close work. One I had seen before but had thought it was purely ceremonial, for appearances at the Fae Court. Its handle was made of malachite and mother-of-pearl. Her hair bounced on her head in curly red ringlets and she appeared to be in a good mood, which put me on my guard. Though I currently thought Midhir was behind all this, Flidais had shown herself in the past to be a willing pawn of Brighid's. I doubted she was truly our adversary, but neither did I trust her.

"How did you get here, if you don't mind my asking?" I said as she approached. "The tethers are all shut down by pandemonium."

The huntress shrugged. "I used an Old Way."

I blinked. "It wasn't guarded?"

"No. Why would it be?"

"Because they're all guarded or destroyed. All across Europe."

"Not the one I used."

"Where is it?" I asked, because I couldn't remember any in this vicinity.

"Underneath Windsor Castle, down amongst the earth left over from the days of William the Conqueror. It emerges in the dungeon or basement or whatever they call it these days. Is it catacombs?"

"It was probably the cellar," I advised her. "How long ago did you use it?"

"Only minutes ago. I traveled directly here, because I was informed by Odin's messenger that you were in some dire need."

"Our dire need is to get off this plane. We have to escape the Olympians."

"Ah, yes. I've heard you provoked them somehow and the Morrigan is dead as a result. What did you do?"

"I put Bacchus on one of the Time Islands."

Flidais rolled her eyes. "That would do it. And for that the Morrigan is slain."

Her comment stung, and I knew it would settle into a corner of my mind and leap out at me from time to time, stinging me anew, but I pretended that I felt nothing. "Can you take us to the Old Way?"

The expression of amusement faded. "Oh. I suppose."

"What's the matter?"

"When I received your message from Odin, I was rather hoping you'd asked me here to help you fight the Olympians."

"If there wasn't a way to avoid the fight altogether, that's precisely what I would be asking, since you know this area better than anyone—with the possible exception of Herne. But I don't relish standing toe-to-toe with a true immortal. I'd rather withdraw and try diplomacy."

Flidais snorted. "The Olympians are not diplomatic—or haven't you noticed? They talk through their differences only when killing isn't the best option. Unless you can give them a good reason to let you live, you're alive just until they catch up. Or as long as I'm fighting on your side."

Ignoring her last comment, I said, "I might be able to think of something if we can get them to listen. Escaping the plane would take killing us off the table. They'd have to talk. Through intermediaries, of course."

"You'd rather run?" Scorn thickened Flidais's voice as she flirted with calling me a coward. "They are on our turf—or as close to our turf as we're likely to get. Let us show them what the Irish think of their arrogance. We have some time to prepare. My divination says the Olympians are on their way but won't be here until after dawn. We can give them a fight and win."

It was gratifying to hear that her divination corroborated the evidence of my augury, but I said, "I prefer to live up to the fighting-Irish stereotype only when I'm cornered or when the odds are skewed in my favor.

There's no upside to taking them on, Flidais. They're as fast as we are, if not faster. And, as you pointed out, they killed the Morrigan."

"But because it was two against one, correct?"

I nodded, though I doubted it was true. From what I could tell, the Morrigan held them off and conducted a mental conversation with me for precisely as long as she wished. She died only when she stopped trying to live.

"We can do the same thing to them," Flidais assured me, "one by one. Use the strategy their Roman puppet favored so much: divide and conquer."

Or, I thought, you could be pretending to help us now, and then you'll quietly sit back and do nothing while Artemis and Diana hunt us down. There was no proof Flidais wasn't the one scheming against us, other than my vague inclination to view her as one who participated in the schemes of others rather than initiating them herself. But I voiced a different thought: "Why are you so anxious to meet them in battle? Might you have a personal agenda?"

Flidais scoffed. "I have never met them, so I don't know what that could be."

"You're essentially the same goddess, except that they're virgins and you're not. Maybe you're trying to prove that chastity is overrated."

"That's self-evident, Atticus," Granuaile pointed out. "Or at least it is to everyone who's enjoyed a good diddle."

"She knows what I mean," I said. "Perhaps Flidais is seeking validation that she's better than the Olympians instead of pursuing the strategically wiser option." She wouldn't be able to dance around calling me a coward if I turned her eagerness for battle into self-aggrandizement.

Narrowing her eyes at me, Flidais let out a slow hiss of breath before saying, "All right, let's go to the Old Way." She waved at her chariot. "Follow and I'll take you there."

"Hold on," I said. "How did you get that chariot and team up through the cramped cellar of Windsor Castle?"

"I didn't." She flicked a finger at her ride. "This is but one of many chariots I keep hidden throughout the isles. The stags live in the area and came when I called."

That was far more sensible than what the Olympians were doing—but, then again, they couldn't shift planes the way Flidais could, so it would make little sense for them.

We followed Flidais through the damp mist of the dark before dawn, the air like wet cloth on our faces. As we loped at an easy pace through the park, we stayed alert for any sign of the Olympians—or for any sign of betrayal.

We received a sign before we reached the castle. A dull thump pounded the air a half mile ahead of us, and a faint shock wave buffeted our faces soon afterward. We stopped running and watched a pale cloud of dust rise into the sky. It wasn't difficult to discern the source. I hoped no one had been in residence.

Granuaile said, "Was that . . . ?"

"An explosion? Yeah."

<Biiig bada-boom.>

We turned to Flidais and she shook her head. "It wasn't me."

"I didn't say—"

"Speech wasn't necessary. You think I arranged the destruction of the Old Way to keep us here."

"No, I don't. But someone else did. Someone from Tír na nÓg. Do you have any idea who might be responsible or who might have ordered such a thing?"

Flidais whirled on me with a flash of anger in her eyes. "Just what is it that you suspect of me?"

There was quite a long list, but voicing my suspicions would be counterproductive. I chose my words with care, leaving her little room to take offense or to escape telling me something useful.

"I suspect nothing, but I wonder plenty. If you have no ideas regarding who might have blown up part of Windsor Castle to prevent us using the Old Way to get back, then we are dealing with someone extremely clever. Who amongst the Tuatha Dé Danann would be able to arrange an explosion on this plane less than an hour after you used it? Or, more to the point, who was following you in Tír na nÓg and saw you leave that particular way?"

Flidais frowned at my last sentence. The idea that she might have been followed disturbed her more than anything else. The challenge faded from her eyes and she looked away, considering the problem.

"I suppose Ogma could have done it. His designs have been inscrutable for a long while."

The thought chilled me but had occurred to me before. Granuaile gasped, because it hadn't occurred to her.

Flidais continued, "But Midhir has been keeping to himself recently. He has a mind for such things. And he is a patron of that Fae lord you shamed during your visit to Court, the one in charge of the rangers. What did you call him?"

"Lord Grundlebeard."

"That's it."

"What's his real name?"

"I never knew it. The irony is that no one ever paid attention to him until you singled him out for ridicule. Everyone calls him Grundlebeard now."

"Bollocks. Now we don't have any choice but to stay and fight."

"It is the best course, Druid—your pardon. At Court you are always Siodhachan, but I know you use other names outside it. Do you still go by Atticus, or do you have a new name?"

"Atticus is fine."

<Maybe you should change it to Swoony McMushy-pants.>

Granuaile choked back a laugh and then coughed to mask her amusement, while Flidais's lips pursed in an effort not to smile. She'd heard Oberon's comment too.

"All right, where do you recommend we fight?" I asked, pretending my hound hadn't said anything. "Not near the castle, I hope. That's going to be flooded with British security in short order. In fact, I bet we're on a satellite camera right now and someone's going to be reviewing this and wondering who the hell we are. We should stay underneath the canopy and maybe go invisible for a while."

Flidais scowled at the sky. "I have heard of these satellites. Perfidious creatures." I didn't question her word choice, and neither did Granuaile or Oberon. Now was not the time to explain orbital surveillance to a being who had yet to use a computer or a cell phone. Satellites, to her, were as magical as the Fae were to humans. "Yes. We will return to the forest and sort ourselves for a defense."

Helicopters and distant sirens sounded behind us as we turned our backs on Windsor Castle and jogged through the Home Park toward Windsor Forest again. Once underneath the canopy, we dropped our camouflage and returned to the small clearing in the middle of the forest. Three marijuana plants grew nervously on the western perimeter, seemingly aware that they didn't belong there, dreading the day when they would be harvested and smoked by a bearded and half-baked local.

<What's the plan, Atticus?>

Still working on it, actually.

Flidais left her chariot and stags plainly visible just underneath the trees, a clear signal that she was now involved and doing a bit of hunting of her own. We entered the forest together from the northwestern side of the clearing, creating one trail, but after about a hundred yards we decided to split up our forces.

"Before we do, however," Flidais said, "we might be able to take advantage of something." She stared at Granuaile while she said this, and Granuaile understandably grew wary.

"Uh . . . what did you have in mind?" she asked.

"Have you taught her how to modify the camouflage binding, Atticus?" the huntress said. The correct answer would be "yes" if I wished to avoid looking clueless, but since I truly was clueless, there was no use pretending.

"I didn't know it could be modified. It's one of the base spells tattooed into our skin."

"You can't modify the base spell, of course, but you can add your own flourishes on top of it. I'm surprised you haven't tried it."

"I'm full of surprises." And I didn't know why she was speaking of camouflage when Granuaile had the ability to turn fully invisible.

"Yes." The goddess smirked, her eyes taking in Granuaile's clothes. "Well, I have noticed that Granuaile and I could be mistaken for twins if we made a little bit of an effort. That could give us an advantage, so allow me to make the effort."

I'd noticed the resemblance before, as had others. Ogma had mistaken Granuaile for Flidais once while we were visiting Tír na nÓg.

Keeping her eyes on Granuaile, Flidais began to speak a binding in Old Irish. I recognized the words for camouflage at the beginning, but she kept speaking past the point where it should have ended, targeting Granuaile's black outfit and reflecting it onto her own clothing before energizing the binding. Her hunting leathers all turned black.

"Whoa," Granuaile and I said in stereo.

Oberon shuddered. <I just got chills! Coming soon on BBC One, *The Dark Druids of Windsor*!>

Flidais removed the bracer on her left arm, which protected her skin from the lash of her bowstring. That gave her the same sleeveless look as Granuaile.

"All right. Hair next," the huntress said, for that was a significant difference. The color was almost identical, but Flidais had quite a bit more curl and frizz to hers than Granuaile did, and it made her look a bit like an eighties rocker.

"Maybe if we tie it up in a knot?" Granuaile said.

"Yes, but first I need to straighten." Flidais improvised a binding that had simply never occurred to me—or to Granuaile either—and the kinks smoothed out until her hair lay flat and wavy like Granuaile's.

<Great big bears, Atticus, think of how much money she could make in Hollywood! Speak some gibberish and you get Oscar-night hairdos in five minutes!>

"Amazing," Granuaile said, smiling.

"Tie up your hair as you like and I will copy it," Flidais said.

Granuaile gathered and twisted her hair behind her in a practiced series of movements. When she was finished, it was tight against her scalp, pulled back from her ears, and piled in a neat sort of bun on top. Flidais studied it for a few seconds and then produced a matching bun on her head.

"Not bad at all," Granuaile said.

"Here, let's face him," the huntress said.

They turned toward me, side by side, so that I could compare. Same height and build, same skin tone, though Granuaile had a few more freckles. The hair looked identical now. Up close you could tell that Flidais's clothes were made of a different material, but from even a mild distance away it would simply be a black silhouette. Likewise, the minor differences in facial features could be easily distinguished up close, but from a distance in a combat situation, anyone would have trouble telling them apart.

"That'll work," I said. "How shall we proceed?"

"We will appear from the flanks one at a time and throw a knife before going invisible again. We will alternate until we run out of knives—we only have five total, correct?"

Granuaile nodded. She had three, to Flidais's two.

"Then you should go first," Flidais said. "To them it will appear that the same person is teleporting around them. Quite the distraction. Someone should be able to take advantage of that." She arched an eyebrow at me and I nodded.

"If it turns out to be possible, target Diana," I said. "She's probably a bit more invested in this than Artemis is, and anything we can do to slow her down would be good."

With all of us agreed, we separated to lie in wai I continued deeper into the woods on the same path, Flidais took off to my left, and Granuaile melted into the trees with Oberon to my right. Once I'd traveled another fifty yards or so and turned around to face my trail, the directions were switched, with Granuaile waiting somewhere off to my left and Flidais to the right.

I drew Fragarach from its sheath and stood so that I had a good view through the trees. The first gray fingers of dawn were reaching through the canopy.

I cast camouflage as a helicopter chopped the air above the Home Park, probably very near where we had paused after the explosion. These days, British security would be prone to suspect any attack on Windsor Castle as a terrorist strike, and not even in their wildest theories would they suspect that someone was simply trying to slam a door in my face. The two men that Granuaile and I had rendered unconscious by Frogmore House would become a part of the investigation now, and satellite feeds from that area would be scoured. One frame we'd be there and then the next we'd disappear. That would make them start searching in an ever-widening circle, and eventually they'd get here—maybe would even spot Artemis and Diana as they were inbound. That would complicate matters. Our duel required privacy.

I shuddered merely thinking the word. This wouldn't be a duel. There wouldn't be any rules or codes. They would simply come at me knowing that the worst I could do to them was deliver some brief pain and annoyance.

How to placate an implacable foe? The Morrigan's advice came back to me: *Gaia loves us more than she loves the Olympians.* The solution, I realized to my chagrin, was to take hostages—figuratively as well as literally. I am not a fan of taking hostages, since it's an act of desperation and so rarely works, and when I kicked Bacchus through a portal it was more to save my life than anything else. But now I could see how the Olympians would view it as a hostage situation. Right now my leverage was tenuous: On the one hand they said they wanted Bacchus back, but on the other a couple of them were doing everything they could to snuff me. The leverage could change—they knew that if they took Oberon or Granuaile I'd give them anything. There might, however, be a way to increase my leverage—or to at least make them talk, which was the entire problem, from my point of view. It wouldn't be pretty, but it had a better chance of working than expecting the Olympians to be reasonable without significant encouragement. It made me wonder why the Morrigan, or the rest of the Tuatha Dé Danann, or anyone else who'd ever had occasion to fight the Olympians, hadn't thought of compelling them to talk. Perhaps in some cases it was simply not an option for them, but more likely it never occurred to them that there was any way of winning other than through force of arms.

Communicating with Albion through my tattoos, I introduced the elemental to the concept of storage units, in case my plan turned out to work.

Chapter 23

I should be confident of what's to come, but somehow that confidence has fled. With Atticus here and Flidais too, and the theoretical aid of Herne—I'm not sure if he's coming back—we ought to be a bit more evenly matched. But nothing went the way I expected it to the last time we tried to ambush the Olympians. I am strategically ill equipped to deal with them. Unless I land a powerful blow to the head with Scáthmhaide, I don't have a way of taking them out. My knives will only annoy them, and they are so very annoyed with us as it is.

Atticus claims that I fight better when I'm angry, and if that's true, I'm sure he's right about the effect but not the cause. When I fight, I am occupied not only with the exertion but with the manner in which I win—a distinction that Atticus believes pointless. In battle there is no moral high ground, he says, only high ground that puts either you or your enemy at a disadvantage, depending on who occupies it. I privately disagree. People can lose—or die—with dignity. If I could give them that, I would. But I admit that I cease to care if my own dignity is wounded first. With anger comes a remarkable clarity of purpose, a stillness from which many paths to victory lie in front of me. Some paths are much less dignified than others, and the distance to travel much shorter. I need only choose one and take the first step. But I do not have that clarity of purpose yet with the Olympians, for I think they have some just cause to be incensed with us. Though messing with the dryads on Olympus was ultimately a successful stratagem—it gave us the time to complete my binding to the earth—I always knew we would have to pay a price for it.

Perhaps my insecurity stems from the knowledge that for the majority of this journey I have been watched and judged from afar by beings who, if my current run of luck holds true, may prove to be my adversaries someday. Or it could come from the fact that Oberon and I nearly lost our lives the last time—in almost no time at all.

My experience thus far has shown that battles in martial-arts and action movies always last longer than the real thing—especially when there are gods involved in the real thing. When you're watching in the theater with your salted popcorn and high-fructose corn syrup, the battles linger and slow-motion sequences pay exquisite attention to killing blows and masks of rage, a celebration of violent death intended for people like me who (until recently) customarily do nothing more violent than buy butchered meat at the grocery store. Once the movie hero and villain finally have their showdown, they discover that they're evenly matched and there is time for a long, beautiful silhouette sequence in front of a dawning sun as the soundtrack composer mashes down some organ keys and a boys' choir sings whole notes until they drop dead from hypoxia. What makes such shots exceedingly silly is the weeks or months of preparation it takes the actors to rehearse the battle so that they *don't* accidentally kill each other. If they wanted to truly go at it, they wouldn't need to rehearse.

Like all true battles on the individual level, it would be ugly and anguished and over before the cinematographer could focus. I have learned that our emotions and adrenal glands won't have it any other way.

I heard the goddesses approach before I saw them, and that saved me from further worry. I had to clear my mind for combat as best I could. The rolling tumble of hooves announced their arrival at the edge of the clearing, where Flidais had left her chariot.

<They're here,> Oberon said. Holding Scáthmhaide in my left hand and a knife in my right, I cast invisibility on myself and camouflage on Oberon. I also activated the strength and speed bindings worked into the silver and iron knotwork on my staff.

Lie down, Oberon, and their shots should sail high. Don't attack unless they draw near.

<Don't worry about me,> he replied. <I almost think barking would be a better distraction than trying to bite them.>

You're probably right.

I saw flashes of movement and heard a hushed conversation, and then the huntresses left their chariots and proceeded on foot into the forest, bows ready. Artemis took point, studying the undergrowth ahead and watching the trail for booby traps, while Diana trailed behind, looking up and around for the expected ambush.

When Artemis reached the point where we'd split up, she said as much to Diana. Diana told her to keep moving ahead, so Artemis did. I let her pass, and when Diana drew even with me, I threw a knife at her head and shed my invisibility. The knife dropped in flight and sank into the side of her ribs, because her right arm had been raised to fire her bow, exposing her side. *"Ha!"* I shouted, then flipped the invisibility back on and hit the ground as an arrow from Artemis sailed overhead.

Flidais popped into view and threw from the other

side, as Diana spun to face where I'd been. She'd just grasped the hilt of my blade to yank it out when Flidais's knife thunked somewhere in her back, missing the quiver. Another *"Ha!"* echoed in the forest, and Artemis whiffed with her second arrow as Flidais disappeared.

That was my cue. Rising to my feet, I dropped my invisibility and tossed another blade into Diana's chest. I blinked out and pitched forward to the ground, but Artemis didn't take a shot this time. She was distracted, perhaps, by something near her—most likely Atticus sneaking up from behind.

Diana sank to her knees, and Flidais's second knife overshot her. I rose, reappeared, and threw my last knife into the belly. She looked to be in genuine pain, but none of the wounds were fatal. She'd be up and fighting in no time once she pulled those free. We had to finish her before that, and I took three steps before something punched me below the ribs and knocked me back off my feet.

As I fell, I saw a black-feathered shaft sprouting from my abdomen. In my haste to lay out Diana, I hadn't gone invisible or dropped to the ground. Atticus hadn't distracted Artemis after all; instead, she had shot me. My real-life fight had been even shorter than I had feared.

Chapter 24

I was sneaking up on Artemis and had perhaps fifteen more yards to go when Oberon shouted in my mind: <They shot Clever Girl!>

I yelled "No!" and tumbled forward as Artemis whirled around and loosed an arrow overhead. Realizing that I had already drawn too close to her for archery, she drew a hunting knife and threw her bow in my direction as I came up out of my somersault. The bow did no harm as it bounced off me, but it did reveal my position. Artemis shifted her feet and presented her right side, blade forward, as her left hand snaked down her thigh and drew another knife from a sheath there. She lunged forward, wickedly fast, and managed to gash me across the chest, right underneath my collarbone. She'd probably been going for my throat but had misjudged due to my camouflage. I backed up and set myself. Though I wanted nothing so much as to help Granuaile, there would be no rushing past Artemis.

I told Oberon, *Stay with her. I'll come as soon as I can.*

<I will.>

Artemis taunted me, realizing that she had scored a hit. "You are not so skilled at this as the Morrigan."

"Neither are you," I retorted. "You only defeated her because she allowed it." That must have struck a nerve—

it was, perhaps, a doubt she'd already harbored about that duel—because she snarled and charged in. Her left arm was raised and her dagger pointed backward, blade held flat against her wrist and forearm like impromptu armor, while her right was cocked back, ready to strike. I took a risk in the interest of ending it quickly—any sort of protracted fight would not work in my favor— knowing that she would wound me but hoping that it wouldn't be instantly debilitating or fatal. I swept Fragarach clockwise toward her raised and extended left arm and followed it with my body, shuffling right and planting my right foot so that I could also pivot clockwise. My sword took off her hand at the wrist and I kept Fragarach moving, whipping it down and around as I spun so that it would catch her as she passed me by. It did catch her, right across the quads of her left leg, but it didn't cut through bone because my strength was gone, leeched away, since she'd caught me too. The knife in her right hand, a bit tardy, still sheared off a slab of my left lat as she thrust at me while I was spinning. I sprayed blood and she sprayed ichor and we both had a good howl over what we had lost. The difference was that she went down, thanks to that hack at her leg, and I remained standing.

It occurred to me that the Morrigan had almost certainly not used camouflage during her battle—how else would the huntresses have been able to target her right side so specifically? Artemis couldn't see through mine very well, if at all, so that meant she wasn't getting any help from Minerva or Athena. That supported my theory that the Morrigan had fought to lose. I'd bet money with the Einherjar that after she had said what she wanted to say to me, she had simply stopped fighting and allowed herself to be cut down.

Artemis rolled away to create some space between us and I let her, because I wanted to check on the noise behind me, where Diana was cursing loudly in Latin. She had risen from the ground and removed all the throwing knives, only to be skewered by an arrow from Flidais. As she reached up to tear it loose, another hit her high and toppled her backward. A shimmering effervescence in the air hinted that perhaps Herne and his hunters were manifesting to provide their promised help, though they were taking their own sweet time at it. Daytime is a notoriously rough stretch for ghosts to do their thing, however, so the fact that he could manifest at all now spoke volumes about his power.

A brief glance was all I could afford. Artemis had regained her feet when I turned around, and considering how fast the Olympians healed, I bet her leg would be just fine in another sixty seconds. My back wouldn't heal anywhere near that fast, but neither would she grow another left hand. Her stump had already stopped leaking; I hadn't, though I was working on it. I stalked toward her, not even attempting to be quiet, and she set herself. She looked to be favoring her left leg, but the tiniest of quirks at the edge of her lips gave away that she was faking. She was already just fine, and the surface cut was for show. She'd shifted the grip on her right-hand knife so that the blade pointed down, and if she crossed with her fist the blade would trail behind, slashing as it went. She was presenting her weak left side, willing to give that up and take more damage there so long as she could counter with her undamaged right. Well, fuck that, I wasn't going to bite.

I came in hard and dropped at the last second, sliding under her haymaker and sweeping her legs out from under her. It was the kind of dirty slide tackle that would get you a red card in football. The momentum from her swing tumbled her across my hips, her right arm stretched out to break her fall, and my right arm, swinging Fragarach down, chopped hers off above the elbow.

I thought that would end it, because what would she do, stump me to death? Nope. She rolled over, down my legs, effectively trapping them, and then scissored her right one to kick me in the face and break my nose. My head spun like I'd drunk way too much tequila, and my vision swam with spots as my skull hit the ground. I think I may have blacked out for a few seconds, because, the next thing I knew, Herne was shouting at me, not only fully manifested but also fully annoyed.

"Oi, you dizzy bastard, wherever you are! What d'you want me to do with her?"

Head pounding and spots still obscuring my sight, I raised my head to see Herne and one of his hunters struggling to keep Artemis immobile. They were both trying to keep her legs wrapped up and were having some difficulty. I dispelled my camouflage before speaking.

"Chop those off," I said, indicating her legs, "but not the head."

"I was hoping you'd say that."

I rose shakily to my feet and lurched my way toward the spot where Granuaile had fallen. My healing process had stopped the bleeding, but my back and head hurt, until I remembered that I could control that. I shut off the pain as unhinged curses in Greek and Latin followed me, interspersed with wet, chunky sounds as the ghosts methodically removed the limbs from Artemis—and from Diana too. Another of Herne's huntsmen and the pack of hounds had subdued Diana, while Flidais looked on with approval.

Oberon, is she alive? Are you okay?

<She's alive but says it hurts a whole lot. They got her in the middle, Atticus. I'm okay.>

Relief shuddered through me and I paused to collect myself. I had been so worried that she'd been killed outright, as Tahirah had so long ago. *Thank you for staying*

with her. Ask her to drop your camouflage and her in-
visibility so I can help. It's safe now. I resumed walking
and tried to shake off the clouds in my head.

<All right. Hey, there you are!> he said as I drew
closer.

Where are you? Bark, please.

Oberon barked and appeared at the same time off to
my left. He was standing watch over Granuaile, who
had an arrow in her, just underneath her ribs and slightly
left of center. Blood welled around the shaft and she
clutched it, tears streaming down her cheeks and her
breathing labored as I arrived.

"It hurts so much, Atticus," she gasped, the last syllable hitching in her throat. "I didn't think it would hurt
this much."

I lay Fragarach on the ground as I crashed to my knees
next to her. Oberon made room. "You have to find your
nerves and block them," I said. "Remember the binding? Block the pain signals. You shut off the electricity
down there and then you can get to work."

She winced. "Gah, I can't believe I forgot that!"

"Shock makes you forget a lot of things. I didn't remember it until recently myself."

"You're hurt?"

"I'll heal. And so will you."

"Okay," she whispered. "Okay. I can do this."

"Absolutely."

She took a few more quick, shallow breaths, closed
her eyes, then spoke the binding I had taught her. She
sighed in relief when it worked, then smiled weakly at
me through watery eyes. "Ohh. That's so much better.
Thanks."

"Sure. Now we can melt these out of you."

"No. I already looked. The head and shaft are synthetic composites. We can't unbind them."

"Fuck."

"No, this is good. It's good, Atticus."

"What?"

"I needed this. I needed to get hit hard and learn how to heal from it."

"But you can't heal with that thing stuck inside you."

"We'll get it out. Go deal with the Olympians."

"They're down already."

"There will be more very soon, and you know it. Hermes and Mercury at the very least."

"But—"

"Atticus. Seriously. I've got this." She reached across with her right hand, clutched my shirt, and gently pulled me down to her lips. She kissed me and then said, her eyes mere inches from mine, "I'm stable inside and comfortably numb. I'm not leaking stomach acid or anything, and I have the internal bleeding stopped. All I need is for you to get me the hell out of here. You have a plan for that, right? Tell me you have a plan."

"I have a plan," I said, and remembered that it was true.

She smiled, new tears sheeting down from the corners of her eyes toward the tops of her ears, and I went all melty. "I knew you did," she said. "I'll do better next time. Now go."

I rose from her lips but froze before getting to my feet, seeing the arrow again and the sodden bloody circle on her black clothing. I couldn't leave her there. Some very old instincts told me that was impossible.

<You look like you just drank some bad beer, Atticus.>

Granuaile heard and laughed once before she realized that was probably not a good idea with an arrow in her diaphragm. "Atticus, go. I'll be invisible and safe enough for a while. Don't worry about me."

I ducked back down and kissed her again. "All right,

I'll go. But only because you would kick my ass if I stayed."

"Take Oberon with you. He doesn't want to stay here."

Is that true?

<Actually, she's the one who wants me to go. She told me so.>

She wants to deal with this alone. That's okay. Speaking aloud, I said, "All right, let's do this." Oberon trotted next to me, tail wagging, and I gave him some love.

Thanks to Herne and his boys, Artemis and Diana had been turned into copies of the Black Knight, resting faceup on the forest floor with no arms and no legs. Their limbs were nearby but not close enough to heal, and I could see that, beyond the initial squirt of ichor, the Olympians' remarkable regenerative processes had stopped the bleeding and they made very tidy torsos. The Morrigan's prescience about Herne's ability to help us was well warranted; I doubted I would have fared so well had he not been there, even with Flidais around. Artemis most likely would have locked her legs around my neck while I was unconscious and snapped it. I thanked Herne for his assistance, and he nodded but said nothing. He and Flidais helped me haul the pieces of Artemis over to where Diana lay and spread them out so that they were only a few feet apart.

I stood between the two bodies and the goddesses glowered up at me. I didn't mock them or rub my victory in their faces. I kept my expression dispassionate as I set my plan in motion. //Druid ready for storage// I sent to Albion. //Ten pieces / My position / Leave large pieces for last//

The earth's magic cannot be used to harm animals of a certain biological complexity. I can use it all I want to give myself an advantage in battle—speed and strength and camouflage and so on—but I can't use it directly against an enemy or a critter that wants to eat me. It's an immutable law and tattooed directly into my skin. But the immortal nature of the Olympians, I realized earlier, provided me with an interesting loophole. They couldn't truly be harmed in any permanent sense by the earth; even when decapitated, their heads retained consciousness without oxygen, so I—or, rather, Albion—could do some things to them we'd never be able to do to any other creature.

Underneath the arms and legs of the huntresses, the forest floor began to bubble and shift. Gooey globs of what geologists call London Clay rose up and encased their limbs in a dark-brown slurry with little fossils sprinkled throughout. This was then coated with a layer of chalk and topped with gravel, which Albion bound together and then smoothed into solid rock.

"What is this?" Diana asked, swiveling her head from side to side, watching the process unfold.

"Your fate," I said. "You will be interred in the earth until you agree to cease hunting me and my friends. No earthquake from Poseidon or Neptune will cough you out of the ground. You will remain in darkness, unheard and undying, until I decide to release you. You'd better hope I don't perish in the meantime."

The clay began to ooze over their torsos, and, once they felt it, their expressions lost much of their vinegar.

"I will cease hunting you and your friends," Artemis said.

My eyebrows shot up at the quick capitulation. "You have my thanks. Diana?"

Her defiance returned. She tried to spit at me and missed. "I will never stop seeking your head," she snarled.

I sucked in air past my teeth. "Wow, never is a *very* long time. Artemis, thank you very much for offering, but I hope you will forgive me if I don't quite believe you yet. I will be more inclined to do so a bit later, perhaps. You and I will speak again soon."

The clay had moved past their shoulders now and was creeping up the columns of their necks. Diana continued to glare at me while Artemis rolled her eyes down for a nervous look. "I am in earnest, Druid. I will swear it."

"Again, I thank you, but you lack credibility at the moment." And there was no way I was letting either of them loose right after they'd shot Granuaile and tried to kill me too. "We've defeated you three times now," I reminded them. "Once in the Netherlands, once in the English Channel, and now here. It didn't have to be this way. You might wish to consider while you're underground if all this was worth it for the god of drunken assholes and five dryads who were perfectly healthy when last I saw them. Save for the past few days of self-defense, I have never assaulted you directly and have strived to amend my trespasses. Can you say the same?"

//Finish now// I sent to Albion, and the clay flowed to envelop the heads of the two huntresses, who screamed curses at me until the gunk cut them off. Once they sank out of sight—mute hunks of rock, safe from any attempt to retrieve them—I looked up in response to a small flutter of wings above. Hugin and Munin stared down at me from the branch of an elm.

"Yeah, I thought you'd show up now. Tell the Einherjar who bet against us to pound sand, Odin. We survived." The ravens squawked but said nothing intelligible.

Laughter bubbled up from the throat of Flidais. "That was amusing, Atticus. And well done. How fares Granuaile?" I wondered why she had not shown any more concern before now.

"She's wounded but stable until we finish here."

"Are we not finished?"

"Not quite. Will you follow me to the edge of the clearing? You too, Herne?"

"Certainly," Flidais replied, and Herne said aye.

"We mislike riding in the sun," he said, "but will endure for the sake of our guests."

The sun had a proper start on the morning now, and the cloud of debris from Windsor Castle was clearly visible once we reached the edge of the pasture. Helicopters were still circling around the Home Park but had yet to stray this far.

"Shouldn't be much longer," I said. "If Odin was watching that all unfold, then I'm sure the Olympians had some eyes on us as well."

The ankle-winged boys didn't keep us waiting. Less than a minute later, they zipped in from the south and hovered at twelve feet to deliver their decree from on high.

"We bring an urgent message from Jupiter and Zeus," Mercury boomed.

I squinted and held a hand over my eyes to shield them from the sun. "You guys want to talk to me, get down here. I'm getting a crick in my neck looking up at you."

They floated down but kept themselves a foot off the ground so that they were still looking down at me.

"Zeus and Jupiter demand the release of the huntresses."

"No," I said. "We're not doing this again. I'm not going to do a long-distance negotiation with the gods of the sky. I want a face-to-face." I purposely turned away from Mercury and locked eyes with Hermes. "I want you to bring Zeus and Jupiter here to negotiate in good faith, safe conduct guaranteed on both sides, or so help me we will set the earth against all Olympians and none of you will ever be able to set foot on this plane again. Is that understood, Hermes?"

The Greek god nodded but said nothing. Mercury

couldn't stand the lack of attention and said, "I, not Hermes, deliver messages to Jupiter, Druid."

Oberon. Take a risk for me? Pee on the Roman's leg and then run.

<Why?>

You're a guest here too, see.

<I don't, but I hope I'll see a T-bone later.>

"I know that, Mercury," I replied, "but I respect Hermes. He's not a jumbo ox box, for one thing."

Mercury blanched, and then his complexion colored to a dyspeptic ochre. "What was that?" he said betwixt ground teeth. He didn't know what a jumbo ox box was, but he was certain he didn't like being called one. While he worked himself up to a rage, Oberon trotted up behind him and lifted a leg. A yellow stream of urine splashed against Mercury's right leg near the back of the knee and trickled down his calf, wetting one of his wings. "What?" he said, flinching away and twisting to see what had happened.

Run now!

<Wauugh!> Oberon said, as he bunched his legs and leapt away from the swing of Mercury's caduceus. It grazed his ribs but did no damage.

"Cur!" Mercury shouted, and gave chase, cruising above Oberon's back. He swung and whiffed again as Oberon juked to the right.

<Yikes! He acts like he's never been peed on before!>

"Herne?" I said. "He's attacked a guest." I waved at Mercury, and before the god could process that he'd overstepped his bounds, he had three ghosts on top of him, preventing further flight, and that was just for starters. The hounds leapt at his ankles and tore off his wings with their teeth. They shook the feathers like bird dogs as he fell screaming to the ground. Hermes tensed, ready to fly to Mercury's aid, but I advised him to stay out of it. "You have a message to deliver, remember?"

That gave him pause and he wafted higher, out of reach. He snarled as he watched Herne and the hunters dismember Mercury into god cutlets. At my signal, Albion did his part and began to coat the various parts into the crust of the earth.

The bags around Hermes's eyes glowed red, and his musical voice said, "There will be a reckoning, Druid."

"What do you *reckon* this is, Hermes?" I pointed to Mercury, who was now being covered in clay and hollering about it. "This is what will become of all Olympians who seek to put me in my place. I will place them underground in pieces for eternity, unable to heal and unable to die. I don't wish that, however, and I'm sure the Olympians don't wish it either. Nothing has been done that cannot be undone. So, please, get you to Zeus and Jupiter too, and ask them to come speak in peace so that we can live in harmony again—or, at the very least, aggressively ignore one another."

Hermes turned his red-rimmed eyes to Flidais. "The Tuatha Dé Danann condone this behavior?"

Flidais cleared her throat before answering in formal, diplomatic tones. "The violence is regrettable and we have no wish to give offense to Olympus, but it is our view that the Druids have acted solely in self-defense and they have the right to defend themselves."

Hermes snorted in disbelief. "They sundered five dryads from their oaks. You believe that was done in self-defense?"

"It was necessary to contain Faunus if we were to escape Bacchus," I said, unsure that Flidais knew all the details about that episode, "so, yes, it was self-defense, and the dryads were returned unharmed, as Olympus demanded."

Hermes ignored me and said to Flidais, "What say you?"

"I say merely this: The Druids do the earth's work on

this plane, while the Tuatha Dé Danann are bound by old oaths to remain in Tír na nÓg as much as possible. We therefore wish them to remain alive and free. Can I be clearer?"

I almost blurted out, "No shit?" but schooled my expression to make it seem as if I had expected her unequivocal support all along. In truth, I'd been expecting an assertion of neutrality, even though she and Manannan—not to mention the Morrigan—had already intervened directly.

The Greek god huffed and his eyes flicked once more to Mercury—or, rather, to where Mercury had been. The earth had swallowed him completely, and his cries could no longer be heard.

"I just want to talk," I reminded him.

"You might not like how the conversation ends," Hermes said, before rising higher into the sky and winging south toward Olympus.

Chapter 25

While Hermes went to go tell his dad on me, I glanced at Flidais and said, "I was impressed by what you said. Is that truly what the Tuatha Dé Danann wish for us— to remain alive and free?"

"Perhaps not all of them," Flidais admitted, "but it is the position of those who matter. It is what Brighid wishes."

So Flidais remained the staunch ally of Brighid. "I'm relieved to hear it. Please give her my kindest regards." That would serve as a thank-you without placing me in her debt.

"I will. What's next?"

"Well, I sure wish Perun were here."

"You do? Why?"

Once I explained, she offered to go get him. He'd been hiding out in Tír na nÓg with Brighid's permission ever since Loki had destroyed his plane.

"How are you going to get him?" I said. "The Old Way under the castle is rubble now."

"It's not the only one around here."

"It's not?"

"Herne's oak does double duty. It's tethered to Tír na nÓg but it's also an anchor to an Old Way. Why do you think we kept influencing England's monarchs to plant new trees in the same spot when the old ones were ripped out?"

"What? You did?" The enormity of her omission hit home. "I mean, why didn't you tell me earlier?"

She grinned, unrepentant. "I wanted to fight. And it was right to do so. The Olympians needed a lesson. But we can leave now if you wish."

Earlier I would have jumped at the chance, but this was an opportunity to preserve our hides for more than a few hours or days. "No, I want to see this through. But if you could take Granuaile and Oberon with you— she needs help with the arrow—that would be great."

Granuaile was fine with the idea and gladly limped into Flidais's chariot once we went to fetch her. She wobbled and looked a bit peaked, but, true to her word, she seemed to have it under control. I gave her a kiss and wished her a speedy recovery. Oberon, however, flatly refused to leave me, and I didn't have the heart to fight him on it.

After leaving Granuaile in the care of Goibhniu, who would saw off the arrowhead to allow the shaft to be withdrawn, Flidais came back before Zeus and Jupiter could arrive. She exited her chariot hand in hand with Perun, the Slavic god of thunder and her current snogging companion.

He looked rejuvenated and spoiling for a fight. His adventures in tailoring were also getting a bit wild. The V in his tight belted tunic plunged precipitously and ended just above his belly button, allowing what appeared to be red shag pile carpeting to spill out. His pants were tucked into blue calf-high boots with a flared top. He looked like a superhero from the seventies. He smiled and gave me a manly hug, which felt like being wrapped up in a throw rug and stomped on. Vertebrae popped and my wounded back sent me an outraged query, wondering what the hell I thought I was doing, allowing myself to be crushed like that. "Atticus! Is good to see you. Why does Flidais bring me here?"

"We need you to appear big and intimidating."

"Ah, you need to scare peoples with face of rage?"

"That's it."

He smiled at me. "I can do this. Will be fun. Look." He crossed his arms and the atmosphere darkened around him. His eyebrows drew together and his eyes, normally blue, flickered with the blue and white of lightning as he glowered down at us. He flexed everything and grew bigger.

<Gah! Whatever you did, Atticus, apologize! He's breaking bad!>

I didn't do anything, Oberon. This is performance art.

<Are you sure?>

Perun's visual promise of doom relaxed, and he grinned. The sky brightened immediately. "Is good, yes?"

I nodded enthusiastically. "That's perfect."

Perun had moved on to greeting Herne, and I was reminded again that he was one of the nicer gods I'd ever met—at least, when he wasn't stirred to anger. He was going to provide me a bit of an edge in the coming psychological warfare. When they arrived, Zeus and Jupiter wouldn't be able to intimidate us with muscles and thunder when we had plenty of that on our side. And I thought it would be important for the Greco–Romans to see that we had a thunder god throwing in his lot with us. They'd accord Perun some respect and perhaps pause long enough to give me a serious hearing. Without him, I'd expect the Olympians to pummel us into submission without bothering to talk.

The current popular image of Zeus as a cheerful, avuncular type perplexes me. I know it comes from a silly kids' movie, but I'm not sure they could have gotten it more wrong. Zeus was never avuncular. He killed his father, raped his sister, and then married her, calculating

that sanctified incest was marginally better than the un-
sanctified kind. After that he conducted a series of what
are generously called "affairs" with mortal women,
though sometimes tales will admit he "ravished" them,
which is to say he raped them. He turned into a swan
once for a girl with an avian fetish, and another time he
manifested as a golden shower over a woman imprisoned in a hole in the ground. His actions clearly paint
him as skeevy to the max and the most despicable of
examples. He's not the kind of god that belongs in kids'
films. He's the kind that releases the kraken.

Thunderclouds condensed and roiled above us, signaling that the gods of the sky had heard my words fall
from the lips of Hermes. The messenger god rocketed
out of the southern sky and hovered six feet above us,
safely out of our reach.

"Zeus and Jupiter approach," he said, then darted
sideways like a hummingbird.

The Olympians knew how to make an entrance. A
deafening thunderclap boomed in our ears, causing
Oberon to yipe, and two lightning bolts struck the
ground not ten yards away. Zeus and Jupiter stood in
their place. Lightning continued to rain down around us
and clouds boiled directly above, which was odd since
we could see blue sky not all that far away.

By now I'd grown used to the differences between the
Greeks and Romans and could immediately tell the two
apart. Zeus, the uncredited god of sexual deviancy, had
wrapped a thin sheet of polyester material around his
waist, like a towel, but was otherwise naked—and was
visibly aroused by the opportunity to confront us. His
beard, oiled and entirely white, was tied underneath the
chin and fell to his sternum. His hair still had a dash of
pepper in it here and there, and this fell in oiled waves
down his back. Jupiter was dressed (or undressed) in
much the same way, but his white beard was cropped

close and oil-free. His hair seemed unnaturally black by comparison, with some graying only at the temples. Perhaps he'd been using Just For Gods hair cream.

Their eyes glowed with menace, and both sets locked on me.

"Enough of this, Druid," Jupiter growled. "Release Bacchus and the others now."

The Olympians, I had noticed, were not the sort for small talk or pleasantries. They just showed up and demanded that you jump to serve them.

"Thanks for coming to talk, Zeus and Jupiter. Look, I'm not the bad guy here."

"You have imprisoned members of our pantheon, have you not?"

"Yes, but that's only because they were behaving like ass napkins. There's something beyond our petty squabbling that requires your attention. It's Loki and Hel and the end of the world as we know it. Despite what Michael Stipe might think, you will not feel fine when it gets here. You should poke your head outside Olympus once in a while. See, if Loki finds me and manages to kill me, Ragnarok will begin. And most of the Norse gods who were supposed to act as a check on that have checked out prematurely. The threat of Loki is real. He's destroyed the planes of two thunder gods already by himself—Perun's of Russia and Ukko's of Finland."

The Olympians flicked their eyes to Perun, who gave them the barest nod of confirmation. The exchange surprised me, because I thought the Olympians would have known about Perun's plane already, but apparently they hadn't been paying attention to recent events.

"If Loki is able to unite his power with that of Hel and Muspellheim and pull off Ragnarok," I continued, "Olympus goes down in flames with the earth. So the world could use my help and yours. What do you say we put aside our differences for a bit and fight a common enemy? Odin's with us, I can assure you of that." Name-dropping couldn't hurt at this point.

Jupiter's expression of impending wrath modulated into a frown of concern. Zeus's leer underwent a similar transformation. At least they were listening, I thought. But there was no give in Jupiter's tone as he uttered his reply.

"We cannot put aside differences until our pantheons are whole again," he said.

"Okay, I'm sure we can work something out. Let's talk so everybody wins. But, first, could you maybe dispel those storm clouds?" I jerked a thumb at the sky. "That's weird and it's going to draw attention."

"Attention from whom?" Zeus snorted, and glanced toward Windsor Castle and the distant helicopters buzzing like flies around carrion. "I care not what the mortals think."

Oberon said, <Uh, too late, guys. Incoming fireball.>

My hound's gaze was fixed on the northern sky. Following it, I saw a familiar orange meteorite with a heart of white phosphorus headed our way. "Aw, *damn* it!"

Chapter 26

Get right behind me and stay low! I ordered Oberon, and then I shouted, "Don't kill him or Ragnarok begins!" a few scant seconds before Loki landed in our midst and sprayed his surroundings with fire, just to make sure we noticed him. My cold iron amulet protected me and my body shielded Oberon. Perun didn't think fast enough to protect Flidais and she hadn't expected such an attack, so she got tagged badly and screamed as flames engulfed her. Perun and the Olympians weren't harmed by the fire but didn't like the intention behind it; Hermes avoided the fire altogether by flying above it. Zeus and Jupiter called down lightning bolts on Loki from their portable storm clouds overhead but didn't know from experience that he was as immune to them as they were to his fire. Perun did know, however, and he'd obviously been thinking about how to handle Loki Flamehair if a rematch became necessary. He summoned wind and snuffed out Loki's flames as if they were candles.

The mad fucker just laughed that insane laugh and pulled his sword out of his ass. Zeus, now afflicted with acute priapism, gasped and asked him to do that again. Jupiter slapped him to the ground and barked at him to get his priorities straight. Obviously there was some tension between them.

Perun had the right of it. Neutralization was more important than defeating Loki right now. But Perun had already crouched down to aid Flidais rather than press his advantage. Before I could step into the fray, Herne called up his lads; Loki's initial fire burst had set the edges of the clearing aflame, and since it was all part of Windsor Forest, that shot Loki right to the top of Herne's list of people to kill.

"For the King's Forest!" he yelled. He and his hunters charged, confident, hounds at their heels, and Loki grinned and waved them on.

"Yah! Yah! Yah!" he said, a wide smile of malevolence splitting his face. That didn't seem right; the charge of an armed ghost cavalry should have scared the scars off his face. Behind him, a giant hound, six feet tall at the shoulders, winked onto the clearing and woofed, then vanished as suddenly as he'd appeared.

"Herne, wait!" I called. But it was too late. The first huntsman, eager to strike a blow for England, did nothing to avoid the sweep of Loki's sword, thinking it would pass through him as all other weapons did. But Loki—father of Hel, Queen of the Dead—didn't swing an ordinary hunk of steel. When the sword met the huntsman's form and continued on, a ripping noise like someone's jeans tearing announced that something untoward was happening. The nameless huntsman and his horse split apart and exploded into puffs of floating blue ectoplasm, then faded entirely from view. Loki didn't just wound the ghost; he annihilated him completely. Herne and the other hunter almost followed in short order, having charged in too far to escape Loki's reach in time, but they managed to muster a defense and were merely knocked off their horses. The spectral hounds, unable to process that the rules had abruptly changed, kept right on going. They nipped at Loki from all sides, and his sword could dispatch only one at a time. "Fff-fff-ffucking dogs!" he spat, kicking ineffectually at them.

<Hey! I heard that!> Oberon said.

A few more frantic stabs of Loki's sword ended the poor pooches, but they had drawn blood and he limped slightly. It did much to subdue his confidence, and by that time Herne and the remaining huntsman had regained their feet and approached him warily. Loki took them in and looked annoyed. As successful as he'd been thus far, he had not come here to fight ghosts. Hel must have placed an enchantment on that sword to make it effective against the undead. I wondered if it had a name.

Loki backed up, keeping space between himself and Herne, and rested his twitching gaze on me. He raised a bony finger and waggled it in accusation.

"Y-y-you nah, nah-t dwarf con, con, sssstruct," he said, repeating the accusation he'd made back in Poland. True. I'd told him that months ago simply to distract him, and it had worked far better than I ever imagined it would. He could have figured out the truth easily if he had bothered to listen to the dwarfs or asked his daughter, who wanted nothing so much as to please him, but apparently he was determined to do things his way and in his own time. The jerking finger panned to my right. "Zeusssss. Ju-Jupiter. No fff-friends tih, tih, to dwarffffs." I supposed that was his way of building a case against me. "Who you are?" Loki said, and I couldn't tell if it was a question or a statement. "Fffffind out. I wuh, wuh, will!"

<I think the trickster's figured out you tricked him,> Oberon said.

Herne and the remaining huntsman had had their fill of caution. Windsor was on fire and they needed justice. They pressed their attack, weapons held high, and

Loki's giant sword crashed down onto Herne's and slid down its length. The antlered ghost was brought to his knees by the force of the blow, but Loki did no lasting damage. On the upswing, though, he tagged the other huntsman, and the ghost paffed out of existence, decompressed as the blade's magic sundered the ethereal binding of his form.

Herne saw this and the great sword raised high, ready to fall on him anew. I ran to his aid, since the Olympians would clearly do nothing but watch. I didn't want to kill Loki yet, but I wasn't averse to hurting him, and Herne didn't deserve to be sent to eternity by an avatar of madness. The sword fell and Herne leapt out of the path of the downstroke, attempting to tumble so that he could rise and take a swing at Loki's ankle. It was an excellent strategy and might have worked, except that blue smoke rose out of the ground all around the giant and took shape as *draugar,* the undead minions of Hel. And the Queen of the Dead herself rose with them, behind her father, as tall as he and stinking of rot and pestilence. Her right side was a vision of loveliness and her left a wasted husk of a corpse. Without ever glancing our way, she placed her right hand on Loki's shoulder and grated in Old Norse, "Come, Father, we have much to discuss." Then she and Loki melted back into the earth and left us with a dozen blue *draugar* to fight. Herne cursed and I cursed with him. I didn't want the two of them to confab, ever, and now it appeared as if they would and Loki would learn who I truly was. And it was all because Ukko had freed both Loki and Garm at someone's urging. Garm had clearly healed, tracked Loki here, and told Hel where to find him on Midgard.

"Blood and shite and fifty-seven severed cocks!" Herne roared, swinging his sword through the neck of the nearest *draugr.* "I'll be spanked by all the men of Scotland before me mates are wiped out and no one pays for it!"

He kept going like that, slinging curses and lopping off heads, and I joined in lest he be overwhelmed. The *draugar* had not been armed and had little defense against our weapons, but anyone could use help against odds like that. Oberon pitched in by knocking a couple of them down, giving us the time to finish them off.

Once the *draugar* were decomposing into ash at our feet, I turned in disbelief to the Olympians, who hadn't stirred an inch to lend us aid. Zeus closed his eyes in perverse pleasure for a moment before flashing me a crooked grin. "Who was that tall woman who appeared just now? She wasn't half bad."

"Bloody git," Herne whispered.

Chapter 27

"That was Hel," I explained. "Loki's daughter. And now that they're together, Ragnarok could start at any time."

"And what, exactly, would that entail?" Jupiter asked, clearly trying to decide if he should care or not. "You said something about Hel and Muspellheim, but I am unfamiliar with their legends. Why would the nightmares of the ancient Norse trouble the modern world?"

"Okay, fair enough. I'll lay it out for you."

"We should move before we talk," Perun interjected from where he knelt next to Flidais. "Innocent peoples come." He pointed east; there were now four aircraft heading our way, silhouetted in the early-morning sun.

"True," I said. "Let's move deeper into the forest. Would that be agreeable to you?" I raised an eyebrow at the Olympians.

Zeus and Jupiter exchanged glances and gave each other a tight nod.

"All right, give me a moment."

If the fire on the edge of the forest took firm hold and began to spread, we'd have firefighters here in addition to investigators. Aside from that, of course, I couldn't bear to let it continue; these were trees for which the Wild Hunt of Herne had perished, and I knew that somewhere, later, I would find the time to be very upset at their passing. With help from Albion, who was much better at moving earth than I was, I bound turf and dirt from the forest floor to the trunks of the affected trees, smothering the flames before allowing the earth to settle back down. While I did this, Zeus and Jupiter finally deigned to be helpful and transformed their thunderclouds into a thick fog that hid us neatly. Mist swirled and shrouded us as the thump of rotors whipped the air above. They'd have to put someone on the ground to find us now, and I figured we still had some time before that happened, if it happened at all.

I led the Olympians to the place where the huntresses were buried and silently asked Albion to move Mercury underneath the ground to somewhere near them. Perun and Flidais followed, though Flidais moved gingerly and only with Perun's help. She would heal fully from the burns eventually, but I knew from experience that it would take an uncomfortable while.

"Right," I bellowed over the noise of the choppers, which I hoped would move away soon. "You wanted to hear why you should care about the Norse. Let's start with Hel, whom Zeus found so alluring. Hel commands legions of those semi-corporeal zombies called *draugar,* who don't go down easy unless you behead them, and I have sources who tell me that they now have access to modern automatic weapons. She can also command the dead, so every person her army kills is a potential recruit for said army. Her forces will quickly build into something that can't be stopped before you add on anything else, but there's more. The sons of Muspellheim are fire giants—sort of like Loki but without an off switch. They just love their fire and magma and want to share it with everyone. And the frost giants are going to join in too, so you're going to have elemental upheaval on top of the zombie apocalypse. And then there's Jörmungandr, the world serpent, who will presumably pop up somewhere and start shit in the ocean. And we may or may not have to deal with dark elves. Humans won't stand a chance against them. Well, maybe Chuck Norris would. But you know what humans are like. They'll panic and start shooting one another, because they're going to think their enemies are responsible for it all. Or else they'll go into Doomsday mode, assume that the only rule is anarchy, and do something unthinkable to people. Some trigger-happy idiot might even launch a nuclear missile, and then it's over. It's going to be one hell of a bloodbath, guys. When all the humans die—or so many of them it won't make any difference—what's going to happen to you and all the rest of the gods who depend on their belief?"

"Bah!" Zeus exploded. "We go to kill Hel and Loki now and this never happens."

"Who's 'we,' Zeus? Do your powers work on any other plane but Olympus and earth? I know Hermes and Mercury can travel to other planes and return, but are you certain that they remain immortal while they're cut off from this plane and the source of their worship?"

Zeus flicked his eyes to Hermes, and the god of thieves gave a tiny shrug. I pressed my advantage. "Have you ever called forth lightning on a plane other than this one or Olympus? And even if you have, did you not notice the part where Loki thought your thunderbolts were kind of cute?"

Zeus glared at me and said nothing. Jupiter jumped in. "Fine. You kill them both."

"He's not so easily killed, as you just witnessed, and neither is Hel. I certainly don't want to confront them on their turf, where I'll be weakened and they'll be strongest. Come on. You guys are smart. What we need to do is help out Odin and the rest of the good guys and make sure the right side wins when they make their move. Look, I've already managed to take out Fenris—

he was supposed to kill Odin and wreak bonus havoc.
What if Poseidon and Neptune went looking for Jörmungandr and we took him out as well? That would
make Loki and Hel all kinds of worried. They'd crawl
back to their dark holes and shake their fists and say,
'Curse you, unexpectedly effective alliance of powerful
beings!' And then we'd all have ice cream or something.
What do you say we cooperate on this so that we can all
have a future?"

"You mean everyone but Bacchus, I suppose?" Jupiter
said.

"No, I'd be delighted to live in a world where Bacchus
and I can coexist. Seriously. You know, we did so for
more than two thousand years. It's only recently that he
decided I needed to die and I disagreed."

"Tell me why."

"Gladly. This is truth or I am the son of a goat: Some
of his Bacchants tried to make a move on a city under my
protection. I killed a few of them because they were slaying innocent humans. Bacchus took offense—probably
because it was a Druid who did it and you Romans have
always hated Druids—and it escalated from there. Had
his Bacchants not invaded my territory in Arizona, he'd
still be living in blissful ignorance of my existence. But
after I called him some names, he swore to you that he
would kill me, and so here we are. All I want is to be left
alone and I'll do the same to you. I left you alone for
two thousand years and I can do it for two thousand
more. I'll tell you what: As a sign of good faith, I'll return Mercury to you now."

I asked Albion to release Mercury from the earth, and
he complied. Five boulders rose from the ground, the
rock and chalk and clay crumbled away from Mercury's
body parts and melted into the turf, and the overall effect was to make me look like a boss.

Jupiter grunted, staring at the pieces of Mercury,

whose eyes burned with hatred. "Good faith? Are we in a negotiation now?"

"Yes. A treaty of sorts. The Treaty of Windsor, if you will. Hear me out, please?"

"Go on," Jupiter said. Hermes, who had been hovering safely above, floated down to Mercury's chopped limbs and began squidging them onto the torso until they held and began to graft together.

"I'll release the goddesses and Bacchus as well for nothing more than a sworn oath that they will not pursue vengeance against me or my associates. I want the same oath from all the Olympians, and you can have mine in return. I have demonstrated for millennia that I can control myself and not seek revenge for wrongs done against me, so I'd like to see you do the same."

"That would give you permission to behave as you wished in the future if we promise not to pursue vengeance."

"No. I'm asking for amnesty for my trespasses to date, not diplomatic immunity for the future. If I break my oath and mess with you, then I should be punished— though I hope we would talk before we let it get this bad again. By the same token, should any Olympians break their oaths, they can expect to disappear. But let's not focus on what could go wrong. Things are wrong enough as it is. Let's focus on what could go right. Your pantheon will be whole again and have an exciting new challenge coming in the form of Loki's traveling horror show. You will win much good karma for helping the Norse. Also, if we win the fight up here in this part of the world, then your people in Greece and Italy are saved and so are you. If we lose, then it's the kind of loss we won't live to regret."

I paused to let them respond. Jupiter didn't speak to me, however. He stroked his beard contemplatively and spoke instead to Mercury. "You have heard his words.

You know what is at stake. Will you, in exchange for your freedom and a similar pledge from the Druid, swear to hold the Druid and his associates blameless and seek no vengeance on them?"

Now that he was whole again—and perhaps because he'd had a small taste of what awaited him if he refused—Mercury had little problem agreeing to such an oath. At Mercury's words, Zeus cast his eyes to Hermes and chucked his chin by way of a question. The oiled beard lifted up exuberantly as a result and then smacked wetly against his chest. Hermes nodded his assent, albeit grudgingly. He was uncommonly taciturn for a messenger.

"All right, Druid," Jupiter said. "You have an agreement in principle thus far. I cannot speak for all the Roman gods, but I have some hope that I can persuade them."

"The same applies to the Greeks," Zeus added.

"Excellent. If you would not mind, I would like you to start by persuading Pan and Faunus. They are currently preventing me from shifting planes."

"No," Jupiter said. "If you are able to shift planes, then you will be able to abandon the huntresses and Bacchus."

"I am in earnest and wish there to be peace between us. I won't abandon these proceedings. But I must also have the ability to escape should any members of your pantheon choose to attack me before taking their oath. Think of this as your demonstration of good faith. Halt the pandemonium and I'll render you the huntresses directly afterward."

Zeus spoke to Hermes. "Where is Pan now?"

The messenger god's eyes rolled up for a moment and then clinked back into place like slot-machine tumblers. "Here on this isle." Interesting—and logical. Hermes was clearly able to locate any member of the pantheon he wished at any time, which would allow him to ferry messages. It would not be a far stretch to imagine that he could locate anyone he wished that way. If that were so, then perhaps the Olympians hadn't been working with anyone in Tír na nÓg after all. Well, aside from that ambush in Romania. They could have simply followed Granuaile on their own and thus found me.

"Fetch him here immediately." After glancing at Mercury, who was visibly improving but in no shape to fly yet, he added, "and if Jupiter agrees, Faunus too, wherever he is. All possible haste."

Jupiter gave his consent to summon Faunus, and Hermes flitted away into the mist. We spent perhaps ten seconds simply staring at one another, which was nearly unbearable since I felt that Zeus's persistent erection was also staring at everyone.

"You should really call a doctor if that lasts more than four hours," I said, and instantly regretted it.

Both sky gods said, "What?" in unison, and I shook my head by way of telling them to never mind.

"If you're wondering how long it will take them to get here," Jupiter said, "it shouldn't be longer than a few minutes."

"That's truth," Zeus agreed. "Hermes is very quick about such things."

"That's reassuring to hear. Perhaps he will be able to bring the rest of the Olympians here and we can ratify the treaty this very day."

Zeus gave a noncommittal shrug. "It depends on whether or not we are whole again. I will not summon them until Artemis is returned."

"Nor I, until Diana and Bacchus are returned."

"Fair enough. But will you do so if we continue to follow through on our promises and reach a new understanding?"

Zeus said, "I will. I wish to be a part of this battle against Loki and Hel."

Jupiter did not verbalize his agreement but nodded.

Hermes returned with Pan first, who looked amused at our meeting more than anything else. Hermes disappeared into the mist to find Faunus next.

Pan required little persuasion to stop spreading pandemonium throughout England. The entire exercise for him had been one of mischief more than malice, and he'd never been particularly cheesed off about the temporary abduction of the dryads south of Olympus, since he preferred to frolic around Arcadia in any case. He simply liked to fuck with people, and Faunus had given him a great excuse to follow his fancy.

"It's done," he said in Greek, a half smile twisting his features. The horns peeking out through his hair were stubby things rather than the curled rams' horns I've seen in some artist depictions, and his other goat bits were anatomically correct. "Do as you wish and live in peace so long as you leave me to do the same."

"Gladly," I said.

Faunus, when he arrived, took a bit more convincing. Some of those dryads had been his particular favorites.

"They're perfectly healthy," I reminded him, speaking in Latin. "And if Bacchus hadn't persuaded you to spread pandemonium throughout Europe, it never would have been necessary for me to abduct them in the first place. He drew you into his personal conflict, and while I might question your judgment on that score, I don't harbor any ill will against you or any dryad. I simply did what I had to do to escape Bacchus while doing as little real damage as possible."

"Three months of worry about my dryads was pretty damaging," he fumed.

"For that I am sorry. But you have caused me great personal hardship of late and may consider yourself avenged already. Can we exchange forgiveness and move forward in peace?"

Faunus clenched his fists and didn't answer right away. He glanced at Jupiter and saw no sympathy in his hard eyes. His shoulders slumped and he sighed. "Yes," he said.

My own shoulders relaxed. I hadn't realized how tense they'd been. "Thank you. A moment while I check, if you please."

Windsor Forest was an old wood and had been bound to Tír na nÓg long ago, though not by me. I put my hand to an alder tree and concentrated, searching for the tether that would allow me to shift away. It was there, strong and vibrant, waiting to take me wherever I wished. I breathed a soft sigh of contentment.

"Excellent," I said. "I will bring the huntresses back and allow them the opportunity to end their hunt of me and my companions. If they refuse to end it, then I hope you will understand that I cannot release them."

Neither of the sky gods had a problem with this, to my surprise. "On her own head be it," Jupiter said.

I asked Albion to bring up Artemis first. When the rock and clay cleared away from her face, she was even more ready than before to swear an end to it all.

"Pride and arrogance led me to overstep my provenance," she said, addressing me without prompting. "I should have been more modest and attentive to my own responsibilities than to take another's grievance as my own. I have lost my hounds and my dignity as a result."

"Fairly spoken," I said. I proposed the oath to her and asked her to swear it before Zeus, who stepped clearly into her view, boner and all. Artemis winced in disgust when she saw it pressing against the fabric he'd wrapped around his waist, but she swore the oath. I asked Albion to release her completely, and all the earth crumbled away from her body. Hermes descended to put her back together as he had done with Mercury. The Roman messenger had now healed sufficiently to stand, though he wasn't quite ready to fly yet.

Diana was not nearly so ready to capitulate. She flatly refused, in fact, vowing instead to slay me and feed me to the crows before violating my bones in ways yet to be determined. Artemis implored her to reconsider, but Diana would have none of it. Jupiter even leaned on her a bit, demanding that she give up her hunt in the interests of Olympus. Diana suggested that he fornicate with Faunus. I probably shouldn't have taunted her and kicked her head back in the Netherlands. And there was no telling what Flidais had said to her while I was blacked out.

Jupiter's face purpled and he whipped his head around to me. "Do with her as you will, Druid," he said. "I will fight for her no more, though I still wish to see Bacchus freed."

I nodded thoughtfully, silently thanking her for making me seem reasonable by comparison, and then said, "Perhaps Diana will think better of her words if given sufficient time to mull them over. Shall we return here, say, once a month, to inquire whether she has changed her mind?"

"That is a noble idea, though I think it far too generous," Jupiter said. "Once a decade should be sufficient."

"I would rather be too generous than not in such cases."

"As you wish."

<One day, Atticus was amazed to discover that when Jupiter said, "As you wish," what he really meant was, "I love you.">

I almost laughed. *Gods, not now, Oberon.* It would be impolitic to show amusement as a cursing Diana was walled up in clay and rock once again and sent back into the earth to marinate in her frustration. I asked Albion to move her elsewhere, far away from this spot but remaining underground, and to keep her out of reach of anyone who might decide to attempt digging her up.

"And so we come to Bacchus," I said. "I'm afraid that he is beyond conversation at the moment. He is deep in his madness, a rather murderous sort."

Jupiter frowned. "How do you know? It's been weeks since he disappeared."

"I sent him to a land of slow time. It's been weeks for us but a fraction of a second for him. As far as he knows, I just got finished kicking him in the chest. So when you pull him back here—and it will be you who does it, not me—he will be furious. Can you control him?" Jupiter assured me that he could. "And assuming that goes well—a dangerous assumption, I know—will you both call the rest of the Olympians here to cement our alliance against Loki and Hel?"

Zeus nodded enthusiastically and looked excited, and Jupiter agreed in more reserved tones.

"Just in case—should I be forced to leave—how do I contact you?"

Hermes looked up at my question and rose from the side of Artemis, who was mending quickly. "You can summon winds as a Druid, can you not?"

Thinking of Fragarach, I said, "To a limited extent, yes."

"Summon a westerly wind, then," Hermes said. "Invoke the names of Iris and myself, and speak to us as it blows past you. Zephyrus, god of the west wind and husband of Iris, will hear and tell us."

"Fair enough." I swiveled my head around to check on Flidais and Perun. "You might want to leave before I do this. He's about ten gallons short of a keg, if you know what I mean."

Flidais shook her head. "I wish to witness on behalf of the Tuatha Dé Danann."

"All right," I said. "Jupiter, I'm going to open a portal right here." I traced my finger in a vertical circle, describing a hoop through which a circus animal might jump. "Bacchus will have his arms splayed toward you thusly." I demonstrated by raising my arms forward and a bit out from the sides. "Reach in and pull him back through by his right arm, because his left one is broken. Do not put your leg or any other part of your body through the portal, or you risk being caught in the same slow timestream. I need you to do this as quickly as possible so that I can close the portal behind him, because it drains the earth to keep them open. Okay?"

"It shall be as you say."

I checked everyone's position before I began. The last thing I wanted was for someone to push *me* into the portal. But no one was trying to sneak up on my six.

Oberon, please go put one of your paws on that tree over there. If we have to bail on this thing, I want you to be ready.

<I am so ready! Ready for a beach in Argentina.>

Me too.

"Here we go," I said, and created a binding between this plane and the Time Island where I'd kicked Bacchus. I scooted away to the side and headed for the tree, ready to shift away if necessary. Jupiter reached in and pulled out the personification of an unchained tantrum, green-veined and still roaring in rage.

Chapter 28

The Romans acted surprised when the god of madness would not be reasoned with. Bacchus *threw* Jupiter at Mercury—or tried to, anyway—because Jupiter was off balance and holding on too tightly to his arm. Jupiter didn't let go, however, and pulled Bacchus down with him as Mercury scrambled out of the way. I closed the portal while they tumbled in the mist, Bacchus continuing to bellow his primal vocalizations over Jupiter's loud demands that he calm down, until Jupiter managed to pin him on the ground.

But that was just the beginning, because then Bacchus twisted his head and saw me. His face began to cycle through several colors—pink, green, brown, purple—as he bared his teeth and let go with more decibels than I thought vocal cords could manage. The helicopters had turned away but could still be heard until Bacchus drowned them out.

My amulet thunked against my chest, and I wondered what he'd just tried to cast on me. One by one, the heads of Artemis, Mercury, Hermes, and Zeus all jerked as if someone had punched them in the face, but they didn't look any different afterward, except perhaps a bit annoyed. Jupiter head-butted the back of Bacchus's skull, driving Bacchus's chin into the dirt, and bellowed at him to stop. He didn't stop, though. He turned his head the

other way and saw Flidais and Perun standing there
without any magical wards except for fulgurites protecting them from lightning, and he flung at them the same
spell of madness he had hurled at the rest of us. For
that's what happened: Flidais and Perun went mad and
tried to kill everyone—including each other. Perun called
down lightning, striking down both Hermes and Faunus, and Flidais drew knives that she had recovered
from the assault on Diana and started laying about her,
beginning with Perun. Had she been at 100 percent she
might have ended him, but, damaged as she was, she got
one knife into him before he batted her away to land
nearby. She rose, saw Zeus, and charged him in a manner that wasn't simply batshit but rather a whole *cave*
full of batshit, eyes crazed and drool leaking out of her
mouth. She'd already forgotten that she'd been fighting
Perun; she would now attack whatever she saw first.

"I *told* you Bacchus was a dick!" I shouted. Jupiter
made no sign that he had heard because he was still
struggling to keep Bacchus contained. The demented
eyes found me again and then fell off to my right side.

I wondered for the briefest moment what he was looking at, and then realized with horror what he intended.
I spun around to my right, where my hound was waiting
only three steps away to shift to Tír na nÓg, his paw on
the tree as I'd instructed.

Oh, no. Oberon, stay with me—

My hound flinched and stepped back from the tree,
and I couldn't shift him away without that contact.
Something changed in his eyes as his lips curled back
from his teeth, his ears flattened, and he growled at me.

Oberon? Oberon, answer me. It's Atticus.

He didn't reply. I was getting nothing from him. The
iron talisman around his neck hadn't been powerful
enough to stop the frenzy of Bacchus; if I wanted him
truly protected I'd have to bind his aura to it like I had

mine. The muscles bunched in his hind legs and my heart sank.

Oberon, no!

He leapt at my throat. I was able to sidestep, and we collided broadside as he passed. I scrambled for the tree in the few seconds I would have while he landed and turned to attack again.

Damn it, Oberon! I began to mentally shout his favorite words to him in hopes that it would shake him loose from the thrall of Bacchus. *Sausage! Poodles! Snacks! Treats! Barbecue!*

None of it helped. He bounded after me and I put the tree between us, which would slow him down a little bit but wouldn't keep me free of his teeth for more than an extra second or two. Zeus must have thrown Flidais our way, because she landed behind me with a shriek and crunch of leaves. When she got to her feet she'd probably come after me, being the nearest thing she could kill, or else she'd attack Oberon and wouldn't restrain herself. Bacchus had made a bollocks of everything, and Jupiter still hadn't been able to get him to shut up.

Taking what I considered an acceptable risk, I squatted down next to the tree so that my right side was protected against the trunk, and held up my left forearm crosswise just below my chin. I didn't have long to wait before Oberon barreled into me, taking my arm into his mouth in the instinctive strike at the throat and laying me out flat. His teeth sank deep, and he tore into it, shaking his head in an attempt to move the arm out of the way. In a moment he'd let go and dive in for the kill. I numbed the pain in my arm to keep my head clear.

I put my right hand on the trunk of the tree and found the tether to Tír na nÓg. Tearing my own forearm in the process, I yanked Oberon's head toward the trunk so that he'd have contact with it—he certainly had contact with me already. I heard Flidais approaching, so far gone that she was not merely letting loose with a battle cry but actually ululating.

When Oberon's muzzle hit the tree I shifted us to Tír na nÓg, leaving Flidais and Perun to the dubious mercy of the Olympians. I noticed the quiet first—the Fae plane lacked screaming gods. I resumed talking to Oberon on the theory that his thrall to Bacchus would be severed with the plane shift. When I'd kicked Bacchus into the portal that sent him to the Time Islands, all of his Bacchants came back to themselves after I closed it.

Oberon, stop! It's Atticus! Oberon, no!

His eyes cleared and he went still. <Atticus?>

I smiled in relief. *Yeah, it's me. You can let go now.*

<What? Gahh!> He unlocked his jaws and my bloody arm flopped down. <What happened? You're bleeding! Great big bears, did I do that?>

Yes, but it's okay, it's not your fault. Bacchus drove you mad.

<But I attacked you?>

Don't worry, buddy, I'll be fine. I'm already healing.

Oberon began to hack and spit as best as he could. <I have to get this out of my mouth. Is there water nearby?>

We can shift there. I took him to the river of Time Islands first so that he could rinse out. He kept apologizing to me the whole time, and I did my best to soothe and reassure him. I closed up the skin on my arm quickly and showed him it was all fine, even though it would take longer to rebuild the muscle underneath.

I hoped Flidais and Perun wouldn't be killed by the Olympians in their fit of madness—and I hoped they wouldn't kill each other. As long as they survived, however, I would think that had gone very well. Both Zeus and Jupiter now had reason to believe me, Jupiter owed me one, because he'd said he could control Bacchus and then couldn't, and I could now shift anywhere I wished. It didn't really matter if Bacchus never swore to leave me alone; without the help of the other Olympians, he'd never catch me.

Of course, I was rather saddened that Herne had to pay such a steep price in all of this. I wondered if there was any way I could possibly make it up to him. Perhaps Manannan Mac Lir could do something for him.

Shifting closer to the center of Tír na nÓg, we found Granuaile in Goibhniu's shop, resting on a cot. The arrow had been removed, the wound bandaged, and she was staring at the ceiling, concentrating on her healing process.

Without saying hello, I affected a casual manner, as if I'd done nothing more than wait in line at the bank, and said, "Well, I made it out of there."

Her face lit up when she saw me, which served as a reminder of how very lucky I was.

"Atticus! Good. Now I can stop worrying."

"Not quite yet. Thanks to Bacchus, Flidais and Perun have gone a bit crazy, and we should probably lie low for a while. We need to go somewhere far away where you can heal properly. Preferably a Pacific island or somewhere in the New World. Someplace without an Old Way to get there. Any suggestions?"

Her eyes rolled back up to the ceiling as she considered, then fixed back on me. "How about Japan?" she said. "I've never been there but I've always wanted to go."

"Done."

<Are we going to get some authentic Kobe beef? I heard all the stuff in America that's labeled Kobe isn't the real thing.>

We might. You never know.

"Where's Goibhniu?" I asked, looking around the shop.

"He ducked out shortly after removing the arrow. He hadn't heard yet about the Morrigan dying and seemed pretty upset when I told him."

"Oh. That's understandable."

Something in my tone caused Granuaile to examine my face with concern. "You need to talk about it, don't you?"

"Yeah," I said solemnly. "I do. We will once we get ourselves settled in Japan." The practicalities of making that happen suddenly made me laugh. "Hal is going to shit an ostrich when I call him from Tokyo. But first I'm going to dash back to the cabin and get some clothes and things for us, all right? I'll be back as soon as I can."

I planted a kiss on her forehead and another on the top of Oberon's, then left Goibhniu's taproom to shift somewhere else entirely. I intended to go to the cabin as I'd said, but I needed to make a detour first.

Chapter 29

Lord Grundlebeard was overdue for a visit. He was my best lead on finding out who had orchestrated my hunting and attempted assassination. But I didn't know his real name, and if I asked about him in Tír na nÓg he might hear of it before I could get to him. A better gamble, I decided, would be to seek out Midhir. Either he was the man behind it all anyway or he could tell me where to find Grundlebeard.

If Midhir truly was the mastermind, then I didn't want Oberon and Granuaile along; neither of them had the magical defenses I had, and Midhir truly was the sort of magician who could turn someone into a newt. They'd be safe with Goibhniu.

Instead of shifting to our cabin in Colorado, I shifted to Brí Léith in Ireland, the old *síd* of Midhir. It's near the modern wee village of Ardagh in County Longford. Some people call such hills "faery mounds" today, and some may even harbor a genuine superstition about them but don't understand their true function: Every single *síd* of the Tuatha Dé Danann is an Old Way to Tír na nÓg. In fact, they are the oldest of the Old Ways.

When the Milesians defeated the Tuatha Dé Danann with their iron, they said—thinking they were clever—"We'll split the land with you. You can have the bit of Ireland that's underground." The Tuatha Dé Danann said, "Okay, fine," though in much more heroic language. But of course they didn't live in their barrows forever; they simply used them as the first fixed points for channeling the earth's magic to create the plane of Tír na nÓg and bind it.

Almost all of the *síde* were filled in now, and the Tuatha Dé Danann didn't leave enough artifacts behind to tempt archaeologists to go mucking around in them. But Ireland's elemental, Fódhla, remembered all the interior spaces as they used to be. It would take little effort on her part to restore the interior of any *síd*. And once a *síd* recovered its original space, then a Druid looking to use the Old Way hidden inside could do so.

I wanted to do it this way rather than shift internally in Tír na nÓg to Midhir's land. The internal tether would land me outside his castle or fortress or whatever he called his home, which would doubtless be guarded. The old *síd,* however, long abandoned and forgotten, would put me somewhere inside his walls. That's why most of the old mounds were filled in now; the Tuatha Dé Danann didn't want random citizens appearing by accident in their parlors. I heard it happened a few times to Aenghus Óg in recent decades, whose *síd* at Newgrange had been closed and overgrown for centuries before archaeologists reopened it in the 1960s. By utter chance, a bloke or five had stepped along the precise path to take them to Tír na nÓg, and then Aenghus had to feed the unfortunate sods to something hungry. Couldn't have them returning and telling everyone the way to Faerie.

I took a moment to take in the view and enjoy the sun and air. It had been too long since I'd been home. Fódhla—a poetic name for Ireland in the same way Albion was for Britain, named after one of the tutelary goddesses of the isle—welcomed me back and was only too happy to restore Brí Léith to its former shape. The surface changed only slightly, but underneath it was hollow and spacious again, and the entrance appeared on the south side of the hill. I asked Fódhla to oblige me with a small skylight at the top to provide some light in the inner chamber, and she knocked that out in a few seconds. After checking my surroundings to make sure no one was watching me, I cast camouflage on myself and ducked inside.

It took some time to discover the proper path. Every *síd* was different, and the paths were laid out in such a way that accidental passage was unlikely—but not impossible. As I looked at the ground in the magical spectrum, the path began to show up as a binding once I took the first two steps in the correct order. So there was a significant amount of shuffling to be done, because the path itself wasn't something the elemental could help me find. I stepped and pranced around for three hours, my back and left forearm healing all the while, before a sidestep on the north side revealed the third step to me, and then the fourth, and so on. I paused to draw Fragarach and boost my speed and strength. I fully expected defenses of some kind on the other side. As I wound my way along the path, the dim ambience from the skylight faded until I was plunged into total darkness and the air cooled precipitously. I had passed through to a damp, dark chamber somewhere in Tír na nÓg, most likely a cellar on Midhir's grounds. I froze and silently cast night vision through the silver charm on my necklace. It didn't help me at all. There wasn't any light to magnify.

I smelled mildew and—over a coppery tang—peat and something that reminded me of bitter almonds. The white noise of industrial earth was gone, no background hum of electronics or motors or anything of the kind. But nature was missing too: no wind or water or scurrying of tiny feet. Except that something was breathing softly nearby. Perhaps more than one something. I couldn't locate it; the acoustics were bizarre, and the noise seemed to echo faintly from all sides. The chamber I was in might be stone and rather large.

Slick quarried stone or tile lay underneath my feet, so I was cut off from magic here. I'd have to rely on my bear charm, and it was already draining because I'd never dispelled my camouflage. I let it go, along with magical sight, because the darkness was camouflage enough and I might need the magic for something else—and besides, the magical sight wasn't showing me what waited there. The night vision I left active in hopes that I'd find a minuscule light source to help me survey my surroundings. Not for the first time, I wished I had some way to summon light, or even fire, the way some witches and wizards could. I'd wrap my shirt around Fragarach and use it as a torch if I could. As it was, I had no choice but to explore by touch and hope I didn't wake whatever slumbered in the dark. Or stumble into a trap. I felt like the Inquisition victim in Poe's "The Pit and the Pendulum."

Stretching out with my left foot and feeling with my toes to make sure there was something solid underneath them, I took a slow step forward. Nothing happened, but there was progress. But when I lifted my right leg to take another step, I must have triggered a magical motion sensor, for a loud *fwoosh* announced the sudden lighting of candles all along a high shelf that circled the room—which was, in fact, circular, once I was able to focus. Though candlelight is generally quite soft, so many lighting at one time in total darkness while I had night vision on blinded me for a few moments. I dispelled the night vision and saw that I had lots of company in the room. The light also woke—and blinded—the many, many small creatures that had been sleeping on another shelf below the candles, about waist high.

They were tiny pale-green winged humanoids with

flat black eyes and mouths out of proportion to the rest of the head. Hairless and sleek, they had stumpy legs and thick, overlong arms with large, three-fingered hands. In the middle of each palm—though I couldn't see them yet—they had another mouth. I recognized these guys. I didn't know what their proper name was, but I called them pieholes, because they didn't really care what they shoved into the three they had. Goibhniu claimed that these were the original tooth faeries, but I didn't know how humanity could have possibly transformed these things into stories of kind critters that gave a damn about children's teeth. These could never be mistaken for anything but what they were—the ravenous, swarming bastard spawn of the Dagda and something he humped one day.

I supposed many pantheons had some incurably horny figures in them, viewed by their adherents with everything from amusement to fear. For the Greeks it was Zeus and Pan; in Vedic tradition it was Indra; and for the Irish, it was the Dagda, whose reputation, like that of many pagan deities, suffered somewhat at the hands of Christian scribes. He was sometimes depicted as a rather oafish sort with an abnormally large reproductive organ. It wasn't because he was freakishly gifted in truth; it was merely to mock and stigmatize his sexuality. To the Irish he was unequivocally good, gifted with vast powers, and his carnal proclivities represented his urge to create life rather than an aberrant personality. Sometimes the life he created was a son or daughter of extraordinary magical talent—namely, Aenghus Óg, Midhir, and Brighid. But sometimes the life he created was bloody dangerous, and over the years a vast menagerie of magical self-sustaining horrors was born. Pieholes were one of the worst, and I thought they'd been wiped out centuries ago for everyone's safety.

Unfortunately, once they blinked a few times, the pieholes recognized me as well: I was food and they were hungry. That bitter-almond smell was their collected shit, which ringed the base of the walls in discolored chalky mounds like mine tailings. Their wings snapped up from their backs, and their yawning mouths grumbled with a low rolling sound between a drone and a growl.

"Guys. Wait," I said, foolishly thinking they'd listen. The warning growl stopped in unison and there was a half second of silence before they screeched and launched themselves at me, hundreds of them from all directions, hands outstretched and miniature mouths gaping with sharp, yellowed teeth.

I dropped to the ground on my right side, tossed aside Fragarach, and curled into the fetal position, managing to throw a protective left arm across the side of my face and ear. They fell upon me, and their hands latched on to whatever they could and bit down with those palm-jaws like lampreys, uncaring if it was cloth or raw meat underneath. My cold iron aura destroyed them in a puff of ashes before they could take a bite with their much larger mouths, but that didn't stop them from tearing up two little gobbets of my flesh each and then plopping them wetly back onto my ruined skin as they expired. More of them kept coming; they weren't quick learners. All they saw when their brothers exploded was a clearer path to dinner. Some of them chomped onto the half-masticated pieces of me that didn't have to be torn free, but plenty more kept going for the freshest meat available. My whole left side seethed with them, a boiling mess of blood and cloth and ashes mixed with shredded muscle tissue. I triggered my healing charm and let it draw all the magic it wanted; it wasn't the time for conservation. Even if I somehow survived the onslaught, I'd bleed out quickly if I didn't get the wounds under control. I didn't try to shut down the pain, because there was no point in diverting my limited magic to comfort. The verdict on whether I lived or died would be delivered soon enough.

Had I brought Granuaile and Oberon, they would have been consumed inside a minute. Cold iron was the only thing giving me a wisp of a chance. Hundreds of tiny bites have a way of turning seconds into hours. Teeth scissored through the flesh all along my left side, and then the plosive thump of the faeries' deaths punched each wound before a new set of teeth took another bite. I gritted my own teeth against the scream that wanted to erupt as my substance was gnawed away. No one would hear me over the screeching of the faeries, and even if they did, it probably wouldn't be someone anxious to help me. Apart from that, I was afraid that if I opened my mouth, one of the pieholes would reach into mine with its hand-jaws and chomp down on my tongue.

After an interminable time of sharp, churning pain, the noise and the bites and the deaths ended, leaving me shredded and covered in a thick paste of ashy blood. It drained slowly through the grate in the floor, which I had not been able to see until now—faeries had been everywhere. The floor was indeed a slick quarried stone, sloped gently to encourage the draining of blood—the source of that coppery smell. My thoughts were sluggish and I didn't want to move lest I exacerbate my condition, but I had to do something. My bear charm was empty, and if I didn't get out of there soon, I never would. My eyelids drooped and I wanted to sleep but knew I'd never wake up if I did. How had Midhir fed those damn things? He had obviously fed them regularly or the shit wouldn't be piled so high, and he hadn't schlepped in victims via the Old Way—it had been unused for centuries before I stepped through. Still, he'd maintained a huge swarm of pieholes here to guard it.

That meant it was a weakness in his defenses he'd gone to great lengths to protect.

I half-dragged, half-flopped my left arm off my face and whimpered when I saw the chewed tissue. Though the blood wasn't pumping—my healing charm had shut down most of it and I was functioning on collateral circulation—I thought I could see a faint gleam of bone near my wrist and the top of my hand. I felt a new appreciation for the word *raw*.

There was no way I'd be able to walk the Old Way out of here. My left leg wouldn't be in any better condition than my arm, and I was drifting dangerously close to passing out. Even if I could get to my feet, I couldn't cast magical sight to see the proper path anyway. And that was probably my doom right there; the exit was most likely as plain as day in the magical spectrum if I only knew where to look—the Morrigan had set up something like that at one of her lairs—but all I could see now were very broad hints that I was well and truly fucked.

I turned my head up to the ceiling and could feel that it had been liberally gnawed on. The haircut Oberon had been suggesting had been delivered by faeries anxious to sample my scalp.

The ceiling offered no signs of a trapdoor or any other egress. No ladders rose from the floor to the ceiling. But there had to be a way out besides the Old Way in.

The drain, perhaps? Too small for me. Where was the conveniently human-sized ventilation shaft that appeared in every movie?

Ventilation, I surmised, was supplied by tiny holes no bigger than a sparrow underneath the shelf of candles. They were gaps, basically, between stones. Large and numerous enough for good air flow, far too small for the tooth faeries—or me—to get through.

My attention returned to the drain. Too small to

squeeze through, but perhaps it led to plain old earth below, something I could tap into and replenish myself.

Something else was draining through the grate besides my blood. It thinned out and flowed more quickly near my feet. There was water coming from behind me, but just beneath my feet.

I tried to push myself up using my right arm, but that was a fail; my abdominal muscles, not to mention parts of my back, had been chewed upon and were on strike. I had to pull myself around using only my right side in extremely awkward fashion.

The water trickled out from a source in the rock wall, no bigger than the ventilation holes above, so it offered no escape. It did offer hope, however.

That thin trickle represented the only source of water for the pieholes, so they had been careful not to shit anywhere near it. The space on either side was clear for a few feet, and what it revealed was blessed, glorious bare earth. The quarried stone didn't extend all the way to the walls—it had simply appeared that way on all other sides because the hills of faerie shit obscured the stone's edge.

I should have known there would be earth here somewhere. There could hardly be an Old Way without it—nothing to bind to otherwise. Now all I had to do was drag myself over there before I died. It was probably fifteen feet.

I pushed it as much as I dared and it still took me three or four bloody minutes to inch my way across the slick stone that distance, but the agony of my left side made it seem longer. Based on the look I'd had at my arm and hand, I imagined that my left side looked like ground beef, or like Hel's dead and rotting half. Most of the motor function was gone, so it was all deadweight. I curled my fingers around the edge of the stone and made one last heave before flopping the back of my undamaged right hand onto the earth. Energy rushed into me through my tattoos, and with it came relief. I drank deeply from the water stream to rehydrate, laboriously shut off every source of pain, and drifted off to sleep, healing now on autopilot.

When I awoke an indeterminate time after, the candles had either burned out or the magical switch had snuffed them due to a profound lack of movement. I shivered and a new thrill of pain washed up my spine. I was running a fever and had the chills because my many open wounds had no doubt become infected. I took a drink from the stream to slake my parched throat—I'd been unconscious for a good while—and my bladder informed me it was ready for a blowout special. I had to move.

I tried to lift my left arm experimentally to see what kind of calamity would ensue. Turned out I couldn't extend it properly or raise it far from my side. It was locked into a bent position because vital hunks of my triceps were missing. My leg was in much the same shape; my range of movement was very limited and it sure wouldn't hold my weight. I could rebuild all that tissue in a week provided I ate a whole lot of protein and kept in touch with the earth, but there was no food in this chamber. I had been the food. I couldn't get better until I escaped; I'd only get weaker.

I filled up my bear charm and then reluctantly removed the back of my hand from the caress of the earth. Firmly bearing down on the pain in my side, I pushed myself up with my right hand until I was leaning, awkwardly, on what I supposed I must call my right flank, though I didn't generally think of myself as having flanks. The darkness remained uncomfortably Stygian.

Grunting and sweating with the effort, feeling tugs of tissue that I knew would be screaming at me had I let them, I forced myself to a precarious sitting position—enough that I could take my weight off my right arm for a few seconds. I lifted it from the floor and waved it madly over my head and almost cried in relief when the candles relit. That was a remarkable binding, and I hoped I'd have an opportunity to learn it.

Using my right arm for support once again—a bit unsteady and weak—I looked down and gasped. Scabbed and purulent skin covered most of my wounds, but many were still open. With smaller wounds my healing spell could cannibalize tissue from elsewhere to fill in what had been lost, but in this case I'd lost way too much.

My condition wouldn't improve until I ate a cow or five. Casting magical sight, I scanned the walls for clues. They were made of flat flagstones piled on top of one another and mortared together with lime. I didn't spy anything magical until I looked behind me above the spring. One of the stones was outlined in the telltale white glow of magic. I heaved myself slowly over there and pushed it, breathing heavily by the time I made it.

Crackling and grinding ensued as twenty slabs of stone broke free of the mortar and rotated out into the circular space, forming a stairway beginning directly over the spring and just missing the slope of the first mound of faerie shit. The stones were long ones so that they swung out past the two shelves where the candles rested and the pieholes had roosted. Once safely above the candles, the stones didn't swing out: A bunch of them swung inward instead, creating a narrow doorway through which I could escape, if only I could get there. Natural light filtered from it, which was especially encouraging.

Climbing those steps with only half a functioning body wasn't going to be easy, but I didn't have a choice, just as I didn't have a choice about whatever waited for me up there.

Fragarach still lay where I'd tossed it. The strap to its

scabbard had been gnawed through, but the scabbard itself had fallen off my back and looked intact where it lay near the center of the room. I dispelled magical sight and boosted my strength in hopes that it would allow me to move faster. Dragging myself around was still laborious but quicker with the assist. I retrieved Fragarach and slid it into the scabbard, took time to make a generous donation to the drain, and then returned to the bottom of the steps as the energy in my bear charm dwindled. I paused to rest and fill it back up. I'd have to deplete it for strength again to get up the stairs; I doubted I'd be able to make it otherwise.

Once I was ready, I clutched Fragarach by the scabbard and reached up to the second step, laying it there. Then I placed my hand flat on the step, elbow high, bunched my right leg under me, and pressed myself up to a somewhat vertical if severely asymmetrical position. The movement pulled my mangled left side in new, subtle ways, but the stabbing pain that accompanied it wasn't subtle. I paused to deal with this torture, then improvised a wretched, miserable bunny hop to ascend the stairs. At the top, gasping and sweating, I discovered that the passage was a very short hallway that led to another open door, through which I could see sunlight on stone and hear the chuckle of a fountain. Once into the hallway I was able to brace myself against the wall and knew that the going would be a tiny bit easier. I closed my eyes and smiled, relieved that I'd made it out of that pit. Whatever awaited me ahead, at least I wouldn't literally die at the hands of greedy pieholes.

The open doorway was made of shifted flat stones identical to the ones on the inside of the pit. Hopping through it, I found myself facing a hallway graced with paintings and sculptures and lit by circular skylights spaced periodically down its length. I was standing in a niche with a small stone selkie fountain on one side and a chair on the other, the skylight above me presumably disguising this secret entrance as a reading nook. Or something.

The ground was blessedly bare underneath my feet, and I could feel the magic there—a common feature of all the homes of the Tuatha Dé Danann. With the exception of a few rooms here and there, they would never willingly cut themselves off from power for the sake of interior design. And who needs a foundation when you can bind everything you need to stay still with the earth's help? Their estates also rarely had a second floor; if they did, they were reserved for non-magical guests or those who did not depend on the earth for their power. That meant I wouldn't have to climb any more stairs to find Midhir. Having a steady supply of magic again, I cast camouflage and magical sight. The nose of the selkie fountain glowed white, giving its purpose away, and I pressed it. The stones behind me shifted and the door to the piehole pit closed. Midhir couldn't have used this as a way to feed them, though; they would have flown out if he had. That meant there was some other way to access the room, but I wasn't terribly interested now that I was out of there.

I checked the hall to see if any noises I'd made had drawn attention. Apparently not. There were no signs of magical booby traps in either direction, so I took a cautious hop into an exposed position. Now that I was paranoid about discovery, it sounded abnormally loud. I supposed there was no good way to hop stealthily. Since my left side was ruddy useless, I turned right, holding Fragarach in my hand and using the wall for support, giving it fist bumps as I hopped. It turned to a smooth plaster past the niche, interrupted at intervals by some works of art. The first door I came to led to an unused bedroom. Past it on the left, an open archway hinted at a parlor or library or some other sitting area full of books, and, through that, another room promised a much larger living space that might lead to a kitchen. I hoped I'd make it there and find something to eat. But there was one more door I wanted to check before I crossed the hall and moved on. It wouldn't do to leave it at my back without knowing what was in there.

It was another bedroom—the master suite, in fact. It was tastefully appointed with a sod floor fed by regular waterings and sun angling through a long glass panel on the far side of the very high ceiling. On the near side of the ceiling, a wrought-iron chandelier with those ingenious motion-sensing candles flared to life as I opened the door. Midhir—it was definitely him, for I recognized the Druidic tattoos on his biceps—hung upside down from it, wrapped in iron chains to nullify his magic. His throat had been cut, and the blood had sheeted down his face and turned the grass below a dark red. Unable to cast a healing spell and cut off from all earthly aid by his suspension, he'd bled out.

"Gods below," I breathed, "I'm in deep shit now."

Whoever had done this to Midhir could easily do the same thing to me. I could cast spells past my iron amulet and aura, of course, but wrap me up in that much iron and cut me off from the earth and I was as vulnerable as a tadpole.

I cast a wild-eyed glance back down the hall, expecting a trap of some sort to be sprung. I immediately assumed I'd either suffer the same fate as Midhir or else be framed for his murder. But seconds ticked by and no cries of alarm sounded. No one snuck up in camouflage and punched me in the junk. The phrase *deathly silent* came to mind.

My panic gradually faded as minutes passed and it became clear that the world was unaware that I'd just found the body of an ancient being. Eventually, though, they'd figure it out; if nothing else, once Midhir's body was discovered, Brighid's hounds would be brought in and they'd pick up my scent.

I toyed briefly with the idea of shifting to a hound myself to pick up some scent clues but discarded the idea as unwise when I was so messed up. Hounds can't hop on one side very well. And, besides, once this got out, Brighid's hounds would pick up the scent of whoever had really done this.

Though it was unwise to approach any farther and place myself in the same room as the murder, I spied another tangle of chains, resting on the feather bed. This demanded a closer look, for there were clothes underneath the chains—clothes I thought I recognized. And as a couple of hops improved my angle of vision, I saw that there wasn't actually a body there—just ashes and foppish clothing that could only belong to Lord Grundlebeard.

I had no way of knowing if those were really the ashes of Lord Grundlebeard or if he—or someone—was clever enough to fake his death this way. But Midhir's death certainly wasn't faked. And a powerful magician like him couldn't have been so thoroughly dominated this way except by another member of the Tuatha Dé Danann.

Though I knew it was all conjecture, the deaths of Midhir and Grundlebeard suggested that they had indeed been involved in the hunt for us. They'd kept an eye on Granuaile through divination or else had spoken to someone who did, and then they'd communicated with vampires and dark elves and Fae assassins and shuttled them around the Old World where they'd be most likely to run into us. They'd even told the Olympians where to ambush us back in Romania. And maybe they'd told Ukko where to find Loki, thus setting him free and possibly accelerating the beginning of the end. In that sense, this ending for them felt like justice.

But they hadn't been the true bosses. They'd been something akin to executive assistants, a layer of insulation from where the real orders originated, and once Granuaile and I had escaped their net, these two, who could point fingers and name a name, had to be eliminated. Something else clicked into place: It had always bothered me that Faunus began to spread pandemonium throughout Europe at the same time that Perun's plane was destroyed by Loki. But Grundlebeard could have easily sent a message to Faunus to begin as soon as I arrived at the Fae Court and then made up a cover story to match. He'd probably been the one to send that pod of yewmen after us as well—at someone else's orders, of course. But now that someone had drunk his milkshake, and Midhir's too.

Thinking of milkshakes reminded me of the kitchen and my dire need for protein. There was no good I could do by lingering in the bedroom, but I could do myself all kinds of good if I found something to eat. My stomach clenched and rumbled at the thought—genuine hunger pangs. If I fed it, perhaps I'd be able to think more clearly.

The parlor-cum-library, when I hopped through it, turned out to be one of my favorite rooms ever. A tree grew in the far corner to my right, its trunk allowed to stretch up through a hole in the ceiling and spread its canopy there. The floor was a lovely trimmed lawn. Starting on either side of the tree, walnut bookshelves lined the walls, oddly but fabulously filled with nothing but graphic novels and manga. Centered in the room, a copy of Alan Moore's *V for Vendetta* was set precisely in the middle of a matching walnut coffee table set low to the ground, Japanese style. The room invited you to pick a graphic novel and read on the grass, perhaps leaning against the trunk of the tree. But the placement of *V for Vendetta* bothered me. It hadn't been casually laid near one of the edges, which would indicate that it had been left by a reader. It was aligned squarely in the center, so that the table edges acted like a frame, directing one's attention to the cover. Perhaps it was a message of some kind? If so, intended for whom? For whomever found Midhir's body? If Midhir had been killed to conceal the identity of the real person behind my hunting, was this message intended for me? Or maybe Midhir's death had nothing to do with me at all. The vendetta might have been against him rather than me, and this timing was entirely coincidental. Regardless, it only increased my suspicion that there was a trap here somewhere and I had yet to spring it.

I hopped forward to take a peek around the corner into the next room. It must be special in some way, for, unlike the rest of the floors I had seen, this one was covered with marble. The ceiling was high and frescoed with lots of naked flesh, but my view of the room—clearly a large one—was blocked by square marble pillars around the perimeter. It suggested an entertainment room of some sort; the middle would be entirely open and servants would circulate in the space behind the pillars, darting between them to refill plates and glasses and take away empties. It was much longer than it was wide. Looking straight across from my vantage point, I could see a wooden door directly opposite me; across and to my left, on what I would call the north wall, were double swinging doors with portholes in them, the kind that one sees in restaurants to allow servers to open them with elbows and shoulders as they're carrying trays of food. That's what I needed. A refrigerator full of protein. Or a safe way out of here. So far I had seen no friendly red EXIT signs, but the sight of the kitchen doors made my mouth water. I made sure to top off the reserves in my bear charm before stepping onto the dead marble floor.

Hopping with a purpose, I made for the first pillar to help me keep my balance. My bare foot sounded like a sad trout flapping against the marble floor. I paused at the pillar and peered through the space between it and the next one at the center of the room. As best as I could tell, it was a room for hosting large orgies—the sort of room a realtor might diplomatically label as a "pleasure garden" or a "hedonist's salon."

Couches and divans and overstuffed pillows lined the edges of the room and encouraged lounging, shall we say, as broad marble stairs led down to a sunken area in the middle that had been quartered, the sections separated by catwalks that met in the middle at a circular stage equipped with a stripper pole. One quarter was a deep koi pond intended for swimming *au naturel,* another was a sumptuous spa, and another was a shallow tub filled with thin red liquid that I guessed was melted gelatin; it was probably meant for Jell-O wrestling but had with neglect dissolved into a wretched little fuck-puddle. The final quarter, roughly catercorner from me, was of a similarly exploitative nature; it was a mud-wrestling pit, and it was occupied. Not by wrestlers or anything human or Fae but rather by the manticore we'd seen guarding the Old Way at Dubringer Moor. He was chained with thick steel cables to three different pillars on the far side of the room. I froze and watched him; his eyes were closed, head resting on his front paws. Perhaps I'd surprised him in a nap? Or perhaps he was dead. The outline of his ribs was showing underneath his red pelt, and while it was unlikely that he had died of starvation in the three days since we'd seen him in Germany, it was possible. Dying of thirst would be more likely if he had been chained here all that time. Something had to be wrong with him; I couldn't believe he wouldn't have heard or smelled me long ago if he were hale.

I looked at him through my faerie specs and saw that he still had an aura; he wouldn't have one if he were dead. So he was sleeping or pretending to sleep—or truly unconscious.

If nothing else, he represented proof that Midhir and Grundlebeard had been involved in our hunting.

And the proof that he represented a mortal threat was also plain: Small piles of ashes dotted the room, mute markers testifying to the death of numerous faeries.

Prudence and a profound disability to move quickly dictated that I should simply try to find another way out rather than hop across in front of him, chained or not, so I turned around and spent ten minutes discovering that the path through Midhir's sex room was the only practical exit. Past the selkie alcove, the architecture afforded nothing but another couple of unoccupied bedrooms. I toyed with the idea of laboriously unbinding the substance of a wall so that I could squeeze through the hole into the proverbial sunset, but there was some bad juju about it in the magical spectrum—either a ward or a trap, I wasn't sure which. It was advanced binding of the sort the Tuatha Dé Danann were capable of, but I didn't know if it was Midhir's work or the work of whoever killed him. The bindings were tightly coiled, like the ones Aenghus Óg had placed on the mind of the late Tempe police detective Darren Fagles; if I tried to unbind them, it would set off an alarm at the very least, though I wouldn't be surprised if something more violent happened. Insane as it sounded, I thought it best to risk the sleeping manticore. I might be able to sneak by him, but there was no way I could fight off anyone summoned by an alarm.

Returning the way I had come, I nervously filled my bear charm once more before stepping onto the marble and then employed my lopsided pogo dance to reach the first pillar. The manticore hadn't moved. It still lay motionless in the mud.

Lacking the luxury of time—my magic was steadily draining now due to the camouflage spell—I hopped to the next pillar in three bounds and paused to check on the manticore. Motionless still.

I had a much larger space to cross now. Though I was tackling the short width of the room rather than the length, it was still a damn big room and the pillars were clustered at the corners of it. A matching pair to the two on my end awaited me perhaps thirty feet away, and it was behind those pillars—or, rather, to the left of those pillars on the north wall—that the kitchen doors waited; beyond them, straight ahead on the east wall, was the door to a mystery room. It was a long way for a one-legged, one-armed dude to go without any support, but I didn't have much choice. Taking a deep breath and praying to the gods below, I pushed off from the pillar and lunged forward, hoping I didn't wipe out.

The manticore woke when I was halfway across. The eyes snapped open, wide and alert, and searched for me. Though I was camouflaged, it wasn't perfect invisibility, and he was able to spot my movement if not my clear outlines. No doubt he heard me moving as well. The black spiked tail rose up into the air behind him like some unholy cobra and fired venomous barbs in my direction. Some of them sank into the upholstery of a long red leather sofa facing the koi pond and blessedly shielded my lower body, and others missed to either side. But one struck me high on the right arm, and the pain that exploded there was unlike anything I've ever felt.

Worse than the tooth faeries eating my left side. Worse than the Hammers of God throwing a knife in my kidney. Worse than dark elves setting me on fire in Greece. It was nerve-searing, caustic agony that shut my motor function down, and I spilled forward onto the unforgiving marble, screaming. Fragarach flew from my grasp and skittered across the floor.

I triggered my healing charm but feared it was already too late. I began to convulse with involuntary muscle spasms, helpless to stop them and unable to pluck out the thorn with either hand—my left was useless and my right hand couldn't reach the side of my own right shoulder. I managed to glimpse the thorn before a convulsion jerked my head away; the skin and flesh around it were dissolving and blackening—not like they would in acid but more like in a base, as if the toxin would do double service as a drain cleaner. It was ruining the topmost band of my shape-shifting tattoos—the one that let me return to my human form. So if I somehow managed to survive long enough to shift to an animal—not a bad idea, since as an otter or a hound I might be able to reach around and rip out the thorn with my teeth— I would never be able to shift back. I'd be stuck.

And I was stuck anyway. No one knew where I was. No one would arrive in time to help me with a convenient vial of manticore antivenin, because no such thing existed. I had to figure something out before I died an ignominious death, cut off from the earth in Midhir's seedy sex hall. The venom was a vicious cocktail of biological agents—nothing against which my cold iron aura would be any use. A searing alkali to burn and dissolve my skin, an inflammatory akin to concentrated capsaicin to keep all the nerves alight and to swell soft tissue, and a fast-acting tetanus analog to lock up my muscles. It wasn't actually tetanus or I would have been able to fight that off easily; it was a different molecule causing all the trouble. It paralyzed the manticore's victims in the most painful manner possible—imagine an epic charley horse in every single muscle—and then he would eat them whole and alive as they screamed their way down his gullet.

The leather couch provided cover from further missiles, but the manticore hadn't bothered to fire any more or even to rise up out of the mud. He knew by the noise I was making that he'd scored a hit, and that was all he needed to do. And he'd played me very well, very patiently; at no point had he ever been asleep. He had simply waited until I made myself an easy target.

I had to escape to another headspace if I was going to manage anything, and I thought Dante would serve me well. Though Druids have to learn different languages to manage their magic and communication with elementals, we also have to memorize large bodies of literature as a method of dividing our consciousness; it allows us to take others with us when we shift planes, for example. The body of work is a template for thoughts and a world unto itself, and we can slip ourselves or someone else into it. Granuaile had absorbed Whitman so far, so she could take one other person with her when she shifted. I had *The Odyssey* in the original Greek on tap, *The Iliad* in Latin, the complete works of Shakespeare, Dante's *Divine Comedy,* and Dostoyevsky's *Brothers Karamazov* in Russian, along with a bunch of bardic tales in Old Irish, which was my first project when I was a wee lad. I was maxed out now; active human memory can't handle much more than seven things at a time without significant risk of loss. But headspaces also have other uses—especially in situations like this one. They can be the happy place you need to find when your mind or body is decidedly unhappy. Dealing with the virulence and pain of the manticore's venom, therefore, could be left to my primary headspace. Removing the thorn would require cool thoughts in another, and getting access to more power before my magic ran out would have to follow directly after.

The thorn was not a straight spine but rather held small sacs of poison along its length, and these were pulsing and delivering more of the manticore's evil shit into my flesh. I had to remove it before the poison overwhelmed my ability to break it down; I was barely keeping pace as it was, fighting to keep the muscles of my right side unlocked and my diaphragm from freezing up. I slipped into Canto V of *Purgatorio*, and the rhythm of it existed outside the pain and the contractions and the havoc being wrought on my system:

> Là 've 'l vocabol suo diventa vano,
> arriva' io forato ne la gola,
> fuggendo a piede e sanguinando il piano.

Yes. In purgatory, souls burn away that which afflicts them and, passing through the crucible, become whole again. Bind the thorn to the back of the sofa and ignore the fact that you can't blink or move your eyes and your throat is closing and your organs are edging toward failure.

> Quivi perdei la vista e la parola
> nel nome di Maria fini', e quivi
> caddi, e rimase la mia carne sola.

And as the poetry flowed through that part of my mind, calm waters next to burning shores of my agony, I could concentrate on my goal and craft the proper binding, croak it past the swelling tissues of my throat, and feel the thorn retreat from my arm, flying a few yards to sink into the back of the sofa. The pain dipped for a brief moment, as a burn will when ice is first applied, but it returned soon enough, as the already savaged muscles on my left side tore and contracted and my tissues continued to swell. I could conceivably fight off the toxin now and break it down if I had enough magic to fuel the healing, but I was running low and had to access the earth's energy buried underneath the marble floor. Sticking with Dante but skipping to Canto IX, I recalled a passage that spoke of marble and sundered stone, an appropriate backdrop for what I wished to do.

The marble floor did not have the same security bindings I had seen on the walls of the back bedrooms; it was plain marble, malleable to sufficient force, and that was probably because Midhir couldn't imagine anyone trying to escape his pleasure dome. I spread out my hand, fighting its desire to curl into a fist, and focused my mind on the swirled-milk pattern underneath it. The marble was dolomite rock with very low silica content— primarily calcium-magnesium carbonate that I unbound in a microscopic area and then strived to reapply as a macro to a larger area the size of my hand. My voice gave out, however, and I coughed in the middle of the unbinding and had to start over. I gasped for breath and the pain nearly intruded into my calm headspace, but the poetry kept flowing.

Trembling and wincing, I carefully tried again, and this time the macro took hold. The marble underneath my hand became brittle as it broke down into its component minerals, and I could pull it apart, chunks of calcium and carbon and magnesium. I had to reapply the macro binding one more time because the first hadn't gone deep enough, and that drained my bear charm completely. Without magic to fuel my body's war against the venom, the poison raged through my veins and I could feel it destroying me, burning and at once paralyzing. My muscles spasmed involuntarily and my giblets howled to me of their torture; I imagined I could hear my liver and spleen screaming a duet, taxed far beyond their ability to filter the blood. I clutched another handful of crumbling marble out of what was now a shallow hole, tossed it away, and managed to scoop one final handful before my fingers seized up completely and wouldn't let go. At the same time my diaphragm locked in place, which meant I had already drawn my last breath.

The bare earth was there, underneath my hand; all I had to do was supinate my forearm, twist my wrist so that the back of my hand could make contact and draw energy through my tattoos. But my biceps wanted to flex and curl my hand away. Shaking and twitching from the effort, I attempted to roll my wrist clockwise. The pull of my biceps actually kept my hand down in the hole, the meat of the palm braced against the edge.

I strained but couldn't do it—a simple rotation of the wrist I typically performed without thinking was now impossible for me with all my will put into it. But there was some give in a few of my longer muscles along the uninjured side of my back. I threw my left shoulder as best as I could to flip and roll over faceup, and at first I thought it wasn't enough. I was on my side, my hand trapped in that hole, and my vision started to darken at the edges. But the inexorable tug of gravity pulled me down past the point of no return, and physics was able to turn my wrist in that hole where my will could not. Once the fine filigree of knots that formed the border of my tattoos touched the earth, the magic rushed in, all I needed and more, balm for my pain and energy to fight the pestilence and unlock my muscles. I began with my diaphragm and took a glorious, heaving gasp of air. After a couple more breaths I lay there quivering and slowly relaxing my body, laughing softly with relief. I'd be worthless for much else until I got the infection completely neutralized, but at least I knew that I'd continue to breathe, until something else killed me.

A voice pressed into my consciousness; it didn't merely

bang on my eardrums, it probed into my brain with un-welcome fingers.

~Hrrr. How is it that you still live?

I craned my neck around but saw no one nearby. I managed to rasp, "Who's there?"

When the voice answered, I realized that the sound my ears heard and the words my brain decoded were not the same thing at all. What my ears heard was like one of those YouTube videos where cats try to make human noises—in this case, a very big cat. But in my head I heard the words in English, except with a disturbing vibrato to them, a low, thrumming, malevolent purr.

~There is no one here but us, you fool. You may surmise that through process of elimination.

"Is this the manticore?"

~I knew you would figure it out. Now please explain why you have not died.

"How about you explain what you're doing here?"

~You persist in asking the obvious. I am here to kill whatever enters the room.

"Volunteered, did you?"

~Hrrr. I detect sarcasm in reference to my chains. Vexing and counterproductive.

"Well, it's vexing to be shot with poisonous barbs too, so suck it, uh . . . manticore."

~ I am called Ahriman. Who are you?

Ever since Odysseus told Polyphemus his name was Nobody, it's been a rule that you should never give a predator your real name. So I replied, "I am Werner Drasche." Neither of us might ever escape this place, but if we both did and he went searching for the arcane lifeleech, the result would work out for me regardless of who died. I certainly was in no shape to finish off Ahriman the manticore myself.

~There are very few who can survive my sting. How did you accomplish this?

"I heal fast. Obviously." Not as fast as I might wish. And the danger wasn't behind me; I was simply behind a couch. I estimated there was at least ten feet of space between the edge of the couch and the nearest pillar. That was ten feet I wouldn't be covering quickly, and Ahriman would easily perforate me when I tried— perhaps more than once. Fragarach lay in plain sight in the midst of that span, so I'd need to pause to pick it up. Or I'd have to crawl the whole way. If I moved slowly enough, the camouflage might keep me invisible. I doubted it.

And it wasn't as if I had the strength to make any kind of move yet. If I tried to do anything but lie there and break down the toxins in my bloodstream, my liver would lead a mutiny. I was still desperately hungry and now in dire need of a drink as well, but the kitchen might as well be on another plane.

~Why are you here?

"Shall we trade questions and answers?"

~Hrrr. Very well. But one at a time, and I go first. "Why are you here?"

"I came to visit Midhir, the owner of this estate, and found him dead. Who imprisoned you here?"

An angry roar preceded his answer. ~One of the Irish gods, but I do not know which one. He or she wore a shapeless covering and had an odd voice.

My jaw dropped with the implications of that. As the goddess of poetry, Brighid could speak with three voices at once. Ahriman asked his next question before I could follow up.

~I am supposed to kill whoever comes to visit Midhir. I can reasonably conclude that this Irish god wishes you dead. What have you done, Werner Drasche, to inspire the wrath of the Tuatha Dé Danann?

"I wish I knew. I suppose I must threaten them some-how, but I cannot imagine why. I have no designs against them and wish only to be left alone. Tell me, if the person who imprisoned you was covered completely and the voice was strange, how did you know it was an Irish god?"

~Hrrr. The god told me as much. "You now serve me and the Tuatha Dé Danann," the god said. But I did not accept the mere words. The truth of it was supported by the method of my capture. They used earth magic to render me immobile and to encase my tail in a wooden box, a hardwood not easily splintered. Then a squad of giants—I heard them called Fir Bolgs—shackled and muzzled me. I killed two of them despite my handicaps, yet here I am.

Interesting. Granuaile and I had thought the manticore was acting willingly as a mercenary, but obviously this mysterious god had chosen to make him an unwilling conscript.

~For a time, Ahriman continued, ~I was stranded on this plane and left to guard a certain tree; I was to kill whoever appeared. Someone did: A man, a woman, and a dog almost stepped through. That man had a sword and a scabbard—a scabbard that looked identical to the one I now see near the red sofa behind which you cower. I wonder—were you that man?

Telling him the truth would do me no harm; he still thought I was Werner Drasche. And confirming the truth would perhaps earn a measure of his trust, which might allow me to deceive him with something else. "Yes, that was me. So under what conditions might you be set free?"

~Killing you is the condition of my freedom. I do wish you would come out from behind that couch so we can get it over with, but you are probably determined to make me wait. Where are your companions?

"They are elsewhere. Listen, Ahriman, this god is being extremely careful to cover his or her tracks. You are wise enough to see that someone so careful would hardly let you live to speak of your role in this. If you kill me, you cannot hope to live much longer—you will be killed once you do this god's dirty work. So why do we not agree to set each other free instead?"

Something between a laugh and a purr rumbled out of the manticore's throat. ~I thought you would propose such a scheme. You may as well beg for mercy. You would have the same chance of securing my agreement. No, Werner Drasche. You are prey, and that is the end of it. There will be no escape for you. Remain behind your couch and die like a coward, or attempt to flee and I will shoot you with many more of my tail spikes. How many of them hit you the first time?

"Only one."

~I thought as much. And you barely survived, judging by the squalling I heard. Two will suffice.

I couldn't argue with that. "Who's feeding you while you lie in wait?"

~The same Irish god who captured me returns every so often to minister to my needs.

That was a ticking clock. If the person who killed Midhir found me like this, I'd be toast for sure. At the moment, my future toast status was only highly likely.

Ahriman continued. ~But I do not require daily food and drink, so if a day or two passes, I will not suffer much beyond boredom. The suffering of others, however, is capable of invigorating me. Hence the properties of my venom. Your pain was delicious, by the way, and it lasted for far longer than that of most humans. I am pleased that you have survived to feel that pain again.

He finished by making a couple of juicy smacking noises. He was licking his chops, and somehow he sounded smug while doing it.

"Have you heard of Wheaton's Law, Ahriman? It goes like this: *Don't be a dick*. I know it's a tough one, and I have broken that law myself more times than I would care to admit, but I think it's a law that every being should try to observe, regardless of faith or position on the food chain."

Ahriman made no comment except to chuckle deep in his chest. ~Hrr-hrr-hrrr! Silence fell after that. Apparently he had no more questions, and he was content to wait for me to make a move.

I was a physical wreck, so I wouldn't escape through acrobatics of any kind. I had to come up with a magical solution.

That red couch deserved my eternal gratitude. I loved that couch and promised it in a fit of sentimentality that, if I survived, I would buy one just like it and build a memorial. Perhaps I could move it along with me through a series of bindings, screening my slow crawl?

It was risky. There was no such thing as a kinda-sorta binding. Either you bound something or you didn't. So if I bound the leather on the end of the couch to the far wall to make it move, there was no telling how fast it would travel—or how far it would continue to move on after I broke the binding. If I didn't break the binding at precisely the right time, it could wind up leaving me exposed to more fire from the manticore.

I looked down at my right hand, still resting in the hole and clutching a handful of crumbled stone, and it occurred to me that a wall of marble would protect me far better than a floor. If we were back on earth on bare ground, I could ask an elemental to create a wall for me, but elementals always remain on earth even though their magic can be tapped, and they wouldn't be able to help me with dead, quarried stone anyway. Despite the time it would take me, the wall was a much safer option than gambling with the couch. And it would give me something to do while my body continued to purge the man-

ticore's toxins. I rolled myself over so that I was
facedown again, in the original position of my fall.

Beginning with the hole in front of me, I modified the
unbinding spell so that the affected area would be a thin
sliver of stone, only as wide as the thickness of a finger-
nail; the length was about six inches, starting from the
ragged, crumbled edge of my hole and extending toward
the pillar. I repeated it twice more, at ninety-degree an-
gles, so that when I was finished I had "cut" a rough
square of marble, with the hole side looking chewed up.
Those three cuts I bundled together in a macro and then
proceeded to the second operation.

Looking at the flat surface of what was now a marble
tile, I mentally selected the right third of it and then
bound it to the inside edge of the cut floor facing the
manticore. The effect, when I completed it, was that the
tile wiggled up off the ground and then flipped so that it
stood facing the center of the room, but the newly bottom portion of it was bound to the rest of the floor. It
left a small crater of exposed earth—they pour no cement foundations in Tír na nÓg, since it's tectonically
stable, lacking actual tectonics. As more marble left the
floor and became my shield wall, I would be left with an
easy source of magic to tap.

I tacked the tile binding onto the end of the slicing
macro and then cast the whole thing as a new macro. It
executed much faster, and I grinned when the next tile
cut itself and clacked into place. I repeated it again and
again, creating a trough of earth and the tiniest of walls,
only four inches high above the surface of the floor.

Once this self-erecting wall appeared beyond the edge
of the couch, however, toxic thorns fired into the upper
lip of the wall—Ahriman's reflexive response to movement, perhaps. The barbs bounced off in a wholly satisfying manner. A few more sailed high, presumably in
case I was trying to get across using camouflage. The

manticore waited for me to scream, but when I didn't and the marble squares kept rising and clicking into place all the way to the pillar, his voice pressed into my brain as his growls filled the room.

~Hrrr. What nonsense is this?

"It's a modified Cask of Amontillado. Treat your foe like Poe."

~Explain, Werner Drasche.

"Call me Montresor if you like. Explanation won't be necessary if you will be patient."

In response, several thorns thunked into the ceiling above. Ahriman had tried to ricochet them down on top of me, but they were too sharp and plunged deep into the sexy fresco, pumping their venom into hapless plaster fornicators. Ahriman roared his frustration— impotent rage in the Hall-O-Love.

My base completed to the first pillar, it was time to practice masonry without mortar. First I unbound some more of the marble around my hand so that I would have a squared edge near me, adjacent to the side that had just been sheared off. I began on a new set of macros for what I supposed must be thought of as skinny bricks, or perhaps really beefy tiles. Since I now had two sides of the squares exposed, I needed only two cuts for squares in this row, and then I had to bind the bottom of each square to the top of the foundation. When that binding executed, the tiles flew off the ground to land on top of the wall, adding six inches of height. As the row passed the couch and proceeded to the pillar, Ahriman divined my purpose and moved. Cables stretched and slithered across fur, and squelching noises from the mud reminded me of gastrointestinal discomfort. He did not bother announcing his intention; he merely fired more of his poison barbs over the couch at as steep an angle as he could manage. He had raised himself to im- prove his chances—and they weren't bad. The thorns landed mere inches beyond my mangled left side. There was no need to inform him how close he had come. Continuing to build the wall and simply not screaming in agony would let him know that he failed.

He gave up after a short while and I could hear him pacing, wet splortches mixed with the clank and rattle of his confinement. I continued to cannibalize the floor to build the wall, a bit higher than I had originally intended to cut off the manticore's field of fire. I didn't want him to be able to nail me from afar once I started moving toward the kitchen door.

Gods below, I hoped there was something edible in there.

The last of the poison had been broken down and a modest skin covering had closed the wound on my shoulder, but my tattoo wouldn't heal up all on its own, and I was running on fumes. Once the wall was completed to my satisfaction, I began to drag myself along the ground, using my right arm and leg. Ahriman heard me moving and he lost it. He didn't speak; instead, he roared and attempted to pull free of his chains, though he had doubtless tested their strength long before and found them sufficient to restrain him. He made quite a ruckus back there, but it didn't stop my long slog to the kitchen. After picking up Fragarach and realizing how profoundly unable I was to use it right then, I had occasion to reflect that crawling away was not my most heroic moment.

Ahriman spoke one last time, as I pushed open the kitchen door and hauled my body out of the sex hall. That half-human voice slithered into my head, menace in every syllable.

~I may die here, Werner Drasche. But if I am freed, I will hunt you.

"Okay!" I called back, and let the door close behind my feet. I hoped that, if he did escape somehow and found me instead of the arcane lifeleech, it would be far enough in the future that I would be in better condition to fight him.

An important step to improving my condition would be to eat something. Magic could boost my base strength, which was barely keeping me moving, but it couldn't boost low blood sugar or stop the growling in my belly, and since the kitchen had been tiled, I was now subsisting on my bear charm until I could find some other source of energy.

The kitchen appeared to be well stocked, and should it prove to be the case, I silently swore to give Brighid a fruit basket and no explanation whatsoever.

Since Tír na nÓg lacked electricity, food was kept safe in iceboxes—the enchanted sort one could find at the goblin market. Midhir had three huge ones and a prep area made entirely of wood; his faery servants wouldn't have appreciated the modernity of stainless steel. The cutlery and cookware were bronze, copper, and glass.

In the first icebox, I found a cold roasted chicken with only a single drumstick missing, so I counted it as a major score. I pulled it off the shelf, laid it out on the tile floor, and tore into it.

Finally able to think of the future, now that I had something on which to chew, I tried to salvage some useful information from my debacle of a shortcut. Whoever had rolled through here was an utter boss. Judging by the bodies and ash piles and by the fact that I still hadn't heard a sound beyond those made by Ahriman or myself, it was quite likely that we were the only living creatures in the compound. If that was true, then I could have walked in the front gate and avoided becoming a chew toy for the pieholes. I would have had to face Ahriman no matter what, though, if I wanted to learn what happened to Midhir.

I knew how the Tuatha Dé Danann tended to think,

and this slaughterhouse probably didn't even count as a massacre to my adversary's way of thinking. No, this was self-preservation. A strategic retreat, even. Bagging the Druids hadn't worked out, so it was time to withdraw and tie up loose ends like Midhir and Lord Grundlebeard. Now that we had the help of the Olympians, Granuaile and I couldn't be confined to earth anymore through pandemonium. So far as I knew, no other pantheons possessed that particular power. Whoever was behind all this would plot something else, for sure, and we'd have to remain paranoid, but at least the vampires were getting some payback, the dark elves had much to fear from the Ljósálfar, and our freedom of movement was restored. Or would be, once I healed.

A slow smile spread across my face, past a cheek full of chicken. As messed up as I was, it felt good to be alive. I didn't want to stop living anytime soon.

I wolfed down the entire chicken and most of a leftover ham before my stomach issued a cease-and-desist order. Bloated but already feeling a bit better, I thought it was time to try standing again. Wedging Fragarach into the handle of an icebox, I hauled myself to an upright position and hoped that no other mortal surprises awaited me as I searched for an exit.

Midhir's palace sprawled extensively, but I didn't bother to explore it all. My errand had already been completed and I didn't have the strength, so it was time to take my leave. I spied more ash piles as I moved through rooms; someone had made sure there would be no Fae witnesses to Midhir's demise. There was a lush courtyard in the center of the estate, with a tall ash tree casting much of it in shadow. It was tethered to the network but only outward bound; no one could shift directly into the center of Midhir's world. I didn't want to shift anywhere in Tír na nÓg, because I didn't want to appear crippled in front of all Faerie and because whoever was behind it all might be encouraged to finish me off. I needed a few days of food and healing—and some new clothes—before anyone laid eyes on me. So I shifted to my cabin above Ouray, Colorado, which had a stash of food and extra duds, in addition to a very strong elemental. Granuaile and Oberon would be worried about me being gone so long—especially since I'd promised them I'd be right back—but I wasn't anxious to see them while I was so messed up.

Unfortunately, I didn't have any choice in the matter. They weren't waiting for me back at Goibhniu's place but rather pelting out of the cabin toward me.

"Gods, Atticus, where have you been?" Granuaile cried.

<What she said! And, great big bears, what happened to you? That's a disastrous haircut.>

"Why are you here?" I asked.

"You said you were going to the cabin and you'd be right back. Where did you go?" She ducked underneath my right arm and draped it over her shoulders so that I could lean on her for support. Her hair smelled like honey and vanilla, and she was wearing strawberry lip gloss. I probably smelled unspeakably bad and felt acutely embarrassed. She was wearing a pale-blue blouse and some jeans that looked new—definitely different clothes since I'd last seen her stretched out and healing from an arrow wound.

"Wait. How long has it been?"

Her jaw dropped in shock and she searched my face to see if I was joking. My question worried her more than the sight of my injuries.

"Atticus, it's been two freaking days. Freaking as in I was freaking out."

"That explains why I was so hungry." And no wonder that they'd left Goibhniu's taproom. He would have told them to bugger off eventually and promised to let them know if I showed up.

<If you're still hungry, I could totally help you eat something.>

"I want to know where you went," Granuaile said, helping me hop through the cabin door, "but first tell me what you need."

My eyes welled a bit, a harbinger of impending schmaltz. I did my best to control it and said, "Actually, I think I'm all right. Or I will be. I'm glad you're here. We're safe now."

"We are?"

"Well, for a little while, yeah. Still up for Japan?"

"Are you?"

"It's as good a place to heal as any."

Chapter 30

We spent five days in Japan, not being hunted. It was blissful—or at least as blissful as five days could be when you're waiting around for your muscles to rebuild. We weren't bothered by vampires or dark elves or Fae, giving additional weight to my theory that our mysterious enemy in Tír na nÓg had been using Old Ways to ferry assassins around. And it was there, on the third day, in a rock garden with a fountain gurgling the eternal poetry of the elements, that I found time to tell Granuaile what had truly happened with the Morrigan, how she had discovered the limits of godhood and had chosen to slough them off; how she had kept her word and found a way for us to survive while giving the middle finger to convention, which said she could behave only in prescribed fashions; and how she had never truly been defeated.

On the fourth day, after I appeared to be at least cosmetically okay, I summoned the west wind using Fragarach. Shortly thereafter we were paid a visit by Hermes, who informed us that Bacchus was under control and that all the Olympians would swear to leave us alone, whenever I was free to hear their oath. Both Flidais and Perun had survived their fit of madness, and Flidais had pledged herself to find some way to restore or replace Herne's hunters. In nautical news, Poseidon and Neptune had reached out to Manannan Mac Lir in a new spirit of brotherhood to search the sea together for Jörmungandr, in hopes of giving us an advantage before the onset of Ragnarok.

That was so hopeful and so much better than the way things could have turned out that I allowed myself to feel a smidgen of hope. Yes, Loki and Hel were probably plotting some intensely evil shit now where we couldn't get to them, hiding themselves from the eye of Odin, but it wasn't just me trying to fill Thor's shoes anymore. The Olympians could be counted on to jump in with gusto.

Aside from that visit, we spent our days either in Zen-like calm in natural surroundings, healing and relaxing, or else baffled by Japanese television at night, which offered more "what the fuck?" per hour than anything in the United States.

"I don't understand a word they're saying, but I can't look away," Granuaile said as we lounged in a very tiny hotel room on the fifth day, a Tuesday morning. There was space to sleep and little else. "What are they going to do with that badger and the shaving cream?"

"I don't know," I replied, shaking my head. Even though I could speak Japanese, I didn't quite understand what the two fast-talking young men in skinny jeans and Muppet T-shirts intended. "Something crazy."

"Forget French. I need to learn Japanese next."

Oberon yawned at the foot of the bed and said, <If I can't quote it later, I don't want to watch it. Atticus, let's go walking in the forest. That mountain where we shifted in looked pretty nice. We can be hounds, and Granuaile can practice being a cat without too many smelly things to bother her.>

I blinked repeatedly to break the spell of the show. "Oberon's right. We need to get out of here."

<There are trees to pee on and tiny animals to chase!> Granuaile's eyes hadn't moved from the TV screen.

"Wait, what's happening? Is that a baby? That's a baby! Atticus, what the fuck are they doing with a baby?"

"Come on, let's go." I thumbed the power switch, and Granuaile flinched as the picture winked out.

"No! They had a badger and a baby! I need to know what happens!"

"Listen to yourself. It's already happened and it's pointless. We have more important things to do."

<The aforementioned trees and tiny animals!>

"What Oberon said," I agreed. "You're all healed now, and I'm probably eighty percent. Let's get some exercise."

We escaped our cubicle room, checked out, and fled Tokyo for Mount Fuji, hiking along one of several well-trod paths to the summit. Though there were plenty of other hikers making the trek with us, birdsong wafted amongst the leaves of maple and beech trees in the broadleaf zone near the base, and we discovered that we were smiling without knowing precisely why. Oberon's tail wagged and his tongue drooped out to the side as he loped alongside and occasionally paused to sniff something next to the trail.

We climbed all the way to the top, thinking we could use a stunning vista to banish the effects of ultra-urban Tokyo. The trees thinned out after a while, then disappeared altogether, leaving a rocky ascent to the summit. Once we were there, a stone post carved with kanji informed us that we had made it to the top, as if we could not figure it out from the fact that there was no more mountain to climb. But that post made me drop my jaw anyway.

Granuaile noticed. "Atticus, what is it?"

"The Morrigan's parting gift," I said. "I forgot about it until now."

"What? You never mentioned that before."

"Because I forgot about it. There's something—or

someone—waiting for us on one of the Time Islands in Tír na nÓg."

"Well, if they're stuck there, then they can probably just wait longer, can't they?"

"I'm sure they can. Not so sure about me, though. Aren't you curious? Who does the Morrigan have stashed away there?"

Granuaile sighed. "We're going to run downhill and shift away right now, aren't we?"

"Yep. Well, I'll kind of limp and stagger instead of run. But we'll go as fast as we can."

Granuaile insisted that we take a few moments to enjoy the view first, since we'd spent so long climbing to appreciate it. The Pacific Ocean caressed the green curves of Honshu's coast and sparkled with reflected sunlight. As long as I didn't look toward the cities, I could glimpse the Japan of long ago, still dangerous and beautiful, where the serenity of Zen and Shinto always had an edge to it—the blade of a katana or wakizashi, usually. Often only a single person's will decided whether the day would be washed in blood or the tranquil ink of calligraphy.

We sent messages of love and harmony to the elemental, and then I tried my best to keep my pace dignified as we descended to the broadleaf zone tethered to Tír na nÓg. Once the trees surrounded us again, we took the earliest opportunity to leave the trail and get out of sight before we shifted away.

We chose a specific destination in Tír na nÓg: the tree nearest the home of Manannan Mac Lir, as safe a place as any for us in the land of the Fae. He and Fand welcomed us, feted us, and, once they heard of our intent to visit the Time Islands, offered the use of a singular canoe that would hold its position in a current without the use of an anchor.

"That island is fairly well known," Manannan said.

"I am fascinated to hear that the Morrigan put someone there."

It was the first time either of us had spoken of the Morrigan. Manannan carefully avoided my eyes, and I could sense that he didn't want to speak of her death. I respected his wishes and didn't go there.

"Really?" I said. "What's so unusual about it? I know it's way upstream, but I don't remember seeing anything there when I was young."

"You wouldn't have. We didn't start putting people in there until—well, it was around the time you retrieved Dagda's cauldron for Ogma down in Wales. Remember that?"

"Yeah. Back in the sixth century."

"Right. Well, you never did hang around Tír na nÓg very much until recently, so it's no wonder you haven't heard of it before now. Some of the Tuatha Dé Danann—myself included—call it Zealot Island. We were bloody sheltered back in the old days, you know. Once we began to have contact with the rest of the world, we were gobsmacked by the intensity with which some people denied the existence of other gods. Lots o' those people are dangerous, but some o' them are so bad they're kind of ridiculous." Manannan smiled with nostalgia. "My favorite character there is the red-faced Puritan who looks like he's a biscuit away from an aneurysm. When I snatched him, he was shouting this frothy sermon about the sublime grace of his god's love, completely unaware of how his body language and voice contradicted every word he said. I know that others have contributed to the island from time to time, but I didn't realize the Morrigan was one of them."

That only increased my curiosity, but we spent much of the time relating the details of our run across Europe. I neglected to mention my visit to Brí Léith, however; since Manannan didn't bring up news of the shocking death of Midhir, I wasn't going to volunteer the information. He knew, of course, that Midhir was dead—Manannan would have escorted his spirit to his final rest. But that didn't mean Manannan knew the details of what had happened or had investigated, or that Midhir's death was public knowledge. It was best to keep silent.

I insisted on cooking in the morning, preparing my signature cheese and chive omelets and serving them with sausages and parsley potatoes. Fand had Blue Mountain coffee from Jamaica that she had sent faeries to harvest on the sly, so it was one of those rare breakfasts you remember long afterward. Bellies full and loving life as we bid our hosts farewell, the three of us set out on the river in the canoe, which Oberon discovered was not designed with a wolfhound in mind. <Yeesh! Shift your weight in this thing and everything moves,> he complained after he nearly capsized us. <I don't think wolfhounds have very good sea legs. I might not be a salty dog after all.>

"Best to lie down and just enjoy the scenery, then," I said. There was quite a bit to see. Zealot Island was about as far upstream as one could get; time moved slower there than almost anywhere. Though narrow, the island sprawled for a decent distance, so there was a rogues' gallery lined up on the beach who would most likely fight to the death if they were left enough time to do so. An English crusader stood right next to a fighter for the Caliphate, for example, and they didn't even know it. Millennia would pass before they could turn their heads and register that an enemy stood nearby.

Metal posts offshore rose all the way around the island, supporting an elaborate system of catwalks and machinery far above it. I didn't know what the contraption was for, but I was sure Goibhniu had something to do with it. We'd go see him next.

On the northern side of the island, at the edge of the

beach but by no means under the canopy of trees that dotted the center of the island, a craggy, stooped figure pointed an accusing finger at us, mouth wide in accusation and eyes burning with rage. The Morrigan had obviously plucked him from a cold environment, since he was bundled up in warm clothing and wearing gloves with the fingers cut off. He looked utterly alien standing on that balmy beach.

"Gods below," I whispered. "What in nine hells was she thinking?"

"Who is it?"

"I can't . . ." I trailed off, my mind spluttering to a halt like an AMC Gremlin. Granuaile paused the boat in the river, using the binding Manannan had taught us. She let me stare for a while to get my thoughts in order before she asked again.

"Atticus? Who is it?"

I shook my head. "No. I don't know how this is going to go. I mean, now that I see him there, of course I need to get him out, but it might turn out to be a terrible idea. Or a great idea. Depends on whether he wants to help us or not. But if it winds up being a terrible idea, I don't want you involved. It's safer that way."

Granuaile crossed her arms. "No. That's not going to fly. I can take care of myself, as you well know. Tell me who it is."

"You misunderstand. I know you can take care of yourself, and I'm not worried about that at all. I'm more worried about you killing him than the other way around. He'll say something atrocious and you'll have no choice but to destroy him. No, I'm sorry. This is a private matter, and I'm going to keep it private until I know his state of mind."

Granuaile cocked an eyebrow and bobbed her head at him. "You can't tell his state of mind by looking at him?"

I gazed at his snarling expression again. "It's not as

easy as you might think," I said. "He kind of looks like that all the time. That could be joy we're looking at. I simply don't know."

We returned to shore and found Goibhniu at his smithy, working on a personal project. Swirling rods of wrought iron outlined a threatening figure with flowing black hair.

"Is that . . . ?"

"The Morrigan," Goibhniu said. "Aye. Me mum isn't too happy about me makin' a memorial, but she can get stuffed. The spirit feckin' moves me, y'know. The Morrigan gave me nightmares all the time, but I already miss her. Gonna put rubies in the eyes and enchant Fae lights behind 'em to make 'em glow."

"Outstanding."

"Kind of you to say." He removed his goggles, wiped his hands on a cloth, and came over to shake my hand with a smile on his face. "Good to see you alive, Siodhachan. Heard a bit about that business with the Olympians, owing to your friend there." He nodded to indicate Granuaile and then turned his grin on her. "Hello, you. And, Oberon, it's always a pleasure."

Oberon barked and wagged his tail as Goibhniu rubbed his head.

"Looks like you've healed up well," he said to Granuaile, then included me with his next sentence. "Will ye be havin' a beer with me? There's a lot of rumors swirlin' round about what exactly happened, but I'd like to hear it from you, and, besides, we have business to discuss."

He must mean the bounty on the vampires. "That would be wonderful."

"Delighted," Granuaile said.

"Brilliant. Don't worry, Oberon," Goibhniu said, "I have something proper to eat over there too."

<How come Goibhniu isn't running everything? He seems to have his priorities straight.>

We followed Goibhniu out of his smithy to his brewery and taproom next door, which was decorated in dark wood and brass. There were a few Fae hanging out inside, but they exited quickly after they saw me. I shared a condensed and edited version of our escape from the Olympians while Goibhniu pulled draughts for us and ladled out some bowls of lamb stew from the kitchen. We three ate at a booth, while Oberon ate his behind the bar. I finished with the uneasy truce struck with Zeus and Jupiter, as we sopped up the remainder of the stew with some bread.

Goibhniu shook his head in wonder and raised his glass. "*Sláinte,* laddie. I love the way you make everybody dance."

We clinked glasses and then I said, "What do you know about Zealot Island?"

The smith blinked. "I know it's feckin' tough to get anybody off it once they're on."

"Why?"

"Time moves so slowly there that when you swoop in to pluck them out you're likely to break their bones. Some o' them haven't blinked in hundreds of years."

"So why put anyone there?"

"We only put assholes there, until I could figure out a way to get 'em out safely."

"Oh, so you *can* get them out?"

"Wait. Are you saying you killed a bunch of people to experiment?" Granuaile asked at the same time, a hint of outrage in her tone. Goibhniu answered her rather than me.

"Well, yeah, but, like I said, they were assholes. Vikings, mostly, what were going around raping and pillaging the Irish coast back then. But, come to think of it, we're still putting assholes there. Only now we can get 'em out without killing 'em. Mostly."

"What do you mean, mostly?" I asked.

Goibhniu shrugged. "It's a tricky business. Have you been out there and seen the rig I set up?"

Thinking of the bizarre machinery erected over the island, I nodded.

"Well, I can snatch 'em out with that. The time bubble has a low ceiling. We sweep what amounts to an ultra-soft mattress in behind 'em and then scoop 'em up. Thing is, you're practically guaranteed to break their legs, because we hit them first to make 'em fall backward and usually they have their legs locked up. Sometimes we get additional breakage, but it's hardly ever fatal anymore."

"Can you get someone out for me?"

"Who?"

I shot a glance at Granuaile, who was listening intently. "I'd rather not say," I replied, "but he was left there by the Morrigan."

Goibhniu's eyes rounded. "She said someone would come asking about that someday, but I never thought it would happen now. And I certainly didn't think it would be you."

"Do you know the person I'm talking about?"

"No, I don't. She only told me that she left someone there and that far off in the future somebody—not her—would ask to get 'im out. She paid me in stupid huge pots of gold to get this guy off the island and make sure he healed up all right."

"But you don't know who it is?"

"Nope. She said whoever asked about it would identify him."

That gave me pause. Considering how long ago she must have put that man on the island, she had been flirting with the idea of her own death for a very long time. Or she had divined some purpose for him far beyond his own era.

"All right, I need you to go around to the north side

and look for an old man in winter clothes pointing at the shore in mid-shout. Can't miss him. Epic eyebrows. That's the guy."

"Done," Goibhniu said. "Or it will be in a couple of weeks. Takes that long."

"Good enough," I said. "What news from the yew-men?"

"Ah! I'm thinkin' we need another beer for that. This is good." He collected our glasses and went back to the tap and checked on Oberon, who had fallen asleep behind the bar after wolfing down his lamb stew.

"You heard what they did the first night, right?" the god of brewing said as he deposited the old glasses in the sink and fetched some fresh ones. "Took out every vampire in Rome. It was a sort of cooperative enterprise from several different pods. They split up from there and took a day to find new targets. Meantime, the rest of the world's vampires wake up at night and some of them realize that they're hearing nothing from their leaders. A few go to find out what's happened, and then it's chaos. Lots of different reactions. Some are battening down the hatches and increasing security until they know more. Some are sending minions to Rome to seize the city for them and take control. Others are claiming that fighting over Rome is a moot point, as it's no longer the center of vampiric power—which is a fair point— and then they claim that their city should be the new capital, or whatever you want to call it."

"Huh. Which cities?"

"Istanbul, Las Vegas, and Paris are the names I've heard." I'd half expected to hear Thessalonika in there, which would mean Theophilus was making a play, but then it made sense that he would let others step forward. He was the sort of leader who moved in the shadows, safely out of reach. In that he was very similar to his mysterious counterpart amongst the Tuatha Dé Danann.

Goibhniu brought over our draughts, and I noticed it was a different beer than the first. "This is my Bally-shannon Blond Ale," he said.

We clinked glasses and took an appreciative sip. "Did the yewmen get any more after Rome?" I asked.

"Oh, aye," Goibhniu said, nodding. "They've been making hits just about every other day, spreading throughout Italy. It's driving the bloodsuckers crazy. They're upgrading their daytime security and hissing at one another, and I'm over here eatin' popcorn and laughin' me ass off."

"So what's the count?"

"They're able to hit around twenty to thirty a night, but that's only every other day. So right now we're at a hundred sixty-two vampires who are finally dead for real."

That was a fraction of the world's vampires, but, so far as I knew, they hadn't ever suffered a loss like this in my lifetime. And it came in territory they'd long considered safe, to vampires who were amongst the most powerful of their kind.

"That's quite a bit of bounty to be paid. Can I bring you that money plus an estimate for more when I pick up my man from Zealot Island?"

"Sure, that would be grand. Want to see the heads or shall I destroy them?"

"Destroy them. There's really only one I'm interested in getting at the moment, but I doubt he'll be in Italy. He'll be one of the lads sending in minions."

Goibhniu frowned. "Who's this?"

"The name's Theophilus. He's the one who all but wiped out the Druids back in the old days. It was his idea to use the Roman legions. His organization."

A spark of genuine anger flashed in the eyes of a god

whose good nature was rarely disturbed. "I didn't know that. When did you discover this?"

"Not long ago. While I was binding her," I said, nodding my head toward Granuaile. "He's after us again. That's why I wanted to push back against the vampires now. Keep him busy. But it would be even better if we could take him out. I think he's more powerful than he lets on."

"Hmm." Goibhniu tapped his glass in contemplation and peered through slitted eyes at me. "You know, there's a hundred more yewmen at the Morrigan's Fen with nothing to do."

Granuaile saw what he meant immediately. "You think we could recruit them to join in?"

"Quite possibly. Say that I can. Where should I send them?"

"Break them up into four pods," I said. "Send one each to those three cities you mentioned and one to Thessalonika. Free range after that."

"Hell yeah," Granuaile said.

Her keenness for the idea surprised me. "Aren't you concerned about the collateral damage to their thralls? I thought this was the kind of thing you found distasteful. Immoral."

"Normally it would be. But I've had time to consider. Time to be hunted, I should say. I suppose my view grew darker after you died, Atticus—"

"Hold on," Goibhniu interjected. "You died?"

"Long story," I waved a hand to dismiss it and let Granuaile finish.

"When the decision is either your life or theirs, it ceases to be complicated. There are issues of dignity and justice to consider, but when it comes to vampires and their thralls, I think I can put that aside. Any one of them would kill me without hesitation, and it's naïve to think that they'll change their minds and wish me well someday if I just leave them alone. Those thralls not only are in the business of defending monsters but wish to become monsters themselves. I want to protect life, and they want to eat it. It's not as if we have a difference of opinion on politics or religion, where violence would be an unacceptable solution. Vampires want to end me. Since abandoning the planet isn't an option, my only choice is to end them first."

I nodded and did my best to keep my expression neutral, though privately I was saddened. Granuaile's generosity had once been unconditional; now it was tempered with a soupçon of bloodthirstiness. But battle hardens you and leaves little room for ethical niceties, and since becoming a full Druid she had seen far more conflict in a month than I saw in my first few years. I'd always known that such scarring would occur eventually, but I'd hoped she could experience the wonder of her new powers unsullied by violence for a while longer, during which she could revel in her connection to Gaia and perhaps let that smooth away some of the anger she had always felt for her stepfather.

I think his fundamental selfishness had shaped her in a manner simultaneously beautiful and dangerous. Her determination to defend the earth was a direct result of what she perceived as his criminal trespasses against the planet—and it behooved her to punish that behavior. I had felt that outrage too, in my youth, and so had many other Druids, and there was no denying that Gaia needed her champions. But during the Industrial Revolution I realized that such outrage was poisoning my spirit. There was nothing I could do to stop the world from changing, so I had to change with it and seek a balance. I didn't think Granuaile was completely unbalanced yet, but I could see which way the seesaw was tipping, and I wished it would go the other way.

Skipping over her words without comment, I said, "What's going to happen to the Fen now?"

"Not sure," Goibhniu said. "It's not exactly prime real estate. Right gloomy swamp, it is, so no one's leaping after it. You remember the old hag Scáthach? Trained Cu Chúlainn?"

"Sure."

"My bet is she'll pop in there."

"Huh. Didn't know she was still around. What about the Morrigan's duties?"

Goibhniu took in a deep breath and sighed heavily through puffed cheeks before answering. "Manannan will take care of those who die—he was already doing half of it anyway. But I don't expect anyone will take over choosin' the slain or fuckin' people till they bleed. People will still pray to her, of course, and she'll probably act from time to time from beyond the veil, just like Lugh Lhámhfhada does, but we'll never see her like again."

Perhaps it was the high alcohol content of Goibhniu's beer, but his words hit me palpably and I suddenly missed her. She'd made life more poignant for the Irish. The terror she inspired gave peace its serenity; the pain she caused gave health its lustre; her failure to love made me grateful for my ability to do so, and I realized, far too late, that though I never did or could have loved her as she might have wished, I should have loved her more.

"To the Morrigan," I said, throat tight with emotion as I raised my glass.

"Aye, the Morrigan," Goibhniu said, lifting his glass and clearly as overcome as I was. Granuaile joined in with a bit of puzzlement but politely declined to notice out loud that Goibhniu and I were tearing up. We knew it was the end of an era; the sun cannot shine as bright without a proper darkness to counter it. The world had gone a bit gray.

Epilogue

We had two weeks before Goibhniu's apparatus over Zealot Island would produce any results, so we took the opportunity to fulfill a long-overdue promise. Without telling my hound what we intended, the three of us shifted to a certain Irish Wolfhound Rescue in Massachusetts. It was the same place where I'd originally found Oberon, and we were hoping that they'd have another suitable hound to adopt. Oberon had been alone far too long, and we had a promise to keep.

Tall chain-link fences stretched away on either side of the main house, with expanses of green grass behind them—acres of turf that served as a massive dog run for a pack of wolfhounds. Seven of them barked and gamboled back and forth as we approached. Oberon's tail wagged and he woofed a greeting to them.

<Hey, I remember this place! Wow! Look at all the hounds, Atticus! Am I going to get to play with them?>

I hope so. We need to let Granuaile go first and see if one of them is a suitable match for the two of you. As we paused outside, Granuaile smiled at me and gave me a quick kiss.

"Fingers crossed," she said, and left us to go inside.

<Match?>

We need to find a wolfhound bitch who will get along

with both you and Granuaile, and there's a chance we
won't find one here.

Oberon leapt and twisted in the air in extreme excitement. He kept spinning around as he spoke. <Great big
bears, Atticus! You're not kidding? You're finally adopting a bitch?>

Maybe, Oberon, maybe. And I'm not adopting her.
Granuaile is, if she can find a smart one that you both
like. And, by the way, she has to like you too. You need
to be a gentlehound and win her affection by yourself.
We're not going to adopt one unless she genuinely gets
along with both of you.

Oberon's enthusiasm wasn't dampened in the least by
my cautions and disclaimers. He spun around so fast he
was making me dizzy, and the independent enthusiasm
of his tail eventually overbalanced him and he wiped
out. Undeterred, he leapt back up and tried to execute
something gymnastic, for which wolfhounds are decidedly not renowned. He wiped out again. Realizing he
felt too awesome to stand right then, he wriggled around
in the grass of the front yard, every inch of him in motion.

<This is the best day ever! It's the best idea you've ever
had! It might be better than sausage! Wait. Is it? YES! I
think it is!>

Well, to be fair, Oberon, sausage wasn't really my
idea. It was just my idea to feed it to you.

<Oh, this is better, Atticus, it's totally better!>

Are you saying you'd give up sausage for a compan-
ion?

<Well, yeah, who wouldn't?>

That admission made me feel more than a little
ashamed. *I'm sorry we waited so long, buddy. And, re-*
member, we might not find the perfect bitch here today,
but if not we'll keep looking. It's a quest now.

<C'mere, you!> Oberon rolled over to get his feet un-

derneath him and then he leapt at me, tackling me to the ground.

"Auggh!" I cried aloud, half in alarm and half in amusement. "Shit! Oberon, get off me!"

<This is so exciting and I am so happy and I need to thank you properly! Hold still!> I tried to twist away, but the bulk of his weight pressed down on my chest and I had no leverage. Still, I managed to turn my hips around in time for Oberon to start humping the side of my leg.

"Gah! Ha! Oberon, stop!" It was simultaneously horrifying and hilarious, and I couldn't keep from laughing. "Someone's going to see!"

<Let them be jealous! You're the best friend ever and I don't care who knows it!> The wolfhounds behind the fence seemed to be barking encouragement now, and that, combined with the joy in Oberon's voice and the picture we must have made for any witnesses, was all it took for me to lose it. I laughed uncontrollably as he humped my leg, helpless to defend myself from his enthusiasm. The hounds barked, I laughed, and Oberon humped until Granuaile appeared behind the fence with an older woman and saved me.

"What in the world? Oberon! That's enough!" She sounded mortified. It was not the first impression she wished to make on the owner of the ranch. I'm sure she must have reinforced her verbal command with a telepathic one, because Oberon finally ceased and apologized—to her, not me.

<Sorry, Clever Girl. I'm just so happy!> He stepped off and spent maybe two seconds in contrition before he started spinning around again. I rolled away and tried to get my laughter under control but couldn't, because now I was embarrassed and so was Granuaile and that was funny too. Luckily, the owner of the ranch wasn't offended or shocked. When Granuaile explained that

Oberon was unusually excited and didn't normally behave that way, the woman nodded in sympathy. She knew very well what wolfhounds were like.

With the show over, the hounds inside the fence turned their attention to Granuaile and the owner of the ranch. They crowded around Granuaile and jockeyed for a position underneath her hands, since she was doing her best to pet all seven with only two limbs. Eventually she isolated one from the others, a cream-coated hound with kind brown eyes.

"Could I spend a bit of time with this one?" Granuaile asked, to which the owner nodded. As Granuaile and the owner walked back toward the house, all the hounds followed, not just the one Granuaile had asked about.

Oberon stopped spinning and pricked up his ears as they passed out of sight. <Hey. Where are they going?>

They're going to chat for a little while. She'll make a decision soon enough. Flop down and I'll give you a belly rub while we wait.

<Okay!> Oberon dove and skidded across the lawn as he twisted to present his belly. I began to scratch him and tried to avoid getting swatted by his tail, which wouldn't stop wagging.

Now, remember, buddy, regardless of which hound we adopt, she's not going to know how to speak at first. We have to teach her.

<Oh, that's right!> Oberon said, and that's all I had to say to keep him occupied, because he began to catalog all his favorite movies and rank them according to their potential for language acquisition. He was going to start with *Pulp Fiction* but dismissed it for fear that she would keep asking him what Marsellus Wallace looked like. Somehow, from there, he wound up choosing to begin with *Pride & Prejudice* starring Keira Knightley, because there was an Irish wolfhound running around in it. Eventually Granuaile and the owner of the ranch

emerged from the house with the cream-colored hound on a leash.

All right, buddy, time to be on your best behavior. Sit up and don't move. Follow Granuaile's lead.

<I will be the very picture of propriety.> He posed like a show dog, perfectly still except for his tail, which swished madly across the grass.

"Hello, Oberon," Granuaile said aloud, clearly for the owner's benefit. Dog owners were used to people talking to dogs and wouldn't find it strange. "This lovely lady is Orlaith. Would you like to say hello?"

Oberon gave a short bark of affirmation, but mentally he said, <Would I! She's so beautiful! Can I sniff her ass yet?>

Granuaile must have answered him, for there was a pause before he said, <Okay.>

Orlaith approached, nose aquiver and tail sawing the air, and Oberon rose to his feet, similarly enthused. He was very patient as she snuffled all around his face, and then she did a quick once-over of his torso before sliding down to his posterior.

<Aaaaand . . . we have target lock!> Oberon said. Orlaith's rear end was of course next to his snout now, and he turned his head to get a good whiff of it. Swinging around his head meant pulling his shoulders along and then his rear legs, which drew him away from Orlaith's nose. She tried to get in closer, and that had the same effect, pulling her ass away from Oberon. In no time they were circling each other, pursuing what for them was a heady fragrance, and Granuaile let go of the leash. Their tempo sped up, and I wondered how long they could maintain it without crashing. Soon they weren't even trying to sniff, they were simply chasing each other in circles with their mouths open in doggie smiles. <She's on my tail! I can't shake her!>

Granuaile laughed and looked at me. "She likes him."

I grinned and nodded. It was pretty obvious from the hound's behavior, but it was good to have confirmation of Orlaith's feelings from Granuaile. I would be very careful not to tap into Orlaith's head for a few weeks, to make sure she bonded properly with Granuaile.

Oberon heard the comment, of course, and said, <She does? I like her too!>

I asked Granuaile, "Do you think you'll get along with her?"

"Oh, yes, no problem," she replied. "Orlaith's quick and very sweet."

Oberon broke out of the circle and took off across the lawn, Orlaith hot on his heels.

<She's too fast! I can't hold her! Waaauuuugh!> Oberon tumbled across the grass and Orlaith quickly followed, a giant mess of fur and splayed legs until they rolled out of it, and then Oberon was chasing *her* around the lawn instead.

The owner of the ranch chuckled and said, "Well, they certainly seem to get along."

Granuaile clapped her hands together in delight and gave a little squee. "Yes, they do. We'd like to adopt her if that's okay." She introduced me to the woman, who was named Kimberly. Her mother had owned the ranch during the time I'd adopted Oberon, and now she looked after it. We couldn't tell her Oberon had ever been there, of course, because he was far older than any normal wolfhound now. But we could show Kimberly that we were pretty good with hounds.

Oberon, come on over here and be brilliant for a second so this lady will trust us with Orlaith. Aloud I said, "Oberon! Here, boy!"

<All right, coming.> He scampered over, Orlaith close behind, and stopped in front of me.

"Sit," I said. He sat. "Lie down." He did so. "Belly rub." He rolled onto his back.

\<You're not going to make me go get you a beer, are you?\>

No worries. "Come to heel." He got up and moved to my right side, facing the same way I was facing, and wagged his tail. Orlaith did the same thing with Granuaile, standing on her left side, though Granuaile hadn't said anything aloud.

Kimberly let out a low whistle of appreciation. "Well, I guess you know your hounds," she said.

\<She's easily impressed.\>

We filled out paperwork with Kimberly and made a generous donation to the rescue, then we left with Orlaith and shifted through Tír na nÓg to our cabin in Colorado, where Orlaith would have plenty of time to bond with Granuaile and begin to learn a few words here and there.

You'll need to be very patient with Orlaith on the talking thing, I explained to Oberon. *You've been with me many years now and probably don't remember how tough it was at first.*

\<Oh, I do, Atticus! Don't worry, I'll be nice. When do we get to talk?\>

When Granuaile thinks she's ready. It will probably be a while, buddy. Bonding them too soon might overwhelm Orlaith, and I needed to remember to remind Granuaile of that. *You can just enjoy her as she is in the meantime, right?*

\<Absolutely! She's awesome!\>

The days passed quickly with training and play until it was time to travel back to Tír na nÓg. I'd asked Hal Hauk to start liquidating some of my assets and converting them to gold, and one of his pack members, Greta, was tasked with delivering it to the cabin. It was her second trip there—a rather long one from Tempe—and she made it clear that she hated the drive. She turned her car around on the road and honked, never getting out. Once I walked around to the driver's side, she rolled down the window and dropped a heavy sack on the ground in front of me.

"A giant bag of gold I can understand, but making me drive up here to deliver those Girl Scout Cookies and whiskey? That makes you a whole new species of asshole," she said, then stepped on the accelerator and peeled down the hill, leaving me in a cloud of dust. I coughed a bit but grinned. I knew what to get her for the holidays. I hefted the sack and, after bidding farewell to Granuaile and the hounds, took it with me to pay Goibhniu and thereby finance the stealth war against vampires.

When I got there and paddled the canoe out to Zealot Island, Goibhniu had already extracted its inhabitant from the slow time and placed him on a makeshift bed on the barge. In keeping with his promise to the Morrigan, he'd called in Fand, who was leaning over the man, lending her healing powers and the miraculous bacon of Manannan Mac Lir's hogs to his recuperation—for, as expected, he had broken quite a few bones in the shock of removal. She smiled as I approached and said, "Ah, here he is! Your savior. I'll let you two talk." She winked at me and whispered, "He's doing very well considering his age, even with our help." Her surprise and curiosity about his identity were unspoken but clear.

It wasn't a mystery to me why he healed so fast, but I felt it best to keep his identity a secret for a while longer. Ignoring her nonverbal query, I simply said, "Thank you." She complimented my new haircut with a faint trace of sarcasm and took the hint, leaving us alone.

A weathered visage underneath a pair of bushy white eyebrows scowled at me in querulous confusion, one gloved hand holding up to his mouth a strip of bacon, which he gnawed on with gusto. He was having trouble placing me—my haircut was quite severe. I'd had to shave my head because most of the hair on the left side had been torn out by the tooth faeries, and now there was only a couple weeks' stubble showing. His curt voice was laced with irritation as he spat in Old Irish, "Say something, y'poxy pile of shite." A small chunk of bacon launched itself from his teeth by way of punctuation.

Normally, such a greeting would elicit from me an assertion that I had enjoyed the company of his mother the previous evening, but, considering who it was, I toned it down a bit. "The good news is that you're still alive after all these years. The bad news is that you're still alive after all these years."

The eyebrows writhed in sinuous fashion atop his brow, wrestling for dominance on his face, until recognition hit him and they drew together in their customary configuration, a severe roof over an angry grimace. "You? Bloody Siodhachan!" Little bacon-flavored flecks of spittle flew from his lips. Deciding this wasn't enough, he hawked up something gross and spat on the deck before continuing, "Gods damn it, how long was I on that thrice-cursed island? Nobody will tell me. You've gone and cocked everything up again, haven't ye?"

My old archdruid literally hadn't aged a day since the Morrigan put him on the island, and he was still as charming as ever.

Acknowledgments

In case you might be interested, I've included a couple of goodies on my website (www.kevinhearne.com) that couldn't appear in the book. The first is a Google map of the run across Europe. The second is a much longer retelling of *The Wooing of Étaín* by Atticus. Links to both can be found on the appropriately titled Goodies page.

Special thanks to Colin Wagenmann in Germany for his insights regarding German geography and for expressing existential quantification in *Deutsch*. I'm also grateful to Michelle Drew and William Cathcart in the UK for info regarding Windsor Park and Frogmore House, and to Heather Blatt at Florida International University for her invaluable help with Middle English. Dr. D. Forrest Taylor coached me a bit on toxins and their effects. Any inaccuracies are of course my fault and not theirs.

To belay speculation, the similarity betwixt my surname and Herne the Hunter's is entirely coincidental—unless it isn't. I know my ancestor arrived in "the Colonies" in the sixteenth century from London and could conceivably be related to an historical Herne (if he existed), but I lay no claim to that and frankly think it far-fetched. I simply found Herne a fascinating and irresistible figure because he illustrates the principle that stories (and perhaps gods) can take on a life of their own.

I cannot say enough good things about my alpha reader, Alan O'Bryan, my agent, Evan Goldfried, and my editors at Del Rey, Tricia Narwani and Mike Braff. Words simply fail, so we tend to drink a lot and sing the praises of a literate populace. Seriously. We're not bad singers. And we have sung songs about you. Someday we will form our own heavy metal band called Thë Grätüïtöüs Ümläüts and sing of death and linguistics. Our first single will be "(Die)acriticäl Märks."

Many thanks to you for reading and for spreading word of the series to your friends. It's the only reason I get to write more.

Last but certainly not least, I'm grateful to my family for their love and support.

Author's Note

Novellas related to series are often stand-alone adventures or only tangentially related to the overall plot, but this one was conceived and written to be an integral part of the Iron Druid Chronicles. It's really book 4.5, set six years between the events of *Tricked* and *Trapped*, and there are references in both *Trapped* and *Hunted* to events that occur in this novella. We've printed it here at the back of book six because novellas are rarely printed and sold separately, and also for the very practical reason that this was written after *Trapped* was already completed and well into its production process. This was the earliest point we could get it into print at no extra cost to you. Thanks for your understanding, and happy reading!

Two Ravens and One Crow

and

One Crow

An Iron Druid Chronicles Novella

What would it be like, I wonder, if humans could slobber as freely as dogs? There's no social stigma for dogs when they slobber and it looks like a lot of fun, so I envy them that freedom. I've certainly wanted to slobber at various times—there are situations where nothing else makes sense—but despite having lived for 2,100 years and in many countries around the world, I have yet to find a culture where it's even mildly acceptable, much less looked upon with approval.

I guess some things will never change.

Despite the universe's refusal to change enduring truths according to my will, lately I've been wishing I could train a Druid in a five-minute karate-movie montage rather than the necessary twelve years. After ten seconds of futile effort trying to solve a problem, the initiate would abruptly improve or learn the lesson and her expression would fill with wonder, and I would award said initiate a cookie or a tight nod of approval. The initiate would bask in the glory of an achievement and then move on to the next difficult challenge for another ten seconds, and so on, until a triumphant swell of music and a slow-motion high five signaled victory and completion. We would smile the radiant smiles of actors in fast-food commercials, merrily chuckling as we ate enough grease to make our hearts explode like meat grenades.

But training my apprentice, Granuaile, wasn't like that at all. Shaping her mind for Druidry was rough and monotonous for both of us, yet shaping her body was fraught with peril. The peril was the sort Sir Galahad had faced at Castle Anthrax: stupefying sexual tension.

Every winter solstice, I gave my apprentice an entire wardrobe of loose, shapeless sweats, and she kept buying herself tight, formfitting outfits to wear in the summer months. I had trained my Irish wolfhound, Oberon, to help me through it and be my Lancelot whenever Granuaile made my jaw drop, which was more often than I would care to admit. She'd go through her kicks and lunges and various stances and build up a sweat, then I'd start thinking about other ways to get sweaty, and shortly thereafter I'd need to be rescued.

Can't I have just a little bit of peril? I would ask Oberon through our mental link.

<No, it's too perilous,> he'd say, and then I'd have to give him a snack, which would force me to tear my eyes away from Granuaile and redirect my thoughts into less prurient channels. It might sound silly, but it was self-preservation.

Granuaile picked up on the pattern after a while, unfortunately.

"Sensei?" she asked.

"Yes?"

"Why are you always leaving about halfway through a workout to give Oberon a snack?"

<To hide the evidence of his BLISTERING PASSION—>

"What? Well, he's a good dog."

<To sequester the sight of his UNTRAMMELED LUST—>

"Granted, but he's a good dog all the time, and the

only times you interrupt what you're doing to give him a snack are during workouts."

<To conceal the tower of his CARNAL DESIRE—>

"I reward him sometimes for using big words. And sometimes I reward him for shutting up."

<To delay the dawning of his ENORMOUS LONGING—>

Now would be a good time to shut up.

<I'd better get a snack.>

Deal.

"So what did he say just now?" Granuaile asked.

"I'm sorry, but that's classified information."

Oberon chuffed, and Granuaile's eyes narrowed. She knew the dog was laughing, blast him, and now she'd be determined to find out what he thought was so funny.

I was saved by the arrival of an extremely large crow. It spat out "Caw!" at Klaxon-level volume, landing on top of our trailer. It startled us all, including Oberon, who barked at it a couple of times. The bird's eyes glowed red and he stopped, tucking his head down and retracting his tail between his legs.

"Morrigan?" I said.

The red glow faded from the crow's eyes as she tilted her head and spoke in a throaty rasp, "Surprise, Siodhachan." The Celtic Chooser of the Slain would never call me Atticus. The head bobbed once at my apprentice. "Granuaile."

"What's wrong?" I asked, because the Morrigan did not make social calls. I belatedly realized that I should have offered her refreshment or adhered to some standard of hospitality, but thankfully the Morrigan was too focused on her mission to notice my awful manners.

The crow rustled her wings and announced, "We have business to attend to. You will be gone for at least a week but perhaps two. You won't need to bring anything, not even a weapon. Shift to your bird form and let us be gone."

"Wait, wait. I'm going to need more of an explanation than that. Can't my apprentice come, or my hound?"

"No. Definitely not. Our business does not concern them."

<That's fine with me. I'll happily stay behind,> Oberon said.

I glanced uncertainly at Granuaile, and she shrugged.

"You say we'll be gone two weeks?"

"At the most. But we must begin immediately. Make haste."

Arguing with the Morrigan would be unwise. Spending at least a week with her—maybe two—would not be any wiser.

I'm doomed, aren't I?

<Yep. It was good to be your hound.>

"You're not doomed," the Morrigan said, and I belatedly remembered that she could read my mind now—or at least hear thoughts that I projected. "But you will be if you don't hurry up."

I turned to Granuaile. "Take a few days off if you wish. You've earned it. But continue to practice your languages and work out every day."

"Okay, sensei. Maybe Oberon and I will head up to Durango." Our place in Many Farms was just over a hundred miles southwest of there. She fingered her hair, dyed a brown so dark it might as well be black. "I can get this mess fixed up. It's time."

Her roots were beginning to show again, which meant mine were too. Our ridiculous fake identities had served us well in this remote location; we kept to ourselves and no one really gave a damn about us. Aside from the embarrassment of our assumed names—the trickster, Coyote, had fixed it so we had to call ourselves Sterling Silver and Betty Baker in public—we liked living and training in Many Farms. Taken all around, Coyote had done us a solid, and he in turn was mighty pleased about the way his renewable-energy projects were coming along, thanks to my help. Six years had done him and the tribe a world of good; the coal mine was shut down forever now that Coyote's ventures were creating lots of jobs.

"All right. You know the drill, right? If I don't come back—"

"I'm supposed to call Hal Hauk, I know," Granuaile said. "He's got your will. But you won't make me do that."

"I sure hope not. See you later." I ducked into the trailer to undress before I shifted, and the Morrigan squawked impatiently.

<Hey, Atticus, bring back some wildebeest flanks, will you?>

Where do you think I'm going? I said as I threw my shirt into the hamper.

<I don't know. I've just always wanted to say that. It makes me sound like a boss when I can casually order up some wildebeest. Or it sounds like something Dr. Seuss might say: *We're going to have a feast. A feast! On some wonderfully succulent wildebeest.*>

If you wanted to go hunting for wildebeest, you should have said so. Listen, watch Granuaile for me, will you?

<I always do.>

Divested of my clothes, I triggered the charm on my necklace that bound my form to a great horned owl and hopped over to the door.

Thanks, buddy. I'll have to owe you that snack. Though I'm sure Granuaile will completely spoil you while I'm gone.

<She always does.>

I hopped down from the trailer doorway and hooted

a good-bye to Granuaile. The Morrigan flapped her wings noisily and launched herself to the southeast.

Come, Siodhachan, her voice said in my mind. I shuddered and took wing after her. I didn't like having her in my head, though at the moment I had to admit it was convenient. Unlike the Morrigan, I couldn't speak like a human while in bird form.

<So what's the emergency?> I asked her. We were flying toward Canyon de Chelly, where we could find a tree bound to Tír na nÓg and shift out of the state.

You need to repair your tattoo, the Morrigan replied.

<You mean the back of my hand? That's been messed up for six years.> Ever since I'd been chewed on by a giant locust—courtesy of Coyote's attempt to save the world—my ability to heal myself had been damaged. Colorado (the elemental, not the state) had taken care of what few needs I'd had since then, because I'd known all along that at some point the Morrigan would have to be the one who doctored my tats. The problem with that was that, unlike most doctors, the Morrigan didn't agree with the credo of "First, do no harm." The rest of the Tuatha Dé Danann thought I was dead—at least, I hoped they did—so I was stuck with the Morrigan as my ink slinger.

You have procrastinated long enough.

I stopped flapping my wings out of shock and dropped like a stone for a second before I recovered. The Morrigan was not a type A personality who worried about procrastination—hers or anyone else's.

<What's really going on? Have you seen something coming? Some reason I'll need to heal?>

One thing at a time, Siodhachan.

<Fine. What's really going on? You're not worried about procrastination.>

She didn't answer. She kept flying as if I hadn't said anything and allowed me time to realize that she wasn't going to answer any more questions, whether I asked them one at a time or not. This was highly unusual behavior for the Morrigan. Usually she couldn't wait to tell me about all the dire shit that was about to befall me. Pronouncing my imminent doom held a certain relish for her. I couldn't understand why she was being so closemouthed now, but my curiosity was piqued.

We shifted from Canyon de Chelly to a deserted patch of Tír na nÓg, where no Fae would see us, and then from there to a damp gray fen in Ireland, surrounded by yew trees, that the Morrigan called her own. She led me to a barrow that I suppose I should call her *home* or *estate* or perhaps a simple *dwelling*, but those words don't really fit the feel of the place so much as the word *lair*. The Morrigan was a bit too savage to live in a *home;* she could rock a *lair* like nobody else, though. Bones, I noticed, were a strong decorative motif. Skulls too. Perhaps that subconsciously tilted me toward the word *lair* instead of *home;* few homes are so abundantly adorned with bones—especially ones that the owner has quite probably gnawed on.

We flew straight through an open portal into a longish tunnel lit by torches, until we emerged in a large chamber with a table and a single chair. It had a pitcher resting on it and a lone goblet made of carved and polished wood. Clearly the Morrigan was unaccustomed to entertaining visitors.

The Morrigan shifted in midair so that her feet touched down lightly and gracefully next to the table. I tried to do the same thing and discovered that the graceful bit was something that one achieves only after much practice. My momentum was far greater than I had judged it to be, and I stumbled toward the table. I panicked as I realized that some very vulnerable body parts were about to be squashed into the edge of the table, so I twisted as best as I could and instead smashed my hip against it. Did I mention the table was stone? My entire leg went numb and I crumpled to the ground at the Morrigan's feet with a pained groan.

The Morrigan laughed hysterically. I'd heard her laugh before, but it had always been evil-genius laughter, not genuine mirth.

It really was ground that we lay on, and not tile or marble or anything else. There was nothing to prevent us from contacting the earth here. And nothing to prevent me from blushing, because the Morrigan was laughing so hard that she couldn't breathe. Tears streamed from the corners of her eyes. She sounded almost girlish, but I carefully refrained from noting this out loud and did my best to banish it from my thoughts as well.

Seeing that she would be at it for some time, I took the opportunity to examine my surroundings a bit better; it would distract me while I waited for the pain in my hip to subside. (If I drew any power to smoosh the pain, the Morrigan would feel it and laugh all the more.)

There were two other entrances to the chamber, equidistant from the one we had used. They were lit similarly and lined with bones on the walls. A wrought-iron chandelier with candles in it blazed above our heads.

The chamber was circular, I now realized, the very center of a barrow-mound with three entrances. It seemed like an awful lot of effort had gone into building such a plain room. There wasn't even a hearth with some questionable stew bubbling in a cauldron.

"What is this place?"

The Morrigan took her time in answering. Once she had wound down, she said, "It is a place for rituals. For mortals it is a place of mystery and dread. Now, thanks to you, it is a place for laughter."

I chose to ignore that last bit. "I see no thornbush here." The tattoos that bound us to the earth had to be made with a living plant; Gaia would be present in our minds and direct the process.

"The ritual spaces are all hidden. Come." She rose to her feet and brushed dust off her body. I rose too, limping a little, and followed her down the passageway to our left. After maybe ten yards she paused and faced the bony wall to her right. "The doors are easily seen with your magical sight. Mortals would never find them."

Before I could shift my sight to the magical spectrum, she touched an inconspicuous knob of bone, which pushed in like a button, and a section of the bone wall sank backward and then shifted left with a hiss of air. Pneumatics. The Morrigan must have seen the surprise register on my face.

"I know you think me old-fashioned and resistant to change," she said. "And that is probably not without merit. I still prefer the sword to the firearm. But I think I may have learned something from you. Many somethings. Come."

She stepped through the door into a humid indoor garden ripe with oxygen and floral scents that tickled the nose. A glass ceiling turned the chamber into a sort of conservatory; along the top of the walls, near the ceiling, bindings carved into the surface spoke of abundance, fertility, and harmony. And, underneath those, bindings that meant the above were to apply liberally to all living things in the room. It was the sort of general, nontargeted binding that my cold iron aura had difficulty suppressing; I'd have to ward specifically against it if I didn't want to fall prey to it, but, honestly, why would I bother?

Wait. As Hamlet said, *That would be scanned.* Harmony with the Morrigan?

More alarming: abundance and fertility . . . with the Morrigan?

I needed to change the subject quickly, even though

the subject was only in my head. The Morrigan might spot it there.

"You know, Morrigan, I've been meaning to speak with you about how I got this wound," I said, gesturing to my scarred right hand. "You were nearby at the time. You could have stepped in and prevented it, yet you didn't. I could have died, and you would have broken your word."

The Morrigan blew air through her nose in a sort of halfhearted snort, and a corner of her mouth turned up. "Why are you paying attention to what might have happened? Tell me what *did* happen."

"I suffered unnecessarily."

The mention of suffering caused the Morrigan to close her eyes in pleasure and make a yummy noise. "The necessity can be debated. But you lived. I never broke my word."

"But it was an awfully close thing, Morrigan. A skinwalker tore out my throat—"

"And you healed," she finished. "I have been faithful in my promise to you. I never promised that you would remain free from injury or suffering. For one thing, that would have interfered with my sex life."

I flinched and took a step back. The Morrigan noticed and laughed. "Speaking of which, Siodhachan, how is yours of late? Do you even have one?"

"Yes, I have one," I replied. I did my best to keep my tone matter-of-fact rather than sullen. It was more difficult than I thought it would be.

Her disbelief was clear. "You keep a mistress in that tiny town?"

"No. We head into Farmington or Durango on the weekends, or Gallup and Flagstaff on occasion. We both have various partners in these places willing to, uh, spend time with us."

"Your gift for euphemism continues to thrive. But I

think I have heard of such modern relationships. There is a colloquialism for them, yes? They are boogie calls."

"Boogie? Oh! Nice try. You were very close. They're known as booty calls."

"That's what I said. Booty calls."

"You said boogie—" The Morrigan's eyes flashed red for the briefest moment, and I cleared my throat. "Pardon me. I must have misheard you. Quite right."

"So your apprentice has these booty calls as well?"

I shrugged. "As far as I know. It's not really my business. She's had a steady boyfriend or five over the years. She got a marriage proposal, too, which she rejected."

"And you were not jealous?"

"It's not my place to be jealous, because I have made it very clear to her that we cannot have a relationship beyond that of master and apprentice."

"I didn't ask about your place or anything regarding propriety. I want to know how you *feel* about her dalliances. Are you jealous?"

I considered. To claim I was completely indifferent would be dishonest. And there were times, perhaps, when Granuaile was a bit too eager to share her conquests with me. After she first met her boyfriend in Durango, she reported that "he was so hot that he damn near made my ovaries explode." But that was as it should be; there was no reason for Granuaile to settle for anything less than hotness. Neither should she settle for anything less than joy. I hoped she would find someone to provide that for her since I couldn't. For my part, I had not been trying very hard lately, and despite the general truth of what I'd told the Morrigan, I hadn't made a booty call in quite some time. There were many beautiful, delightful, intelligent women in the area, especially in the college towns, but somehow they all fell short of Granuaile in my eyes, and I had been choosing to do without rather than settle for a sort of surrogate. It wasn't celibacy, I told myself. It was high standards.

"No," I finally said. "She is my apprentice but isn't mine in any other sense. I am a tad envious of her partners, perhaps, but nothing more. I am happy for her happiness."

The Morrigan scoffed openly. "Happiness? Neither of you is happy. Your auras scream of repression."

"That's okay," I said.

"It is not. Sexual repression is conduct unbecoming a Celt."

I shrugged. "Better that than having to deal with guilt ferrets."

"What are guilt ferrets?"

"They're bastards. They cling to your neck and tickle and bite and generally make you miserable, which is a pretty good trick for a metaphor." They were also impervious to logic—perhaps their most diabolical power. There was no cause for me to feel guilty about any liaisons with other women, since Granuaile and I were not in a relationship and monogamy was not required, but the guilt ferrets attacked me anyway every time.

"I dislike guilt," the Morrigan said. "It is regret and recrimination and despair over that which cannot be changed. It is like eating ashes for breakfast. It is the whip that clerics use on the laity, making the sheep slaves to whatever moral code the shepherds espouse. It is a catalyst for suicide and untold other acts of selfishness and stupidity. I cannot think of a more poisonous emotion."

"I don't like it either," I admitted.

"So why do you bother to feel it?" the Morrigan asked.

"Because an inability to feel guilt points to sociopathic tendencies."

The Morrigan made a purring noise deep in her throat,

and her hands rose to pinch her nipples. "Oh, Siod-hachan. Are you suggesting I'm a sociopath? You always say the sweetest things."

I took a step back and raised my own hands defensively. "No. No, that wasn't meant to be sweet or flirtatious or anything."

"What's the matter, Siodhachan?"

"Nothing. I'm just not being sweet."

The Morrigan's eyes dropped. "Fair enough. Looks to me like you're scared stiff."

I looked down and discovered that the sodding abundance and fertility bindings weren't messing around.

"Ignore that guy," I said, pointing down. "He's always intruding on my conversations and poking his head in where he's not wanted."

"But what if I want him?" The Morrigan had an expression on her face that was almost playful; it humanized her, and for a moment I forgot she was a bloodthirsty harbinger of death and realized how stunningly attractive she was. She reminded me of one of those old Patrick Nagel prints, except very much in three dimensions and far more sexy. I found it difficult to come up with a clever reply, perhaps because most of the blood that used to keep my brain functioning well had relocated elsewhere.

"Well, um. Uh. Pretend I'm saying something witty right now. Also: nnnn—" I couldn't say no. I wanted to, but I was physically unable to say it. I kept trying. "Nnnn . . ."

The Morrigan laughed and drew closer, taking me into her hand. I tensed up, expecting pain. She chuckled a bit more about that and leaned forward to whisper in my ear.

"Relax, Siodhachan. You have nothing to fear. You saw the bindings for harmony in this room. They work

on me too. There can't be harmony if you're terrified,
now, can there? So we will do it your way. This once."

Harmony, I discovered, could be horrifying. That was
what kept me from saying no. There couldn't be open
disagreement in the presence of these bindings. Com-
bined with fertility and abundance, what the Morrigan
currently wanted was precisely what the bindings
wanted. I was the one out of harmony, so I felt the force
of it. I thought of simply exiting the room, and managed
a single step before my legs refused to move any farther
in that direction. "Do we have to do it at all?" I said,
desperately.

"You need it. So do I. And I can play nice when I want
to." Her words fell on my ear in soft warm puffs of
breath, and she stroked me gently to prove she spoke the
truth. My eyes closed and then snapped back open as I
realized what was happening.

"But . . ."

"Shh."

"Weren't we supposed to be in a hurry?"

"I allowed for some wiggle room."

She kissed me, preventing any other protest, and
played nice. But the physical pleasure didn't come with
a side of emotional fulfillment. A zoo full of guilt ferrets
bit me the whole time.

A Druid's tattoos aren't the sort one gets in a parlor
from an excessively pierced person. The needle has to be
living—in other words, a thorn from a live plant—and
Gaia must be present. She guides where the ink goes and
creates the binding that allows us to tap into her magic.
Alone it took me about a week to get in touch with
Gaia, but together with the Morrigan we were able to
enter the trancelike fugue state and meld our minds in
only five days. Touching up the tattoo on the back of my
hand took an additional two, and during that time we

were able to speak of the Morrigan's progress on her cold iron amulet, amongst other things. One needs a distraction or five when getting stabbed repeatedly with pointy bits. Gaia doesn't let you turn off the pain; gifts and talents earned without pain are so often taken for granted.

"So it's been six years," I said. "Are you about ready to bind your amulet to your aura?"

A hint of red crept into the Morrigan's eyes and she didn't respond at first, so I was going to let it slide and pretend I'd never asked the question. She surprised me by answering a few minutes later, just as I was about to introduce the topic of crocheted superhero plushies and their excessive cuteness.

"I don't know if I'll ever be ready, Siodhachan," she said. "The trick is winning the favor of an iron elemental. As I have said to you before, I am unskilled in the arts of currying favor. If I curry anything, it is fear. But I cannot scare an elemental into binding cold iron to my aura. All I can do is scare them away."

"But I thought you were making progress with one. The last time we spoke of this, you were feeding it lots of faeries and it was pleased with you."

"Yes. Well, shortly thereafter I lost my patience and it fled. The same thing happened with two others. What is that American game you like so much, where a player gets three chances to succeed?"

"Oh—I think perhaps you mean baseball."

"Yes. Baseball. I have struck out, Siodhachan—is that the correct phrase?"

"It is."

"I have witnessed a couple of those games in crow form, because you find it so fascinating."

"Really? Who did you see?"

"I misremember. My attention wandered, but I believe

one team was inordinately proud of the color of their socks."

"Oh, yes! Boston or Chicago?"

"Boston. That was it. Many fine Irish people there. I perched on top of a large green wall, and I can understand your attraction to the game. The players suffer greatly yet mask it with stoicism."

"You liked the suffering? Well, that's not why I enjoy it, personally."

"How can you not appreciate their inner struggles? Whether they strike out or allow the opposing team to score or commit any number of other tiny failures, they are filled with doubt and self-recrimination and outright fear that their careers have ended, that they have lost the talent or skill that earned them the opportunity to play professionally, and with dread at the possibility that they have publicly shamed themselves. It is magnificent drama. It is little wonder that people pay to watch it and swill cups of poorly made beer while gobbling up those tubes of low-grade meat paste covered in ketchup and mustard. What are those called?"

"Hot dogs."

"Why? Do they contain dog meat?"

"I certainly hope not. It's just an idiomatic term."

"Americans are a strange people."

"Granted."

"But the despair, Siodhachan! It is so very succulent. They strike out and return to their bunker area, you know what I mean—"

"It's called a dugout."

"Their dugout. They sit on a bench, curse their luck, and loudly accuse the opposing team of having Oedipal relationships with their mothers."

"What? Oh, that took me a second. Thankfully, Morrigan, motherfucking is not nearly so common in America as baseball players would have us believe."

"I am relieved to hear it. But then they chew gum or sunflower seeds or cancerous wads of tobacco and try to forget their failure, even though it gnaws away at them. They tell one another lewd jokes and speculate about the sexual orientation of the umpires. All of it is an attempt to lift their spirits to the point where they can compete successfully at their next opportunity. The true beauty of the game is in the dugout, Siodhachan." She paused and swallowed before continuing in a subdued tone. "And that is where I am, regarding the binding of my amulet. I have failed and I need to convince myself that I can succeed the next time."

"I don't think there's any question, Morrigan. You can."

"I think you do not see my problem. To men I am either sex or violent death. Sometimes both. Occasionally I am a healer of battle wounds. But I am no one's friend."

"But, Morrigan—"

"Hush, Siodhachan. There is nothing you can say to alter the truth of matters. You have been more kind to me than anyone in my long life, but even you fear me. You are a wonderful lover, but I have taken you as I have taken all the others. I understand that I am not given friendship because I give none. It is truth, and I must face it here in my dugout."

I had no ready reply. Perhaps the single tear trailing down her face stunned me to silence. Perhaps there is nothing one can add to the truth if it is properly told.

The Morrigan sniffled once and wiped the tear from her cheek. "I would not share my emotions were we not bound with Gaia in a room of harmony. You see? I cannot give my trust or anything of myself without the aid of magic. All I do is take."

"Well, I think you should take me out to a ball game or five after this. I will admire the grace under pressure and you can get off on the despair in the dugout. Great fun for the both of us. I'll spring for the Cracker Jacks and maybe buy you a jersey. What do you say?"

"You want to simply . . . spend time with me?"

"Yeah. It's what friends do. How does it sound?"

The Morrigan smiled and her eyes glistened. "It sounds like a gift. I would be grateful."

"We are going to Norway now," the Morrigan announced as soon as we left the room of harmony, abundance, and fertility and stood in the hallway of bone. Her tone immediately returned to the cold, businesslike rasp I was used to, and I was on my guard again.

"Why?"

"For an exquisite meal. And a rendezvous with certain gods who very politely requested a word with you."

"Which gods?"

"They wish to introduce themselves."

"They're not Norse gods, are they?"

"They are."

"I can't see them!"

"You must. I have given my word."

"That's not *my* problem."

Her eyes locked on mine and glowed red. "Oh, I rather think it is, Siodhachan."

After our heart-to-heart talk in the binding room, this severe return to her old, implacable self was a bit jarring. "Could we maybe go back into the room of harmony and discuss this?"

"No."

"Morrigan, I'm supposed to be dead, remember? If the Norse find out I'm alive, they'll just want to kill me all over again."

"Some of them are already well aware of the deception."

"That's the same as all of them."

"No, it is not. Come. You will be safe."

This statement, meant to put me at my ease, utterly failed to reassure me. I remembered that the Morrigan's definition of safe varied widely from mine. Hers included excruciating pain and severe injury just short of death. Mine included beer and a recliner chair. The fact that she felt it necessary to repair my healing capability before we made this trip suggested very strongly that she knew it would be dangerous.

Hand in hand, we used one of the yew trees in her fen to shift from Ireland to Tír na nÓg and from there to an evergreen stretch north of Oslo. We took our bird forms and flew into the city until we banked down a narrow alley, where the Morrigan shifted to her human form as the last rays of sunlight moved off to the west and left us in darkness. I shifted as well and felt doubly naked without a sword over my shoulder in enemy territory. No one witnessed our metamorphosis, nor did anyone spy our public nudity. The Morrigan unbound a locked access door, and we stepped into the back room of what looked like a tailor's shop.

"Padraig," she called. "We are here."

I cast a questioning glance her way. That wasn't a Norwegian name.

"There are plenty of people outside Ireland who pay me respect, Siodhachan," she said. "Don't look so surprised."

"Of course," I said.

A short lad with a florid complexion bounded through a black curtain that presumably led to the front of the shop. His eyes grew wide when he saw us and he started to bow to her, but the Morrigan stopped him.

"Never mind that," she said. "We don't have time. Just fetch our clothes."

"Right away!" he blurted, joy writ large on his features, and he fled back through the curtain.

"How cute," I said. "You have a fanboy."

"Minion."

"A matter of nuance. Why not simply cloak yourself in darkness as I've seen you do before?"

"We are to arrive without bindings or wards of any kind. No magic is allowed."

"What? That's insane! First no sword, and now no magic?"

"They are bound by the same rules. Make sure you follow them."

"Forgive me, Morrigan, but these Norse gods, whoever they are, might not feel as bound by the rules as you do."

"This is a formal summit of deities. They would not dare to cross me. Nor will we cross them."

Padraig returned before I could register any further objections. He held a black evening dress made of silk and lace in his left hand and a tuxedo in his right. He sort of threw the tuxedo at me and then grandly presented the gown to the Morrigan. His eyes drank in her body, and his breathing was already labored. The Morrigan surely noticed this but made no comment.

Since I was certain she wasn't carrying any cash on her, I didn't particularly want to see what form of payment Padraig was expecting for these rather expensive clothes. I began to dress as quickly as possible, hoping that I'd be able to exit and wait outside before I had to bear witness to something tragic.

Unfortunately, the dress was a much simpler affair to don than a tuxedo. It slipped over her head, and with a couple of tugs here and a zip there she was ready. The dress was stunning; the black silk was a flat matte in some places but shone with highlights elsewhere. A curling vine pattern of lace interrupted the silk and hugged her curves, allowing her porcelain skin to show through. Starting over her left breast, the lace curved between them and then underneath, tracing its way in a spiral around her torso until it reappeared above her right hip, where it fell in a serpentine wave down the front of her thigh. The dress ended just above the knees.

"You didn't forget my shoes, did you, Padraig?" the Morrigan said.

A brief flash of panic crossed Padraig's face as he realized he may have committed an unpardonable sin. "No, no!" he said, hands up in a placating gesture. "I simply couldn't carry them along with the dress and tux. I'll go get them and be right back."

He bolted through the curtain again.

I cocked an eyebrow at the Morrigan. "Do I get shoes too?"

"He might forget," she replied. "How shall we punish him?"

"Let's not and pretend we did," I said. "Let's leave the poor man alone."

"That would be unkind, Siodhachan," she said. "He prayed so fervently for my favor. He's fully aware that there will be a price for it."

"What if he's unable to pay?"

"Oh, they are always able to pay. Was it Shakespeare's Shylock who was so eager to extract a pound of flesh? I'm like him. I'm happy to carve off a pound. Or two. I never seem to have a scale handy when it's time to take what's due."

Padraig returned with a pair of black shoes for me and some sandals for the Morrigan—the type with lots of leather straps on them to wind around the calves. I dragged a chair over from a desk piled high with receipts and invoices. I parked myself on the chair and squeezed my feet into the shoes. I'd rather have remained barefoot, since anything I wore on my feet would cut me off from the earth, but the Morrigan seemed to have arranged matters so that I would be at my greatest disadvantage when I met whomever we were meeting. My bear charm was just below full, since I'd charged up in the forest before we took wing and only used a little bit of it to transform back to human in the city. It felt good to have something available even though the Morrigan kept insisting I wouldn't need it. That was simply too trusting of her—yet more unusual behavior.

I didn't understand what was going on with her. On the one hand, she had nearly wept at the idea of going to see a baseball game with me. Now she spoke of carving pounds of flesh from a man who'd been praying to her. It was like she had swerved toward kindness and sanity for a moment, but now she was overcorrecting and trying to be extra-special savage. I feared what she would do to Padraig; I wanted to tell him to run for his life, because this was the Morrigan that gives Irishmen nightmares. Sandal straps twined sinuously around her calves, she addressed Padraig in a silky tone, if the silk was draped over a knife blade.

"Everything appears to be in order, Padraig. You have done well. Are you ready for your payment?"

"Oh, yes, I'm ready, very ready," he said.

The corners of the Morrigan's mouth twitched upward in idle amusement. "Take off your shirt, Padraig," she said in a husky whisper, and suddenly I felt warm as she began to employ her seductive powers on the poor lad. I've always thought them more powerful than those of succubi, but she hadn't needed to use them on me back at her lair-o-bones because the fertility bindings accomplished the same thing. I was partially protected from her wonted powers of seduction by my cold iron amulet, and in this case they weren't even directed at me, but Padraig was utterly helpless. He was practically panting as he tore at his shirt and wrestled himself out of it.

"Yes, Morrigan!" he cried. "Oh, goddess!" The front of his trousers twitched and strained as if one of Ridley

Scott's alien babies were trying to erupt from it. The Morrigan placed her hand flat on his chest, just underneath his right collarbone, and he shuddered at her touch. Then her fingernails turned long and black, almost into talons, and she dug into his chest with them and began to slowly rake across and down to his left. Padraig cried out, and both his hands clutched at the Morrigan's wrist—not to pull her hand away but rather to force it deeper. Blood welled underneath her nails and began to run down his ribs and belly; Padraig moaned and wailed and his hips began to buck uncontrollably as she tore at his chest.

I wondered if he had any customers in the front of the store. Tailor shops are not usually so fraught with pain and ecstasy.

Padraig screamed when the Morrigan's nails sheared off his left nipple. She pulled her hand away then; Padraig let go of her wrist and fell to the floor, jerking and trembling.

"We can go now," she said, stepping over Padraig's twitching body and through the black curtain, leaving me alone with a man having a bloody epic orgasm on the floor.

I wanted to kneel and heal up his chest but suspected that the Morrigan would object in violent fashion. I didn't know what to do. "Well, thanks! Um. Have a nice day!" I finally said, and followed after the Morrigan. Once through the curtain, I saw that the shop was empty and the Morrigan was heading for the front door. "Aren't you going to help him?" I said. I had to raise my voice to be heard over the noise Padraig was making.

She stopped and turned, perplexed by my question. "I just did, Siodhachan."

"He's losing a lot of blood and he sounds like he's in pain."

"Yes, but he's also in pleasure. He'll live. And, besides, he asked for it."

"He asked to be mutilated and—whatever else that is?"

"He will ejaculate for five more minutes and then pass out."

I blanched. "Is that even possible?"

"Yes. When he wakes, he will experience the most intense period of creativity he's ever known. His designs will make him one of the most sought-after tailors in all Europe."

"Oh. So that's what he asked for?"

"Yes. I'm not a goddess of craft, like Brighid, but I do what I can."

"He didn't ask to lose a nipple and be permanently scarred, did he?"

"People who court my favor know what kind of goddess I am," she replied. "And there are still plenty of people willing to make Faustian bargains. They tend to focus on the results rather than the costs to achieve them."

She turned away, signaling an end to the conversation, and I sighed in defeat. I hoped Padraig would think it was worth it in the end.

We exited the shop, closing the door on the tailor's rapture and ruin, then hailed a cab. The Morrigan told the driver to drop us off at the corner of Kirkegata and Rådhusgata.

There's a seventeenth-century building at that location that currently houses one of the finest gourmet restaurants anywhere. It's the sort of place where you have to dress up to walk through the door and even the toothpicks are posh. Dinners are served in four to six courses, and there's not only a professional waiter but a professional sommelier at your elbow.

At some point the building had been painted a belligerent shade of mauve—it was *mauve*, damn it, and proud. It was a generous two stories tall, with frequent narrow white-framed windows blessedly interrupting the Great Mauve Wall. Above a gray cornice loomed a black-shingled roof, which had architecture of its own, allowing for an attic room or three and their concomitant windows. Movement up there drew my eyes, and I spied two enormous ravens perched on the eaves, seeming to look straight at me with equal parts gravitas and gloom. Each one of them had an eye that gleamed white.

"That's an overdose of Poe, isn't it?" I said.

The Morrigan, seeing the ravens, gave a short bark of laughter. "There's no Poe involved at all. Use your head, Siodhachan."

I remembered we were supposedly meeting members of the Norse pantheon and said, "You don't mean *he* is here—"

The Morrigan slapped me. "I said use your head, not your mouth."

"But how can he—"

I got slapped again.

"Right. Sorry."

The Morrigan took a deep breath and closed her eyes, clenching her fists at her sides. It was the first sign I'd seen that she felt the least bit nervous about this encounter.

"How do I look?" she asked, and I wondered again at how she could be simultaneously so ruthless and insecure.

"Fearsome. Deadly. A bit delicious."

She smiled. "You always know what to say. Let's go. And, remember, no magic."

Once inside, we were greeted with a large smile by the maître d', an impeccably scrubbed and barbered man dressed in black-tie livery. He ushered us to a window table in the Cleopatra Room, where waited none other

than the goddess who gave her name to Friday. She rose
to receive us.

Frigg glowed the way stained glass does; she had that
sort of beauty, very colorful and beatific yet flat and
gauzy with the suggestion that you're missing quite a bit
of depth. The question was whether the depth was carefully hidden or if it was simply missing.

She appeared cordial yet tense, like a little boy who's
being forced by his mother to be nice to his aunt Ethel
or else, except that Aunt Ethel is the one with the hairy
mustache and it's all he can do to keep from screaming
when she arrives and wants a kiss. The pleasant expression on Frigg's face, with a ghost of a smile, didn't reach
her eyes; they were cold and unfriendly. She wore a
royal-blue sheath gown circled with a wide black sash
just beneath her ribs. Circling her neck was an extremely
shiny something, set with enough diamonds to feed several families and a stable full of ponies for a year. I was
about to check her out in the magical spectrum when
the Morrigan grabbed my jaw and yanked it right to
face her. She spoke in Old Irish so Frigg wouldn't know
what she said.

"Remember what I said about magic?"

"Not supposed to use any," I managed to say while
she had an iron grip on my chin.

"That's right. None. But you were about to cast magical sight, weren't you? See my eyes? They're brown instead of red because I can't use magic right now. Pretend
they're red, Siodhachan. I'm watching you."

"Got it."

She let me go and then I felt like the little boy, except
I'd failed to greet Aunt Ethel properly and received a
royal chewing out as a result. I blushed and muttered a
quick apology in Old Norse to Frigg for my manners.
"Call me Atticus, please."

"Thank you for coming," she said, then waved a hand at the chairs across from her. "Please, sit."

I pulled out the Morrigan's chair for her, and after she was seated I took the spot nearest the window. The sommelier showed up to welcome us to Statholdergaarden and discuss wine before we could say anything. Frigg ordered a bottle of Australian Shiraz, surprising me somewhat. It must have shown on my face, because she explained the order afterward.

"One gets so tired of mead from the teats of a magic goat every night. Not that I'm complaining about the quality—I dare anyone to find a better brew flowing from the udders of a she-goat—but one does need a bit of variety now and then. The food and drink here will be a welcome change."

I was completely unprepared to answer her. Not only had I not drunk the same thing every night for centuries, I had never made small talk about goat teats before. I realized that my mouth had dropped open after the Morrigan reached over and pushed up on my chin. My teeth clacked together audibly, and then Frigg's face turned crimson, realizing she'd introduced an awkward topic of conversation. The Morrigan seemed determined to embarrass everyone tonight.

Unsure of what to say, I kept silent and waited. I couldn't think of a safe topic of conversation—not even the weather, because that might be interpreted as a reference to Thor. I didn't want to embarrass myself or anyone else, and I didn't want to earn another rebuke from the Morrigan for saying the wrong thing—like, for example, inquiring after the missing occupant of the chair next to Frigg's. There was a place setting there, and Frigg had asked the sommelier for four glasses, but there was no other sign of the last member of our party. Unless you counted the two ravens on the roof.

I suppose there was a statistical non-zero probability

that this could be a coincidence—two normal ravens just happened to be perching on the roof of a restaurant in Oslo where I was about to meet unnamed Norse gods—but I felt it was fairly improbable. It was far more probable that I was about to have an extremely uncomfortable formal dinner with two deities who had a long list of reasons to kill me.

Granuaile asked me once how it could be possible for all the world's gods to be walking around without anybody noticing. The answer was (and is) simple: cosplay. Most gods cosplay as humans when they visit earth and do their best to stay in character. If they perform miracles here and there, they're always small things that no one outside the local area will notice. But, more than anything else, they don't show themselves because humanity doesn't truly believe they ever will. We imagine them chilling out in their heavens or nirvanas or planes of punishment, and they're generally expected to stay there. And if they're going to work their divine magic on earth or pull a deus ex machina, then they act through surrogates or from afar. In a sense, deities are incapable of showing themselves because most people don't believe they'll meet their gods before they die. I am a notable exception to the rule. The ancient Greeks and Romans believed they could run into the Olympians, though, so that allowed Zeus and company to start all kinds of shit in the old days.

The silence lengthened. I couldn't believe Frigg's entire repertoire had been exhausted on goat teats and mead, but for the nonce, at least, her speech was on hiatus. Taking a deep breath, I employed the architectural-history gambit: "Why is this called the Cleopatra Room?" I asked.

The Morrigan pointed up. "The ceiling," she said. Craning my head back, I saw an elaborate stucco on the ceiling. Back in Arizona, they just sprayed stucco on the outside of houses and called it an exterior. But long ago, back when this building was originally constructed, artists used it as a medium to create permanent bas-relief sculptures. This one—undoubtedly one of the finest I'd ever seen—depicted the suicide of Cleopatra, who'd famously decided to leave this world by snakebite. Seeing it made me immediately miss Oberon, because I knew he would find the opportunity for parody irresistible, and I knew what he would say if he could see it now, complete with the voice of Samuel L. Jackson: <Enough is *enough*! I have *had* it with these motherfucking snakes on this motherfucking ceiling!>

"Beautiful," I said, and hoped my smile would be interpreted as art appreciation rather than amusement at my hound's fondness for movies.

"Yes," the Morrigan agreed.

Our scintillating conversation was blessedly interrupted by the sommelier, who returned with the bottle of Shiraz. He poured a little out for our suspiciously missing homie, then left us to fill the silence once again. We had nothing, so we drank a bit and speculated about all the different flavors we could taste in the fermented grapes. The Morrigan opined that it had a layered flavor, stony but finishing with a lush *réglisse*. Frigg tasted spice, whatever that meant; I doubt it was an allusion to the planet Arrakis. I am not proficient in the language of wine, so I was just about to suggest there was a faint top note of mango chutney when Frigg's eyes shifted over my shoulder and her expression softened. She rose from her chair, and the Morrigan and I followed suit. Turning to follow Frigg's gaze, I saw a tall man in a tuxedo approaching our table. Gray hair flowed about his head and down to his shoulders, but it wasn't thin and receding; it was somehow virile and imbued with badassery. The simple black eye patch over his left eye didn't make him look like a pirate but instead communicated wisdom—

precisely the prize for which he gave up his eye. It spoke of his suffering and his willingness to sacrifice—to stop at nothing—to remain the wisest of the wise. His epic beard was a bit surprising and somewhat intimidating: I'd expected an unruly carpet flowing down his chest, but it was a densely packed and trimmed affair, almost like topiary, which gave his features the weight of a carefully constructed edifice that few men could pull off. Most guys grow beards that do nothing for them other than communicate to the world that "this is what happens when you don't shave." The beard of Odin told you that he wasn't a hippie or a barbarian or a fantasy author but a god who could bring order to chaos.

He took his wife's hand and planted a kiss on it. Then he turned to the Morrigan and nodded to her once. "Morrigan." She nodded back. Then his eye swiveled to face me, and I could *feel* the frost of his hatred; I had to suppress a shudder. "So you are the one," he said. "Slayer of the Norns and Freyr and so many others." His voice reminded me of whiskey—and I don't say that just because I'm Irish. His words were rich and smoky and quite possibly had been aged in oak barrels for years before he spoke them. "Since I recovered, I have watched you from Hlidskjálf, unable to believe what I saw. Despite ample evidence to the contrary, I saw nothing in you that suggested you were capable of defeating us. But now, seeing you in person, I can perceive your essential nature. You are deceptive."

"Frequently," I admitted. "Hello, by the way. I'm honored to meet you."

Odin's hands curled into fists at his sides. "Honor!" he growled. "You cannot speak to me of honor when you have none!"

Frigg placed a delicate hand on his arm. "Let's sit down, shall we?" The tension drained from Odin's shoulders, and his fists unclenched. We all sat, and as we did so I realized that Odin and I had something in common: We were both under the complete control of the woman sitting next to us. I admired Frigg's good sense. Sitting down made it much more difficult for Odin to lunge across the table in an attempt to snap my neck. And seating the Morrigan directly across from him would serve as a reminder that, should matters come to blows, she would be the one choosing the slain.

The waiter appeared, an earnest man intent on regaling us with specials and options he'd been at pains to memorize, but Odin stopped him and spoke in the modern Norwegian language. "We will all take the full six courses," he said. "If there are options, please leave it as chef's choice. And please inform the sommelier that we also trust his judgment regarding wines for the remainder of the evening. We have much to discuss and do not wish to be distracted with decisions to make." A credit card appeared in his hand. "This will assure you that we will pay for whatever you serve."

The waiter bowed, took the card, and said, "Very good. I'll return shortly with the first course, which is crayfish from the fjord and—"

Odin waved him silent. "We'll figure it out when we eat it, my good man. Forgive me if I am being rude. I assure you we will tip generously."

"Very good," the waiter repeated, and went away to orchestrate what would no doubt be a very large bill. Odin returned his gaze to me and his language to Old Norse. Before he could enumerate the reasons I deserved to die, I jumped in. I had much to answer for, but I wouldn't passively accept whatever he wished to say—especially regarding my supposed lack of honor. I like to think I have a smidgen of it, at least.

"Odin, wise as you are, I am sure you have already noted that I twice held Gungnir in my hands and twice refused to target you personally when I could have done so. In both cases, I chose to do that which would secure my safety and nothing more. You sit here before me today because I stayed my hand. Twice."

"And you think because you spared my life twice that you are honorable?"

"The entire reason I came to Asgard was to honor my promises. I killed only those who seemed bent on killing me. The Norns tried first but killed Ratatosk instead. Having no choice, I slew them and then went to the hall of Idunn and Bragi. I could have slain them, but I left them alone."

"But you stole one of Idunn's golden apples! Your honor is the honor of a thief."

"A thief who keeps his word. You tried to kill me for it shortly thereafter. I could have taken your life. Instead— with great reluctance, I might add—I took Sleipnir's."

"There was no honor in that decision. It was strategically the best course of action, because it occupied the attention of the Valkyries as well. Had you slain me outright, they would have pursued you to avenge me."

"Even so, my point remains: I responded with violence only when it was first offered to me."

"Ha! What violence from Thor prompted you to bring a party of men and giants to Asgard to slay him?"

"That is a separate matter. But, again, I was keeping my word."

"You promised to kill Thor?"

"No, I promised to provide transportation to Asgard."

"So in your mind you have done us no wrong?"

"I did not say that, Odin."

We paused as the waiter brought out the first course. The crayfish was there, but so was a small trout roulade. I sampled it and discovered that the chef knew what he was doing. If this was to be my last meal, I couldn't ask for a finer one. None of the gods touched their food. They watched me eat and waited for me to continue.

"On the contrary," I continued, "I believe I acted shamefully during that second trip, and I deeply regret what happened. I apologize to you both, though I know the words are inadequate."

Odin snorted. "They're worse than useless. It's insulting that you would even try to pay for what you did with a meaningless phrase."

"How would you suggest that I pay? Paying with my life is not an option."

I expected an argument here, but Odin surprised me by agreeing. "No, it's not," he said. "There's not enough of you to pay the blood price."

"Blood price?"

"It's a common enough concept."

The waiter swooped in and cleared the first course away before depositing the second in front of us, a seafood soup garnished with avocado and other goodies. Once he left, Odin changed the subject.

"We will speak of blood later. What I would like to know is why you're alive."

"Why didn't I die before the Common Era, you mean? How did I manage to live long enough to vex you?"

"Precisely."

"I occasionally drink an herbal tea that renews my cells and reverses the aging process."

"Interesting." Odin looked down at his soup and, deciding it looked good enough to eat, picked up a spoon. Frigg, the Morrigan, and I did the same, and we slurped up a spoonful or two before Odin asked another question. "And this tea you drink—is it readily available in these modern supermarkets? Or is it something you invented?"

"No. I got the recipe from Airmid, one of the Tuatha

Dé Danann. She's long dead now, however. Tragic circumstances."

"A tragedy! Forgive me for noticing, but they seem to follow in your wake."

"You're forgiven. May I ask you something?"

"Of course." His spoon hovered over his bowl as he waited for my question.

"How did you find out where I was?" My cold iron amulet normally shielded me from divination; not even the Norns had seen me coming.

"Hugin and Munin found you a couple of months ago, working out in the desert with that apprentice of yours."

Mentioning Granuaile wasn't an accident. It was a subtle threat, but I pretended not to notice. "Oh. About the ravens. Which one . . . ?"

"Did you kill? Hugin. I languished in dreams of the past for years, attended by Frigg and unable to function in the present. But eventually Munin remembered Hugin and laid an egg. The new raven, when he reached maturity, became Hugin again. I awoke, sent the ravens abroad in search of you, and, once you were found, I watched from Hlidskjálf."

"I see. And how many of the Norse know I'm still alive?"

"Only Frigg and myself."

"Why didn't you tell them all?"

"That is related to the blood price of which we will speak further. If you would not mind, I would like to know precisely how you learned the recipe for this brew of eternal youth."

I shrugged. "I already told you. Airmid taught me."

"Yes, but why? Why you and no one else?"

I put down my spoon and exchanged glances with the Morrigan. She knew the answer, but no one else did. "Oh. That is quite a story."

Odin gestured at the table. "We have four more courses."

"It is not that long, but it is a story I have never shared before and I am reluctant to share it. It has a certain value."

Odin's eye bored into mine. "Understood. Consider it a part of what you owe us."

"Very well." I saw the waiter and sommelier approaching. "I will begin once we've been served the third course."

The third course was pan-fried pike with a side of white asparagus and some other assorted vegetables artfully arranged on a white plate, drizzled with a beurre blanc. The sommelier, an older gentleman with thinning hair but crisp movements and a steady hand, served us all a glass of chardonnay. After that, I had to share a secret I thought I'd never speak aloud.

In the days when the Tuatha Dé Danann were puissant in Ireland, the most famous physician of the time—if I may use the modern word—was Dian Cecht. During the First Battle of Mag Tuireadh, the king, Nuada, lost his right arm in battle, and he applied to Dian Cecht for remedy. Despite his victory over the Fir Bolgs, he was no longer fit to rule with such a disability.

Together with the craftsman Creidhne, Dian Cecht fashioned a magical silver hand and arm for Nuada; once it was attached, it functioned just like a regular arm would, and Dian Cecht's fame grew ever greater throughout Ireland. People began to call the former king Nuada Silver-hand, for it was truly a miraculous sight and all who saw it were amazed. In public, Nuada was mightily pleased and recognized the fame his silver hand brought him. But in private—well, there were issues. It repelled his wife, who did not want it to touch her. And whether he wore it or not, Nuada could not help but feel incomplete and out of balance. Despite the miracle of the silver arm, he was diminished.

But Miach, son of Dian Cecht, felt Nuada's pain and dared to help him. He was an extraordinarily talented and empathetic healer, who avoided conflict with his father whenever he could. But in the case of Nuada, he could not withhold help when it was in his power—and his power only—to give it.

Over nine days and nights of chanting and ritual, he managed to regenerate a new arm and hand of flesh and blood for Nuada. The king was whole again and could return to the throne. Miach had surpassed his father, however, and Dian Cecht was not the sort of man who suffered such things in passive silence. Indeed, rather than feel pride for his son's accomplishment and broadcast it far and wide, he was consumed with jealous rage and confronted his son with a sword.

Miach protested that he did not want to fight and bore only love and goodwill for his father, but Dian Cecht was beyond reason. His first stroke grazed Miach's skin, but his son healed it immediately. Such a display only drove Dian Cecht to further violence. Despite Miach's attempts to dodge, his father's second attempt stabbed him in the gut—but Miach healed even that. Dian Cecht became more animal than man when he saw. His third stroke cleaved all the way down into Miach's brain, and that overcame his son's ability to heal. He died, and then Dian Cecht threw down his sword in horror at what he had done.

His horror was not a fraction of Airmid's, however. Airmid, sister of Miach, was quite a healer in her own right and a powerful Druid. Her rage was such that she did not attend her brother's funeral for fear that she would kill her father. Instead, she waited until the funeral had ended and everyone had gone home, and then she visited her brother's grave to pay her respects. She wept for three days and nights on his grave and sang him songs in broken sobs. She wept for love and loss and memories she could no longer share but had to keep in trust for them both, and she wept for all the memories that would never be now that he was dead. Exhausted, she collapsed next to his grave and slept.

When she woke, a wonder greeted her eyes. Out of Miach's grave, watered by her tears and the blood of Miach's body, grew 365 herbs of medicinal power. Possessed with a purpose, realizing the gift before her, Airmid spread out her cloak and began to test and catalog the herbs, examining their qualities and preserving in her mind their unique properties. But before Airmid was finished, Dian Cecht, possessed by grief and guilt, came to visit the grave of his son.

He saw Airmid's cloak spread on the ground and the world's medicinal herbs laid out in order upon it. He saw the herbs themselves growing from the grave in the shape of Miach's body, and his jealous rage rose again.

"Even in death he mocks me and renders my life meager in comparison!" Dian Cecht roared. He tore at the herbs growing in the earth, then yanked Airmid's cloak from the ground and snapped it in the wind, scattering the herbs into the sky. Because of this deed, it is said that no one alive knows the sum of the earth's herblore.

It was at this point that Airmid lost her composure. Wielding a stick as her weapon, she attacked Dian Cecht, battering him about the face and body with all the strength a Druid could bring to bear, until he crumpled to the ground. Throwing down the stick, she picked up a boulder and raised it over her head, intending to bring it down upon her father's head. But a voice from Tír na nÓg stopped her.

"Airmid, no!" it cried, and she froze. It was the voice of Miach, calling her from beyond the veil. "For the love you bear me, do not slay our father!"

The rock tumbled from her fingers, and she left Dian Cecht bleeding on the ground to heal himself. She picked up her cloak and walked away from the grave without speaking a word. She did not speak to anyone for nine days, in fact, and the first person she spoke to was me.

I was in the twilight of my normal lifetime and dwelling on my approaching death. I wasn't decrepit or arthritic, for Gaia sustains us well, but my physical prime was four decades gone at the least, and the prospect of a steep decline into death's embrace had somewhat soured my disposition. I was drinking alone at an inn when Airmid entered, searched the room, and picked me out. She saw the signs of morbidity in my aura, no doubt. But she also saw the tattoos on my arm and knew I was a Druid.

She sat down across from me with a satchel and said, "Old man, indulge a young woman. What would you do to have your youth again? To feel the bounce of vigor in your step, to feel the hard wood of your cock again, and to nevermore lose it to the ravages of age unless you will it?"

I did not know who she was. She was robed and gloved, so I did not even know she was a Druid, much less a member of the Tuatha Dé Danann. "Do you jest or do you ask in all seriousness?" I said.

"I am in earnest," she replied. "I truly wish to know what you would be willing to do for a gift like that."

"I would kill for that," I said. Men have killed for far less.

"Then I have a proposal for you," she said, and withdrew a sheaf of skins from her satchel, filled with all the herblore she could remember from before Dian Cecht threw her work to the wind. "I am a Druid, and I have discovered a blend of herbs that, when slightly altered with a simple binding and brewed as a tea, confers the blessings of youth on he who drinks it. That secret and so many others are contained in these pages. They are yours if you kill a man for me."

I perused a few of the pages and realized that the herb-lore set down therein was far beyond my ken. I examined her aura and saw no hint of deception there or in any gesture of her body. That is no guarantee of honesty, for we can all be deceived easier than we would like to think, but so far as I could tell she was making me a genuine offer, and I was desperate enough to accept. But I had to ask: "Why not simply kill him yourself? I can see that you are a powerful Druid."

"I cannot kill him, because he is my father."

"I must kill your father in exchange for this herblore?"

"Yes. What say you?"

"Who is your father?"

"Dian Cecht of the Tuatha Dé Danann."

She recounted for me the story of her brother's death and told me how she managed to classify and catalog 327 of the 365 herbs before her father destroyed her work. "A Druid doesn't forget," she said. "I have spent the last nine days writing down this lore and experimenting further. This new tea of youth is the best of my discoveries, but there are more."

"I am engaged," I said. "Tell me where to find him."

Legends say that Dian Cecht died of a terrible plague. To the bards who told it that way, it seemed like an ironic and just ending for a villainous physician. The truth of his end involves a terrified chicken.

Airmid directed me to Dian Cecht's house. When I arrived there, he was not at home. I approached it in camouflage and disabled his few simple wards, went inside, then put them back together. Since I was over sixty, I didn't feel equal to besting him in a fair fight, and I dislike fair fights anyway. I needed an advantage, so I greased down the floorboards near the door. Once he closed it behind him, I would spring from hiding and the uncertain footing would negate any advantage he had in speed.

The entrance to his house was a kitchen and dining area. A hallway from this led to other rooms, and after I was finished with my preparations, I hid around the corner and sat in the hall.

Hours passed, during which I had ample opportunity to reconsider, but I convinced myself that, in a very real sense, it was either him or me. If I didn't kill him, I would die—eventually. If I did, I wouldn't die, period. I had killed men in battles but never plotted a murder before. It didn't sit well with me, but neither did the prospect of gasping my last breath.

When Dian Cecht finally came home, he brought a chicken with him to pluck for his dinner. He clutched it tightly against his chest with one hand—his sword hand. When I leapt out of my hiding place and shouted, "HA!" with my own sword drawn, I killed him. Or, rather, the chicken did.

He let go of the chicken to reach for his sword, and the creature exploded from his grip and slapped him several times in the face with her beating wings as she pecked at him. In his attempt to shy away from the chicken and also draw his weapon, he slipped on the greasy floor, cracking his head open on the edge of a worktable near the door as he fell. He was dead before he hit the ground. And that's when I first met the Morrigan. Though I had never crossed swords with Dian Cecht, the intent had been there, and thus our confrontation had fallen to her sphere of influence. She had chosen Dian Cecht, not me, to be slain, and she let me know.

She couldn't choose him for death against Miach, because Miach had never tried to fight back. And Miach thwarted her again when he made Airmid promise not to kill her father. I was an acceptable work-around, however, and she said at the time we would meet again.

I thought she meant she'd choose me to die in battle soon; I had no idea at the time that our association would last so long.

I took the chicken back to the inn where I'd met Airmid and had them cook it for me. She came in as I was finishing up and I told her that the deed was done.

"Where did you cut him?" she asked.

"I didn't use my sword," I said, then pointed at the bones on my plate. "I used this chicken."

I told her what had happened and she seemed pleased. True to her word, she gave me the sum of her notes and showed me the binding I needed to use to create Immortali-Tea, as well as several other bindings for other special brews. And that is how I not only gained the secret to eternal youth but gained the herblore of the greatest herbalist ever to walk the earth. Plus a great chicken dinner.

Odin set down his fork and dabbed his mouth with a napkin. He looked at Frigg and said, "I hope the fourth course won't be a chicken dish."

"I don't think it is."

"Good." He turned to me and said, "I can see why you prefer to keep that story to yourself. It is a terrible thing to be henpecked."

The fourth course was a veal sirloin stuffed with morel mushrooms and another attractive arrangement of vegetables on the side. I tore into this since I'd never enjoyed a bite of the third course, occupied as I was with the story. The gods enjoyed their wine but didn't touch the food. Apparently they don't do veal. Perhaps they would have enjoyed chicken after all.

"I have had much time to ponder the ramifications of your actions in Asgard," Odin said as I was eating. "And much time to ponder my response. In the old days, there would be no question—we would have killed you and any known associates. But this is a different time, and the simple vengeance we crave would not serve us well in the long run. We would rather, instead, that you serve us well."

I stopped chewing. "I beg your pardon? Are you suggesting some sort of indenture?"

"No. A blood price. Ragnarok is coming soon, and since you have killed or assisted in the killing of many gods who were to fight on our side, we wish you to take their place."

I very nearly choked and needed to drink a bit to clear my throat before I could speak. "You want me to take the place of gods?"

"Not entirely by yourself. It would be helpful if you could recruit some others. You clearly have the powers of a classical hero, and your assistance would be invaluable. All that matters is defeating the forces of Hel and Muspellheim: Next to that, our vengeance is a trifling matter. Fight with us, and the blood you shed on our behalf will expiate your debt. That, and one other thing."

"What?"

"I would appreciate the return of Gungnir."

"Promise not to throw it at me again?"

A flicker of irritation crossed Odin's face. "Yes."

"Okay, sure, I'll return it. I have no use for it. Send Hugin and Munin to visit me in Arizona three days from now. I'll tell them where to pick it up."

"Thank you. And Ragnarok?"

I thought about Hel and her attempt to kill me near Kayenta. I thought about the world overrun with *draugar*. Even people who were preparing for the zombie apocalypse would have trouble with those things. "If the shit goes down, Odin, I'm on your side."

"Excellent. Will you fight with him, Morrigan?"

The Morrigan, like Frigg, had remained silent for much of the meal. Now she gave a thin smile. "I'm afraid I'll have to miss that particular battle. The Valkyries will have to suffice."

Odin's expression darkened. We had killed twelve of the Valkyries when we raided Asgard. I don't know how many remained, if any. To change the subject, I said, "Can I ask what happened to Thor's hammer?"

"Why?" Frigg asked. "Did you promise someone you'd steal it?"

The nastiness of the question surprised me. We'd been getting along so well. But I tend to react when provoked. "No," I said. "If I had, it would already be in my possession." Frigg seethed and Odin chuckled softly.

"You were supposed to keep *my* anger in check," he said.

The fourth course was cleared away—the waiter making sure we were all okay, since the gods hadn't touched the veal—and the fifth was laid before us. Five different well-aged cheeses were attractively presented on a white rectangular platter with crackers and fruit compote. Some were sliced in triangles, some in thin, translucent pieces. It was a superlative achievement in both geometry and dairy. The sommelier served us something from Italy; I didn't quite catch it.

"Mjöllnir rests in Gladsheim," Odin said once the servers had retreated.

"No one wields it now?"

The Norse gods frowned as if I'd asked something particularly inane. "Like who?" Odin said.

"I was thinking maybe some other, later aspect of Thor. The one from the comics is popular right now."

Odin scoffed. "Popular, perhaps. But he is not worshipped, and you know what that means: He can't muster magic enough to manifest himself! He has to be played by a human actor in his own movies. He's nothing but cheap entertainment. Surely you know this."

I did know it, but it never hurts to let possible antagonists think they are smarter than you.

"Well, if he can't do it, then surely some other aspect of Thor can?"

"They are all comfortable in their current situations, and none is as strong as the original. I wouldn't want a single one of them at my back. No, Thor's responsibility is now yours."

"Mine? You want *me* to face the world serpent?"

"Or find someone else to do it, yes."

This twist in the conversation reminded me uncomfortably of Cleopatra on the ceiling. I looked up and examined it again past the glow of the chandelier, and, while I did, the gods directed their attention to the cheeses.

The artist had taken quite a bit of license; Cleopatra reclined, leaning on her right arm, while her left hand held a snake up to her breast, inviting it to bite her. I thought the snake would have simply bitten her hand when she reached to pick it up, but that was the least of the odd choices the artist had made. For some reason, he had decided to give Cleopatra European features and provide her with a Rubenesque figure; my archdruid would have described her as "festively plump." She also appeared to be dressed in Greek style rather than anything Egyptian. Though still quite beautiful as a work of art, the inaccuracy bizarrely exposed what I think is the true tragedy of Cleopatra: No one really understood her or her decision. But maybe some could empathize with the feeling of being trapped by circumstances. I certainly could.

"I can't agree specifically to a cage match with Jörmungandr," I said, "but I will fight on your side against Hel, see if I can recruit additional aid, and return Gungnir to help make amends for my wrongs against you."

Odin opened his mouth to reply but closed it again as

the sommelier arrived to bring us a dessert wine for the final course. It was to be a macaron filled with Bavarian vanilla and strawberries and served with champagne jelly, and he assured us it would arrive shortly. But I never got to try the macaron. Never got to hear Odin's stifled reply.

As the sommelier drew close behind me to deposit a glass over my right shoulder, several things happened in quick succession in a fraction of a second. The Morrigan's left hand blurred and pushed me so violently from my seat that my head hit the floor while my ass was still in the chair. Glass tinkled. The sommelier cried out and fell backward, to hell with the wine. The report of a rifle cracked in the air. Odin and Frigg lurched to their feet.

After the second passed, the Morrigan's words floated down to me as I struggled to stay low but get in a defensive position. "There, Siodhachan," she said, amusement in every word. "I saved your life. Now you can stop whining about our agreement."

Someone had tried to shoot me in the head through the window and had shot the sommelier instead. Since he'd taken the bullet in the hip and had been standing behind my right shoulder, that meant the shot had come from the roof across the street and had been aimed more or less at the top left side of my face.

The sommelier clutched at his hip and loudly informed the room, in case they missed it, that he'd been shot. Upper-class squeals and calls for emergency personnel filled the restaurant, but I blocked that out and kept my eye on Frigg and Odin. It seemed insane to me that they would go through that whole charade of a dinner just to kill me anyway—especially since they didn't have Gungnir back and didn't know where it was—but I had to suspect they were responsible, because they had good reason to kill me and they were the only ones who knew I was here, apart from the Morrigan. I ruled the Morrigan out as a suspect, because she could have killed me anytime she wanted to in the last two millennia without any witnesses. The only possible reason to arrange it like this would be to blame it on the Norse—but why would she have cause to do that?

Still, she obviously had known the shot was coming, or she wouldn't have known when to push me. She must have divined it and, in so doing, might have seen other things.

"Who pulled the trigger, Morrigan?" I asked, watching the two Norse gods and keeping my back to the wall.

She shrugged. "I don't know. I foresaw the attempt on your life, but the assassin is shielded from my sight. Tracking him or her down should provide us some after-dinner entertainment and will aid digestion." She calmly rose from the table and tossed her napkin down. "Shall we begin?"

"No, wait," I said. "How do we know they didn't order it?" I gestured at Odin and Frigg. Odin was looking up at the ceiling rather than at me or anything else. It was an odd moment for art appreciation. Frigg spoke instead.

"Of course we didn't order it. Odin is sending the ravens now to follow the shooter."

"Well, then, Odin's using magic, isn't he? I'd like to use some to heal this poor guy, if it's all right with you." Our waiter and the maître d' had crouched down next to the sommelier, who was telling his colleagues that, if he died, he wanted all his worldly goods to be given to his hamster. I didn't think it would hold up; he wasn't of sound body and might not be of sound mind anymore.

"No, let me do it," Frigg said, coming around to help the sommelier. Her necklace flashed in the light of the chandelier. "He's one of ours. You three go find the assassin."

"Go find someone who wants to kill me accompanied by a god who wants to kill me?" I said.

Odin tore his gaze from the ceiling and spoke. "I don't want to kill you; I want you to die horribly in Ragnarok. But not until you tip the scales in our favor."

"He will," the Morrigan said, but it was unclear whether she was speaking of tipping the scales or dying horribly. Or both.

Frigg knelt down next to the sommelier and laid a hand on his forehead. His eyes rolled up, locked on her face, and he quieted. The maître d' rose to attend to other matters; there were customers to calm and emergency services to greet. Our waiter remained next to the sommelier.

Even if Frigg and Odin weren't directly behind taking a shot at me, it had to be someone they knew. I sincerely doubted Odin had been careless enough to reveal this meeting in someone's hearing, but if it hadn't been a careless word, then the security leak had to have come from some other source. Before the Morrigan could stop me, I triggered the charm on my necklace that would cast magical sight. Through that filter, I saw the white nimbus of magic around Odin's gray head. Two strong ropes of it wound away and through the ceiling, which I assumed were his connections to Hugin and Munin. The rest of his body looked completely human; he was doing nothing but communicating with his ravens.

Frigg was another matter. Her entire body was suffused with a soft white glow, though at the moment it was concentrated in two places: her right hand, placed on the sommelier's forehead, and around the necklace she wore. Her hand was clearly serving as a chill pill for the panicked shooting victim, but what was that necklace doing?

I moved away from my position on the wall, figuring it was safe now and the Morrigan would slap me out of the way of any further shots. As I crouched down next to Frigg and the sommelier, a hint of annoyance crept into her tone.

"I told you I would take care of him," she said.

"You're taking excellent care of him," I agreed. "I wouldn't dream of attempting to do any better. I'm curious about your necklace."

Her left hand drifted up to touch it. "My necklace?"

"Yes. What purpose does it serve?"

Exasperated now, she ground out, "It is personal adornment. Is this some sort of trick or an attempt to make me feel stupid?"

"Forgive me, I meant to ask what magical purpose it serves."

"None. My magic comes from within."

"Then why is it awash in magical energy?"

"What?"

"Confirm it for yourself. Morrigan, Odin, please look at Frigg's necklace. It is not merely jewelry, is it?"

The Morrigan's head tilted slightly to one side and Odin focused his gaze on the necklace. The Morrigan spoke first.

"It is enchanted with something, but it is not a binding of the Tuatha Dé Danann or the Fae."

"No, it is not," Odin said. "It is Norse magic." This horrified Frigg so much that she took her hand off the sommelier, who abruptly remembered that he hadn't finished panicking properly.

"Wauuggh!" he cried, and Frigg returned her hand to his forehead to shut him up.

"Odin, get it off me," she said, using her left hand to sweep her hair away from the back of her neck and reveal the clasp of the necklace. "I want to take a good look."

Sirens began to wail in the distance; police and ambulances were on their way.

Odin came around the table and unclasped the necklace. As soon as he did, the magic glow extinguished.

"That's interesting. The magic is gone," I said. "Odin, would you mind clasping the necklace together again for a moment?"

He did so and the magic glow returned. The Morrigan said, "Interesting indeed."

Odin unclasped it, the glow faded, and Odin placed it on the table.

"Does the magic return every time it's clasped?" I wondered aloud. Odin connected the two ends together once more, but nothing happened.

"No. Only when it's worn," he said. "Clever work."

"Do you know what the spell does?" I asked.

"It is a tracking spell. A locator."

"And who would want to know Frigg's location badly enough to enchant her jewelry?"

"I do not know," he replied. "But I dearly wish to find out."

The waiter, who'd been focusing on his friend and keeping silent, and thus had been ignored until this time, made an unwise decision to speak up. "You people keep talking about magic and calling one another by the names of gods. Are you mental?"

"Frigg, if you please?" Odin said. His wife sighed and placed her left hand briefly on the waiter's forehead. He collapsed next to his friend. Frigg's eyes flicked up to mine.

"Don't worry," she said. "He's merely in oblivion. An effective talent for healing but surprisingly useful for occasions like this as well."

The sirens outside grew loud and car doors slammed. Lots of people got shouty.

"We should make our exit now," I said.

"Allow me to camouflage us," the Morrigan said.

"Not me," Odin said. "I'll use my own methods."

I still felt sorry for the aging sommelier who had an inordinate fondness for his hamster. Why had Frigg not sent him to oblivion? She somehow inferred what I was thinking and said, "Go. He will be fine."

"Meet you outside," the Morrigan said.

The slight tingle of camouflage settled over my skin, and I began to thread my way past customers and staff and then police and paramedics until I was in a bit of free space on Kirkegata. The Morrigan's sandpapery voice entered my head.

Across the street, Siodhachan, she said.

Turning my head, I saw that the Morrigan and Odin had dropped their concealment and were staring at me from the other side of the street. The sensation of camouflage left me and I became visible as well. After waiting for another couple of cars to pass on the street, I jogged across to them.

"The assassin is athletically gifted," Odin informed us. "He's leaping from roof to roof, which is quite an accomplishment when one considers that they are sometimes of differing heights. And my ravens have just witnessed him leaping across an entire street."

"So not human, then."

Odin shrugged. "He is not a dark elf. I have seen such feats from berserkers, however. Some of the Einherjar can perform like that. This one may have been granted some strength—but by whom? We need to catch up quickly before he goes someplace my ravens cannot follow."

"How are we going to do that?"

"We'll go to the roof of this building," Odin replied, as if that made everything clear. The Morrigan and I followed him inside a four-story brick building, and we climbed until we reached the blessedly flat rooftop. "He went that way," Odin said, pointing to Kirkegata. There were very few flat roofs ahead, and even if I could bridge the distance between them and leap over streets, the steep shingled surfaces on some of them didn't look as if they'd offer a safe landing.

"Unzip me, Siodhachan," the Morrigan said. "I'll go as a crow and join Odin's ravens." *I want to see what's going on for myself,* she added telepathically as I moved to unzip the back of her dress. *I dislike being dependent on others for my intelligence.*

When she shifted to her crow form and launched herself into the night, I was left alone with Odin, who took the opportunity, out of sight and hearing of Frigg and the Morrigan, to tell me how he really felt.

"I like looking at you about as much as a jötunn's yawning asshole," he began.

"Right," I said.

"I'd rather spit you like a hog, roast you with thyme, and feed you to my wolves than track down this assassin. But I can't have the Morrigan thinking I don't keep my word. I promised a peaceful meeting and now it's been ruined."

"I understand that completely."

"I also don't like the fact that someone used Frigg to track us. That question needs answering. So we're going to pull a Johnny Cash. Have you heard of him? American singer?"

"Yeah, I know him. The Man in Black."

"Good." He turned to the north, put two fingers between his teeth, and whistled a rather haunting series of notes. The night sky answered with the neighing of horses.

"Oh, no," I said.

"What's the matter, Druid, afraid of horses?"

"Well, these are fairly special ones, aren't they? So special that they have no physical presence?"

"That's entirely in their favor. Smoother ride." Odin's tuxedo morphed before my eyes. The jacket lengthened to a long trench coat and turned skull gray. His shirt turned to a tunic, his pants became breeches, and his shoes grew up his calves and hugged them as leather boots—all of it gray. His face weathered and shrank in a bit, turning gaunt and tough. The architecture of his beard unraveled and became an untamed mane. His teeth flashed white in the darkness. "Haven't done this in a long time. Should be fun, even with a pile of weasel shit like you."

"Kind of you to say."

Blue-green lights approached from the northern sky; in a matter of seconds they resolved into the outlines of spectral horses and hounds, and they came to a halt more or less on the roof.

"Up you go, then," Odin said, leaping onto the back of a horse. Even though only the outline was there and I could see through the damn thing—I saw Odin's leg dangling down the other side—the Norse god appeared to be sitting on something very solid.

I approached one of the horses and mounted it against all visual evidence that it would be possible. I was simultaneously relieved and skeeved that something extremely horsey supported my weight.

"The Wild Hunt rides!" Odin said, his face alight with savage joy. He kicked at his phantom stallion and the whole pack of us leapt forward, floating just above the rooftops. His mouth rounded and he bellowed out the old Johnny Cash chorus about ghost riders as we sort of slid across the skyline of Oslo. A few of the extra horses neighed along, and some of the hounds bayed at the stars.

Riding a spectral steed was much like hopping on one of those moving walkways in the airport; it was as smooth a ride as Odin promised. But I confess it freaked me out a little bit. I was quite used to flying as an owl, but it felt completely alien to be floating above the world in human form. Having additional horses and a pack of blue-green ghost hounds keeping pace with me only highlighted the fact that our party should be coursing on the ground rather than in the air.

We quickly gained on the two ravens and one crow, who were following the shooter. The Morrigan's voice slipped into my head. *I see him. He is dressed like a modern mercenary. Black body armor and boots. He left the rifle back on the roof across from the restaurant.*

I didn't answer. I looked at Odin's face to see if he had any reaction to receiving the same news from his ravens. His expression, formerly excited, had turned into a sour frown.

"What's the matter, Odin?"

He scowled at me. "I'm missing my spear, damn you to Hel," he said.

"That brings up an excellent point," I replied. "What are we supposed to do when we catch up with this guy if we don't have any weapons?"

"The hounds will bring him down," Odin assured me.

Beware, the Morrigan said. *The shooter hasn't seen me or the ravens yet, but he heard the hunt and knows you're behind him.*

I was unsure what she thought I should do with this information. There were no reins on my unreal horsie. I couldn't turn or slow down or speed up. For all practical purposes, I was on an amusement park ride called the Wild Hunt and locked into my seat. Sort of.

The assassin came into view, head and shoulders highlighted by moonlight but otherwise as difficult to see as the Wild Hunt. He landed on a flat roof ahead of us and turned, a handgun in his right supported by his left. He methodically squeezed off a few rounds in our direction, and the third one shot Odin out of his seat. With a whuff, he toppled backward and I followed his trajectory, seeing him land awkwardly on a rooftop below.

The Wild Hunt continued on and I swiveled to see his arms scrabble for purchase, so I knew he wasn't dead. And then I got punched backward too, understanding that I'd also been shot down only when I was already falling toward a street, not a nice comfy roof.

It was in situations like this that I truly appreciated my charms, which I could activate with a mental command rather than speaking the bindings aloud. I triggered the charm that would allow me to shape-shift into an otter, then oriented myself legs down, falling inside my abruptly overlarge tuxedo. It acted as a bit of a parachute so that the impact, when it came, was merely painful rather than fatal. The squealing tires I heard approaching would have been fatal if they had run over me, but, thank goodness, modern Norwegians are reluctant to run over formal wear that rains down from the sky. While I gave out soft little otter moans and tried to assess how badly off I was, I heard a car door open and close and some hurried footsteps approaching to see if there was a dude inside the tuxedo. I struggled toward the collar and managed to poke my head through it, though I didn't feel like moving at all. I'd been shot between my ninth and tenth ribs on the left side, which meant he'd pretty much destroyed my spleen. I triggered my healing charm and projected mentally to the Morrigan, hoping she would hear me. *That fucker shot me. Odin too.*

I told you to beware, came the reply. *Now you know why we had to fix your tattoo. Coming around.* I heard a quick sequence of gunshots from above. The woman— for it was a woman—who had nearly run over me startled and made a wee squeaky noise and looked up. Then she looked behind her as cars began to honk. She had yet to see me.

What about the assassin? I asked the Morrigan.

The hounds of the Wild Hunt are tearing him apart.

He just discovered through experiment that bullets do not affect the incorporeal.

But now we won't know who's behind him, I said.

I think the answer is coming.

The nice lady who didn't run me over finally looked down and spotted me. She was wearing a large yellow name tag on her sweater, presumably from work, that read *Linda*. She squinted through a pair of large spectacles and bent forward a bit to make sure she wasn't hallucinating.

"Oh! It's an otter! A cute little otter! What are you doing here? Wait. What am I doing here? Ahhh! Stop honking! Go on, little otter. Move. Out of the street now." She made shooing motions, as if human hand signals were universally understood by animals. I rolled over onto my back and tried to look pathetic, which didn't tax my thespian talents in the least. Linda shrewdly noticed I was not well. "Hey. Are you all right? You don't look so good. Poor thing."

I gave a mournful little otter cry to push her sympathy button. Magic or no, getting shot takes something out of you; I wanted a ride out of there, and it worked.

"Oh! You must be ill. I'll take you to the vet if you promise not to bite me."

I didn't know what kind of promise she expected me to make as an otter. I was beginning to suspect Linda might have some issues. Still, she was a kind soul and more likely to help me than the average person. I repeated the wee moan and closed my eyes. That did it. She picked me up, keeping me wrapped in the shirt, and took me to her car; it was one of those tiny European jobs that look like a doorstop with wheels. The coat and pants she left in the street. She nearly dropped me when she realized I was bleeding.

"Oh! Oh, my goodness! Please don't die!"

She completely ignored the honking cars behind her

now; they didn't bother her anymore. She had a mission. She opened the passenger door and gently laid me down in the seat before running around to the driver's side. Safely ensconced with my line of sight obstructed by the dashboard, I never saw the attack coming. Linda didn't see it coming either, because she was looking at me when it hit.

A figure in black dropped out of the sky and rammed its fist down onto the hood of Linda's car just as she hit the accelerator. The front end stayed put and the rear leapt up, tumbling me painfully from the seat into the tiny area where people were supposed to stretch out their legs. This did nothing to improve the condition of my spleen.

Linda screamed as she was thrown forward and the driver's side air bag deployed. The honking behind us ceased, the drivers realizing that something serious was happening ahead and the stoppage of traffic wasn't due to one person's whimsy.

"Out of the car!" an angry voice bellowed. It may have been a woman's voice; it was speaking modern Norwegian. Linda was either too disoriented or too wise to comply.

Under attack, I sent to the Morrigan.

I saw. If I forget to tell you later, thank you for a lovely evening of mayhem.

Um. You're welcome?

Wincing with the effort, I managed to extricate myself fully from the tuxedo shirt and crawl back into the passenger seat as the driver's side door was yanked open and Linda was torn from the vehicle by unseen hands. She should have worn her seat belt.

I shape-shifted back to human and gasped as my insides rearranged. It didn't improve my situation except that I could better see what was going on. Steam rose from under the hood; the car was totaled and wouldn't be running anytime soon. The figure in black, I saw, didn't intend to rip me from the car too; he or she intended to pick up the car and throw it somewhere with me still inside—a godlike variation on vehicular homicide. I couldn't tell much about the attacker, because he or she was outfitted not only with black mercenary body armor but with a black ski mask as well. Absolutely none of the clothing was made of natural materials, so I couldn't bind anything. I fumbled for the door release as the figure lifted the car from the front corner, grabbing on to the well of the wheel with one hand and latching on to the front bumper, perhaps, with the right. It's frightening to be in a car as it leaves the ground. There's a fundamental sense of wrongness to being airborne in a car that isn't performing a movie stunt.

The Morrigan dove out of the sky, shifted midair, and kicked the person in the jaw. The car dropped back to earth, I banged my head somehow, and then I got to watch the Morrigan throw down with this strange assailant in the middle of the road. Naked. Weaponless. And with a growing crowd of witnesses.

They both began to move faster than the eye could track, blurring in motion as they landed blows and kicks on each other. That made the assailant a god in disguise; nobody human was a match for the Morrigan. That made me think of vampires; I supposed a sufficiently old one could match her. The Morrigan acknowledged this by disengaging for a moment to wipe some blood away from her lips. She smiled, both her teeth and eyes now red, and said, "Oh, you're delightful, whoever you are."

I wish somebody could have filmed it at high speed so I could later appreciate the martial arts involved; the few people trying to capture this fight at night with cellphone cameras were going to be disappointed. The Morrigan and the anonymous figure fell to't again, trading audible blows yet unable to do significant damage to each other.

I opened the car door and slid out into the street without camouflage, wishing to preserve what magic I had left. I clutched my open wound, which I hadn't closed up yet because the bullet was still inside and needed to be extracted. My emergence caused some comment among the general public. Some variation of "That man is naked and bleeding!" could be heard rippling through them, but this spectacle was only momentarily diverting compared to the woman who was naked and fighting.

Linda, however, who was thankfully okay if a bit rattled, found my exit both fascinating and horrifying. "Who is that? How did he get in my car? I don't know who that is! I swear he's not mine! I was not driving with a naked man! Which is kind of a shame, really, now that I think about it. Look at that, eh? Yum!"

There was very little I could contribute to the fight. I was in no condition to match speed or strength with them, and I had parts that were extremely vulnerable right now. Despite my winning record against pagan gods and vampires so far, I didn't relish facing off against one that could go toe-to-toe with the Morrigan. I was also supposed to be in hiding, so the increasing number of camera phones was making me nervous. I left the scene with an odd gait that tried to minimize impact and headed for a dark alley between buildings. No one tried to stop me until I entered the alley itself.

A gray figure loomed out of the darkness, and moonlight glinted on his brow and the ridge of his nose. Blood covered his tunic and some of it had seeped through his coat as well, high up on the right side of his torso. "Where are you going?" Odin said.

"Oh! Away, I guess? I hadn't thought it through too much. Whoever that is out there, if he was able to track me he wouldn't have needed to enchant Frigg's neck-lace, and, besides, I'm not in any shape to fight."

Odin grunted. "Neither am I. I suppose our business is concluded and you're free to go. But don't you wish to find out who wants to kill you? I do."

"I figured someone would send me a memo. Where's the Wild Hunt?"

"I dismissed them. The hunt is wonderful above the rooftops but not so ideal among the civilians at street level."

"Good call. Speaking of which, if you'd like to get the fight moved into this alley for closer observation, I could probably manage it. There would be no civilians unless they followed."

"Do it." Odin's appearance began to shift from the Gray Wanderer to the impressive tuxedo-clad authority figure.

I reached out to the Morrigan with my mind. *Move into the alley behind you. I'm here with Odin.* I didn't get an answer, but the nature of the battle changed. Morrigan altered her tactics and managed to grab hold of her opponent and toss him or her across the street and into the alley where we waited. The assembled crowd gave a collective gasp. The figure landed with a whuff of breath at our feet. Odin bent down and tore off the ski mask with his left hand, revealing the assailant to be female after all.

I didn't recognize her at first, since her hair was mussed, her nose and mouth bloodied by the Morrigan, and I was looking at her face upside down. She recog-nized me, however, and pushed and pivoted on the ground and tried to sweep my legs. I hopped over her kick like it was a jump rope, but I hadn't sped up my movements yet and she was much faster than me. Up on her feet before I knew what she was about, she punched me in the solar plexus and sent me sprawling backward in the alley. She would have followed up had Odin not interposed himself and grabbed her by the throat with his left hand. She roared and flailed at him, but he did not let go, and his grip was unbreakable. For a guy who wasn't in shape to fight, he seemed to be doing quite well for himself.

"You *will* submit! Freyja! Cease this instant!"

Freyja, the Norse goddess of war and beauty, had more than the average number of reasons to hate me. We didn't need to interrogate her to figure out what she'd done and why. I'd killed her brother and made a truly terrible decision to offer her in exchange for the aid of the frost giants. She would loathe me forever and want me dead, Ragnarok be damned. Odin pinned her against the wall, her feet lifted off the ground, until she stopped struggling and went limp. Then he let her down and loosened his grip but did not let go.

"We will discuss your betrayal at length back in Asgard," he growled.

"Who is betraying whom, Odin?" she spat, blood flying from her lips. "Making deals with a murderer of your own kin—"

"In Asgard!" Odin roared. She quieted, clenched her jaw, and squeezed her eyes shut, unwilling to look at me unless she could kill me. I got to my feet but held my tongue. There was no apology I could make that would balance my ledger with her.

The Morrigan, bloodied and bruising, appeared in the background.

"It was a pleasure to meet you, Freyja. It was a proper meeting indeed." She gave a bloody grin. "I hope we get a chance to meet again." Freyja did not respond.

Odin turned his head to face me. "I cannot begin to express my dismay . . ."

"No need," I said. "Our agreement holds. Give me a few extra days to heal and arrange the delivery of Gungnir. I will tell your ravens where. And I will be there to help at the end of the world, if the world doesn't kill me first."

He nodded curtly. "Leave us now, if you will."

I was only too glad to oblige. *Morrigan, we need to take the cell phones of the witnesses. We can't have a record of your fight or my existence hitting the Internet.*

Done. Go and heal, Siodhachan. She strode forward and planted a bloody kiss on my lips. *Call me soon. I would like to catch a baseball game.* She cast camouflage on herself and vanished from view. Shortly thereafter, cries of dismay could be heard in the street as people watched their phones leap out of their hands, pockets, and purses and smash to pieces on the sidewalk. No one could prove that gods fought in the streets of Oslo; it was all hearsay.

I left Odin and Freyja in that dark alley and recovered my pants and tuxedo jacket from the street, ignoring the curious queries of bystanders. Getting dressed allowed me to hail a cab a couple of blocks away to drive me out to the woods, where I could shift away to safety.

After some time to heal and some scouting in southwestern Colorado, I found a place in the woods that I could use as a sort of safe house. It was definitely a fixer-upper, an old miner's cabin nestled in the mountains above the wee hamlet of Ouray, but the solitude was perfect. The only people who ever came up the road nearby were 4x4 Jeep tourists, and they never stopped at the cabin. They sometimes stopped at Camp Bird Mine a short distance below, but mostly they were on their way to enjoy the wildflowers of Yankee Boy Basin. Also, their traffic was limited to the summer; the road was impassable once the snows came, and those didn't begin to melt until late spring. I could shift directly there, however, because the entire area was full of pine and spruce, and once I bound it to Tír na nÓg, I could appear within a kung fu leap of the front door.

I made arrangements to buy it through my attorney, Hal Hauk, and decided to use it as a drop point for Gungnir. The paperwork took longer than I would have wished, but once I finally had the keys to the place and was assured no one but me would be poking around in there, I shifted to Canyon de Chelly and hitchhiked back home to our trailer in Many Farms. My apprentice and hound were quite happy to see me and full of questions about what had happened.

I held up the back of my right hand. "The Morrigan fixed my tattoos, among other things," I said. "Has everything been okay here?"

"Fine until a few days ago," Granuaile said. "I think something must have died nearby, because we've had ravens circling the place, but I can't find it and the damn things won't go away." She pointed to the sky where two black-winged shapes soared above. As my eyes found them, the ravens banked and dove toward us. They landed on top of my trailer, much as the Morrigan had, and peered at me from the roof.

"Okay, that's really weird. It's too bad you don't have a bust of Pallas," Granuaile remarked.

<Or crackers. I hear birds are wild for crackers.>

"I know who these birds are," I said.

"*Who* they are? You mean these are shape-shifters?" Granuaile asked.

"No, these are Hugin and Munin. Odin's ravens." I pulled out a marked-up map of my real estate purchase and showed it to the birds. "Odin," I said, addressing the ravens for his benefit, "I will leave Gungnir at the cabin on Midgard that is marked on this map." I pointed at a circled area. "It will be there by this evening. The cabin is unoccupied and will be unlocked. I will leave Gungnir in the closet of the master bedroom. Safe travels." I folded the map and tossed it on top of the trailer. The ravens squawked and one of them hopped over to grasp the map between its talons. They flew away with another hoarse cry, and I was quite nearly back to peace and seemingly interminable training.

<Huh. Guess they didn't want a cracker after all. Another myth busted.>

"That was Hugin and Munin?"

"It sure was. Granuaile, if I ever get restless and yearn for action in the remaining years of your training, I want you to remind me of this episode."

"Not sure what the episode was yet, but I will, sensei."

<Hey, Atticus, that reminds me! You wanted me to remind you that we need to get barbecue in Atlanta!>

I did?

<Well, somewhere in the South. You said I would get pulled pork and beef brisket.>

I seriously don't remember this.

<That's why I have to remind you, see.>

I smiled. *You are a very clever hound.*

<And you are an excellent food provider.>

Well, don't get all mushy on me.

"When do I get to hear the details of this episode?" Granuaile asked. "It sounds like Odin is back."

"He is. I'll tell you everything later tonight. It's actually not over yet; I have one more detail that needs my attention. Continue your training and pretend I'm not here for now."

"Aye, sensei."

Gungnir was buried in the earth near our trailer and encased in iron to protect it from divination. With the help of the elemental Colorado and the iron elemental, Ferris, I retrieved it with little trouble. I inspected it to make sure it was in good condition, being careful not to touch the spearhead engraved with runes, lest my aura nullify its magic.

This spear had shed a whole lot of blood, and now that I was returning it to Odin, it would shed a whole lot more. But people who truly want to shed blood will find a way to shed it, just as people who wish to do good will find a way to be a benediction to their neighbors.

Building and growing are so much harder than cutting something down. I once spent twelve years training an apprentice to accept the magic of the earth, only to see him beheaded by the forces of Al-Mansur in Galicia. After I lost Cíbran, the hopelessness of training an apprentice had overwhelmed me for far too long, and I'd had serious doubts about taking on Granuaile and several thoughts along the way of giving up.

But the meeting with Odin reassured me and gave me new hope. Now that we were sort of on the same side and he would keep my fake death a secret, I could face the remainder of Granuaile's training with a bit more confidence that we would not be discovered and summarily destroyed.

I had less confidence, however, in my ability to avoid distraction where Granuaile was concerned. After weeks of tiptoeing around the Morrigan's severe mood swings, I wanted nothing so much as to talk with Granuaile, to enjoy her mind and sense of humor and appreciate a well-balanced personality. It wasn't that Granuaile was serene or at peace with herself yet, but she was walking along that road and it was a joy to sense that and appreciate it, whereas the Morrigan was lost in the apeshit wilderness. Right now, it would be far too easy for me to forget myself and smile at Granuaile in a way that communicated how much I cared for her.

The weather wasn't giving me a break on the physical side of things either. It was still hot outside, and Granuaile was still wearing very tight workout clothes. She

had begun a series of advanced tai chi forms while I was
retrieving Gungnir from the earth.

<Atticus, I should warn you that you're in terrible
peril.>

Come on, not yet. She just started.

<No, it's true. We're out of snacks. I now have no in-
centive to rescue you from your animal desires.>

What? How can we be out of snacks?

<A perceptive question! Granuaile noticed the short-
age a few days ago. "We're running low on snacks," she
said. I heard her quite clearly. But then she did nothing
to fix the problem. I can only conclude that she *wanted*
the snacks all gone. And from that we can deduce that
she doesn't want me to save you anymore. Holy revelation, Druidman! She's on to us!>

I didn't want to believe him, but I also have a suspi-
cious nature. I turned my head and saw that Granuaile's
forms were perfect. She was mesmerizing. And, soon
enough, she caught me watching.

*Gods below, I think you're right! Quick! To the Geek-
mobile!*

<Let's go!>

We had recently traded in Granuaile's hybrid SUV and
bought a new one with a bright-green paint job that the
manufacturer called "Lime Squeeze." It looked like Mountain Dew, the drink of choice for nerds, geeks, and dorks
everywhere, so it had earned the name of Geekmobile.

I tossed Gungnir into the back and opened the back
door for Oberon so he could hop inside.

"Hey, where are you going?" Granuaile asked.

"We need supplies," I said. "Running down to Chinle."
And also to Canyon de Chelly, where I could shift quickly
to the cabin near Ouray and drop off Odin's spear.
Oberon and I might go hunting while we were there.

"I want to go!"

"No, continue your training. Target practice with the

throwing knives, and don't forget to work with the staff. We'll get into some new martial-arts stuff tomorrow, I promise. And I want to hear how you're progressing in your Old Irish." I closed the cab door and started the engine before she could talk her way inside. We kicked up some dust in my haste to escape.

<How many more years do you have to train her? Like five hundred?>

Only six.

<Doesn't matter. You're going to need to come up with another plan. Not that I object to snacks.>

I know. I'm running out of ideas, though.

<You could draw a mustache on her with a Sharpie while she sleeps.>

She has a mirror, Oberon.

<All right. Take her to get her hair cut and secretly pay off the stylist to give her a mullet.>

That would probably work, except that she would murder the stylist. It would never work. There was more to Granuaile than her hair.

<Oh, yeah. Well, that's all I've got. At some point you two will go all Discovery Channel on each other, and then you'll feel so guilty you'll wear hair shirts and sleep in iron maidens. You're doomed.>

His words reminded me of my promise to fight on the side of the Norse in Ragnarok, when and if it came. *We're all doomed,* I said. *But for now I think I'll count my blessings.*

<Oh, let me help! Blessing number one: me!>

He stuck his head between the front seats and deftly licked my ear, delivering a classic Wet Willy. I shied away and laughed. *Always, buddy,* I said.